More praise for *The Indian Lawyer*

"James Welch, in his novels on Indian life, has proven himself to be one of this country's finest writers. And now, in perhaps his most important book, he has given us an unforgettable morality play rooted in the opposite worlds of prison and mainstream middle-class life. What is so impressive about this book is its steadfast refusal to take the easy way out of the moral dilemmas it presents. With unfailing insight, *The Indian Lawyer* leaves us with a renewed vision of the hard chore and exacting cost of remaining human in the face of crushing odds." —Rick DeMarinis

Praise for *Fool's Crow*

"A novel that in the sweep and inevitability of its events, in the human persuasiveness and variety of its characters, in the scrupulous authenticity of its cultural reconstruction, and in the sheer flow and strength of its prose, is a major contribution to Native American literature." —Wallace Stegner

"A tale that is not only remarkable for its beauty of language, but for the way in which [Welch] makes something new of an oft-used theme. . . . [It] may be the closest we will ever come in literature to an understanding of what life was like for the western Indian before the cataclysm of the last century." —Dee Brown, author of *Bury My Heart at Wounded Knee*

"Welch has written an extraordinary novel . . . [that] plunges the reader with startling abruptness wholly into an Indian world, a world in which reality is idyllic and bitter, hard-edged and magical." —Louis D. Owens, *Los Angeles Times Book Review*

Praise for *Killing Custer*

"The Great Spirit must have created James Welch so that he could tell of the Little Bighorn from the viewpoint of the tribes that

fought there. With Paul Stekler this lyrical writer of the West now adds *Killing Custer* to his tribal count."   —Dee Brown, author of
Bury My Heart at Wounded Knee

"For those who may wonder about the 'Custer Had It Coming' bumper stickers they see in the West, James Welch provides the answer, in a book which reads with the same poetic prose that has made his novels American classics."   —Tony Hillerman

"James Welch's *Killing Custer* is a moving and thoughtful meditation on the history of America's wars of conquest and dispossession, and on the necessity—and the difficulty—of recovering that history, and making it a part of living memory for modern-day Indians and whites."   —Richard Slotkin, author of *Gunfighter Nation*

THE
INDIAN
LAWYER

James Welch

W. W. NORTON & COMPANY
New York · London

For information about permission to reproduce selections from this book,
write to Permissions, W. W. Norton & Company, Inc., 500 Fifth Avenue,
New York, NY 10110

The text of this book is composed in Bodoni Book,
with the display type set in Craw Modern.
Composition and manufacturing by RR Donnelley, Bloomsburg
Book design by Guenet Abraham.

Library of Congress Cataloging-in-Publication Data

Welch, James, 1940–2003
The Indian lawyer / James Welch.
p.   cm.
1. Siksika Indians—Fiction. I. Title.
PS3573.E44I5   1990
813'.54—dc20   90-6894

ISBN 978-0-393-32938-4 pbk.

W. W. Norton & Company, Inc., 500 Fifth Avenue, New York, N.Y. 10110
www.wwnorton.com

W. W. Norton & Company Ltd., Castle House, 75/76 Wells Street,
London W1T 3QT

2 3 4 5 6 7 8 9 0

To the members and the staff, past and present, of the Montana Board of Pardons, with admiration.

C H A P T E R O N E

It had happened a little less than a year ago in the
library on the high side. He felt the shank go in and it
surprised him. He knew in a split second what had happened but it surprised him and then it pissed him off. He
was the cautious type and he had let himself get stuck like a
fish just off fish row. A couple of guys on the unit had given
him a little shit for that. Harwood, the old con, getting
stuck like some fish. He had to know that the Indians were
going to try it some time. In the library yet. He hadn't been
on the job for three weeks when it happened. But he got
nine days in the infirmary out of it. That wasn't too bad. He
even managed to score some Tylenol 3, which he sold to the
inmate who brought the mail.

But then he had to go to max. In the old days he would

have gone to a Protective Custody Unit, which had its good points, but he would have picked up a jacket, probably as a snitch although he had never snitched anybody off. Once you got labeled you might as well serve the rest of your shift in PC, because somebody in population would get you. But that was the old days. Now they made you go to max for protection and there were some bad dudes there. It was the new policy to discourage inmates from vegetating in PC. There were no treatment programs, no school, no jobs in the PC units, just the opportunity to fuck the dog all day. Ah well, it might have been tempting in the old days to go PC, to avoid all the hassles in the yard, the chow hall, the other units. But he was better off in population as long as he stayed away from the fucking Indians.

Harwood closed his eyes and snorted, almost laughed. Here he was, thinking about staying away from the Indians, and Little Dog was sitting right next to him. But Little Dog was all right. He didn't really run with the rest of them. He ate with them and sometimes watched television in the dayroom, but most of the time when he wasn't working he stayed in his house and read. He'd been busted back six months ago from the dairy dorm for paraphernalia. They hadn't found the shit.

Little Dog's house, or cell, was only a couple of doors down the corridor from Harwood's. One morning he dropped by to borrow some toothpaste and Harwood had glanced up and down the corridor, looking for the setup. Nothing seemed out of the ordinary, just the usual migration to the showers, and so he squeezed some toothpaste on Little Dog's toothbrush. Little Dog smiled and said thanks, but Harwood didn't go to the showers that morning. Since then he'd decided that Little Dog was okay, that he wasn't interested in the Indian games.

"What are you, some kind of fence, Harwood?"

Harwood sat up straight in the metal chair, pulling his long legs in. He didn't look up.

"How about it, Harwood?"

"Yeah, some kind of fence, Beasley."

"We gotta keep this area free of shit, Harwood, in case we need an emergency exit. I guess your legs classify as shit, don't they?"

Harwood folded his arms across his chest and smiled. He knew Beasley. Most of the time Beasley was assigned to the library; in fact he had been on duty the day Harwood got stuck. He had wanted to write Harwood up for fighting but he was talked out of it by another officer. Everybody knew Beasley.

"Hey, Little Dog—remember that time down in the chow hall when I wrote up one of your soul brothers? Do you remember what he did?"

"Farted."

"That's right. He farted in the chow line. You know what that's called, Larry? Insolence. That's what I put in the report. Insolence. Class Two. Let's see." Beasley scratched his head. "What happened to him? I can't remember."

"Locked him down. Fifteen days." Little Dog was studying the papers on his lap. His GED. Certificates of successful completion of the addictive diseases program, aggression control, World of Work, Twelve Steps. He hadn't gone through the Intensive Treatment Unit for chemical dependency—that might be a sticking point—but he had done all right this time in. No way they could deny him parole.

"You know what Harwood is, Larry? A walking Class Two. A walking, talking, farting Class Two. Oh, he thinks he's getting away with it, pulling down those easy gigs. What was it before the library, Harwood—that's right, you were a book-keeper over in Prison Industries. Hear that, Larry? You smokes get sent out to the dairy dorm, bust your asses out there in the cold, and Harwood here is a bookkeeper. And now he's up for parole. I don't know—sounds to me like there's a lot of prejudice—"

The door to the hearing room opened. Harwood and Little Dog looked up.

"Wait right there, Bill. We'll get a disposition sheet out to you in a couple of minutes." The hearings officer closed the door behind him.

"How'd it go?" said Harwood.

Shanley threw himself down in the chair, leaned back, and exhaled.

"How about it, Shanley?" Beasley had his feet up, scrap-ing the bowl of his pipe with one of the keys that dangled from a chain at his waist. "You gonna celebrate the Fourth with the kids? That'd be nice, wouldn't it, take the little ones to the lake, eat hot dogs, drink a little beer, maybe mess around with the wife a little."

"I don't know," said Shanley. He looked at Harwood and his eyes were wide. "I'm damned if I know what went on in there. I think I did okay—I answered all their questions, damm it!"

"That's all you can do," said Harwood. "Don't worry, you're a first-timer, you've done all right." Shanley didn't belong in the close units on the high side. He should have been in the letter units on the low side. Low security. As usual the prison was overcrowded, so they stuck a guy like Shanley in with the heavies. Harwood had tried to watch out for him, to teach him the ropes, but Shanley was just too innocent. As a result he'd been bulldogged numerous times, raped twice, and Harwood suspected he was having his wife send him money to pay off the heavies, probably the Indians, since they controlled the unit. All because he didn't belong on the high security side. At least Harwood had made sure he didn't become somebody's old lady.

"Well, what's it going to be, Shanley, long sheet or short sheet? We're going to miss you down there in the kitchen. You got a real touch with those sweet rolls. I almost hope they set you back. How long you been in, Shanley?"

"Thirteen months, twelve days, not counting sixty days jail time."

"Hooo," Beasley breathed. "That's a pretty good stretch for checks. You must have been laying some pretty serious paper. What's that on—five years? You know, most guys, they'd give a suspended or deferred, slap their wrist a little— but you, you must be some kind of badass. Like Harwood here. How long you been down this time, Harwood, five, six years?"

"Close to seven, Beasley. That's on a forty-year beef reduced to thirty by Sentence Review. Fifth felony, second armed robbery, persistent offender, declared dangerous. And an escape, two years consecutive to the thirty. Anything else you need to know, Beasley?"

"Hey now, don't get testy, Harwood. I'm just making conversation, that's all, trying to ease the tension. I know you guys are a little nervous when you come up. You're a little nervous, aren't you, Larry?"

Little Dog knew better than to get drawn in. He'd done all right this time and he wasn't about to blow it by telling Beasley to fuck off. He wanted to go home. It'd been nearly four years and it had been three years before that. In fact, he'd been on the outside only two years out of the last eleven. He was tired of the joint and tired of the juvenile home and foster homes. He was ready to go back to the reservation and live with his grandmother. He held up his GED diploma. "See this, Officer Beasley? This is my ticket. I got a good training program waiting for me on the res and I'm going to make it."

Beasley laughed. "That's the spirit, Larry. Hell, nothing's going to stop you this time. You just lay off the sauce, you'll be okay. See that, Harwood?"

The door opened and the hearings officer entered the small holding room. He waved a piece of paper and smiled. "Short sheet, Bill. You did a good job."

Shanley let out a deep breath and slumped back on the chair. He had done some hard time. He accepted Harwood's hand, his eyes glittery. "When can I leave?" His voice was small, apprehensive.

"Well, I'm going to have to read you out, check out that job plan once more. It's a little shaky, but I don't see why we can't get you out of here the end of next week. I'll come by your unit tomorrow. We'll get the ball rolling then."

Shanley stood and the tears came. He couldn't help them. He tried to read the disposition sheet. He turned away from the others.

"Want to sit here for a while, Bill, kind of get it together?"

"I'm all right." Shanley wiped his eyes with his sleeve. He shook the hearings officer's hand. "Thanks."

"You earned it. Good luck." The hearings officer turned to Little Dog. "Larry?"

Little Dog straightened his papers and stood, following the

officer into the hearing room. The door chunked behind them.

Shanley looked down at Harwood. "Thanks—thanks for helping me. I don't know if . . ." His voice caught and his "Good luck" was barely a whisper.

Harwood listened to Shanley's steps echo down the hall. It was late in the afternoon and the building had turned quiet. A couple of officers talked in low tones in the muster room next door and Harwood couldn't see or understand them. Beasley was reading the newspaper, his feet up on the desk. Suddenly Harwood felt empty inside. He knew it was hopeless, an exercise in delusion. That morning he had actually felt good. He had gotten his library job back and he spent the morning unpacking a couple of crates of books from some church group in Billings. They weren't the kind of books he would have read, mostly inspirational, self-help stuff, but he had unpacked them and glued on the little envelopes that held the checkout cards. Then he spent the afternoon up to three-quarters of an hour ago typing the names and titles on the checkout cards. It was a good mind-numbing job and he thought of Patti Ann and he thought he would get a chance to be with her shortly. That's how much he deluded himself. They had been married for nine years and he had spent seven and a half of them locked up, counting jail time and prison time. At least he had that going for him. Maybe they would think he had served enough time; maybe they'd cut him a little slack because he'd been shanked. His prison record was pretty good—no write-ups the last couple of years; he'd completed ADSP and the follow-up program even though he didn't have a drinking or drug problem; he'd gone through aggression control; he'd even had several one-on-one sessions with the shrink, Larson, to see why he liked to point guns at people. He knew he interested Larson because he wasn't like most of the other inmates—he was bright and clean-cut and had a degree in economics as well as an A.A. in bookkeeping. He'd been interviewed by a couple of student psychologists who also couldn't figure out why he pulled the shit he did. He liked Larson, he was an old pro, and Harwood had tried to level with him, but he just couldn't explain his motivation. It came out sounding like he was a thrill-seeker or some bullshit thing like that. Larson figured it had something to do with power, he'd told Harwood that much, but he couldn't understand what was behind it. Most of the other inmates were pretty easy to figure out, the patterns were there—poverty, abuse, history of criminality in the family, impulsiveness. But Harwood was something else. He came from a good family, he had a normal childhood, and he hadn't committed a crime until he was twenty-four. By that time he'd been working two years in the accounting department for a small chain of grocery stores in Montana and Idaho. He'd gotten good evaluations. Things were looking rosy. So why now, at the age of thirty-seven, was he doing his second stretch for armed robbery? Harwood used to laugh and throw up his hands at Larson's frustration. If you couldn't laugh you'd end up crying. There was a lot of laughing in the joint.

Harwood put all that old business out of his mind and concentrated on Patti Ann. What was it—a little over a month since she had last come down to see him? Jesus! Harwood looked at his watch. 4:35. She was here now, waiting for him in the visiting room. Waiting to see if he made it. He glanced over at Beasley. Shit, if it had been any other officer Harwood could have him call over to the visiting room and tell Patti Ann he would be a little late. Ah, Christ, it didn't matter. The news wasn't going to be good anyhow. Harwood shook his head and wished there was a window to look out of. There were never enough windows.

What would she be wearing today? Maybe that white dress with the little straps. Yeah, she'd be wearing that, it was his favorite. Sexy and innocent-looking at the same time. And the high heels, the burgundy ones. He liked the way her legs looked in that outfit. She'd be nice and tan, slender but healthy-looking. God, she was probably going nuts wondering what was happening to him. She knew his hearing was today but she didn't know it would be the last one of the day. She'd driven all the way over from Helena and if they were lucky they'd get half an hour together. It wasn't going to be a very happy visit, so maybe it was just as well. She can come back next month, thought Harwood, when things were back to normal.

He heard the muffled sound of laughter from the hearing room and then the door opened and Little Dog came out beaming.

"We'll do your release papers tomorrow, Larry. We should be able to get you on a bus by the end of next week, maybe sooner. It's all been cleared with your parole officer. Okay?"

"Sooner the better. I'm going to make it this time. I'm done with this shit."

"Just don't set your sights too high, Larry, at least not initially. One day at a time, just like the old song. Get adjusted out there. Good luck to you." The hearings officer shook Little Dog's hand, then turned to Harwood. "Come on in, Jack."

The first thing Harwood noticed was the carpeting, wall to wall. He hadn't walked on carpeting in seven years. Then the bank of windows that looked across the courtyard to a twenty-foot-tall cement wall. Some view.

"You want to sit here, Jack?" The hearings officer pointed to a chair across the table from the three board members. It was set back a way from the table. "Jack, these are the members of the board who will conduct your hearing—Mr. Berglund, Mr. Higgins, and Mr. Yellow Calf. Jack Harwood."

"How you doing, Jack?" The man in the middle leaned forward with a smile.

Harwood glanced down at the nameplate. Peter Higgins. He was the chairman, the one you had to look out for, that was the word in the yard. He came down hard on the bullshitters, so shoot straight. "Not bad, Mr. Higgins."

"Good, that's good. Let's see—" Higgins picked up a loose-leaf notebook. "Five felonies, two armed robberies, one escape. Two probation violations, one parole violation. That sound about right, Jack?"

"Unfortunately, that's correct."

"Unfortunately? What do you mean, unfortunately? Fortune has nothing to do with it. You're up to your ears in the life of crime, Jack. You're a big-time hood."

Harwood shrugged.

"Okay, instant offense, holding up a savings and loan in Helena, two fall partners. Where are they now, Jack?"

"Hartpence is still here, Williams got out a couple of years ago. Williams did good time."

"He also rolled over on you guys, didn't he? I seem to remember reading that he cut himself a deal with the county attorney's office. You remember that case, Bob?"

Berglund had been rolling his necktie around a pencil. The question caught him by surprise. "Williams. Yeah, we paroled him two years ago. He snitched these guys off and Judge Howard gave him a reduced sentence. He was the driver."

Higgins looked down at the thick notebook. It held all the cases the parole board was to hear at the prison that month. The other members of the board had identical notebooks. As they studied them, Harwood took the opportunity to glance behind him. The hearings officer and the executive secretary were talking. Flaherty, that was the secretary's name, Walt Flaherty. He was a good guy. He treated the inmates well, answered their questions, didn't act like a honcho. Harwood looked out the windows. A yard crew was working on the small strip of grass in the courtyard. Seven of them.

"Have you ever had a gun stuck in your face, Jack?"

Harwood was surprised at the suddenness of the question but not the question itself. He remembered his first parole hearing. He knew they liked to come from all angles, trying to trip you up.

"Just once, Mr. Higgins. One of the arresting officers this last time pointed his revolver at me. I guess both of them did but the other one was behind me."

"Can you imagine how that poor woman in the savings and loan felt, some jackass comes along and sticks a gun in her face? She must have been terrified. She probably still has nightmares!" Higgins's voice was beginning to rise. "All because a big-time hood like you is too damn lazy to go out and earn his money like decent human beings, like that woman!"

Remorse. That was the key. "I think about it all the time, Mr. Higgins, believe me. If there was anything I could do—I just thank the Lord—"

"This was your second armed robbery, Jack. Why don't

you tell us about the first one." Berglund had a calm, level voice. He was a rancher from Miles City, a tall balding man who had put in several years in the state legislature, who had pushed for better treatment programs in the prison and who had been a key player in getting the funds to build the new prison. Now, he liked to joke, his appointment to the parole board was punishment for his past political sins.

"There's not much to tell, Mr. Berglund," said Harwood. "I didn't need the money, I was a decent hardworking human being—" Harwood glanced at Higgins. "I guess it was just an impulsive thing, you know, one of those things you do—"

"Impulsive?" Higgins's voice was strained with wonder. "You call going to a bar, buying a sawed-off shotgun, picking up a fall partner at his home way out in Rimini, returning to Helena, gassing up your car, then holding up the Colonial Inn—impulsive?"

Harwood glanced over at Sylvester Yellow Calf. He was leaning back in his swivel chair, studying the notebook in his lap. He was a big man, good shape, good-looking. Harwood had never seen an Indian in a suit and tie before. He knew Yellow Calf was a lawyer in Helena and a former basketball player. In fact, Yellow Calf had played for the University of Montana while Harwood went to school there. Harwood didn't pay much attention to sports but the fact that Yellow Calf was a lawyer in Helena did intrigue him. That was Harwood's turf, that was where Patti Ann lived.

"I guess 'impulsive' is the wrong word for it, Mr. Higgins. I don't know, maybe 'fascination' would be a better one. I kind of became fascinated with serious crime, not just shoplifting or writing a bum check. I don't know, maybe it became kind of an obsession, I just knew I had to try it. So my friend and I held up the Colonial."

"How much did you get?"

"A little over two thousand."

"And how much from the savings and loan?"

"Twelve."

"Okay, Jack, the million-dollar question—why? And don't give me any more of that fascination bullshit. You might be able to con a couple of student psychologists but you're talking to us now." Higgins swept his arm around the room. "We're all adults, nothing goes beyond this room, you know that. So why not level with us?"

Harwood hesitated. For the first time since deciding that he wasn't going to make parole anyway he felt a kind of pressure to answer the question well. Were they taking this hearing seriously? Jesus, he might actually have a chance. "Okay, I'll try to explain it all, Mr. Higgins. That first time was pretty much like I said. I'm sure it's in your records there—I had graduated from UM and had taken a job in the accounting department of the grocery chain. I was in training and not making a lot of money but I was getting by, I was single then. I didn't have much going for me socially so I started hanging around this particular bar in Helena. I never had a drinking problem but it was a place to go, to spend the evenings. To make a long story short, I met a couple of guys I shouldn't have. They'd done time over here and they were into some petty shit, mostly burglaries. One night I went with them— that was the night we hit the Steinhaus, got over four hundred in cash, a thirty-eight that was behind the bar, and a couple of cases of booze. Those guys were pretty elated but I was scared shitless. They tried to give me some of the money but I wouldn't take it. I stayed away from that bar for a couple of weeks. I thought I was through with it. But one night I met them in the parking lot at Buttrey's. I don't to this day know why but I let them talk me into riding around with them. They were drinking beer and started talking about doing time here in Deer Lodge. They told me all about the way guys are bull-dogged, beaten up for not playing con games. I was fascinated—there's that word again, Mr. Higgins—and kind of scared. It was like there was a reason for telling me about this scary shit. There seemed to be a threat behind it. Anyway, we hit the Cenex that night and got a bunch of tools and some cash. One of the guys said there was supposed to be a lot of cash around but we couldn't find it. Turns out the sixty dollars we did get was money from a football pool. I don't know, a week or so later one of the guys and I robbed the Colonial."

"That's a pretty major step, Jack, going from burglary to armed robbery," said Berglund. He was shaking his head. "I don't understand how a fellow like you could get involved in burglary, much less robbery. As far as I can tell, you had no juvenile record, no priors. Let's see, the judge gave you five, five, and twenty, all concurrent, and suspended fifteen." He looked up from his notebook. "That's a curious sentence, Jack, kind of harsh and lenient at the same time."

"I did fourteen months on it, built up a lot of good time. I was earning day for day toward the end." Harwood smiled. "I thought I learned a pretty good lesson there."

"And what happened?"

"It's a fairly old story. My employer wouldn't take me back because I was a criminal, and I couldn't get bonded, so my career as an accountant was over almost before it started. I couldn't even get a job as a boxboy with that chain. I ended up paroling out to a housepainting outfit in Helena and made some decent money that summer. But it wasn't a career."

"Isn't that about the time you got married?"

"Yeah, I painted her house that summer. She was in the process of getting a divorce and she was fixing up the house in order to sell it. I helped her do some other stuff on my time off, then I helped her move when she sold it. We got married that winter—nine years ago." Harwood looked at the backs of his hands, which were resting on his knees. "She's a good woman."

"Doesn't she work for the state?"

"Human Resources—she's in records."

"Children?"

Harwood knew they had this information in their notebooks, but this was part of their game. "She miscarried twice, had to have a hysterectomy after the second time. I was already in here when that happened. It was a pretty bad time for her. That's when I decided to walk away. I wanted to go to Helena to be with her."

Higgins had been leaning back in his swivel chair, studying Harwood's reactions to Berglund's questions. He glanced over at Sylvester Yellow Calf, who had Harwood's jacket spread before him. He was reading a trial transcript. Higgins looked beyond Yellow Calf to the twenty-foot-high wall on the other side of the courtyard. It was sliced in half by the shadow of the administration building. Higgins's stomach growled. Last case of the day, and it was a tough one. He listened to Harwood explain his escape and how he was picked up in Helena two days later at the hospital. It appeared that he did just want to be with his wife, because he had to know that

would be the first place they would look for him—and there
he was. He was still in his prison khakis when the cops
walked in on him. That escape was probably the reason he
was still in the joint. Escapes were mandatory consecutive
sentences. They could have paroled him before now without
the escape. It was hard to get a handle on Harwood. In some
ways he was about as decent an inmate as they'd heard today,
for several months for that matter. The word was that Harwood took some of the weaker inmates under his wing—no
sex, no bulldogging, just protection. And he was certainly a
lot brighter than your run-of-the-mill inmate. And that's what
irked Higgins. Pissed him off, in fact. He didn't have to pull
this crap. He should be out taking care of his wife, going to
work, paying taxes. Peter Higgins felt his jaw tightening and
he had to tell himself, Easy, go easy.

Berglund was beginning to wind down. He was old and had
a weak heart. He'd only been back from triple-bypass surgery
for three months and Higgins worried about him. At least the
new hearing room was air-conditioned, not like the old one
where you had to keep the doors closed and locked for security reasons and it got to be an oven in there. This was pretty
plush. Even the flags looked crisper in here.

Sylvester Yellow Calf laid the file on the table and waited
for Berglund to finish questioning the inmate. He too could
tell the old man was about finished for the day. His usually
level voice was becoming flat and tinny. And they had put in a
long day, seen a lot of inmates. Sylvester sneaked a look at his
watch. 5:10. Not too bad. He probably was going to make it
back to Helena by 6:30. Took about an hour if you hustled.
He hated cocktail parties and he should be laughing at himself for being anxious about this one. But it was a big one.

Finally, Bob Berglund slumped back with an audible, grateful wheeze. He automatically reached in his shirt pocket for a cigarette before he remembered they weren't there anymore. He'd had to give them up.

Sylvester looked at the inmate, Jack Harwood, almost for the first time since he had glanced up when Harwood entered the room. Clean-cut, short hair, no headband, no bandanna, no tattoos. His khakis were ironed, maybe even starched, and the running shoes looked brand-new.

"Mr. Harwood, I've been reading the transcript of the savings and loan robbery trial. Just a couple of things, let's see." Sylvester flipped back a couple of pages. "Here we are—in response to a question by the prosecuting attorney you state that you have no desire to cooperate with the court, that what's done is done, and here, I quote: 'I've already ruined my fucking chance for a decent life, you're going to flush me anyway, I'm not taking anybody else down.' Then you refused to answer any more of the prosecuting attorney's questions. Just a couple of things, Mr. Harwood. First, why did you request a jury trial if you weren't going to cooperate with anyone, including your own attorney—and second, what did you mean by the statement 'I'm not taking anybody else down'? That almost sounds like there were more of you than got charged for the robbery."

Harwood laughed, softly, to the whole table. "I may have been a little melodramatic there. That prosecutor was a bulldog. No, there were just the three of us—Hartpence, Williams, and me."

"You're sure? No other accomplices?"

"That's the way it went down, just like on your police report there."

"It also says in the transcript that only three thousand dollars was recovered—that's out of twelve thousand. What happened to the rest of the money?"

"That's always puzzled me, Mr. Yellow Calf. I can't imagine what happened to the rest of it. We put the athletic bag with the money in it in the trunk of Williams's car. When they busted Williams the next day, they only found the three thousand." Harwood laughed and lifted his eyebrows as though the joke was on him.

"C'mon, Jack, you were the man. Those other guys didn't have enough brains between them to make a good breakfast. All right, tell me this—tell me what you think happened to the money."

Harwood began to realize that things were getting out of control. It was clear that Higgins didn't like him, and now this Indian was getting smart. Harwood almost laughed again but caught himself. Be sincere, be straight, level with them. As much as you can.

"You're not going to believe this, you're not going to want to believe this—" Harwood glanced quickly at Higgins, who was examining his fingernails. "I don't think Williams got away with it. He knew the consequences—Hartpence is a pretty mean dude." Now Harwood looked into Yellow Calf's eyes. "I can only guess it was the cops. They're the only ones besides Williams who had access to the car and the money. That's the only way I can figure it."

"For Christ's sake, Harwood!" If so much wasn't on the line, it would have been comical to see Higgins explode. He was a small man with a shiny face and round eyes that always seemed full of helpless fury. He had abandoned his clip-on tie earlier that afternoon and now even his neck was bright red.

Yellow Calf jumped in quickly. "Jack, you don't expect us to believe this, do you? You know, as Mr. Higgins has already pointed out, all we want out of you guys is the truth. You have already been to trial, you've been found guilty, you're serving your time. We can't do anything to you if you tell us the truth. We just want the truth. Do you understand that, Jack? Do you want to try again?"

Things were definitely fucked. Just like that. Even Berglund was looking at him with mild disgust.

"You've done pretty well in here, Jack. No write-ups the past two years, you've completed some programs, you're working. You were kind of a smartass early on but you've cleaned up your act considerably. That's to the good—but there are two or three areas we need to address in considering your case. One, you picked up a felony, the escape, while you were in here. That doesn't look good. That makes it hard for us to parole you on your first appearance. And law enforcement doesn't want you back in the Helena area. We have notes from the county attorney's office, the sheriff's department, the police department. But mostly they—and we—believe that you got away with the rest of the money, the nine thousand dollars. That's not a hell of a lot of money, Jack, but you put us in a very awkward position. How will it look to law enforcement, to the people in Helena, if we just parole you without your having to account for the money?"

"I sure wish I knew what happened to that money, Mr. Yellow Calf, I'd sure tell you." The jig was now up. Harwood had tried to sound sincere, to act sincere, but he knew Yellow Calf had detected the small sarcasm in his voice. Practically seven years in the joint and he still couldn't tell them. But what if he did? What would happen? What about the statute of limitations? Didn't that run out in seven years? He'd have to look that up tomorrow in the library. One thing about a prison library, it has a good legal section. And good jailhouse lawyers. For a couple of packs of cigarettes he could have one of them review his case. Be kind of fun to ask this Indian lawyer right now about the statute of limitations, get a little free legal advice from the adversary. But even as Jack Harwood thought this, he felt his spirits sinking rapidly.

"Anything else you'd like to tell us, Jack?"

Harwood stared at Yellow Calf. Yeah, I've been shanked by the fucking Indians. Don't I get some points for that, some good time, combat pay, a Purple Heart? Harwood wanted to tell this Indian fucking lawyer that. It seemed only human to take that into consideration, but he knew the board wouldn't. They had that information in their notebooks but for some reason they chose not to bring it up. Neither would he. Neither would he forget Sylvester Yellow Calf.

He turned to the chairman and smiled. "I guess that's about it, Mr. Higgins. I'd like a chance out there. Things have changed and I'd like to see what it's like."

Higgins had regained his composure. Now he just sounded weary. "You want to step outside? We'll get a disposition sheet to you in a minute."

Harwood stood and thanked the board, smiling, brisk. He waved to Walt Flaherty. "See you in the yard, Walt." The old con code—don't let them see you sweat. Just like in the commercial.

Patti Ann Harwood sat at a small round table in the visiting room, watching the families—the parents, the children, the wives, the girlfriends. It was getting late and most of the children had grown tired of seeing their fathers, their stepfathers, their mothers' boyfriends. Some had gone outside to play; others twisted and whined on plastic chairs; still others, the smaller ones, slept on jackets or small blankets on the concrete floor. The initial enthusiasm had long since worn off and the conversations were by turns desultory and intimate.

Patti Ann had been sitting, waiting, for an hour and forty minutes. She knew Jack would probably be a little late but this was ridiculous. She'd already had the duty officer call over to the hearing room. Jack was the next case, but that had been at least an hour ago. It was bad enough having to see him like this, once a month because he wouldn't let her come any more often, but now there were only twenty minutes left. There was so much to say—Patti Ann caught herself—there was usually nothing to say because to say things out loud made each visit more painful than the last. Patti Ann could feel herself slowly, inexorably slipping to the edge of Jack's life. What could he tell her of his life in the prison? What could she tell him of the outside world that didn't fill him with regret, even pain? The small talk—she had become pretty good at it but it didn't go anywhere. When she left the prison after each visit she felt insignificant. She didn't have a family with Jack, she didn't have a life with Jack. She lived alone, a prison widow.

She dug into her purse, found her cigarettes and plastic lighter. As she lit up she glanced around the room at the other women. Years ago she had scorned them and pitied them. Most of them were unattractive—fat or skinny, hard-looking or puffy, stringy hair or pathetic, glamorous bouffants; some of them had tattoos on their knuckles and arms; most of them were on general assistance, relief, child care. These were the ones who came to visit most often. They lived in downtown Deer Lodge, sometimes two to three families to an apartment. Some of them worked but most found it more profitable to stay on assistance. That way, too, they could visit their men at every opportunity.

In the beginning Patti Ann had looked down on them, especially those who met their men in prison through sisters or girlfriends or former boyfriends and husbands, pen-pal organizations, church groups. These were the saddest to Patti Ann. Losers on the outside and losers on the inside. They fulfilled their men's needs while they were in prison but when they got out the men usually dumped them. Who needs an unattractive divorced woman with two kids that aren't even yours?

Even now Patti Ann could see these women scattered around the visiting room. And today she didn't feel very different from them. She was nervous and fitful, mildly depressed. At first when she heard that Jack was scheduled for his parole hearing this month she had been elated, despite his cautions. She had walked around her apartment looking at the furniture, the pictures, the rugs, the small things, trying to see them as Jack might when he walked in for the first time. She had even bought a bright new comforter for the double bed. Then she thought of looking for a new larger apartment until she realized that he had been living in a cubicle smaller than her bedroom. Jack had called a couple more times and spoken to her with a quiet sobriety and she did come to realize that he might not make it. But he had been in for seven years—how could the parole board turn him down? She had waited for him, they had to know that. If she could have had a child perhaps she could have waited forever, but all she had was herself, every night in the small apartment, herself.

Patti Ann had been watching a family, and the inmate smiled at her and waved. It took a second for her to realize that the gesture was directed at her. She smiled awkwardly and tried to place him—slight, sandy hair, a little obsequious even at this distance. Yes, Stanley, Stanley—no, Shanley, Bob? Bill? The little guy that Jack tried so hard to protect. Jack had introduced her to him last winter. Now he gave her the thumbs-up and she remembered that he was up for parole too. He had made it. She smiled and nodded, and then she smiled and nodded to his wife, who was also slight—in her sleeveless blouse, tight jeans, and sneakers, she looked like somebody's little sister, but there were three children at the table.

Above the murmur of the late-afternoon conversations Patti Ann heard the electric gate roll open. She was surprised that she was that attuned to the nuances of prison noises. She looked toward the open door and she saw Jack enter the visiting room. He dropped his pass on the duty officer's table and looked at her. He did not look happy.

She stood and watched him pick his way between tables, once stepping over a sleeping child, and she moved forward and hugged him and gave him a small kiss, the kind the officers allowed. She knew before asking but she asked anyway.

"They turned me down," he said, and he lowered himself wearily onto a plastic chair.

"But why?" she said. "How could they . . ."

He unfolded a sheet of paper and handed it to her and then sat back and watched her read it. "Nature of crime," he said. "Also, they don't parole repeat violent offenders on their first appearance."

"But you're not violent, that's ridiculous!"

"Seven years ago I stuck a gun in someone's face. That makes me violent. Listen, we've been all through this. I warned you, didn't I? I told you not to get your hopes up. You've seen how this system works. You make a couple of mistakes and they make you pay. They don't care how long it takes, just so long as you pay." Harwood leaned forward, shook a cigarette out of her pack, and lit it. "So I'm paying," he said glumly.

"Well, what do you have to do now? What else?"

"It's on there, near the bottom." Harwood nodded toward the piece of paper on the table. He noticed the full ashtray. She was smoking too much again.

Patti Ann picked up the disposition sheet. Under Recommendations, in longhand, it listed reduced custody, continued clear conduct, advanced aggression control. But it was the top of the sheet that caused her heart to sink. Parole denied, pass to discharge of sentence. Such clinical, dispassionate language—a couple of phrases that probably meant nothing to the parole board but meant everything to Jack, and to her. She set the piece of paper aside and sighed an almost contented sigh. Parole denied. And she suddenly recognized the source of her earlier depression. It startled her, the utter simplicity—she had been afraid that Jack would be paroled, that he would come home to her apartment, to her life! She had made a life. She had a routine, a couple of friends, she sewed in the evenings and she had been to bed alone more than she had with Jack or any man. She looked at Jack as though he were an object and she saw a familiar face, a small smile fading as the eyes narrowed in puzzlement.

"What's wrong?" he said.

She shook her head and tried to smile. Today, for the first time since he went in, she saw an inmate sitting across the table, wearing khakis and running shoes like the rest of them. He even had that look, that edgy don't-get-too-close look that some of the longtimers had. But it was the uniformity of it all, the cinder-block buildings, the maze of sidewalks, the guard towers, the dirt parking lot in front of the administration building, the inmates in their khakis and blues and watch caps, the officers in their blue blazers and maroon ties, the glint of the ribbon wire on top of the endless Cyclone fences—all of it was colorless in its monotony and now she saw that lack of color in her husband and it scared her and made her angry.

"Jack," she said. She leaned forward and put her hand on his knee. "I need you out of here. Things are getting too odd for us. I can't deal with you being in here and me out there. Every time I drive home from here, I look at the streams, the pines, the mountains—the world just seems too big, too much to handle every day. I think I won't see you again." She lowered her head and looked at her hand. "It frightens me so much when I think that someday I might like it that way."

Harwood covered her hand with his own. He glanced at his wristwatch. They had only ten minutes left. "You have to be strong for a little while longer. I know this is a blow but we have to weather it out. We can if we stay strong."

Patti Ann looked up into his face and it was familiar again

but it would always be changed by what she had seen earlier. She had seen what prison actually does to a man; she had seen the dull gray edges of resignation, and she wondered if she could ever look at her husband again without seeing that. She sighed and nodded her head.

Harwood stubbed out his cigarette and leaned away from her. "You smoke too much, you know that?"

She smiled, then laughed softly. He had said that to her when he first met her, when he painted her house. The world was different then.

"You're also very pretty. You didn't wear my favorite dress, though. How about it—next time?"

"Okay." She had deliberately not worn that dress. It was an innocent-looking sundress, a little short with delicate shoulder straps, hardly striking on the street, but in here she felt naked and vulnerable. Part of her discomfort came from the way Jack had stared at her last time, as though he were one of the gang and she a prime piece. Now he was memorizing her from top to bottom and she tried to understand his unabashed lust, but all she could feel was a vague shame at the unnaturalness of it. She was his wife.

She became aware of a change in the noises that surrounded them and she glanced around and saw that visiting hours were over. The women were gathering kids and toys, some were giving their men a last-minute thrill, a squeeze here, a tongue there, a small packet of dope. But most seemed just weary and relieved that it was over for another day.

Harwood stood and took her hand and brought her to her feet. Amid the milling, he hugged her close and kissed her hard. She felt his hand on her butt and just as quickly it was gone and he was walking her out the door to the electric gate.

"I need you to do me a favor," he said quietly as they waited for the other visitors to assemble at the gate. "There's this guy on the parole board, his name's Sylvester Yellow Calf—an Indian, a lawyer from Helena. You can look him up in the phone book. I want you to find out something about him, if he's married, what law firm he's attached to, what kind of law he practices. Find out who his friends are, what does he do for a social life, things like that. I know this is asking a lot, but I need to know something about him."

Patti Ann had been looking through the metal gate at a shadowy mountain that loomed above the administration building. Although it was late August a small crevice near the top contained a wedge of snow that was turning blue as the light went off it. Behind the right shoulder of the mountain she could see a column of smoke. Now she turned toward Jack, but he was looking straight ahead at the electric gate. Just then the gate buzzed and began to slide open. Jack squeezed her hand and turned to go back across the yard to his unit. She had begun to move with the crowd through the gate when she heard him call her name. She turned but she was caught up in the moving throng.

"I want you to meet him," he called. "Soon. Make an appointment with him, bump into him in the grocery store, anything—just meet him. I'll call you."

By then she was through the gate and she stepped to one side. "Why?" she cried, but Harwood smiled and waved as he walked briskly back to his unit.

CHAPTER TWO

As Sylvester Yellow Calf drove down from Mac-
Donald Pass toward the Prickly Pear Valley he thought of
Larry Little Dog's family. He had grown up with one of
Little Dog's brothers and had played many games of horse
and one-on-one on a rickety basket nailed to a utility pole
in the Little Dog yard. At the time he had envied Donny
and the whole family and had thought up many excuses to
be at their house day and night. There were so many brothers and sisters that Sylvester could barely remember Larry,
who was much younger than Donny.

It was during Sylvester and Donny's senior year that the
Little Dog parents were killed in a car accident. Ironically,
they had been driving to Cut Bank to watch the two boys
play in a basketball game when they ran off an icy bridge.

Donny played that night but he quit the team later to try to keep the rest of his family together. But Family Services got most of the younger brothers and sisters—there must have been a dozen of them, Sylvester thought. Somehow Donny and Larry and a sister on whom Sylvester always had a crush managed to escape and live with their grandmother, which was another irony because Sylvester lived with his grandparents and had envied Donny for having parents.

Sylvester rolled his window all the way down. He could feel the air warm as he descended into the valley. He hadn't asked Larry about Donny because he was afraid of what he would find out. The only thing Sylvester knew about Donny now was that he wasn't an inmate of Montana State Prison.

A familiar feeling of unease began to wash over Sylvester. He had left so many people behind, so many friends and acquaintances, to live in a world that had little to do with his people. He had always been different, even back there on the reservation, and now he was different in a white man's town in a white man's world of briefcases, suits, law, and politics. Even Buster Harrington, the senior partner of the law firm, had begun to push him to become more like his young white colleagues. Harrington had begun to worry that perhaps Sylvester was too different. But a lot of politicians were different. You could even make it a virtue if you called it integrity.

Sylvester glanced at the console clock. 6:35. He should at least go home and change his shirt. Eight straight hours in the hearing room, not to mention the drive, did little for the wardrobe, less for the spirit. Things were a little more tolerable now. He could leave most of it at the prison.

During his first couple of years on the board he would bring the whole disheartening mess home with him—the untreatable crazies who saw hell through their cell floors; the child molesters who were mentally and emotionally children themselves; the abused who became the abusers; the paint-sniffing, brain-fried Indians who hadn't had any opportunities, any chance. Now Sylvester could leave most of it at the prison and he didn't like himself any more for being able to do so. It just made things a little more tolerable.

Sylvester slowed down as he rounded a curve and came into the basin of the Prickly Pear Valley. Far off to the north the sky was dark with a summer storm. A rainbow glimmered faintly beneath it, mostly yellow and green. The foothills were unnaturally golden in the evening sun. Then Sylvester saw the column of smoke to the southeast. It was a soft, puffy cloud above the dark mountains, blowing in no particular direction. A dusty volatility hung in the air over the valley.

〰〰〰

"Hi."

"Hi yourself. You look awful. You just get back?"

"Thanks." Sylvester leaned over and kissed Shelley's cheek. "Just pulled in. Have you heard anything about a fire? I saw some smoke a little south of here."

"Probably a lightning strike. I thought I heard thunder last night."

"It looked pretty big. With a little wind it could take off." Sylvester kissed her other cheek.

"Go wash up. You know where the towels are. I'll call Maggie and tell her we'll be right over."

"Where are the girls?" Sylvester ran some cool water into the basin. His neck was stiff from sitting all day.

"At Mother's—she's going to keep them tonight."

Sylvester splashed his face and looked into the mirror. He did look a little ragged, a little shadowy beneath the eyes. He needed a haircut too.

Shelley came into the small room. "She says we better get our asses over there or there will be no need to come. Don't you love it?"

"Who's this guy we're supposed to meet?"

"You're supposed to meet," Shelley corrected. "His name is Fabares and he's from the Democratic Party national headquarters. I'm not sure what he does, but he's a hotshot—according to Maggie. You've got some soap on your ear."

"Maybe we should drop by my place so I can get a clean shirt." Sylvester had the collar of his striped shirt turned down.

"Forget it. Harrington will hand you your rear end if we don't get there now. C'mon, let's get it over with. Then we can get something to eat."

"I wish this kind of crap didn't happen," Sylvester moaned.

"You know how to make it stop."

"Don't be cruel. I've had a rough couple of days. Be nice to me and I'll make it worth your while."

"Afterwards." Shelley grabbed his hand. "I'll be just as nice as you please, nicer than you deserve. Turn out the light."

〰〰〰

Buster Harrington and his wife, Maggie, lived in one of the many mansions built during the 1880s and '90s in Helena by lumber barons, mining kings, prosperous stockmen and merchants. Many of the mansions had burned down; many had fallen into disrepair; some had been converted into apartments and office space. Most were memories, the ruins of a stone wall, a section of rusted iron fence, a broken bird bath overgrown with weeds all that was left. To those who cared to notice, the mansions along with the downtown blocks on Last Chance Gulch represented a transition from the gold camps of the 1860s and '70s to a real city ten to twenty years later.

The Harringtons' house had been built for a feed and grain dealer who had come all the way from Glasgow, Scotland, made his stake in the gold fields, and settled down to supply the farmers and ranchers who in turn supplied the miners. The house itself, as mansions go, was not oversized—there was no ballroom, no billiard room, just gracious high-ceilinged rooms trimmed in imported woods and brass sconces and fixtures. The centerpiece of the living room was a crystal chandelier which had been imported from Scotland in 1888. Buster Harrington stood beneath this chandelier, an Early Times ditch in his pudgy hand, half-listening to the Democratic headquarters man, Fabares, explain the new law regarding PACs. Actually the law had been around for a while but Fabares was making sure that the hicks in this cowtown understood it. As always the talk was boiling down to contributions, a subject that bored Harrington, and so he excused himself from the circle and went to look into the library.

Maggie was at the far end by the fireplace, showing the small watercolor by Russell and the oil by Sharpe. The women, five or six of them, were standing in attitudes that suggested appreciation of what they were seeing. The lone man, immaculate in a dark blue suit, stood off to one side, sipping at his colorless drink. He seemed more interested in the women. Seeing him made Harrington aware that he had never liked having the Russell and Sharpe pictures in the house. They had been part of a fee settlement with a sheepman right after the Second World War. That had been a landmark grazing case; the stakes were high and the fee was big. For a fresh-faced vet just out of law school the ramifications went beyond the monetary award. Harrington became a Helena force, an instant adviser to Governor Ford (Harrington always found it hard to believe that he had been a Republican in his early days, had met Thomas E. Dewey in 1948, had worn a Dewey button around until that fateful election day), and, best of all, he became a member of the Montana Club, the only place to eat in Helena, then and now.

Harrington took a swallow of his Early Times and walked down to the man in the dark suit. "Buster Harrington." He stuck out a hand. "I don't believe we've been introduced."

"Ernst Lyman," the man said brightly. "I've been admiring the pictures your wife is so gracious in showing."

Harrington tried to place the accent. Northern European.

"These are famous artists. Charley Russell is very famous in my native country."

"Germany, right?"

"Close. The Netherlands—but I am of German stock. I have lived in the Netherlands since before the war. Cowboys and especially Indians are very big there."

"Well, they're pretty big around here too. Almost everybody has a cowboy or an Indian in the woodpile."

"Buster! Stop that!" Maggie, as well as the other women, had been listening.

"What? What did I say? It's true, isn't it?"

"You don't have to be vulgar." Maggie turned to the man in the blue suit. "You'll just have to forgive him, Mr. Lyman. He's a vulgar little man."

This Lyman must be something, Harrington thought, the kind of guy people go out of their way to apologize to—even my wife. But that's the way with foreigners—people need to apologize to foreigners for the least little screwup. As if foreigners had the market on good manners.

Harrington watched Lyman protesting to Maggie—no, he had not been offended, no offense was given, blah, blah. Harrington looked at his watch. 7:10. Goddam that Sylvester. Finally get a guy in here who might do him some good and he doesn't show. Fabares is probably looking at his watch too.

Sipping his drink, Harrington remembered Sylvester's first big case five or six years ago. Sylvester had been with the firm for close to four years and he was struggling, frustrated with the kinds of cases he had been handling, eager for something with meat on it. The big case was fairly simple—an old lady had slipped on the icy sidewalk in front of the Anaconda Company's headquarters in Butte and broken her hip and wrist. Harrington thought the case was probably unwinnable, because the old lady put away enough booze every day to float a battleship. But he thought the company would give her a small settlement just to avoid publicity, so he gave the case to Sylvester and coached him in the psychology of dealing with corporate America. It was a simple case that would give Sylvester some experience in dealing with power and, more important, give him a small victory in settlement.

To Harrington's astonishment, the company (or the Company, as it was known throughout Montana) decided to fight it to prevent such actions in the future. Somehow, and Harrington still did not know how, Sylvester managed to talk him and the other partners into pursuing the suit. And Sylvester took it to court, arguing that the suit had become a class issue, that the little old lady and her husband, a former Anaconda Company copper miner who had been disabled on the job several years previous, and others like them had been persecuted beyond decency by the company ever since the brutal turn-of-the-century days of no safety standards, of silicosis and sulfuric-acid burns, union-busting, terrorism by local deputies, by company guards, and the hanging of Frank Little, the IWW organizer. Sylvester had laid it on and it stuck.

The jury awarded the little old lady 1.8 million dollars, and the story went out over the AP wire around the country how a little old lady who had slipped on a sidewalk and her Indian attorney had brought a historically ruthless monopoly to its knees. The Anaconda Company left Butte and "the Richest Hill on Earth" shortly thereafter, not as a result of the lawsuit, but because it could mine richer hills in South America without the hassle of social responsibility.

Harrington laughed and shook his head. He often did when he thought of Sylvester's audacity and luck in that particular case. He had seen something of himself in his earlier career, and it made him feel good. After that, he thought of Sylvester as a man to be reckoned with and gave him some of the bigger cases with social implications. And now he wanted to give the young man his biggest chance of all. Then Harrington could call it a career. Fuck it all and sleep till noon.

"Pardon me?" Lyman had heard the laugh and thought it had something to do with him.

"What do you do, Mr. Lyman?" Harrington wanted to ask him why he was here. The man was a little slick, a little too well dressed, a little too immaculate. Harrington had learned to hang on to his wallet around guys like this.

"Actually, I am representing my government in seeking a grain deal with your state. It is not a big deal—we still get most of our grain from Canada—but if we are able to find more outlets, who knows?"

"You don't look like a wheat farmer to me, Mr. Lyman."

"No, no," laughed Lyman. "I am from Rotterdam. I am more in the shipping business. You might say I am doing a favor to my government."

"And in return you will ship the grain."

"If a satisfactory deal can be worked out. Dog scratch dog, eh?"

This time Harrington laughed. He wanted to wink at Maggie but she had turned away. Where in the hell had she dug this guy up? He glanced at the Russell and the Sharpe. He'd been planning to give them to the Historical Society for a couple of years now. Get them out of the house. Guys like Lyman made him nervous.

"Well, good luck, Mr. Lyman. We need new markets for our natural resources. Enjoy yourself. Have another drink." As Harrington shook the eager hand, he wondered if grain was a natural resource. Then he saw Sylvester standing just inside the room. He had a tall bottle of beer in his hand and a shy smile on his face.

"There he is!" Harrington grinned as he crossed the room. He took Sylvester's hand. "You bastard—where the hell have you been? What is that? Miller High Life! We've got some of that imported stuff, what the hell, Michelob? C'mon, we'll get you a bottle. Where's Shelley?"

"She got waylaid—Mrs. Lukas."

"Oh, Jesus. Well, we can forget about Shelley for the next three hours. One of these days I'm going to have to find out Maggie's secret. She manages to invite every lulu in Helena." Harrington smiled as he and Sylvester skirted a cluster of young men. "Help yourselves, boys. Don't be shy."

Sylvester nodded. "How's it going, Rick?"

"One step at a time," one of the young men called after him.

"God, that's lame. They get younger all the time. Those boys ought to be out selling lemonade on a hot day like this. Who's this Rick?"

"He's in the AG's office. Bright. Remember that brouhaha over in Campaign Practices? He's the one who nailed Whitmere."

Harrington looked back. Now he couldn't even remember which one was Rick. "Let me tell you a little about this Fabares. He's from Democratic headquarters, congressional committee, kind of a point man, supposedly spreading the word about PACs and how to get around them, but I think he really is here to see what kind of shape the party is in—who's weak, who's strong, if we've got our shit together. He's especially interested in the western district seat. We've got to keep a Democrat in there to balance out our losses in the eastern part of the state. He's slick, but what's new about that? He knows his business. And his business on this trip is to meet potential candidates." They had reached the small wet bar, and Harrington wedged himself in between a middle-aged couple. "Harry, give Mr. Yellow Calf one of those foreign beers, will you?" He turned toward Sylvester. "This is Harry. He's an English major up at the college. You're not going to turn out to be a lawyer, are you, Harry?"

"I hope so, Mr. Harrington. Nice to meet you, Mr. Yellow Calf. I never saw you play but my dad says you were something else."

Sylvester reached around Harrington and shook the young bartender's hand. "Good to meet you, Harry."

"We don't seem to have any foreign beer, Mr. Harrington." Harry studied the bottles in the tub of ice. "Bud, Miller's, and Michelob—that's all."

"Michelob—isn't that foreign? Well, let's have one, Harry." Harrington turned to Sylvester. "I can't believe it's not foreign with a name like that."

Sylvester laughed. He didn't care what kind of beer he drank, he didn't drink that much, but when Buster got a notion in his mind there was no dissuading him. Harrington slapped the man next to him on the back. "How's it going, Bob?"

Harry handed the Michelob across the bar. "You still play, Mr. Yellow Calf—I mean shoot around, stuff like that?"

"I haven't touched a basketball in years, Harry. I play a little handball once in a while. How about you?"

Harry actually looked down at his feet. "Aw, just a little intramurals up at the college. I'm not that hot."

"Neither am I anymore. Last time I went home my seventeen-year-old nephew played circles around me."

"You mean up in Browning?"

Sylvester should have been surprised and he was. But he was also used to it. Almost everyone in Montana knew that he had played on the Browning team that went to state two years in a row and won it both times. That was a legendary team, it turned out. That was also a long time ago, and so it surprised Sylvester that a young man like Harry would know about it. A familiar discomfort swept over Sylvester. Without looking around he could tell that people were beginning to look at him, beginning to notice him. There weren't many Indian lawyers in Helena who had been basketball stars at the University of Montana and so a kind of recognition filled the room with low voices and nudges. Many, many times in the past ten or twelve years Sylvester had wished he had never gone to college in Montana. He'd had several out-of-state scholarship offers but he had stayed in Montana to be near his grandparents. He remembered thinking as his coach took him down to the university to register that his grandparents were old and ready to die and he would one day have to go back up to Browning to care for them. That was seventeen years ago and they were still alive. His grandfather had suffered a stroke and couldn't talk or move much, but his grandmother, at eighty-seven, was still going to powwows and giveaways and honoring ceremonies. She was an elder and the first woman to be served at feasts. When Sylvester went home he was treated with respect, not because he had been a basketball player or was now a lawyer but because he was Little Bird Walking Woman's grandson whom she had brought up well.

Sylvester glanced around the room, looking for Shelley. He suddenly felt hot and tired, and he wished they could just go to her place and eat something and sleep. He tried to remember what he'd had for lunch at the prison—some kind of meat that he couldn't cut with the plastic knife and fork and boiled potatoes and corn. What was for dessert? Or was that meal yesterday—or last month? There was always meat you couldn't cut.

He felt a hand on his shoulder and he was being guided

away from the bar. "Anyway, this Fabares is our pipeline back to D.C. That's why I want you to meet him. Excuse me. Help yourselves, boys. See, we're in bad shape. The Republicans are going to win the whole goddam thing this go-round. We've got to plan for the future. Some of our best boys are getting up there—hell, they want to get out and smell the roses one more time before they croak."

Sylvester caught a glimpse of Shelley and Mrs. Lukas. They were in the living room standing in the light of the bay window. A third woman approached and Shelley smiled and extended her hand. She is a good-looking woman, thought Sylvester, warm, gracious, slightly aristocratic. He always felt grateful for her.

"Ah, here we are. Pete! Excuse me, fellas, comin' through!" Harrington had Sylvester by the sleeve, tugging him after him. "How ya doing, Ralph. Pete, this is Sylvester Yellow Calf, the young fella I was telling you about. Sly, this is Pete Fabares, from our national headquarters—I think I told you about him, didn't I? It's quite an honor to have him way out here in Montana."

"How do you do, Mr. Fabares."

"Sylvester, it's an honor to meet you. Buster says some very nice things about you."

Harrington laughed and clapped Fabares on the shoulder as if he had told the best joke of the day. "Hell, every firm in the state is after this young man! He's going to reinvent the wheel before he's done. You can take that to the bank, Pete."

"Along with a few new contributors, I hope." This time Fabares laughed. He laughed quickly, easily, as though he'd spent a lot of time fending off the Harringtons of the country.

"Seriously, Buster tells me you're interested in the possibility of public life, maybe a congressional run, something like that."

Sylvester glanced around at the faces. Ralph Waiters and Ed Vance were colleagues, the others state and local party people. He nodded, trying to encompass the whole group, and felt foolish. Only Ed Vance, his best friend and handball partner, smiled openly. He seemed to be enjoying this.

"Well, I'm really just exploring the possibility, Mr. Fabares. I'm totally new at this, I've talked with a few people, but really it's just a glimmer of an idea." Buster's idea, he wanted to add, but he knew that wasn't entirely true.

"Is there a place where Sylvester and I could talk, Buster? I hate to be so abrupt but I've got to catch that plane to Salt Lake in"—he held his watch up conspicuously—"a little less than an hour."

"Sure. We can go into my study. It's right over there, other side of the staircase."

At the door, Fabares said, "I'd like to talk to Sylvester alone for a few minutes—if you don't mind, Buster." With an ease that astonished Sylvester, he shut the door in Harrington's face. He walked to a tall, draped window and peered through the lace. The sun was down now but the valley to the north took on a golden luminescence before the gray mountains. "God, this is beautiful country," he said quietly. "I was out here once before—advance man for McGovern—but things were so hectic back in those days I didn't really get a chance to see the country. The senator wanted to meet some Indian leaders, so I got some from the Crows and the Sioux, I think. I'll tell you how naive I was in those days, this is really embarrassing, I wanted them to be dressed up in headdresses and buckskins and carrying spears or whatever. I'm from Massachusetts, never seen an Indian, I just imagined they still wore that old-time stuff. Well, they showed up in suits, they handed out business cards." Fabares laughed. "At least they did present the senator with a peace pipe!"

Sylvester smiled. He had been back east enough to know that some people there had a pretty peculiar notion about Indians. He studied Fabares's profile. In the other room, at a little distance, he had looked young, about Sylvester's age, but in the light from the window, he looked to be in his late forties, early fifties. The thick brown hair and round, wire-rimmed glasses made him look athletic, jubilantly healthy, but there was a drawn, creased quality about his face that suggested that whatever he held on to would soon be gone, was already fading.

"What do you believe in, Sylvester?" Fabares had turned away from the window, and in the softening light he once again looked young. There was a challenging tone in his voice.

"Issues?"

"Anything. What's important to you?"

"Well, certainly Indian issues, water rights, mineral rights on reservations, alcoholism, family issues."

"What else?"

"The environment, wilderness, preservation . . ."

"Okay, what else?"

"Generally, the problems poor people face in gaining a voice . . ."

"Okay, let's see, you've got Indians, environmentalists, poor people—with that constituency you just might get elected dog catcher here in Helena. Who else you going to appeal to—the basketball fans, the people you represent in workman's comp cases, liability—according to Buster, you have a tendency to want to take on the cases of the little man against the system. That's all well and good. You'd need those little men and women if you were to take a run at state senator or county attorney—but if you have your eye on something a little bigger you're going to need organizations, special interests, a few fat cats. You've got Buster behind you and that's no small thing. He's made more than a few congressmen from this state—you remember Don Morrissey? That may have been before your time. He had absolutely no name recognition in Montana, he was a schoolteacher from Deer Lodge— two years later he was representing the western district in Congress. That was all Buster's doing. Do you recall what happened to Morrissey? He got back there and reneged on a couple of promises. He didn't even survive the next primaries. The voters had something to do with that, but Buster had everything to do with it."

"How do you know all this about Montana? I thought we were pretty small potatoes in the grand scheme."

Fabares turned to the window again. He spoke slowly, thoughtfully. "There is a grander scheme, Sylvester. Your people knew that better than most. I don't need to get up on a soapbox to tell you that. You've got a lot to protect out here, and I don't mean only the environment. There's a way of life in Montana that has to be preserved. You know what's happening—Peabody is strip-mining the whole southeast corner of Montana, Champion and Plum Creek are clear-cutting western Montana at a rapid rate, corporations are buying up family farms and ranches, they're buying up scenic lands and blue-ribbon trout water for development." Fabares pushed up his glasses and smiled. "You know who's going to suffer? These same people who so vehemently oppose setting aside land for wilderness, for any kind of preservation. They're going to find themselves locked out of land they have hunted and fished and hiked all their lives. Worse yet, they're going to find themselves unable to earn a living, unable to even find themselves a chunk of land they can afford to build a house on. This has happened time and time again, in state after state.

"Montana still has a chance, but things are happening rapidly, in a big-time way. I'd say since the energy crisis, it's been crunch time in Montana. The giants are rearing their ugly heads and they're looking right at this country. They'll come in, take what's here, and leave. And what they leave behind won't be pretty. Montana will be violently, thoroughly raped. And of course the people will love it. That's the sad irony."

Sylvester picked at the foil on the bottle of Michelob. It had grown warm in his hand. "Reminds me of what has happened on the reservations," he said softly. "On my own reservation. The big companies came in and took the oil and natural gas, then capped off the wells and left. Right now, mining interests are trying to open a sacred area in the mountains for exploration and development. As many people on the reservation are for it as are against it."

"That's it exactly, Sylvester, that's it. Montana is becoming one big reservation and all the people in it are the Indians. They make noises about self-determination, but we know who, up to this point, determines what's good for Montana— not the Indians, not the people of Montana, but the special interests, the giants, and their backers. And these backers are the ganglia on the body politic. They are spread throughout and they have interests you wouldn't believe. They would sell out Montana for an opportunity to have a photo hanging on their wall of them kissing George Bush's ass. You wouldn't believe it, Sylvester.

"But—this is worst-case scenario, although it is closer to reality than your best-case scenario. Even here, on the state and local level, the conservatives, the gun nuts and constitutionalists, are posing a real challenge to our candidates. They call themselves the mainstream, and the scary thing is they might be right. This country is turning a bad direction, Sylvester. Those people you wanted to appeal to—the Indians, the poor people, the conservationists—they are on the outside, looking in. And I'm afraid they're going to stay there for the next four years, possibly the next eight years."

"You talk as though George Bush has already won. Don't the Democrats have a chance? We're doing pretty well in this state, especially in the congressional races, the governor's race, most of the key local races. Montana always votes Republican in the presidential race and they probably will this time, but otherwise we're in pretty good shape."

"I'm something of an alarmist, Sylvester. I guess that's part of my job, as well as the cheerleading part. Whatever it takes to get Democrats off their asses, I do. But this time, I'm scared, really scared. I can see all of the social gains we've made in the past twenty years going down the tubes—you get a Republican administration back in there, a conservative Supreme Court—poof! No more legalized abortion, no more desegregation. That's just for starters.

"But I'm rattling on—you know all this, Sylvester, don't you?"

"In a general way. I've talked with Buster and a few local people. I'm aware of what's at stake. I'm just a little surprised that a man of your stature is so negative." Sylvester laughed. "I should be surprised at myself for not feeling more so. Maybe I'm just too damned dumb to realize this country is on the verge of going to hell."

"Like I said, Sylvester, I'm a professional alarmist. I put the fear of God into the complacent." Fabares glanced at his watch. "Well, what do you think? You want to come on board? It's kind of a leaky vessel now, but I think we'll be back on an even keel in a couple of years. And believe me, things are not as bad as I tend to make them out. I'll give you a scoop—when Buster phoned us back in Washington a couple of months ago, we did a little checking around on our own. You've got a lot going for you—great name recognition as a result of your basketball career, law degree from Stanford, well established in a prestigious law firm, member of the parole board, which gives you some record in public service—and above all, you're an Indian. I believe this state, this country, is ready for another Indian in Congress, Sylvester. Do you want to be that congressman? It's about that simple."

Sylvester shook his head slowly. "My God," he said. He sat down in Harrington's swivel chair behind the mahogany desk. He set his warm beer on a coaster beside the green felt pad. Fabares drained off the last of his gin and tonic.

"When do you have to know?" said Sylvester.

"No hurry—two weeks, a month at tops." This time Fabares laughed. He had seen this scene many times in his career. There was always something comical in the reactions to this kind of offer. "We have to get things off the ground. There's always a lot of preliminary work. If you're going to be a candidate in '90 we've got to kick this old horse in the rear end. I won't bother to tell you now what we have to do. It's not an impossible task, Sylvester, but it will require some hard work.

"Right now, I want you to think about it, talk it over with people you respect—I understand you have a very bright girlfriend, what's her name, Shelley? Buster tells me she is old Senator Hatton's daughter. A good man, tough old bird. What does she do?"

"She works in the fiscal analyst's office, analyzes budgets for the various departments and divisions, university system, in state government. She's sort of in charge of giving them the bad news."

"Well, talk it over with her, especially because her life will be changed too." Fabares pulled a wallet out of his breast pocket. "Here's my card. Call me anytime. If I'm not there, they'll tell you where to find me. I'm afraid I'm on the run most of the time."

Sylvester stood up and the two men shook hands.

"I like you, Sylvester. I'm sure the people will too."

Fabares left the room, closing the door behind him, and Sylvester sat back down in the chair. His throat felt scratchy, as though he had been talking a long time, but he had hardly said ten words in twenty minutes. He picked up the bottle of beer—he would have loved a cold one but he didn't have the energy to go out to the party—and drank the whole thing. He felt small in the shadowy room. He remembered those times he'd helped his grandparents pitch their tipi every summer in the backyard. He slept out there every night all summer long and he felt tiny. Every now and then, particularly in summer storms, the shadows had frightened him, just as they frightened him now. Only now he was a big man, a real big man afraid of these shadows and those that lay ahead.

"Are you okay?" Shelley's head floated at the edge of the door. Her slightly curled blond hair framed her face like a burst of morning sun.

"I'm fine," said Sylvester. "Come in here. God, it's good to see you just now. I was afraid to go out there."

She closed the door and crossed the room quickly. She put her arms around his neck and he held her tight. The silkiness of her dress made her feel small and light. Almost without thinking, he straightened and lifted her off the floor. One of her high heels fell off with a clatter.

"You want to do it right here?" she said. "On the desk?"

Sylvester laughed and twirled her around. "Anywhere you want—dining-room table, TV set—"

"Mrs. Lukas thinks you're cute. She has always stuck up for the noble red man. Did you know that?"

"With her money she can stick up for me anytime. Just so I don't have to jump her old bones." Sylvester lowered Shelley to the floor.

"You're awfully giddy—did something good happen with Fabares? He was smiling when he left." She leaned against the desk and slipped her shoe on, looking up at him.

"Mr. Fabares thinks I might be a pretty good candidate for Congress in '90—if I want it. He thinks I'd have a real good chance."

"That's wonderful! I think. Isn't it? I mean, you did want it to be something like that, didn't you?"

"I don't know. I'm kind of dumbfounded—it was so easy. I could actually be on my way to Congress. Can you believe that?"

Shelley picked up an antique inkwell from the desk and held it to her chest. "I think it's wonderful and you could make a good job of it. You have so much to offer, Sylvester, you really do." She stroked the inkwell as though it were a kitten. Without looking up she said, "You could do so much good for your people, I know you could."

"I wish I were that confident." Sylvester sighed and walked to the window. Lights from the various subdivisions twinkled across the valley floor. He looked at his watch. "Not more than four hours ago I was interviewing an inmate who came from a family that I practically grew up in. He was a lot younger so I didn't really recognize him, but one of his older brothers was like a brother to me. Now I don't even know where he is and I'm afraid to find out. More and more I feel like I've gone on my merry way and the people who meant something to me have fallen by the wayside. Other people have come into my life—people I don't feel particularly close to—and helped me make it from one step to the next—from my coaches and teachers and professors to Buster, now to Fabares. They seem to hand me along. I can't remember a time that I had to work hard, on my own, to achieve something. There was always somebody there to open another door, to say, 'Come on in, it's warm in here,' then they seem to shut the door on the faces of people I came from. Sometimes I imagine Donny Little Dog—that's the boy I grew up with— standing just on the other side of that door waiting for it to open again. But it never will. Not for him. Not for the others I left behind."

Sylvester fell silent for a moment. He could see the lights from the airport and the lights of a plane taking off. It could be Fabares's plane to Salt Lake, he thought. Then he looked to the northern sky until he saw a star that he knew. When he spoke, his voice was low, wistful. "You know, when I was home in July for the big powwow, I'd had enough of the celebrating and so I just wandered around the streets of Browning. Almost everybody was out at the powwow so I practically had the streets to myself. I was having a good time visiting all my old haunts until I came to this vacant lot. There was a little kid, about seven or eight, a little Indian kid playing marbles all by himself. He had on a raggedy T-shirt, his blue jeans were out at the knees, and he had on these great big basketball shoes. He was so intent on his game he didn't notice me. I stood and watched him for quite some time with a growing feeling that I had seen him before or had seen a scene like this before. It was so familiar. Even the hot day and the mountains to the west seemed familiar in a way that didn't seem ordinary, not a day-to-day familiarity but something about this particular day. Then this little kid noticed me. He stood up and looked at me—and I saw myself. Years ago I was that kid playing marbles by myself in that vacant lot on that day.

"That's when the thought occurred to me—if that seven-year-old and I were in the same place at the same time and I saw myself in him, why couldn't he turn out to be me? Why couldn't he have the same opportunities, the same encouragement, the same helping hands I had? Why couldn't this kid be taught that he is important, that he doesn't have to fail just because he is an Indian and it's expected of him?" Sylvester turned from the window and looked at Shelley. Her eyes glistened in the soft light. "I never told you this but that incident made me take seriously Buster's urging that I get into politics. I never told you because I still wasn't sure I could do it."

"You can do it. I know you can. I know you." Shelley crossed the room and put her arms around Sylvester's waist. She looked up at him. "You can help that child and more just like him. You're a good man, Sylvester Yellow Calf." She squeezed him. "And next time don't hide anything from me, you hear?"

"Yessum. Can we go home now?"

"Your place or mine?"

"Yours. Do you have eggs? I'll fix us omelettes."

"Like last time?"

Sylvester frowned. "I'm better. I've been practicing that flip."

"Right." Shelley put her hand in his and led the way to the door. "Maybe we'll stop at Burger King on the way home. No offense, Mr. Congressman."

CHAPTER THREE

Patti Ann Harwood drove her Honda Civic up the last ramp and out into the brilliant sunshine of the mid-September morning. She had never parked on top of the downtown parking garage before but she wanted to smoke a cigarette and look out over the small city. She needed to get her bearings before she did this thing. She found a space that looked north and east and pulled in between a pickup and a motorcycle. Before her, far beyond the old buildings, she saw a range of mountains that she'd never learned the name of. The mountains looked surprisingly distinct in the morning light, bright blue-green beneath the scattered white clouds.

She punched in the car lighter and shook a cigarette out of a nearly empty pack. Straight ahead she could see the top portion of the Power Block building where Harrington, Lohn and Associates had offices. She had driven by it, walked by it, scouted it several times before she got the nerve to call and make the appointment. Now the appointed time—9:30 A.M., Friday, September 14th—was at hand and she was not really nervous. She was more irritated than anything about this intrusion into her quiet life. And she was going to have to miss half a day's work. Patti Ann lit her cigarette and rested her head against the seatback. And the game of it—playing detective or whatever—made her feel foolish, which was the source of her irritation.

She had made up her story and now she was going to tell it. And snoop. She closed her eyes and heard Jack's voice again: "I want you to meet him, make an appointment with him, bump into him in the grocery store . . ." That was three weeks ago, the last time she saw him down at the prison. She had put his words out of her mind for the next couple of weeks until he called last Thursday. "Have you talked with him yet?" And she knew exactly who "him" was but she said, "Who?" hoping that they really were talking about someone else.

But Jack said, "The Indian, the lawyer on the parole board. I asked you to meet him."

And she said, "What is this all about? What am I supposed to be looking at or for or whatever?"

Then came the disgusted tone. It had been happening with more frequency lately. He would make some oblique statement and when she didn't pick up on it, an edge of disgust would seep into his voice. She knew it had to do with prison and guards and snitches but she didn't live in that world. She was used to approaching the subject head-on.

"Meet him, that's all. Make an appointment—those law-

yers, most of them, don't charge for an initial consultation—
tell him your mother died and you and your sister are fighting
over the china, tell him a tree fell on your house and the
insurance company won't pay up. Use your head." And it
went on like that until she felt beaten and a little dirty. She
called Sylvester Yellow Calf's office the next morning and
made the appointment.

And here she was, in her best silk suit, new high heels and
freshly done hair. She was attractive and today she was at her
best. Some consolation. She stubbed out her cigarette, looked
in the rearview mirror, and touched her auburn hair.

As she walked to the stairs of the parking garage she
smelled the faint odor of smoke. Most of the fires that had
plagued the Helena area the past couple of weeks were out or
under control. But there were others burning in the wild
mountains and parks of Montana. The yellow haze that usually filled the valley had given way to a high blue sky and a
mild southerly wind. Patti Ann had watched the fire stories on
TV and at one time had thought all of Montana would burn
up. She and her friend Myrna had driven out to the Elkhorns
one evening and watched the orange glow intensify as darkness fell. But now the valley looked nice and the buildings
that lined Last Chance Gulch were clear and solid in the
morning light. Maybe the worst was over.

~~~~~~

"Mr. Yellow Calf will be with you in a moment, Miss
Lowry. He's just finishing up some paperwork. Would you
like a cup of coffee?"

"No thank you."

"Well, if you need anything, just holler. There's some magazines there. I can't guarantee how recent they are."

"I'll be fine." Patti Ann liked the receptionist. She was one of those good middle-aged women who work hard and lead a normal life. The absence of a wedding ring on the woman's finger did not seem abnormal. She could be a widow or divorced or an old maid. To Patti Ann any of those alternatives seemed normal compared to her own deception. She had had to present herself as Patricia Lowry—she had made no mention of a husband, dead or alive. But that was becoming normal to her. She never mentioned a man in her life, not even to the women at work. Myrna was the only one who knew about Jack Harwood, and she could be trusted. Her husband, Phil, was also in prison, in the same unit as Jack. Phil had told Myrna that Harwood had a wife in Helena, and lo and behold, it turned out his wife was Patti Ann Harwood, who just happened to work in the same department as Myrna. The two men were not close but their wives had become friends. They had something in common, a real secret.

Patti Ann looked around the reception room, which was also the typing pool. Two women faced each other across a wide desk listening intently to their headsets, their electronic typewriters punctuating the strange silence of the old building. Human Resources, where Patti Ann worked, was always so chaotic, so fluorescent and noisy, that she almost envied the women at their typewriters. But not really. She had started out as a clerk/typist and she knew how dehumanizing the job was. Still—the light oak paneling, the hanging lamps, the tall windows that overlooked Last Chance Gulch and its many shops and restaurants must be some recompense for spending the day listening to dictaphones.

She heard a door open and she looked expectantly toward the hallway to her left. She glanced at the receptionist, who smiled and nodded.

The first thing she noticed about him was his black hair, neatly trimmed around the ears but full and shiny, parted in the middle and combed back. About the only thing Jack had told her about his physical appearance was that he was tall, an ex–basketball player. As he shook her hand she looked at his and saw how brown it was. She had spent a lot of time outdoors on her days off this past summer and she was still tan, but in her eyes her hand looked as pale as salad dressing. She forced herself to look up and she saw a nice smile with strong teeth, but the eyes were black and set a little closer together than normal in the dark face.

Now she realized that he had introduced himself and she realized that it was she who was holding on to his hand.

"This is Patricia Lowry, Mr. Yellow Calf. She's the one with the problem with the will. She says it's very complicated." The receptionist smiled. "She asked especially for you."

"Oh," said Patti Ann, withdrawing her hand quickly. "I'm sorry. A friend told me you were very good at this sort of thing. It's probably nothing at all."

"We'll see. Why don't you come back to my office." Sylvester had two files in his left hand. He dropped them on the receptionist's desk. "Will you see that Ed gets these, Doris? And tell him I don't think I can make it to handball this afternoon. I'm a little backed up." He swung his arm in the direction of the hallway. "Right this way, Ms. Lowry."

The office was large and bright and simply furnished—an oak desk with a green top, a swivel chair, filing cabinets, and at the other end, away from the windows, a small couch with two matching chairs across a glass coffee table. The only extravagance that Patti Ann could see was a large framed lithograph over the couch.

"It's lovely," said Patti Ann.

"It's the Paradise Valley, down by Livingston. I like the colors."

"It's very wintry."

Sylvester laughed. "It's called February. Good eye."

"Is that where you're from, the Paradise Valley?" Patti Ann had a vague image of a valley where movie stars and writers lived. She had read an article somewhere a long time ago.

"No, no. I'm from the windswept prairies up north—Browning. I'm afraid February doesn't look much like that up there."

Patti Ann thought, Aha, I've learned my first piece of information. But she felt immediately guilty. Such a small tidbit seemed an incredible invasion into this man's privacy. "I don't want to take up too much of your time, Mr. Yellow Calf, really."

"Don't worry, please, sit down. Would you like some coffee?"

"No. Would it be too much bother?"

"Coffee room's right next door. Cream, sugar?"

"Black, please."

Patti Ann sat in silence, the only noise the faraway chatter of the typewriters. They had passed a lot of doors with names on them to get to Sylvester's office, but they were all closed. Again Patti Ann compared it with her own department. The only time a door was even partially closed was when a client was spilling out her life story. This is wrong, she thought, I can't deceive him like this. She felt cold. She pressed her fingers to her cheeks as one does on a cold day.

Sylvester entered, holding the cups before him. He kicked the door partially closed. Patti Ann felt the urge to stand and take the cups from him, but she made herself sit still, perched on the edge of the couch.

"Here we are." Sylvester set the cups on the coffee table, then lowered himself into one of the chairs. "Strained my back the other day. Now then, I hear you have a problem with a will?"

Patti Ann spotted an ashtray on top of a bookcase near the windows. She wanted to smoke but she decided to plunge into her story before she lost her nerve. "My mother died a little less than a year ago. She left a will which left everything to her daughters—I have two sisters—which was to be divided equally. My father died a couple of years earlier. Anyway, everything was to be divided equally except for two things: my older sister was to get the silverware and I was to get some old books which are pretty valuable. My younger sister didn't get anything in particular, just a third of the rest of the estate, which really didn't come to much. She feels cheated and now she wants some of the value of the silverware and books. She wants us to sell them and give her a third of the money."

"Has she filed a formal action?"

"She's in touch with a lawyer, or so she says. She says she'll use him only if she has to. I think she means it."

"I'm getting the impression there is no love lost between you and your older sister and this younger sister."

"She's quite a bit younger. We weren't very close." Patti Ann said this as matter-of-factly as possible, but she felt that familiar hollow feeling that came when she thought of her younger sister. And she felt guilty for using her sister in this crazy story. It was true, she had a younger sister and they weren't close. Patti Ann had quit trying to contact her two years ago, just after Susan's divorce.

"What kind of books are we talking about?" Sylvester had picked up a yellow legal pad from the other chair. "I think we're not talking about *Accounting Made Easy,* right?"

"My father was an antiques dealer back in Minnesota." Patti Ann felt a little self-righteous, for her father had in fact been an antiques dealer. Once again she was sort of telling the truth. "He acquired a private libraryful of books in an estate sale. Among the books was a first-edition collection of William Wordsworth, leather-bound, mint condition. Back in those days, early sixties, it was worth upward of thirty thousand. Now it's undoubtedly worth a good deal more. I haven't had it appraised recently, but it has to have gone up." She watched Sylvester scribble this information on the legal pad. Now she was out on a limb, up the creek without a paddle. What if he knew something about books? She shouldn't have said thirty thousand, that sounded too high as soon as she said it. There were always stories going around when she was growing up about some dealer who happened onto such a treasure, usually rare books or gems, but her father had never come close to such a deal. Oak tables and chairs, sideboards, mirrors and lamps were more his speed. "Do you mind if I have a cigarette?"

"Not at all. I have an ashtray around here." He started to rise.

"I see it." She stood and walked to the bookcase. She felt better moving around. The writing stopped and she sensed his eyes on her back. She hesitated, scanning the titles in the bookcase, and she felt a slight touch of intimacy with this man who had something to do with her husband's being in prison. At that moment. And for that moment she felt like a woman in the presence of a man, and all it implied. The feeling almost overwhelmed her. It had been a long time.

When she turned she caught his eyes before he could look down at the legal pad. He cleared his throat. "Big question, Ms. Lowry—were these unusual bequests a codicil of your mother's will? Did she amend her original will later on?"

"They were in the original will." Patti Ann sat and shook a cigarette out of the pack. She touched the lighter to it and leaned back, inhaling in the same motion.

"No matter. I don't think it makes much difference one way or the other. Sometimes a specific codicil works to the advantage of the defendant—assuming that your sister is bent on suing. By the way, do you have a copy of the will?"

"No, I seem to have misplaced it, I don't know . . . ."

"No problem. We can get one. That's really our first course of action, check it out—it's probably airtight, nothing to worry about. Why don't we do this, Ms. Lowry—"

"Patti Ann." Suddenly she wanted him to call her by her real name—real first name, anyway. "That's my nickname. That's what everybody calls me."

"Okay, Patti Ann, why don't you check around and see if you can find your copy of the will. If you can't, we can send for one and we'll take it from there. Sounds to me like you're on pretty good grounds, so I wouldn't worry too much."

She watched him write something on the pad. She wanted

to ask him what people called him. She couldn't believe he answered to Sylvester. "Shall I call you, then—Mr. Yellow Calf?"

"As soon as you hear anything, or don't hear anything. If they seem to be dragging their heels, call me. We have other avenues." He reached into his jacket pocket and pulled out a small leather case. "Here's my card. It's got my home phone on it too."

"Oh, do you live around here?" And she instantly felt stupid. Damn that Jack.

But he appeared not to notice the pointedness of the question. "I've lived in Helena for ten years now. That's about five or six years longer than I expected to stay." He laughed and shook his head. "I had planned on going back to my reservation and working there, but one thing and another kept coming up. How about you? Have you lived here very long?"

"Twelve years this summer. I came out with my husband from Minnesota. He was a forester. He'd just graduated from the university back there. This was his first job." Patty Ann could remember the excitement of the move, the new job, the small old house they had bought in the flats. They had met at the university as students, he in forestry and she in the General College. She was in the two-year social work program, not because she was committed to social work but because she was not committed to anything and social work seemed at least possible as a career. She was a serious student and got good grades, but when he proposed marriage in the spring of her first year she accepted and they were married a month later and on their way to Montana and his first job. They were excited then, and despite the money they owed on student

loans, they decided to have a baby. They could get by, first on
his salary alone, then when the baby was old enough Patti
Ann could go back to school, finish her degree, get a decent
job. She miscarried at the end of four months. It was a small
tragedy in their new lives together, but the doctor urged them
to try again, they were young and they both checked out as
normal healthy human beings of the opposite sex. The doctor
had a nice hearty laugh and they felt good about themselves
again and had a romantic candle-lit dinner of Cornish game
hens and Mateus Rosé. The second fetus lasted six months
and Patti Ann hemorrhaged severely enough to be placed in
intensive treatment for two days while they pumped her full
of drugs and blood. She recovered but her husband touched
her less and less often—she thought it was because he
thought she was too delicate—until one night after they had
gone to a movie and were getting ready for bed, he said she
should have told him she couldn't have children, she should
have told him at the start, he didn't want to go through life
without children. And when she offered to try again, he
laughed and they slept apart in the same bed for another year.

"Is your husband—still here?" Sylvester Yellow Calf had
a look of mild surprise in his eyes.

"Oh! Oh no!" It took a moment for Patti Ann to register his
question. "Oh no! Goodness, we were divorced almost ten
years ago. No, he went back to Minnesota. I have no idea—"
And then she became embarrassed at her overreaction to the
simple question, but the rush of memories of her first husband had paralyzed her. She had deliberately not thought of
him for years. When something reminded her of him—an old
movie, a picnic site in the forest—she stopped the memory

dead in its tracks. What in the world had caused her to think of him, of them, just now?

She glanced at her watch. Nearly eleven. "I've taken up way too much of your time, Mr. Yellow Calf. I didn't realize it was so late."

"Sylvester," he said as they both stood up. He grimaced. He really had hurt his back playing handball the other day. In all his years of basketball he had never hurt his back. He extended his hand. "Call me Sylvester."

~~~~~~

She stood for a moment just outside the main entrance of the Power Block. The air had the faint odor of smoke, as though a new fire had sprung up somewhere in the state. It seemed these days that you could smell each new fire, could even tell where each was located by wind direction. But today there was no wind and the only visible sign of smoke was a slight graying of the blue sky.

Patti Ann felt both shaky and relieved—but mildly disappointed in everything, from the interview with Sylvester Yellow Calf to the smoke to the way her life was going. She thought of the momentary thrill in the office when she felt Sylvester's eyes on her when she went to get the ashtray and she knew what was wrong—except for two intense years, one with each of her two husbands, she had lived a lifetime without the physical warmth of a man. Two years out of thirty-two. She had been a good girl, never cheated on her men, not even during these past seven years that Jack had been down. She had never put herself in cheating situations—especially after that first year when she realized almost any public place after

dark could be dangerous. She used to go bowling with a couple of girls from the office on Friday evenings and afterward
they would stop somewhere for pizza and beer. Patti Ann was
a little older than Ruth and Laurie and a lot more reserved.
After the third or fourth such outing, Patti Ann had to break
it off because there were too many men in those places, too
many dangerous opportunities. She had been surprised at
how easily relationships could occur in bowling alleys and
pizza parlors. She had thought only bars were dangerous.

For the past six years she had pretty much stayed at home.
She did go out to an occasional movie with her friend Myrna.
She had even tried to go to church with Myrna, but after a
couple of sermons on salvation and repentance she came away
depressed, not wanting to think of Jack—or herself—in those
terms. They were meant for other people, the ones she considered normal. But when had she stopped thinking of herself as
normal? Was it after her first two miscarriages, or after her
marriage to Jack? Or was it when he got sent to prison a little
more than a year after their marriage? After her fourth mis-
carriage and subsequent hysterectomy she knew she was not
normal. The doctor, the same one with the hearty laugh, had
told her he was tired of dealing with suicidal women, if she
wanted to kill herself she'd have to find a way other than
childbirth now.

Well, he needn't have worried. She hadn't even touched a
man since the day Jack had escaped from the prison and come
to see her in the hospital. They had hugged for a long time
and she didn't want him to ever go away. She was still dopey
from the painkillers and when the cops came into the room
and put the handcuffs on Jack she tried to tell them it was all
right, he was her husband.

That had been early in Jack's confinement. He had just gotten out of Reception and was mistakenly assigned to one of the letter units on the low side. When they told him about his wife's hysterectomy and that they couldn't spare an officer to take him to Helena, he walked out the next morning with a farm crew and just kept walking. He never did tell Patti Ann exactly how he did it or how he got from Deer Lodge to Helena. He just did it and she loved him all the more for it.

But he had changed in the last two or three years. He had become secretive and manipulative. She wasn't surprised now that he wanted her to find out what she could about Sylvester Yellow Calf; she just couldn't figure out what he planned to do with the information. She thought it had to do with the fact that Jack no longer got along with the Indian inmates—she didn't know why this was true; she hadn't known anything about it until he got stabbed a year ago. Perhaps he wanted Sylvester's help in calming this situation. She should have come right out with it, told Sylvester that her husband was in prison, was in danger, that he, Sylvester, had turned him down for parole just last month. She had wanted to tell him that her husband didn't deserve to be kept locked up, that he was rehabilitated, that she would keep him on the straight and narrow.

When Jack had called last night, she told him all these things, she would get down on her knees, but he would have none of it. He didn't want Yellow Calf to know she was his wife because he didn't want anybody to know her husband was in prison, it just wouldn't be good for her. Later, he seemed to contradict himself, saying Yellow Calf would find out when the time was right. There was something sinister, secretive, in Jack's voice. She did not think for a minute that Jack was doing all of this for her benefit, or even for their benefit. There was another reason.

And that was how Jack had changed.

And now Patti Ann had better get some lunch, she thought, or she was going to collapse right here—that would be the final indignity, probably what she deserved for taking part in this crap. There was a bakery less than a block away that served soup and muffins. She thought briefly of taking the afternoon off as well, but she needed to save her time off so she could visit Jack one Friday afternoon each month. Her boss was a stickler when it came to time off, especially comptime, so Patti Ann had not missed a work day, except for those Friday afternoons, since she started at Human Resources seven years ago.

What a martyr, she thought. Then she thought she had better go straight home and change her clothes. She had worn her best of everything this morning and in fact had felt quite elegant sitting in Sylvester Yellow Calf's clean Victorian office. Such a contrast to Jack's lawyer's office—what was his name, Rouse, Roush? She had noticed in the newspaper about six months ago that he had been disbarred for suggesting a couple of his female clients might like to work for him in a truckers' motel that he had an interest in.

Oh well, it was fun while it lasted, she thought, as she walked back up the block to the parking garage.

She tried to feel sad or guilty or something negative, but in truth she felt good, almost elated. For the first time in a long time she felt alive, free as a bird, a woman.

〰〰〰

Sylvester looked down at the traffic turning left and right below his window. Last Chance Gulch turned into a pedestrian mall right in front of the Power Block. There were a lot more cars than people, and Sylvester often wondered how the shops on the mall made it. He put his hands on the small of his back and leaned back, massaging the muscles. He had once represented a woman who had a small gem shop not more than half a block from his office. She claimed that some dealer from Seattle had beaten her out of $150,000; Sylvester helped her recover $80,000 and she seemed happy. Maybe all these shops dealt in such figures; but he knew better. He had had the lithograph over his couch framed for $120; he had eaten a hamburger at the Rialto for a buck and a quarter, which included all the coffee he could drink. Sylvester had heard that the rents were kept low to keep these small businesses in place. Helena needed a center and Last Chance Gulch was still it, by hook and by crook. Sylvester's office, six floors up, stood close to the very spot where the first gold discovery was made by the four Georgians who took their last chance in a gulch off the Prickly Pear Valley. Only one was from Georgia but they were called the Four Georgians, and Helena was born in 1864, right on top of the gold fields. Amazingly, the center had held for a hundred years, even after the gold played out. What earthquakes and fires couldn't do all those years, the shopping centers and malls had done in the last twenty.

But the center was restored and the pedestrian mall, with its designer paving, trees, modern antique lamps, benches, and other structures, hung tenuously on.

From his window, Sylvester could almost see the great

basin, or valley, that was called the Prickly Pear Valley. His people, the Blackfeet, called it Many-sharp-points-ground for the same reason the whites called it Prickly Pear. Before the whites came, the valley was a great hunting ground for the Blackfeet. Now it was full of housing developments, government structures, shopping centers, an airport, and farther out, ranches and farms.

The phone rang just as Sylvester saw Patti Ann, auburn hair, light silk suit, walking swiftly toward the parking garage. Even from up here, she presents a striking figure, thought Sylvester. Her hair sparkled in the sun and he caught his breath and turned away.

"Hello?"

"Hi. How's your morning going? Mine's been a mess."

"How so?" Sylvester laughed. He needed to hear Shelley's voice just then.

"Have you ever wanted to just kill somebody? I mean, just strangle them?"

"I think so."

"Don't be so enthusiastic. I thought your people liked to kill people."

"Your people killed a lot more people than my people did. We were bloody pacifists compared to you."

"Picky, picky. Anyway, here's the bad news—Triphammer wants me to work tomorrow morning—could stretch into early afternoon, like one or two. So what do you think?"

"We could still make it. Can't take more than three hours to get down there."

"I know how much it means to you."

Sylvester enjoyed Shelley's manipulations. Now it was he

who wanted to go to Chico Hot Springs; it was he who had begged and wheedled for two weeks, who had arranged for her daughters to stay with her mother, who had painted such a glowing picture of swimming, sex, and wonderful food. "Yes, it means a lot to me."

"I could wring that damn Triphammer's neck for him. You want me to?"

"Let's not get carried away. I've got some stuff I can do around here in the morning. You can give me a buzz here. I'll be all packed."

"Seems like a long way to go just for overnight."

"You want to cancel out?"

"You just be packed, boy. What are you going to do tonight?"

"Nothing. Put some heat on my back. I strained it the other day and it isn't getting any better. I'll read a book."

"When was the last time you read a book? Don't tell me." Shelley paused, then sighed. "Wish I could see you tonight, but I promised the girls pizza and Monopoly over at Mother's. She's feeling faint these days—thinks she won't live past Christmas. Can you believe it? She's fifty-four!"

"Way I feel, I'll be lucky to last out the night."

"Poof! I gotta go. I'm having lunch with Triphammer and a couple of computer guys. That's why I have to be around in the morning—we're changing over to a new fiscal program. Let's see how we can screw that one up. Love ya."

"Love you too." But the phone was dead. Sylvester put the receiver back on the cradle. It was quiet for the moment, no cars turning, no voices, no typing. He stepped toward the window and looked down at the sidewalk leading to the parking garage. He half expected to see Patti Ann again, as though time as well as the noise had ceased.

But she was long gone.

He looked to the flats in the distance. The air had taken on a whitish, smoky tint. The mountains were a long way away.

CHAPTER FOUR

Jack Harwood stayed apart from the other inmates as they made their way down to the chow hall for supper. He wasn't paranoid but he made it a point to be a little to the side and behind the Indians who lived in Close II with him. There was a new kid, kind of a faggy sort, who seemed to have his eye on Jack. He really knew how to attract the weak ones. What the hell was the attraction, anyway? He tried to keep to himself, do his own time, but somewhere along the line one of these pussies would stop by his house and just hang around. Sometimes he had two or three hanging around. It was a Class Two write-up if they came inside his cell, so they just stood around, acting casual and insouciant. But they weren't casual or insouciant—they were scared to death. If a couple of tough guys came by, they would freeze up, flatten themselves against Jack's doorjamb, practically whimper their casual conversation. Jack had to smile at these pathetic characters, but in the end he wound up providing a small protection service—that is, he allowed them to tag along when he went to the canteen or library, even to the shower. He had come close to being butt-fucked himself when he came in on his first beef. He'd been rescued by a guy he hadn't even seen before, a guy he later learned had just been transferred that day from max.

Jack remembered the terror he'd felt while being wrestled into the laundry room off the bathroom, the fear of becoming somebody's old lady—a guard named Rufus had told him all about it with lip-smacking enjoyment when he was on reception—but the guy from max, a short, stocky half-breed with long hair, told them to stop, they were interfering with his toilette. And they did. Later, Jack found out the guy was Paco Morsette, the spiritual leader of the Indian population at that time. Jack never had a chance to thank Morsette because Morsette was transferred back to max later that night. Jack never learned the reason and he had learned not to ask questions. Rufus had taught him that on Reception. You never knew who was a snitch or who had suddenly developed a grudge or a crush or an imagined hurt. Just do your own time, boy, nobody likes a busybody.

Jack glanced to the side and he saw the faggy-looking kid glance away. Great. Another secret admirer. Now what, Rufus? Do I give off a scent that's irresistible to these dinks? Do I look like a father figure? Am I that fucking old?

The inmates from Close II had reached the chow hall and they stood two abreast waiting for the door to be opened. It was 4:27 and the officer on the other side of the door didn't seem to notice them. They were the first shift for the evening meal and they weren't getting in until the wall clock above the cafeteria line said 4:30.

"My name's Peter Quinn."

Jack looked at Peter Quinn. He was a little surprised that Peter Quinn was taller than he was by an inch or two. He wasn't surprised by the pale skin and long dark hair. He could tell a druggie a mile away.

"What're you in on, Peter?" said Jack.

"Oh God, you wouldn't believe it." Peter Quinn not only had a faggy voice—he had a loud faggy voice.

Jack could see several heads turning in front of them.

"They said I robbed a Mini-mart—with a gun, no less."

"Did you?" Jack noticed the Indians at the front of the line were beginning to look around. Jack didn't want this.

"If you want to get technical—I had a gun but it wasn't loaded. It was just one of those pellet guns, the kind that looks like a forty-five, but I didn't even have any pellets!" Peter Quinn ran his long pale fingers through his long dark hair, then shook his head, letting the hair fall where it would. "For crying out loud, the thing wasn't even loaded. I've never even shot a gun!"

By now the whole line had parted. Fucking great, thought Jack as he watched the Indians watch the scene. Some wore dark glasses, almost all wore bandannas around their long hair or around their thigh. A couple were grinning—most were not. Peter Quinn hadn't noticed a thing.

"Look, Quinn, a word of advice. Do your own time, don't fuck with anybody. See those pricks up there?" Jack was looking at them, speaking to Quinn quietly.

"Yeah, what about them?"

"Didn't they teach you anything on Reception?"

"You mean fish row? Oh yeah—they wanted me to take advantage of programs—"

"That's not what I meant. Didn't they tell you to keep your fucking mouth shut and to blend in with the concrete?"

"Ohhh . . . right." Quinn looked around the yard, then seemed to notice the audience he had attracted. Recognition and fright made his face even paler. "I keep forgetting where I am."

Jack kept his eyes on the faces ahead, and one by one they all turned again to the door. "Try to remember, there are some bad people in the joint. They'd just as soon cut you or fuck you as look at you. Keep your head down and watch your back. Think you can remember all that?"

"Oh, God!" Quinn groaned. "I'm dead meat, I swear I am. I'm like that—I don't know why—everywhere I go—even in school—" His voice was rising again.

"Jesus, what's with you?" Jack was getting irritated.

Quinn closed his eyes and nodded rapidly. "Okay, okay, low profile, I gotcha—"

The door opened and the inmates started talking and laughing, pushing their way forward in as orderly a way as possible. Jack could smell roast meat and he could visualize the mashed potatoes and gravy, the green beans, the cherry cobbler, the endless slices of white bread. Now he could hear the clatter of trays and silverwear, plastic glasses and large spoons plunking shit down on plates.

"I'm hungry," said Quinn. He had a pleasant smile on his face. "It's funny, when I get nervous I get hungry. Do you ever get nervous?"

"No," said Jack.

"That's great," said Quinn. "That's terrific. Some guys are just like that, cool as a fucking cucumber. My dad was like that. I hated him for it, but that was a long time ago, I used to think he was subnormal—"

Jack closed his eyes and laughed softly. The kid was going to get along. He was too irrepressibly nuts to jump on and stay on. He'd have a bad time for a while, until the tough guys realized that he just wouldn't stay down, then they'd figure it was too much trouble, there were other, weaker fish to bulldog, to extort from, to fuck. That left drugs. If he was a druggie they might try to get his people to pack drugs in for them. But Quinn would come out all right—Jack had become a student of a certain segment of humanity and he figured Quinn was going to be a survivor, maybe even a capitalist if he had the right people on the outside.

"You don't look like the type," said Quinn.

"How's that?"

"I don't know. You just don't look like the type who ought to be in here, you know?"

"I don't know."

"You're too clean-cut or something." Quinn ran his long fingers through his long hair again and shook his head. "You look like you should be teaching school or being a lawyer. What were you out there?"

"A bank robber."

"That's what you're in here for. I mean, really."

"Let me explain something. You're the fish. A fish does not pry into another person's life history. A fish keeps his mouth shut in the close units; otherwise he gets into all kinds of trouble. Sometimes he ends up getting carried out of here." Jack could see that sudden flush of fear in Quinn's eyes. He had seen it many times before when a new guy suddenly realized where he was, who his companions were, how long it was going to be before he got back to his old haunts, his girlfriend, his buddies. It was a good thing, that moment of recognition. It might keep him alive. It might even keep him from getting hassled in a big-time way. "I don't care, Quinn. I'm not your enemy, I'm not your friend. I'm just a guy doing time. Those guys up there"—Jack nodded toward the head of the line—"they care. Already they're a little curious about you. From the moment you came onto the unit you piqued their interest. They're wondering what you have to offer— sex, money, dope? Do you have a rich daddy who will pay to keep you from getting shanked? Do you have some pals on the outside who can bring in drugs? Will you make somebody a nice old lady? This is how their minds work, Quinn."

Now there was a definite, focused fear in Quinn's eyes. He was finally getting the message.

"I'm not trying to scare you, partner." Like hell, thought Jack. "I think you can make it if you just do like I say—keep your mouth shut and try to look like a concrete wall. You know those lizards that change colors to suit their environment?"

"Chameleons," breathed Quinn in a voice so low Jack couldn't tell if his lips moved.

"That's right, that's the ticket. You just hug the wall and turn gray when these guys come by, you'll do okay. Okay? Now, you see that table over there, near where that officer is standing? That's where you eat. That's where the fish eat." Jack picked up his tray and silverware. Several of the Indians from the front of the line were starting to sit at a big table in the middle of the dining hall. Ever since he'd been shanked in the library, he was conscious of where they were. He wasn't really afraid of them; he couldn't afford to be. He just had to be alert and the pressure was getting to him. The funny part was, they ignored him. And that was dangerous.

All because of that damned nonexistent money, the nine thousand dollars everybody kept harping about. It was true that Jack had gotten away with it; it was true that he had planned to rathole it; but when Patti Ann had her hysterectomy he told her where it was and she used it to pay for the operation. That was to the good. On the bad side of the ledger, everybody—Williams, Hartpence, the Indians, the parole board—they all thought he still had it; in fact, it was Hartpence, saving his own ass, who told the Indians a little over a year ago that Jack had it. It would have been funny, Hartpence the hardass snitching, if Jack hadn't got stabbed. After he got out of max he tried to transfer down, but the cops wouldn't let him go to the low side because of his escape. So he was stuck again in Close II with the Indians. But the Indians ignored him, and that made Jack nervous. It was just like the old cowboy movies. When the Indians hadn't attacked for a long time, everybody in the wagon train got nervous. Only this wasn't the movies and they could get him anytime they wanted, today, next month, next year.

Then there was Patti Ann. She had fought long and hard to keep from using the money. She didn't even want to know where it was. Jack had felt just a little betrayed because he had found, or stolen, the means to keep her out of serious debt. The money had gone to a good cause, a small recompense for the godawful flaw of nature that almost killed her. She wasn't convinced, but he beat her down. Finally, he said he didn't want to be saddled with debt when he got out. Then he told her where the money was—in the shoebox that held the white shoes she wore on their wedding day. She had cried and he had wondered why she had married such an asshole.

Jack sat at a table where he could see both the Indians and the fish-row crowd. He sat with three longtimers who had very little to say to each other. About all he knew about them was they weren't child molesters and they chewed their food well. One of them, Motley, had just come back from the cow camp for threatening an officer but nobody knew what over. The other two had just always been around. On Annual Review status, just like Jack. They had had their parole hearings and been rejected too. So now they waited every year to have their cases reviewed by the parole board; if the parole board liked what they did to improve their situation in the prison, they would get another hearing, another possibility for parole. That seldom happened. Jack dabbed at the lumpy mashed potatoes. Most guys just gave up and waited for their discharge date. Fuck the parole board. But Jack was tired of waiting. He had something waiting on the outside. And now it seemed farther away than ever—unless his half-baked plan worked.

Quinn was smiling and gesturing, both hands full of white bread. Occasionally he would swing his head and his long black hair would spray across his face, then drop obediently behind his ears.

Jack felt a slight pressure on the back of his chair and he turned quickly. Beasley was smiling down at him.

"Looks like your girlfriend is having fun with her food, Harwood. You might have to clue her in tonight between sessions."

Jack sat back in his chair but Beasley was already picking his way between tables toward Quinn's table. Beasley looked down at the fish but he didn't stop until he reached the officer who leaned against the wall. The officer smiled, then laughed, then looked back at Jack. Jack knew what Beasley meant about the food. The inmates took their eating seriously and they didn't like a fish to come in and make sport of one of the highlights of their day. Maybe Jack would tell him that, maybe he wouldn't. Whichever, Quinn was going to get into trouble and he'd end up hanging around the door to Jack's house. But unlike the rest of them, he was a survivor. Jack could tell. He'd survive—if he didn't fuck up too bad at the beginning. Jack would have to stay away from him. Guys like that can take you down real easy.

~~~~~~~~

Patti Ann had just started on the last buttonhole when the phone rang. She had an old machine and buttonholes required all of her concentration. She was saving up for a new Elna complete with buttonhole attachment, but that was a long time in the future.

She stood, careful not to disturb the patterns and material pinned together and spread out on the dining-room table. She hurried to the wall phone just inside the kitchen entrance. She picked up the receiver and said hello.

"It's me."

"Jack!" She knew who "me" was. He'd been greeting her this way for a year now but she tried to sound enthusiastic. "It's so good to hear your voice."

"What are you up to?"

"Oh, I'm sewing a dress-suit for Myra. Poor thing, she doesn't have any clothes."

"I thought you just made her a dress."

"That was for summer. This is a winter-weight suit. We picked out the material last week."

"How'd it go?"

Patti Ann made a face at the refrigerator. They used to have nice conversations, loving, intimate, bright; now, Jack acted like the telephone was a walkie-talkie and they were surrounded by enemies.

"With the lawyer," he said. "The Indian."

"Oh, that went well. He's a nice man—a little formidable, but nice."

"What do you mean, formidable?" Jack asked quickly.

"Oh, he just seems so big—and brown!" She laughed. "He is an Indian after all, but he just seems so healthy and bright. I'm just not used to seeing such a—successful-looking Indian man. Most of the people we deal with are pretty down-and-out. And he was terribly open and friendly—"

"What did you talk about?"

Patti Ann paused. As she had talked about Sylvester Yellow Calf she felt good, as though something exciting had happened in her monotonous life, as though she really had established a relationship with him. Now she came floating back to earth. She had deceived him and that was that. She felt her jaw tighten.

"I told him I had a legal problem, then told him what it was, I won't go into the gory details—"

"Go ahead."

Make my day, thought Patti Ann, but she said, "I told him

it had to do with my younger sister wanting to sue me for some inheritance, a collection of rare books, she wanted half the value or something—I forget. It was all such an atrocious lie! And he believed it all, took notes, questioned me—he said he would help me—"

"He believed you?"

"Jack, what is this all about? I can't do this kind of thing, I'm no good at it. I don't like it!"

"I know, I know. I don't like it either, sweetheart. Believe me, I wouldn't do it if we didn't have to—but there is a small chance that this encounter"—he hesitated for a long second—"and the next one will help me get out of here. I can't do much more time, Patti. It's starting to get to me in a bad way—ever since I got stabbed, I've been—I'm getting paranoid—"

"Jack, can't we do something? Can't we talk to someone? I know they'd listen, they have to listen!"

"Who's they, Patti? I have at least three more years and they are going to make sure I serve every last day of it. They are the jailers, the keepers of the key, and I'm the poor shmuck they've got behind bars. I'm afraid they are not going to listen to a bunch of violins."

"But we must do something!" The frustration that Patti Ann felt every time she talked with Jack was building again and she was near tears. She had been able to tolerate his imprisonment, his being locked away from her, until that day he got stabbed. Since then, she had had sleeping nightmares, waking nightmares, nightmares that occurred when she was leafing through files or shopping at the grocery store. She would see a blinding rush of movement, hear a harsh scream, and see Jack tumbling to the floor, holding his hand out—and she was too far away, always, to grasp it. Now she saw the flash of movement, but by concentrating on the notepad on the refrigerator door, she was able to wipe the rest of it from her mind.

"We must do something," she said softly.

Jack sighed. "There is something, it's a long shot, Patti. I hate to involve you but I don't see any other way. You must see Yellow Calf again."

"Oh, Jack."

"I know. It's crappy—and the worst part is I can't even tell you why you must do this yet. You just have to believe that this is the only thing that can help me."

"But what does Yellow Calf have to do with anything? Couldn't I just tell him who I am and who you are and ask him to help us? I know he would be able to do something."

"Patti, he's one of those people—them—who are keeping me in here. Even if he was sympathetic, there is nothing he can do. I've had my parole hearing and they rejected me. They're not going to turn that around just because we're both miserable." He sighed again, this time an exasperated sigh, and Patti Ann knew that he was losing patience with her.

"What do you want me to do?" she said.

"Just meet him again. It might be a little more difficult this time because I want you to meet him socially, get friendly with him—maybe have a drink, if you can arrange it. This is important, Patti."

"How in the world am I going to arrange that? Jack, he and I travel in different circles. You should have seen his office!"

"It's important, Patti. I have to know more about him. By the way, is he married?"

Patti Ann stared at the refrigerator door. "I don't know,"

she said slowly. "I didn't ask him." She was genuinely surprised, as though that detail had some relevance. "I don't
know," she said.

"Find out. Is he married, does he have an ex-wife, kids,
where does he live, who does he associate with—that kind of
thing. Think of it as a game, Patti, because that's what it
is—just a game. But it might have something to do with me
leaving this place." When Patti Ann didn't respond, he said,
"You want that, don't you, sweetheart?"

"Oh, Jack, I do love you and want you here with me more
than anything. I don't want to spend the rest of my life sewing
dresses for old Myrna."

He laughed. "That does seem like a terrible waste of talent,
doesn't it?"

Patti Ann laughed too and was about to reply when she
heard a commotion on the other end. "Jack?" she said. Then
she heard a loud rattling clatter as though someone had
thrown a metal chair down some stairs. "Jack!"

"It's okay, baby." The voice was breathless. "Listen, I've
got to go. Somebody else wants to use the phone."

"Are you all right, Jack?"

"Yeah, no problem." But the breathing was ragged and
short. "Do you think you can do that for me, Patti?"

"Yellow Calf?"

"Yes."

"Yes."

"Good girl. Love ya."

"I love you too . . ." But he had hung up. Patti Ann listened
to the dial tone for a moment, then she hung up too. She
folded her arms and stared at a Happy Face magnet holding a
grocery list on the refrigerator. There weren't many items on

the list: MILK, DECAF, SUPPER, BLACK ZIPPER. Supper was always the tricky one. Too tempting to get a frozen dinner or a can of something. Maybe a big shrimp salad or something Chinese to spoon over rice. Jack said the rice in prison reminded him of maggots. He expected it to start moving. It was a joke but she hadn't been able to eat rice since; or mashed potatoes, for that matter. She couldn't remember how Jack had described them but it had something to do with being sticky.

She put some water in the teakettle and turned the burner on. As she spooned the last of the decaf into a cup she began to shake. She managed to drop the spoon into the cup and wrap her arms tight around her chest. She closed her eyes but not before she saw the blinding rush, heard the scream, and saw Jack down, his arm raised. She opened her eyes and concentrated on the stove clock. 8:23. 8:23. 8:23. And 8:24. Time to eat, time to eat, time to eat, but she could not think about food. One thing at a time. The unit beneath the teakettle was turning orange and she put her finger close and felt the heat. Black zipper, black zipper.

Then she remembered what it was she wanted to tell Jack. She had listened to a program on NPR the other night while she was working on Myrna's dress-suit. It was all about the biological clock. Patti Ann felt sorry for the women who heard it ticking—but at the same time had felt a surge of joy within herself. She didn't have to worry about that clock because there was no more biology left in her. But these women were roughly her age, many of them older, and they were talking about having children. In some strange way, they gave permission to Patti Ann to have a baby, or a child at least. She had thought often, if fleetingly, of adopting a child, but the odds against it seemed insurmountable—her husband was in prison, she didn't make a lot of money, she'd been divorced once, but the biggest obstacle was Jack himself. Whenever she had hinted at adoption, he had laughed and made a joke about what a fine example he'd be, a jailbird for a father, teaching his son the ropes of a life of crime.

But she had made up her mind to at least go to an adoption agency. That's what those women on the radio had given her, the courage to at least go. And that's what she wanted to tell Jack. What would it hurt? Mightn't it bring some happiness to them to start life anew with a child they could both love? Was that asking too much?

As she poured the hot water into the cup of decaf, she thought of the prospect of Jack's getting out soon if this Yellow Calf thing, whatever it was, worked out. Wouldn't it be nice if they could be a family, a real family. It wouldn't seem so strange to have Jack come home to her and her little world if they could share something.

Yes, she would meet Sylvester Yellow Calf, contrive to have a drink with him, ask him all kinds of questions, trick him, deceive him. Sorry, Mr. Yellow Calf, it's necessary, you understand. She raised her cup in the dimly lit kitchen. Whatever it takes, Mr. Sylvester Yellow Calf.

C H A P T E R   F I V E

Sylvester Yellow Calf had fouled out with 3:12 to play. As he walked slowly to the bench, his basketball career over, the man he had been guarding, Al Childers, trotted over and offered a pat on the rump. It was a nice gesture, a way of saying goodbye after three years of competing against each other. The applause quickened and many people stood. It was all over, even though Montana was behind by only three. Both teams played good defense, and without Sylvester, there was no one to create the plays necessary for Montana to score close in. It was a typical Grizzly team, good inside play but no one except Sylvester to take the occasional outside shot or work it inside.

He sat at the far end of the bench and buried his face in a

towel. It was only the second time in his college career that he had fouled out, and he had to choose the second round of the playoffs to do it. The match-up with Childers had come off and now most of the people were standing. The referee held the ball under the basket and Childers stood three feet behind the foul line, waiting for the applause to die down. Then Childers took a couple of steps up, the ref passed him the ball, and he drained it, just as he had done thousands of time in the schoolyards of Chicago. Several pro scouts had followed him this season and it was clear that he would go in the first round of the draft. Sylvester watched him hit the bonus and he realized that he had not often had the opportunity to watch Childers play. The match-up was so complete that when Childers rested, Sylvester rested; when Childers came back in, Sylvester reentered the game. It was automatic. The coach did not have to tell Sylvester anything.

Now he watched Childers step into a passing lane, steal the pass, and glide down the court for an easy layup. It brought the Boise State fans to their feet in one emotional leap and silenced the Montana side for the rest of the evening. Later in the locker room a reporter told Sylvester that he had out-rebounded and out-assisted Childers, but Childers had twenty-eight points to Sylvester's seventeen.

Sylvester was crushed. He thought he had played better defense than that. He hadn't given up more than fifteen or sixteen to anybody other than Childers in his career. And usually he held Childers around that figure.

After a few more question the sportswriter pronounced Sylvester a "winner" and went off to interview the winners.

"Isn't this the greatest place?"

Sylvester opened his eyes. He had fallen asleep on the too-soft double bed. The early-morning swim in the hot springs had exhausted him.

"God, I'd like to live here. I wonder if they need a maid or a horseshoer or something. I could live here forever, breathing this mountain air, swimming, eating in that wonderful dining room. They're so nice here!"

Sylvester raised his head. Shelley was sitting at the small desk near the window, writing a postcard.

"Who are you writing to?"

"The girls! I promised them a postcard. They think Chico Hot Springs is like a desert outpost, so I'm sending this one." She held up a photograph of the resort with the snowy mountain in the background. "This ought to disabuse them of that notion." She looked out the window for a moment, then returned to her writing.

Sylvester closed his eyes again. He hadn't thought about that game with Boise State for a couple of years at least. It had been his final game and when he recovered from the aches and bruises of a lifetime of basketball, he had concentrated on preparing for law school. He remembered that sportswriter— Ray Lundeen—he'd covered all the games of Sylvester's college career for the Missoula newspaper. He'd covered a lot of Sylvester's high school games before that when he'd been a reporter and columnist with the *Great Falls Tribune* before taking the Missoula job. He liked to think he knew Yellow Calf's "insides" better than any other sports fan, sportswriter, coach, player, human being in the state of Montana. Sylvester's career had been a storied one and he had told the story truly.

Maybe he did and maybe he didn't—but he did have a profound effect on Sylvester's young life.

It happened during Sylvester's senior year in high school. Browning had gone undefeated and was preparing for the state tournament. They had won it the year before and were all but conceded the championship this year. The same key players were back, they were all healthy and they all loved to run. Racehorse basketball. That was the way of good Indian teams—they were exciting, they had fascinating names, and they played with such abandon that opponents were reduced eventually to just getting out of the way. That was the straight skinny, at least as Ray Lundeen knew it. He also knew that most of the white fans around the state, while professing great admiration and even contagious enthusiasm for these Indian teams, wouldn't offer the parents of these kids a cup of coffee in a snowstorm. That was the way of the world, as Ray Lundeen knew it. He had grown up in a midwestern city and had followed the careers of many black players. He had watched them become stars, had stood in crowds honoring their parents at halftime, and had seen them all, with few exceptions, fade back into the obscurity and poverty of the ghetto. He had grown cynical and a bit caustic, a known curmudgeon even as a young reporter. His first job out of journalism school took him to Grand Forks, North Dakota; two years later, on a whim he applied for a sportswriting job in Great Falls. He wanted to sharpen his skills in a small city job before attacking the world of big-time journalism. The drawing card of the Great Falls job was the opportunity to write a weekly sports column, which he did for the next seven years.

It was about halfway through this tenure that he began to notice the name of Sylvester Yellow Calf in the basketball stories being sent down from the Hi-line. By this time he had developed a consuming interest in Indian basketball teams—it had actually started in North Dakota when he covered the divisional and state tournaments and found himself having difficulty masking his bias in favor of Indian teams. In many ways, in their athletic ability, the way they carried themselves, the way they played the game, they reminded him of some of the black teams in his home city.

And he noticed the curious phenomenon that occurred during these games on neutral courts. The fans of the teams not actually playing the Indian teams became caught up in the excitement of watching these players and rooted for them as enthusiastically as the reservation people. But Ray also noticed that when the game ended there was almost no interchange between the two sets of fans. Quite often the only interchange was an act of hostility.

And that hostility, disguised only by metaphor, extended into the newsroom. Once Ray mentioned his discovery to an older reporter on another newspaper.

"It's like being in a monkey cage," the older man said. "At first, you're surprised not only that they can perform their tricks but how well they do it. But in the end, you're in a monkey cage and people get mighty uneasy when they're surrounded by monkeys."

The Browning team went nine and sixteen during Sylvester's sophomore year, twenty-four and one his junior year, and twenty-five and zero his senior year. The only loss in that junior year was a forfeit to an archrival when a Browning player on the bench got hit in the head with a full can of beer. An opposing player tried to wrestle Sylvester to the floor but Sylvester pulled free and threw the player against the stage at the end of the court. By the time the lone policeman, the teachers, and the principal got the fans off the court, the floor was littered with objects and two Browning players were bleeding. The team was hustled off the court, into the locker room to pick up their street clothes, then out to the bus. They put their clothes on over their wet uniforms as the bus lurched out of town, followed by three or four carloads of young men, honking and shouting threats.

But the next year there were no incidents between the two teams, either home or away, and Browning continued to win. They had won the state B championship the year before and were heavily favored to repeat. Sylvester ran the break and led the team in every category but rebounding. Even there, he got more offensive rebounds, usually put-backs after one of his teammates missed. But he distributed the ball, and they were a team every step of the way until Ray Lundeen wrote the column in the *Great Falls Tribune* that changed everything.

The column was in the form of a cautionary tale addressed to Sylvester Yellow Calf. "Dear Mr. Yellow Calf," it began. "You are the heart and soul of the greatest Indian basketball team this state has seen. You have provided thrills and chills, in one way or another, to every basketball fan in Montana, and for that we thank you." It was not a great column, for Ray Lundeen was only a competent writer, but as the column went on it became oddly effective, a sort of paean to all the teams and players who came out of the ghetto or from the reservation to provide momentary pleasure, excitement, diversion to the faceless, pitiful hordes who live in the shadow of the bomb (Montana was the fifth-biggest nuclear power in the the world, he pointed out), who lead lives of "quiet desperation," of bankruptcy and foreclosure, of night sweats and trembling.

"Many of your teammates, Sylvester, will have had their brief moment in the sun and will fall by the wayside, perhaps to a life of drink and degradation—so much a part of Indian experience—but you will, must, carry the torch." And the column went on to praise Sylvester's leadership, intelligence, work ethic, politeness. He ended by calling Sylvester a "winner" both on the court and off, in the past, present, and future, in life—a "winner for all minorities who fight the endless battle for respect and honor."

The principal had tacked the article up on the bulletin board outside his office. Word spread and soon several players were standing at the bulletin board, joking and jostling, looking for their own names. But as they read, they became quiet and motionless. They didn't say much to each other as they made their way to study hall, but they were all thinking the same thing. They had been presented in their youth with a vision of themselves that they might have thought about briefly and offhandedly—they had seen it, the ex-jocks who slept in their clothes, in cars and doorways, who tried to bum quarters off them as they passed on their way to practice. Some of these had been uncles, cousins, even in one case a father.

The more they thought about it the more they realized that Sylvester had been exempted from that vision, that he was a "winner" who would go on to better things.

Practice that afternoon appeared normal. There was the usual thumping and screeching of basketball shoes, grunting, yelling, the steady pound of basketball on hardwood as the sides drove up and down the court; there was also a surprising lack of horseplay, grabbing jerseys, tugging on trunks, fake passes, and circus shots. The coach did not yell at them, as he usually did, for roughhousing because there was none. To all appearances it was a good, hard practice by a good, disciplined team; but the character of it had changed and Sylvester noticed.

He had read the column and that day he felt mostly embarrassment and regret that his teammates had not gotten their fair share of credit. He did not feel that it was a big deal—he had been the main subject of all the stories about the team. Though he was intelligent, even bright, he was too young to understand the way his teammates—and later, their parents and relatives and friends—would take this particular story. He did not feel that he was that much different from the others—they were all smart, athletic, spirited. They would all make it. They would prove to this Ray Lundeen that they were all winners.

But the seed of incipient hostility had been planted, and most of the players were made to feel that they had ridden on Sylvester Yellow Calf's coattails this far. More than one wondered that day if he would be one of those destined to "fall by the wayside." What made matters worse, each of them had plenty of examples within his own family, within his family's circle of friends, of young men of potential who had failed, often miserably. What *did* make these boys different was that up to the point of the article they had determined to succeed, "to rise above," as their guidance counselor often suggested. The irony in this was that they looked to Sylvester, who had been raised in the bald poverty of Moccasin Flat by grandparents, as an example of rising above. They knew that his parents were no good, his mother a barfly who had left a long time ago, his father a wino who had drifted off a long time ago too. Their parents had told them terrible stories about Sylvester's family. Somehow, those stories made him one of them, in spite of his stardom. Now they felt betrayed by this paragon of virtue who would almost guarantee their failure by his success.

But they did not fail in basketball. They were too good a team to come apart in the state tournament; in fact, they played the best ball of their lives, and in the title game when the starters began coming out with a little over three minutes left, the five thousand–plus fans gave them standing ovations. Sylvester was the last to come out, and all the players on the bench gave him the power shake, a couple smiled, one said, "We blew their asses out," but it was a subdued group that watched the final seconds tick away.

Afterward in the locker room they said a prayer in Blackfeet, then the coach told them what they had accomplished as a team—he emphasized "team"—but as he looked around the hot, grimy room, he knew that they were not really listening. Already the term had taken on a distant sound. He had grown up in Browning too. As he finished his little speech he looked directly at Sylvester, who sat at the end of the bench with his head down. The coach did not feel the usual fatherly pride toward his star player; instead, he felt a strange mixture of resentment and pity. The young man still had a long road to travel.

Sylvester had already signed a letter of intent to play for the University of Montana Grizzlies, because he wanted to be within driving distance of his grandparents and because the school had a good Division One basketball program. Mostly Sylvester wanted to get into a school with a decent prelaw program. He had made up his mind that he wanted to at least see if he could hack law studies. He had read an article in a magazine that the guidance counselor had given him about Indian lawyers. The article called them the "new warriors" and predicted that Indian law and water law—both of which figured prominently on reservations—were the fields to choose in the seventies and eighties. The guidance counselor, a young woman named Lena Old Horn, who had thought about a law career herself (and still hadn't given up on the notion), told Sylvester that he had the talent and dedication to be one of these new warriors.

After basketball season, Sylvester grew apart from his teammates, even from Donny Little Dog, who had to quit the team after his parents were killed in a car accident. The team had dedicated their season to Donny and his family, and he had sat on the bench with the players during the state tournament. He and Sylvester had grown up together in Moccasin Flat, had fought, fished, hunted, played basketball, run track, studied together, even chased girls together, although the girl Sylvester wanted was Donny's sister, who was a year younger than they were. She was a shy girl who ended up taking care of the family until Family Services took most of them away. After that, she sank inward into a quiet despondency. She endured Sylvester's teasing attention but did nothing to encourage it.

After Donny drifted away, Sylvester was basically alone. He'd decided to skip track that spring in order to concentrate on his studies. With Lena Old Horn's help, he took two courses at the Blackfeet Community College, one an English course taught by a young instructor named Stanley Weintraub. He was from back east and wore his hair in a ponytail and had a small gold earring in his ear. He was not a stranger to Montana, having worked three years ago on the Flathead Reservation as a Vista volunteer. But that was west of the mountains, near the university town of Missoula. He had made a lot of friends over there, had occasionally sat in on poetry classes at the university. Weintraub was a pretty good poet and he'd hoped to be able to teach poetry at the community college. But there was something about the attitude of the college, the town, the whole reservation that made Weintraub hesitant, almost fearful. His way of treating Indians—as dead-level equals, not to be deferred to, not to be condescending toward, but to be looked at squarely in the eye—did not seem to work here. There was a structure among these people that Weintraub did not understand, much less fit into. And so he became fast friends with Lena Old Horn, one of the other outsiders in town. It did not bother Lena that she was an outsider; she had expected it; it would be the same for an outsider on her own reservation. She tried to explain this to Stan, and when it wouldn't sink in, she let it go and did her job at the high school.

But when Sylvester Yellow Calf came into her office one late afternoon and asked her what a person would have to do to get a law degree, her heart had actually skipped a couple of beats. As he sat there, so tall and handsome in his letterman's jacket, she thought he had been sent to her by a spirit guide. She had heard of him, of course; she went to all the home games with Stan, she talked with his teachers, she knew he lived with his grandparents on Moccasin Flat; there were few secrets a star basketball player could keep in Browning. But to have him come to her and ask about the study of law was too good to be true.

Lena talked with him for an hour, then gave him the article

about the new breed of Indian lawyers. There was nothing really personal in their discussion—she was the guidance counselor and he the student—but when he left she found herself trying to remember if she had given him any encouragement other than professional. She was almost ashamed because she hoped she had; she hoped he wanted to see her again as much as she wanted to see him.

After that first time, he did come again; he came at least once a week, usually after classes, and they talked of different law schools, the advantages and disadvantages of each. She lent him her own brochures and catalogues and he took them home and read them assiduously. A couple of times he seemed overwhelmed by the unfathomable jargon of the law, but she coaxed him back and restored his confidence.

By spring they were friends. He took Lena and Stan fishing at Mission Lake and Four Horns Reservoir. He had to teach them everything, but they were fast learners and soon they were all catching fish. Later in the evening Stan would fry them up while Lena and Sylvester talked at Lena's kitchen table. Only once did things become outwardly awkward—the night Lena asked him about his parents. He had always been so outgoing and polite that she was startled by the way his jaw became rigid. He did not look up from his plate of fish and potatoes. He said that his mother had another family somewhere in New Mexico and his father had been seen a few years ago in Butte. Then he laughed and said they weren't his real parents anyway. Lena did not know what he meant but she changed the subject. She had shamed him deeply, in front of Stan, a white man, an outsider. She should have known better but she had been taken in by his image as a star athlete, an honor student, a role model to all the kids around Browning. She should have known that he was as inwardly timid and vulnerable as any youth who had been abandoned, cast aside by those he loved the most. She had seen lots of kids on her own reservation being raised by grandparents. Sylvester seemed different from them, but she knew he wasn't and she should have known better than to ask him about his family in front of an outsider. She also knew that for him she was no longer an outsider, and this pleased her more than anything in her life at that moment. He would have answered her truly and fully if they had been alone. She knew this deep down but she also knew she would never bring up his parents again.

As for Sylvester, he was in love and confused. He knew that Lena and Stan were more than just friends. He had seen, on the grassy banks of Four Horns Reservoir with a brilliant sun greening up the prairie around them, Stan put his arm around Lena, and it seemed natural out there. In town, in school, one seldom saw teachers, even married ones, touch each other. Sylvester smiled at such intimacy when he saw it because it made the teachers human, just like the kids. And he liked being with Lena and Stan because it made him feel grown-up, even though his grandmother didn't particularly like it. She pointed out that he was neglecting his own people by hanging around with them. Sylvester didn't argue—he couldn't tell her that his own people seemed to have grown away from him ever since the state tournament back in March. His teammates remained distantly friendly but they never invited Sylvester to pickup games or Saturday nights of driving around. Most were involved with track, so he hardly ever saw them after school—except at a distance when he sometimes watched them practice on the football field. The people in town smiled and greeted him—a few even asked if he was going to start for the Grizzlies next winter or if he was staying in shape—but there was none of the old banter, the fond teasing that he had grown up with.

In less than two months Sylvester had become a different person. He had always been a little different—he studied hard, he took care of his grandparents as much as they took care of him, he didn't drink at all, he was always the best athlete even as a little kid—but now without dwelling on it, he knew he had become an outsider to all but the old people. He still went places with his grandmother and grandfather—to honoring ceremonies, to giveaways, to namings—and the elders treated him with kindness and respect, but he did feel that he was becoming distant from these old people and their ceremonies as well. So that left Lena—and Stan. Stan tried to interest Sylvester in poetry—both the reading and the writing of it—but all Sylvester wanted to learn from Stan was how to write a clear sentence, how to put his thoughts into words that would be understandable to that great world out there. In fact, Sylvester was not a bad writer. He would do well in college. So Stan taught him the form of the essay and had him writing on everything from the scalp dance to the Watts riots.

He also became Sylvester's sparring mate on the basketball court behind the elementary school. Although at five-ten he was five inches shorter than Sylvester, he was surprisingly quick and aggressive and not afraid to throw a hip or an elbow. He couldn't shoot and he was a terrible dribbler, but he was a flailing, hacking machine on defense, and Sylvester needed that kind of practice.

But Sylvester found himself becoming increasingly annoyed at Stanley Weintraub. He couldn't figure it out—it wasn't because of the way Stan played or because of the frequent chewing-outs he gave Sylvester over his essays (although none of the high school teachers had ever found reason to yell at Sylvester). It was something else. It was Lena.

Sylvester was in love with Lena in a way that a youth falls in love with a special aunt. And Sylvester resented Stan in the way a youth might resent the uncle who treated his wife with a kind of loving indifference. Sylvester had never been close enough to husbands and wives, to aunts and uncles, to lovers, to know why he felt this way. He had known girlfriends, longing, jealousy, but those feelings were not complicated and eventually resolved themselves with time and new girlfriends and new seasons of basketball.

What he felt toward Lena was not quite sexual even though he found her very attractive. Her small slender body and wide face with high cheekbones suggested vulnerability and strength. He could see her a hundred years ago in buckskins and shawl doing beadwork or dancing a grass dance with other women. But her hair was long and soft, slightly curled under at her shoulders, fashionable. Once, in her office, he stood leaning over her shoulder, following her finger across a course description, and he almost put his hand on her shoulder. It was a reflex action, the way he leaned into a huddle, watching the coach diagram a play on the floor. His hand was inches from her shoulder when he caught himself. He had never touched her because she was an authority figure in school. He had shaken hands with teachers when they congratulated him over something, but he had never initiated the contact. Lena had looked up at that instant, brushed her long hair away from her face, and her eyes were expectant. Now Sylvester felt that had he rested his hand on her shoulder, their relationship would have changed, and he was both sad and glad that he hadn't. He didn't know what he wanted from Lena and so he often became annoyed with Stan for his easy, possessive way around her.

The day Sylvester broke Stan's nose was a cold, blustery, sleety mid-May Sunday. After almost a month of warm sunshine, the day caught Browning by surprise. People were still raking old leaves, planting gardens, washing cars, playing softball in the driving sleet from the north. The wind chill plunged to ten above and the mountains a few miles to the west disappeared and still the people refused to go inside, as though ancestral rhythms told them spring was the time to go outside and stay outside.

Sylvester thought about that day often, remembering all the details, the way the rope clanked against the flagpole at the elementary school, the sting of the driven sleet across his cheek. Stan was playing his usual aggressive game, the one Sylvester had put up with all spring to toughen himself up for college ball. It happened very quickly but Sylvester saw it all the way. He was backing into the pivot, backing the flailing poet off the ball, when Stan caught Sylvester with a knuckle in the back, nothing unusual, nothing to get upset about, and Sylvester wasn't. He simply pivoted toward the basket with his left elbow out and he saw, almost simultaneously, Stan drop to his knee and the ball go into the chainless hoop.

Sylvester drove Stan up to the PHS hospital in Stan's old Volkswagen bus. The sleet was almost too thick to see through and the road up the hill was slick, but they made it and walked into the emergency area just as a doctor was about to leave. Stan held a handkerchief tenderly against his nose but the blood seeped down his sweatshirt, staining, almost obliterating the "Rutgers" across his chest.

Sylvester waited for two hours in the darkening waiting room, looking at dog-eared but barely read magazines. He thought about calling Lena, but what would he say? I've wrecked your lover's nose because I want you for myself. Yes, it was deliberate, yes, I saw it happen, heard the pop, saw the blood and made the layup. Yes, I like Stan but I hate him too. I want him to leave you alone, not touch you or kiss you when he thinks I'm not looking. But I don't know what I want from you, except for you to give me all of your attention, to look at me, to touch me, to help me.

Sylvester drove Stan home, then walked back to his grandparents' house on Moccasin Flat. The area was beginning to be surrounded by government housing, but his grandparents lived in the old section in a house of plywood and tarpaper and boards and plastic-covered windows. The daffodils which his grandmother had planted on each side of the door were bent under the weight of the sleet. Sylvester shook each one, brushed off the sleet, then entered the house.

As he ate the deer-meat stew and frybread, he watched his grandparents watch television. They could get only two channels, neither very clearly, but they watched every night until bedtime, his grandmother working on a star quilt, his grandfather rolling cigarettes and laughing deep in his chest. Sylvester wondered, as he often did when he studied his grandparents, what his mother looked like. There were no pictures of her around the house.

≈≈≈≈≈

At dinner that night, in the rustic dark dining room, Shelley asked Sylvester if he had made up his mind about running for Congress. They had spent most of the afternoon riding horses with the other dudes in the mountains to the east of Chico Hot Springs. Sylvester hadn't been on a horse in many years, and although Shelley had grown up on a ranch she had never been much of a rider. Both were stiff and tired. The soak in the hot springs had helped but it had left them rubbery, too rubbery even to make love before dinner.

"Wonder what they put in these to make them taste that way?" Shelley was holding one of the pencil-thin breadsticks to her nose. "It smells so familiar."

"Garlic?"

"Get out of here! There hasn't been any garlic within ten miles of these things. How's the shrimp?"

"Prawns. Good. You want a bite?"

"God, I grew up on shrimp. My mother loved them. Morning, noon, and night—shrimp, shrimp, shrimp. I think she had some kind of deficiency."

"In Roundup?"

"Sure, frozen shrimp. You can get it there. Oregano! That's what's in these things." She broke the breadstick in half and gave half to Sylvester. "Taste it."

Sylvester smiled and chewed the breadstick. He didn't know oregano from sagebrush but he nodded and watched Shelley cut a piece of steak. She looked up and smiled back. "Isn't it wonderful?" she said. "I miss the country something fierce. I never thought I would."

Six years ago Sylvester had represented Shelley's mother in selling off their ranch in Musselshell County. It was one of the largest in the state; rather, it was three ranches, two of them with contiguous boundaries. It was these two that Mrs. Hatton sold a year after her husband, Mel, had died of cancer.

Mel Hatton had been a state senator for years and the Hattons had always kept a house in Helena. It was a historic house, not far from Buster Harrington's. Not coincidentally, the two had been fast friends and political allies, although Hatton was much more conservative, backing every ranch- and farm-related bill that came up whether it was a good bill or bad. But he had a side that was open to social reform—he had helped his buddy, Bob Berglund, get the funding to build the new prison—and conservation—he argued vehemently for setting aside Wilderness Areas just so future generations could see what Montana and the west used to be like. When he died, Roundup named its dusty little park after him. And Mrs. Hatton moved permanently to Helena. Sylvester's role in selling off the two ranches was enhanced by the fact that although there were several bidders lined up he found another buyer for one of them, a conservancy group that bought up land to protect flora and fauna that would otherwise be endangered. This particular ranch had a large wetlands area that was a nesting ground for ducks and geese and other water birds. Sylvester had gone to law school with one of the directors of the group and after much complicated maneuvering had struck a deal with them. Mrs. Hatton sold that ranch at a loss, which turned out to be an advantage in the overall deal.

She introduced Sylvester to her daughter one day when he went to her house to have her sign some papers. Shelley and her daughters were there because Shelley had just moved out on her husband, a Roundup veterinarian, with whom she had absolutely nothing in common but the two girls. She moved out when the veterinarian became obsessed with owning the ranches and tried to use her to queer any other deals with her mother. It was a hateful time but Shelley was grateful for the opportunity to make the break. She never once looked back.

After that initial meeting with Sylvester she saw him three or four times during the next five years—once in a bookstore where they said "Excuse me" and recognized each other and then at a couple of Democratic fund-raisers. Each time they exchanged as few words as possible, he because he was still uneasy around attractive white women, and she because he was an Indian. She couldn't imagine what she could have in common with an Indian. There were very few Indians around Roundup; the few she saw were ranch hands who drank in a particularly rank bar. So she was always surprised, just as she was surprised when she learned that Sylvester Yellow Calf was representing her mother in the land deals, when she saw him at these functions surrounded by groups of men and women who she knew were prominent in Helena society, at least in Democratic Helena. She knew he was a former star athlete but she couldn't believe that earned him such attention. It made her a little angry.

Then a year ago her mother dragged her to a Friends of the Library fund-raising dinner. She didn't know much about the organization and she knew even less about the program, and so she was once again surprised to see Sylvester Yellow Calf, sitting at the head table. God, the man is everywhere, she thought. And when he was introduced and rose to deliver the speech she thought seriously of walking out, but she was sitting too close to the head table. He spoke in a slow, low-key, dangerous way about the failure of society in general, Montana in particular, to encourage education on reservations. He spoke of the legal status of Indian people, the rights that had been accorded them and then ignored by the federal government. He spoke of the duty of all Montanans to see that

all their children get an equal education. He spoke of complicated Title IV funding issues, of bills pending in the legislature to take such funding away from reservation schools and
spread it equally among all schools, regardless of status. It
was an interesting and provocative speech but not the speech
most of the guests wanted to hear. They wanted more of Sylvester Yellow Calf in the speech; they wanted to know how an
Indian off the reservation could have made such a success of
his life. They wanted to hear about his basketball career.
Above all, since Helena was *the* political town, the state capi-
tal, they wanted to know if he, Sylvester Yellow Calf, had
political aspirations. He laughed the question off as he had
done many times in the past.

Shelley didn't laugh, and she now understood why he was
always a center of attention at the Democratic fund-raisers.
They wanted him to run for something. She was surprised at
her own stupidity. She had often listened to her father and his
colleagues discuss some rising star in the party and how they
could best take advantage of his popularity. She saw Sylvester
finally in terms she could understand. She almost admired
him for keeping his speech impersonal. After the question-
and-answer session ended and the guests were leaving, Shelley caught Sylvester putting on his coat. She started to intro-
duce herself, but he cut her short. He remembered her and
had been wondering how she and her mother were doing. She
thanked him for the speech and he grew shy and hesitant and
looked at her as if he couldn't believe she'd actually enjoyed
it. She hadn't, particularly—at the time she had no interest in
Indian matters, none but a casual Montana interest in Indians
at all—but that wasn't the point.

Two days later he called her and she accepted an invitation

to dinner at the Montana Club. They talked about politics, computers, grizzly bears, hunting (neither of them hunted), the Olympics. They did not talk about Indians or basketball. Whenever the conversation came near either subject, he steered it away, and this puzzled her. They talked about her background, the ranches, her schooling at Swarthmore and later graduate studies in sociology at the University of Pennsylvania. She was the only Montanan as far as she knew at either place. She had met her husband there. He was from Philadelphia but he was going to veterinary school at Cornell. They met at a party and got married at the end of the school year just after his graduation. She told him there were a lot of animals in Montana. They moved to Roundup, where he bought out a veterinarian who just happened to be retiring. Six months later they had a daughter and ten months after that they had another daughter. Their names were Amy and Marty, short for Margaret, her mother's name. She realized that she was talking a lot about herself, and it felt good. She hadn't had a chance to explain herself to anyone for ages. She talked about her job with the state in the fiscal analyst's office. In three years she had risen from someone who couldn't balance her checkbook to a computer whiz. She laughed at herself, and that felt good too.

In fact, she couldn't understand why she felt so comfortable with this man whom she had almost despised a week before at the library dinner. Was it because he was a good listener? He must have listened to dozens of women spill their life stories in his work. Why was he not married? She didn't even know if he had been married, if he had any children, if he socialized with Indians, if he had a woman friend back on the reservation. Did he even go back to his reservation? She knew he was Blackfeet and she knew the reservation was up near Glacier Park. She had been up that way once when some relatives from Oregon came for a visit. She knew the highway went through the reservation but she hadn't noticed it, hadn't even noticed any Indians.

After that first date, he did open up a little, and then a little more, until now, a year later, she knew several of the particulars of his life, but he was just now letting her in on his feelings. She now knew why he would enter politics, why he was dissatisfied with his life of the usual lawyerly stuff of settling claims, personal injury and workman's comp, of representing business interests in land and property deals, of various other forms of litigation. He did some pro bono work for tribes but the big deals, the water rights, the hunting and fishing rights, the mineral rights cases, were usually handled by tribal attorneys and big law firms in Washington, D.C., on retainer. Harrington wanted him to handle as many cases as possible without sacrificing his usefulness with the firm. He wanted the goodwill and he wanted Sylvester to establish a political base with the tribes.

Shelley understood this. She had known that her father met often with representatives of tribal government, even though he was a traditional foe—a large landowner whose interests often ran counter to tribal interests.

And she now knew quite a lot about Indians in an abstract way—their culture, the reservation system, the education system, the role of the feds in Indian affairs. But Sylvester had never invited her to accompany him on his frequent trips up to Browning to visit his grandparents. He told her about them—his grandfather had been tribal treasurer for many years but was not big in traditional life; that was the domain of his grandmother, Little Bird Walking Woman, or Mary Bird. Shelley always wondered where the Mary came from. And she wanted desperately to meet this woman, for she knew she would understand much more about Sylvester. It was almost enough to love him and see him and be part of his life. But she wanted to learn so much more about him. She couldn't believe that just a year ago this man who was now sitting across from her in the lovely dim dining room eating his shrimp had been an almost total stranger.

"Have you decided yet?"

Sylvester put down his fork. He had been quiet for a long time, but so had she. "Haven't we talked about this?" he said.

"Once—a couple of weeks ago. I said you should do it."

"Easy for you to say." He extended his large hand, palm up, across the table. She put her own in it and it looked small and white. She still wore her Swarthmore graduation ring—for professional identity, she once told him. Men still took her for a secretary. Although she was taller than average and wore tailored suits most of the winter and thought herself somewhat imposing, men and some women, heads of departments and divisions, often mistook her for a "gofer" and attempted to send her on errands. Triphammer enjoyed this but he also enjoyed asking her to make her fiscal presentation and he enjoyed watching them squirm as she went over the various elements of their budgets. He liked his assistant but he loved to make her life a little miserable at times.

Must be my hair, she thought, it's too frizzy. "I still think you should do it. I've weighed the pros and cons—I remember how hectic and frustrating life was for Daddy during the legislative sessions. He seldom came home for meals; most of the time he was at the capitol until after midnight, then he was up early in the morning, reading bills and making phone calls. It was such a relief when the session was over and we could go back to the ranch—although later I always had to finish out the school year in Helena. Really, from a month before the session to the end of the school year I hardly saw my father.

"But he did good things overall. I think he helped make Montana a more humane state, although I don't think he was able to help your people much. He couldn't really shake his landowner roots. But you—you could make up for some of the shortsighted things this state, this nation, has done to the Indians. Don't you think?"

Sylvester gently pulled his hand away and sat back. He glanced over at the two couples at the table beside theirs. He had noticed them sit down earlier. The two men wore clean cowboy shirts, Wranglers, and boots. One of them was bald on top, his head white from never seeing the sun. The other was shorter and stockier and making too much noise. One of the wives or girlfriends was small and pretty in a flowery yellow dress; the other was dressed like the men except for spiked heels in place of cowboy boots. She smoked a lot of thin cigarettes. From time to time they would glance over at Sylvester and Shelley. Lately the glances had been longer.

"I think I could help some. I sure could do more than I'm doing now—but would that be enough? Could I get all the tribes behind me? If even one tribe or Indian group decided they didn't want me because I'm a Blackfeet or a lawyer or whatever, it would be disastrous. Then could I get enough support from whites? A lot of them would probably think I was trying to give the state back to the tribes. Would your father have supported me? I might say and do some things that would alienate even a lot of Democrats who thought I would be good for their own interests."

"You would do what you had to do. But you won't be able to do anything if you don't try it." Shelley laughed, but it wasn't her best effort. "About Daddy—it might have shaken him up. He was kind of an old poot about a lot of things but he honestly did have a lot of friends among the Indians. Back in those days, I was the one you would have to convince. I was horribly naive and uninterested."

"Would you have gone out with me?"

"Not on a dare. I saw all the movies. You were a savage and you liked nothing better than to ravish white girls like me. Besides, I was too young."

Sylvester glanced over at the white couples and his heart sank. Shelley had made a joke of it, but there was too much truth in what she said. Sylvester had been stared at enough to sort it out. There were the people who recognized him from his basketball days; then there were the ones who looked at him because he was an Indian, usually dressed up in a fancy suit, and they thought him a novelty; and finally, there were the ones who stared at him and hated him because he was an Indian. Now he was an Indian free and easy with a lovely blond woman. Sylvester could recognize the ones who represented a threat and he was now looking right at them.

"Well?"

"What?"

"You haven't answered my question."

Sylvester leaned forward, trying to ignore the couples. "I don't know if I'm prepared. I know I'm not in the right frame of mind to go after it yet but I think I could get there. But I haven't really talked with anyone since Fabares suggested it. Except you."

"Right. You've really bent my ear. Yap, yap, yap."

"I'm sorry. I'm a quiet person. You know that by now."

The mood of the dining room had changed. There was less noise—conversations had diminished as people drank their coffee, the clatter of the busboys and waitresses had softened. Even Shelley's mood had changed. She sat back and looked down at her plate. Her face, so lovely and glowing a moment ago, seemed older. She was only thirty-three, but just now she had the look that some of Sylvester's divorce clients used to get when he told them the bad news. It was a thoughtful sadness, full of cares about children, the lonely future. He didn't do divorces anymore.

"Shelley," he said softly. He put his hand out again but she didn't take it. "I want to tell you. I don't ever want to keep anything from you. I'm leaning toward it. I want you to know that." But he knew they had gone beyond the issue. She was bitterly disappointed that she didn't know him as well as she wanted to. Sylvester loved her. He really hadn't had many girlfriends in high school and college and in his early years of practicing law in Helena. He had lived in a strange world back then and still did. First girls, then women, found him attractive, and, of course, he was a star. But he was unsure of himself around girls. He'd gone out with Indian girls in college and he'd had a few dates with white girls—he took out a sorority girl from his Spanish class twice, once to a concert and once to a movie. They had sat beside each other in Spanish and often lingered after class, discussing the next day's assignment. They laughed and joked and got along so well that he asked her out and they had fun at the concert, sitting high up in the fieldhouse, the warmth and excitement tingling through their bodies. She was tall and slender and had a quiet grace about her—she didn't seem to him to belong in a sorority and this gave him hope. He felt himself falling in love with her. On the second date, as they were walking home in the late-April evening, she asked him several questions about his life on the reservation. He enjoyed her attention and told her about his grandparents, Moccasin Flat, the poverty, the drinking, the way people coped and hoped for a future. He came alive with answers and loved her for asking the questions. He thought she was trying to understand him, Indians. But on the walk in front of the sorority house, she told him she couldn't go out anymore, that she had to study, that she had a friend back in Virginia. Sylvester spent that night trying to think of what he had done wrong. His roommate, King Johnson, a black football player from Indiana, laughed and said, "You're a fucking redskin, man."

After that Sylvester did not take his dating seriously. There were always girls who didn't care if he was a fucking redskin, or maybe they cared because he was. He didn't question their motives and he didn't go out with girls he might get serious about. If his dates were impressed because he was an athlete, so much the better. He took them out and sometimes he screwed them, sometimes he didn't.

In law school he didn't go out much at all, except to dinner at friends' houses or occasionally to bars with a group of law students. The conversation, intense, often heated, was always about law or politics or sports or movies. The students came from all over the country. Many came from wealthy families; some were there on scholarships or fellowships; some were just squeaking by on loans and small grants. There was one other Indian—a Pueblo woman from Laguna. She was seven years older than Sylvester and she reminded him of Lena Old Horn. She was small and she wore her hair pulled tightly back, which made her cheekbones even more prominent and her eyes darkly oriental. Most of the students were a little afraid of her because she had a fierce countenance in repose and a quick, clipped voice and she was older than most of them. But she and Sylvester got along well. She often admonished him to always think of himself as different, to not get too comfortable among the others, to be wary. She had been chopped off at the knees, she had had her head or her ass handed to her too many times—she talked like that. Sylvester always laughed because he couldn't imagine anyone capable of chopping her off at the knees. Until the night she took him to her apartment just off Middlefield Road after a spaghetti feed at some friends' house. Both had drunk enough wine to feel tipsy, but she drove determinedly and well. They drank another bottle of wine while she showed him pictures of her and her ex-husband and her daughter, who was being raised by her grandparents. Sylvester almost trembled with recognition of such a familiar scene and he almost left the smoky little apartment. He wanted to leave but he sat and drank the wine and listened to her stories of how good her ex-husband had been in bed, at least, and when she stood above him and took off her sweater he knew he should leave. Instead, he ran his fingers over the smooth silk of her bra. Her breasts were larger than he had thought and he felt the hard nipples through the white material. Her body was mature and small and firm. She pulled the turquoise combs from her hair and shook it out. She eased him to her breasts and covered his face with her hair as he kissed and nibbled through the material. It was hot in the kitchen but her dark skin was cool and smooth and he hugged her hips into his chest. He looked up within the halo of her hair and she was watching him, her teeth white and shiny in her smile. The smile never left her face as she pulled him to his feet and led him into the bedroom. She turned her back to him and kicked off her high heels and pulled the black jersey skirt over her head and off. Her white panties glowed in the dark.

They made love quick and hard and brief. Sylvester marveled at how light and strong she was and how many ways she knew to make love. Once, she whispered in his ear and he rolled away and looked at her. She laughed and said he ought to see himself. Then she was on top of him and he felt his cock slipping into her as though it, if not he, knew her secrets.

He left at dawn and rode her bike the two miles to his own apartment. Although he was exhausted and somewhat dazed, he had brief flashes of what had happened and he grinned to himself. The gray, brightening streets of Palo Alto had never looked so fresh. He felt as though he had made love for the first time in his life. He was happy and scared and he didn't notice that he almost ran over a cat that had streaked out from between two parked cars. Later in the week he returned her bike and they were in bed ten minutes after he knocked on her door. They could not get enough of each other.

This went on for the two months until the end of the term. Her name at the beginning of their affair was Anita Talcott; at the end it was Anita Sandoval. She had legally changed back to her maiden name. She was going home for the summer in an attempt to get her daughter, Sunny, back, but she would return in the fall. Sylvester helped her load her car and when she drove off down the hot street he waved and was glad she was gone.

Something had happened during the course of their affair. At first she had been possessive and he liked that. He was ready to be possessed by such a woman. But then she became vulnerable, almost shy when they were in class or just walking on the campus. If they went to a movie or a club in San Francisco she held on to his arm and she smiled quietly when he talked of the many things they had in common. She agreed to everything he suggested. She was his and Sylvester grew uncomfortable in this knowledge. He liked her better when they were in bed, when she threw her head from side to side on the pillow, or rode him, her head back, her breasts pointing to the ceiling. She came in great shuddering gasps, her fist against her mouth, and then she collapsed on top of him, her grin powerful in the dark room.

But she had lost that power in other parts of her life and this disappointed Sylvester. Even her name change, which she had initiated before they met, did not seem to affect her. The only thing that seemed to affect her, besides Sylvester, was her daughter. She once told him that she just wanted to settle down with Sunny, get some kind of job to support them, and protect her from the world.

Sylvester realized that she had given too much of herself to him—as she probably had with other men—and that he now was the one who could cut her off at the knees if he wanted. This power frightened him and so when he waved goodbye, he ran the two miles home and he felt light and fast, as though a hundred pounds had been lifted from his shoulders.

Because they had promised to write each other during the summer, he sent a couple of letters to her grandparents' Laguna address. In the letters he wrote of small things, enclosed interesting campus newspaper clippings about the law school, and ended with "Love." She never answered. And she did not return to school in the fall.

A hundred pounds had been lifted, but Sylvester felt sad. Had she met another man? One she could give herself to—who would cut her off at the knees—or find a way to love her unqualifiedly? Or had she gotten her daughter and found a job, a home protected from the world?

He never really got over his ambivalence toward Anita until he moved back to Montana, to Helena and his first job; even then he had to concentrate on his work, handling divorces, personal injury cases. A couple of times he almost wrote to Anita but he could think of nothing to say. Their affair had been that brief, and he sometimes wished they had remained simply friends. He thought they could have remained good friends.

Sylvester made some friends in Helena, mostly men connected with the law, but he stayed away from women who might want him. He couldn't say exactly why he was so gunshy. He had nothing against the small commitment it would take to enjoy the company of a woman, he just couldn't make that commitment, even if was nothing more than a dinner date. It wasn't until he got to know Shelley, after their first two or three formal meetings, that he understood that love had to be possible, that he had always chosen women who put up barriers, either consciously or unconsciously, between themselves and happiness. And he further understood that he had done the same. With Shelley, he had *felt* the possibility of love and that was enough. So simple. And it had taken him a lifetime to learn it.

Sylvester now suddenly thought of Lena Old Horn. He hadn't seen her since his senior year in college. He knew she was still in Browning. He subscribed to the *Glacier Reporter* and had read a small feature story about her less than a year ago. She was chaperoning a group of students on a visit to the Institute of American Indian Arts in Santa Fe. There was a picture of the students and Lena, but she stood in the second row off to the side, slightly out of range of the flashbulb. Still he recognized her long flowing hair and her small shoulders and he thought about that spring day on the banks of Four Horns Reservoir when Stanley Weintraub put his arm around Lena and rested his hand on her shoulder. Even in the picture she looked as though she were facing into the strong southwest wind as she had that day.

Sylvester glanced over at the table beyond Shelley's shoulder. The two ranch couples were leaving. The tall thin woman in the Wranglers and high heels stubbed out her cigarette and looked at Sylvester. Then she looked at Shelley and her eyes narrowed. She was trying to attract their attention so she could register her disgust.

But Shelley did not notice. She appeared not to notice anything in the dining room but the napkin on her lap. She was smoothing out the wrinkles.

"There is one other person I have to talk to," said Sylvester, breaking a silence that he knew was irretrievable. The table between them seemed to have grown larger. "You know I love you." The words sounded so far away he felt as if he was calling across the windy pothole lakes of his youth.

CHAPTER SIX

Jack Harwood first heard the sound of urgency—the quiet footsteps on the concrete floor, the hesitation, the silent preparation—then he heard the click and hum, the blowing, the loud voice on the loudspeaker rousting the unit. He pulled on his khakis just as the door banged open. The light flicked on, blinding him for a moment.

"C'mon, Harwood, we haven't got all day."

He could hear the running footsteps on the concrete, no attempt now to hide the urgency. He heard more doors being opened and the guards yelling to the inmates inside their houses.

"What time is it?" Harwood padded in his bare feet to the door.

"Just stand there outside the door. You know the drill."

"What are you looking for?" It was too early in the morning to be a standard toss. He looked down the hall and saw other inmates standing outside their doors. Beyond, the window at the end of the corridor was black with night. He heard the guard ripping the blanket and sheet off his bed.

"Maybe you could tell me what you're looking for—I could tell you if it's there or not."

"Shut the fuck up, Jack."

The sound of the guard sliding his hands under the mattress made Jack uncomfortable. Did he have anything in there? They were looking for contraband—booze, drugs, pornographic Polaroids of wives or girlfriends, weapons. Jack looked down the hall toward the guard station. An officer stood on a stepladder, unscrewing a ventilator screen.

"Hey, what's going on, Duds?" Jack peered around the corner.

Dudley was looking at a picture taped above Jack's desk. "She's some looker, Jack. When are you going to straighten up and fly right? Jesus, if I had a squeeze like that I'd be out selling Bibles." Dudley was puffing from his efforts. Like a lot of the guards he was big, his beer belly straining the buttons on the thin white shirt.

"Get me out of here and I'll sell you anything you want."

"Don't talk like that, Jack. It makes you sound like one of these white-collar boys we've got on Lower C."

"What's the problem?"

"Aw, we got word that someone in your cube is packing iron. The source is very reliable, but I'm getting too old for this shit."

"Visitor?"

"That's enough, Jack. Just to answer your next question, if

we don't find it your cube is locked down until we do." Dudley brushed past him and entered the next house.

Down the hall Jack saw Peter Quinn standing outside his door with another inmate, a stocky little guy. Mutt and Jeff, their nicknames. Both were wearing jockey shorts and T-shirts and looking forlorn. They were double-bunked because of the overcrowding of the prison. Jack knew the little guy was being shaken down for his canteen money. It wouldn't be long before the Indians had him sending home for protection money. A couple of years ago Jack might have tried to help him out—but not anymore. Jack didn't need trouble because he had a plan and that plan did not call for trouble with anyone. Especially the Indians.

Shit. If they were locked down he couldn't call Patti. It had been two weeks since his last call to her. He couldn't tell if he had really made his point. She had sounded like she was terrified for him. He had made it, all right, he had done a good job. Throwing a metal chair against the wall during their last conversation had shaken her up. The unknown. He had become a master of psychology, a real terrorist.

The next step was going to be the hardest and he didn't know if he had the heart for it. If he did, things with Patti would be changed forever, even when he got out. If he didn't, he might wind up dead or broken. He had seen too many guys just give up after a while. They might be rejected for parole or brought back on a parole violation—or they might simply tire of the struggle after their fifth, sixth felony. Jack would rather be out on the streets or dead.

The trouble was, the Indians still thought he had the money. He had made the major mistake of telling Bill Shanley one day in the library that the judge had thrown the book at him because he thought that Harwood had ratholed the nine thousand that nobody could find. He had laughed about it. But when the Indians started bulldogging Shanley, he had told them about Jack and the money. Jack didn't blame Shanley. He might have done the same thing in his place. Besides, Hardass Hartpence had rolled over on him before Shanley. Trouble was, the Indians believed Shanley. The games were serious in the joint.

One morning on the way to the chow hall, two of the biggest—Walker and Old Bull—caught up with him. He glanced at them and his heartbeat fluttered in his throat. They were smiling. Walker, the taller of the two, had short hair and a strong lean face. He was from Great Falls, part of a family of strongarm robbers who always had at least one member in prison.

"Hey, Harwood, slow down. We want to talk to you." Walker put a large hand on Jack's shoulder and pressed him close. Jack glanced at the hand and saw a long red welt that ran from the middle knuckle to the bottom of the thumb.

Old Bull stepped to the other side of Jack. He was short and stout. He wore mirrored glasses and a red bandanna around his long hair.

"We were going over to the weight room this afternoon and we wanted to know if you wanted to come along. You're looking a little white, Jack." Walker squeezed him tighter.

Jack knew better than to resist the pressure. "I have to work today. Why don't you come to the library and read a book?"

"You got any good fuck books over there? I'm getting a little horny just holding you, Jack. I ain't nothin', though. You ought to see Leonard there when he gets worked up for some white meat. He gets a little rambunctious, to say the least." Walker laughed and slapped Jack on the side of his head. It wasn't a hard slap but the fingers were strong and Jack felt it. He glanced at Old Bull but Old Bull stared straight ahead, no expression on his face.

"By the way, we were talking with your pal Shanley the other day. It was quite interesting. It's nice to get to know your fellow students, don't you think?" When Jack didn't answer, Walker laughed and pointed to a building identical to theirs—a concrete block, in the shape of an X. There was heavy iron mesh over the windows. "See that unit, Jack? That's for crazies and sex fiends. Lot of old perverts in there, creeps who roll their shit in little balls, child molesters. That's the kind of place that is. Then you got your max, your death row—"

"I've been here before."

"That's right! No shit, you been down before. You know how the game is played. Okay, Harwood, let me see if I've got it right—the strong preys on the weak, just like in nature. The fish eats the worm, the eagle eats the fish, I don't know who eats the eagle, but you get the idea."

They were at the end of the line. Suddenly Old Bull darted ahead, then turned. Jack had to stop quickly to keep from bumping into him. As it was, the part in Old Bull's long hair was less than a foot from Jack's eyes. He smelled after-shave or hair tonic. He could see his own eyes in the mirrored sunglasses.

"The thing is, Harwood, we know you've got nine thousand buckeroos stashed somewhere. We want it." Walker was whispering, his lips four inches from Jack's ear. "Nothing's going to happen to you out here. We're going to give you the day to think about it. Then we're going to come looking for you. No big deal, you just tell us where it is and you've got our protection for the rest of your stay."

"What if I don't have it?" Jack tried to see through the mirrored sunglasses. "I don't have it."

Old Bull raised his face and smiled. Three teeth were missing from the left side of his smile.

"I think Leonard almost wishes you didn't have it." Walker tousled Jack's hair, as though they had been playing. "See you tonight, Harwood. Try to get some religion before then, okay?"

They beat him up twice after that, once that night and then a week later. Neither beating was very serious—they didn't crush his skull or run a broom handle up his ass. They were quick and efficient. Both Walker and Old Bull had done a lot of boxing and they used their fists all over Jack's body, never in the face. Jack told them he didn't have the money. Even after the second beating, as he lay gasping for breath on the bathroom floor, he managed to tell them he had never had the money, it didn't do any good to beat him up. Walker knelt down and patted Jack on the cheek; then he and Old Bull disappeared.

The next day Jack made up his mind to tell the officer at the library what was going on. It took him a long time to walk across the yard to the building which housed the library and counselors' offices. He changed his mind several times during his walk. He tried to imagine what would happen, and it wasn't hard. The officer would ask him if he wanted Administrative Segregation, which was a fancy phrase for Protective Custody, which meant a shift in max. If he took up the offer he would carry a jacket—a pussy, a snitch, a bellycrawler—

which would follow him when he returned to population, if he ever could. His escape made it impossible to transfer to one of the letter units on the low side. But he couldn't stay in Close II with the Indians. The beatings would continue. And when he finally convinced them he couldn't produce the money, he'd probably get stuck or get his head caved in with a hunk of pipe—a message to the rest of the population. There were not enough officers to keep the heavy shit from coming in. Already Jack had seen the shanks made out of spoons, forks, angle iron. Walker had shown him his "little tomahawk"—a razor blade embedded in a toothbrush handle. The periodic shakedowns of Close II produced a few weapons but not all. It only took one.

By the time Jack reached the library he was determined to tell the officer on duty what had happened. He could serve out his shift and discharge from max, if necessary. Maybe he could parole out of there. Maybe he could rejoin population in a couple of months and nothing would happen. Maybe a lot of things. But the officer was Beasley and Jack knew he didn't have a chance. Beasley would ridicule Jack in front of the other inmates and he would be dead for sure. He thought about sending in a kite to talk to one of the counselors that day or getting near the warden or associate warden, but nothing seemed enough. The only way he could get help was by rolling over on Walker and Old Bull and the others and blowing their whole operation. He knew several inmates in the close units who were being bulldogged, beaten, raped. Walker's old lady on the outside was sitting on a ton of money that parents and wives were sending every month to keep their boys safe. Jack could name names and tell the warden and his staff exactly how it worked. He could be the trap, he could spring it and get out. Montana had an agreement with Oregon, Nevada, Minnesota to exchange prisoners. He could get a transfer to another state.

But as Jack looked at Beasley his heart sank. It could take a month or two to get transferred and even max would not be safe. Besides, they could get him in another state if they wanted—it only took one inmate, one letter, one Beasley to alert the bad boys in another prison. Nobody loves a snitch.

Jack worked his shift that day and nothing happened that night. In fact, nothing happened for two months. Jack healed up. He even took up jogging. He stayed away from the unit as much as possible. He avoided the weight room and the gym. He bought a shank from one of the inmates who was discharging and he slept with it under his mattress just about level with his chest. At night he would practice reaching for it until he became good at grasping it, rolling onto his back, and sticking the air. He knew it wouldn't be enough but he was determined to stick at least one of them before they got him.

Then one late afternoon he was pushing a rolling cart full of books back into the stacks. Putting the books back on the shelves was his last task of the day. He enjoyed it because the library was quiet. The inmates were back in their units or at chow, the yard was quiet, and he could think of any number of things that were always on the back burner. That day he was thinking of the night he and Patti celebrated the news of her first pregnancy with him. It was just like in the movies, a candle-lit dinner, the clinking of wineglasses. He looked at her through the burgundy glass and smiled and felt the sharp sting of the shank as it entered his lower back near the kidney. He turned quickly and saw the heavy body of Old Bull disappear around the front of the stacks. He heard the door open, then the slow whoosh of its closing.

He held his handkerchief hard against the sting and felt it get wet, but he made it to the rolling metal gate and the guard in the sally port who activated the gate saw him fall to his knees.

The blade had nicked the kidney, and he bled a lot. They kept him in the infirmary for nine days while they tried to figure out what to do with him. They couldn't send him back to his unit and there were no prisoners in the other state prisons to be swapped just then. Nevada had one, but he was testifying in a lengthy trial and a deal might be worked out to get him back on the street. The warden told Jack he had cashed in a lot of chips to get Jack down there. For what it was worth, Nevada could fuck itself next time they wanted a favor.

So Jack was sent to max for three months. It wasn't too bad. He read a lot of books, watched some TV. He had an hour each day of yard time and he took up jogging again, although the circles were a little tighter in max. He eventually became the swamper on his unit and he had the cleanest floor on max. Above all, he had peace of mind. There were fewer games— most of the cons stuck by themselves. It was kind of a badge of honor to do your own time, not ask for favors, not run games. The guards were tough but they left you alone if you left them alone. So Jack spent a peaceful three months basically by himself. But he managed to make a couple of friends there, guys who had gotten tired of the cheapshit stuff out in population and had elected to get sent to max and serve their shift there. Both were near the end of their sentences, both had served full sentences, no parole, no sentence review, no good time. One of them, Woody Peters, was a bank robber who took up jogging with Jack. The other, Robert Fitzgerald, was a breed from eastern Washington. He had stabbed a bouncer in the parking lot outside a club in Missoula. They were both about the same age as Jack, middle thirties, and admired him for his education and thought he was a dumb-ass to spend his life in the joint.

They discharged within a week of each other. Both were going to Helena, Woody Peters to work for his brother-in-law as a drywaller and Fitzgerald to enter a chemical dependency program. He wanted to get straight with the booze but not necessarily give up the life of crime. Peters gave Jack his sister's address and phone number—if he ever needed anything, or wanted to buddy up for some action on the outside— then both were gone. Three weeks later, Jack returned to Close II.

And now here he was, standing in his jeans out in the corridor, his feet freezing on the concrete floor. He had been back nine months and nobody had bothered him. He still watched his back but he was beginning to think that the Indians now believed that he didn't have the money.

Suddenly he heard a loud crash, the sound of broken glass followed by the pop of a small explosion. He heard a guard yell and then three others were running past him. Duds puffed after them. "Get back in your houses! Stay there, goddammit!" He swung a waist chain and bracelets over his head like a calf roper. Jack saw inmates ducking in their haste to get into their houses. Then he was inside and he heard the bolt shoot. The commotion at the far end of the hall was muffled. Jack stood looking out his window into the corridor for several long moments. His feet were no longer cold but his hands were shaking. Then he saw three guards half-leading, half-carrying Old Bull past his window. Old Bull was in his shorts, trying to keep up, but the ankle bracelets were too short and his feet were dancing and dragging. His face was bloody and his eyes were puffed up, almost closed. It took a moment to register that Jack had never seen him without the mirrored sunglasses, and even in that flash he still hadn't seen Old Bull's eyes.

Jack turned away, then turned back as something else flashed by. It was Duds, his shirttail out and the buttons ripped off the thin shirt. His white belly preceded him. He was holding a revolver by the butt with two fingers, holding it away from his body as if he had a putrid cat by the tail.

Jack walked over to his bed and lay down. He crossed his arms, his hands in each armpit. He stared at the ceiling and watched it lighten as the gray dawn entered his world.

CHAPTER SEVEN

Patti Ann Harwood took a deep breath, held it for a few seconds, then exhaled a nervous sigh that filled her work cubicle. She punched an outside line, then held the receiver in her lap. She could always back out now or later, if this whole business got crazy. She glanced at the scrap of paper, but she had memorized the number in the last three days. She leaned forward and punched the numbers rapidly. Now or never.

"May I speak to Mr. Yellow Calf, please. This is one of his clients."

"One moment, please."

Patti Ann wondered if this was the same receptionist she had met. He had called her Doris. Patricia Lowry. That was

Patti Ann's name. No, she told him to call her Patti Ann. Patti Ann Lowry. Okay.

"Hello?" The voice was strong, as she had remembered, but quizzical, impersonal.

"Hello, Mr. Yellow Calf. This is Patti Ann Lowry. I came to see you a couple of weeks ago about a will?" All business.

"Yes, of course. A sister was disputing it. She wanted a third of the value of some valuable books you received. Something like that."

"Yes, that's right." Patti Ann felt almost thrilled that he remembered. "I can't believe you remember."

He laughed. "Oh, I remember some things, some things better than others. What's up?"

"I hope I'm not disturbing you. I know you have important things—"

"Not at all. I was just sitting here wondering if I should go to lunch or eat this apple that's been sitting in the bottom drawer of my desk for two weeks. Somehow the apple always loses."

"I'm glad I caught you, then." Suddenly Patti Ann couldn't remember how much she had told him the books were worth. Twenty thousand? "Oh, Lord," she said.

"What?"

"Nothing—I'm sorry—I just thought of something." What if she did tell him she'd forgotten how much the books were worth? Clients must forget details all the time. "Oh, I forget how much the books are worth." She felt slightly reckless.

"Thirty thousand," he said. "I have the notes right here."

That was sobering. He knew more about her lie than she did.

"Well, what I'm calling about is I'd like to discuss the

matter further. I sent for a copy of the will and haven't heard anything. It's been two weeks."

"These things take time. You're dealing with the bureaucracy. Red tape and all that."

"But I'd like to get this matter settled. I'd like to discuss our course of action." She hesitated. Did she really want to go this far? But she said, "I'd like to meet with you."

"Sure, I understand."

"I'd like to pay you."

He laughed again. "Well, I haven't exactly swung into action yet."

She heard the sound of paper being moved around. She heard a lot of that in her office. But it was lunchtime and most of the girls were gone. She hated these cubicles. Anybody could listen to anybody if she tried. The cubicles were new, less than a week old, and already she had learned to talk in a low murmur. She missed her old office with its door and green walls. Bureaucracy. She could tell Mr. Yellow Calf some things.

"How about this Friday afternoon? One?"

This was her last chance. She could say no, she could hang up and be done with it. She knew if she went on, she would see it through to the end. Oh, Patti, what are you doing? Jack, Jack, what are we getting into?

"Could you make it then?"

She swallowed and closed her eyes. "This is so difficult, Mr. Yellow Calf—we, the office I work for, has just changed to a new system and we lost a lot of time. I don't think I can take the time off—"

"We could meet after work. Would that be better?"

Patti Ann opened her eyes. "Today?"

"If that suits you. I generally don't get out of here for an hour or so after quitting time anyway. Today is just another day."

No it's not, thought Patti Ann. Today is the first day for the rest of your life. She felt foolish and suddenly dramatic. Go ahead, make my day.

〰〰〰

They met in the bar of the Overland Express, an eating establishment just across the downtown mall from Sylvester's office. She had suggested it. She and Myrna had eaten there a couple of times during Patti Ann's brief liberation from marriage and home, just after Jack went to prison. Actually the Overland was not really a part of that liberation, which took place in bowling alleys and pizza parlors. The lean young men did not come into the Overland.

The sun sat low on the southern horizon and Patti Ann felt a sting in the autumn air as she clicked across the paving stones of the mall walkway. She had decided to be a few minutes late because she knew he would be on time. That way she could look for him in the bar, then apologize profusely for some unavoidable little incident. She pulled up her collar and she couldn't tell if the chill which ran down her spine was from the wind or the anticipation. It was ten to six and the downtown mall was completely deserted.

The bar was old, high-ceilinged, and spacious. A row of windows on the north side let in the evening light. Patti Ann adjusted her collar and stepped around the divider which screened off the entrance. She had remembered the bar as being full of dark wood and gloom, but the light from the windows gave it a rich, intimate look.

Sylvester saw her and stood and waved. He was not alone. Another man, shorter, heavier, with thinning brown hair, stood too. He was grinning, as though he recognized her.

She walked to the table, each step more tentative than the last as she studied the other man.

"Hi." Sylvester put out his hand and took hers. "I was beginning to wonder if we said tonight. Ed tells me I've been doing some odd things lately—premature senility, I believe he called it." Sylvester helped her out of her coat and laid it across the extra chair.

"I'm terribly sorry—"

"No problem. This is Ed Vance. Patricia Lowry." They shook hands, then sat down. "Ed's my handball partner— rival, actually. We also work together across the street."

Ed Vance continued to grin at her and Patti Ann smiled back but she felt uncomfortable. Why was he here? Was Sylvester Yellow Calf playing some kind of game? Was Ed Vance like a witness? Patti Ann felt trapped. They knew her story didn't add up to a hill of beans.

Almost as if he had read her thoughts, Ed Vance drained his beer and said, "Don't worry, Ms. Lowry—I'm on my way out, really and truly. I've just been helping Sly sort out his myriad problems. For a single man, he's waist-deep in life's struggles. Why do I envy him?" He stood and put on his gray suitcoat. "Tacos tonight. My kids are crazy about tacos. See you tomorrow, Sly. Nice to meet you, Ms. Lowry. Maybe you can cheer him up."

The cocktail waitress came just as Ed skirted their table on his way out. He dropped a dollar on her tray.

"Now, what can I get you two lovebirds?"

Patti Ann looked at Sylvester with her mouth open. Then they both laughed, and Patti Ann wondered if she would ever call him Sly. Somehow, a barrier had been pulled down, almost without assistance from either of them, and she felt good and pretty with this man. He made her feel this way. She had felt it in his office and decided now that this was not a mistake—it was okay after so long. Everything but the lie was okay. She almost touched his hand.

〜〜〜〜

E d V a n c e d r o v e east on Broadway, up out of Last Chance Gulch, past the old governor's mansion, past the state capitol building, out to California, where he took a right and began to climb until he reached the twisting streets that had names like Pineview Drive, Alpine Drive, and finally, his street, South Ridge Drive. The neighborhoods were newer here, upper-middle-class, white, professional, boring. Ed definitely found the area dull, but it was a good place to raise kids if they didn't fall off the mountain or get burned up in a forest fire. One of the first fires of the summer had almost swept over the crest of the mountain into the area. At night, people stood out on their decks, watching the orange glow behind the ridge. Some had rented U-Hauls and loaded them with possessions. The developer had hired an extra security guard just to keep an eye on these U-Hauls. During the days the smoke was so thick, Helena was invisible. The heavy drone of borate bombers suddenly turned fierce as the planes dove in to dump their load.

Ed, like his neighbors, took the few days off and sprayed his shake roof with a garden hose. He felt foolish standing up there in his dust mask and shorts, his T-shirt gritty with ash. Then, miraculously, just as the flames were becoming visible on the crest, the wind shifted, and people climbed down from their roofs, unloaded their U-Hauls, and began the cleaning-up. Sylvester had helped Ed hose down the house, the drive-way, even the grass. Later, they sat on the front porch, look-ing out over the smoky valley, drinking beer and eating charred hamburgers, and Ed couldn't have asked for a better friend.

But now, as Ed turned onto his street, he realized that he was, and had always been, jealous of Sylvester's fortunes. Even though Ed was a good lawyer and had handled his cases as well as Sylvester, he would never shine in Buster Harring-ton's eyes. He would always be an associate whereas Sylvester would be a partner within the year. That was the straight dope from Harrington himself. As soon as Sylvester made up his mind to run for Congress he would be jumped up. Of course, his caseload would be reduced severely and much of it would fall on Ed's shoulders.

That wasn't the problem. Ed didn't mind the work. He already handled too much and he would handle more. On the other hand, maybe that *was* the problem. Ed was a drone and Sylvester a star. And there was no really good reason for it. Ed had been at the firm longer, he made a lot of money for Harrington and the other partners, but they just seemed to dump the shit cases on him. Sylvester got more than his share of the plums—he got Ed's share too.

Ed signaled right and turned into his driveway. Billy and Sarah were looking up at a red maple that Ed had paid too much for—but he wanted big trees, instant trees. He wanted the place to look like a home.

He opened the car door, grabbed his briefcase, and swung out. "What's up?"

Sarah looked at him with wide eyes. "This tree is dying," she said.

Ed laughed. "Trees turn different colors in the fall. You know that, Sarah." He ran his fingers through Billy's hair. "You kids know that."

"Nope. It's dying. Mommy noticed it, too."

Ed walked over to the tree and pulled a leaf off. The edges were rusty and crumbled in his fingers. "Shit," he said.

"Daddy!" Sarah squealed with delight. "You owe a quarter!"

"We're having tacos," said Billy.

Ed dropped the leaf and looked up and saw all the leaves were rusty. It's only a tree, he thought. "It's only a tree," he said. "Trees are a dime a dozen. Where's Rolly?"

"He's in helping Mommy make tacos," said Sarah.

"How come you kids aren't helping? You're older than Rolly."

"Mommy told us to get out," said Billy.

"What did you do?"

"Nothing."

"Sure?"

"Billy hit Rolly with a tennis ball. He was bouncing it against a wall downstairs and Rolly just got in the way. Didn't you, Billy?"

"You kids should have your jackets on. C'mon, let's go inside."

"Will you protect us?" said Billy.

As Ed shepherded the kids up the walkway, he thought, Sylvester doesn't have problems like these. Right now, he's probably asking that long-stemmed beauty if she'd like to have dinner with him, then they'll have drinks, and after that who knows what? Why else would he take on a pretty woman with such a small problem? Kids handled wills. Big Indian fucker's going to screw her, sure as hell.

Ed suddenly felt self-righteous. Here he was, going home to his family and tacos, to his upper-middle-class home with dying trees and a wife who kicked her own children out of the house on a cold fall day. All right, Sylvester, have your fun. Slow and steady wins the race. "Oh, God," he groaned.

"What?" said Sarah.

"Nothing. March."

≈≈≈≈

"How did it happen?"

"I guess we both wanted it."

"Isn't it wrong?" she said. She was lying on his arm.

"I think so." The voice was flat in the dark room.

Patti Ann sighed. "My God, my God. It was so good."

Sylvester tightened his hand on her slender shoulder and drew her close. Her lips brushed his ear, then kissed him on the cheek. She was surprised that his cheek was so soft, just as she had been surprised to feel his bare chest. There was hardly any hair there. She had read somewhere in her distant youth that Indians used clamshells to bite off their hair. She had always thought it impossible. Now she figured that Indians didn't have excess hair. There was no need for clamshells. But she had seen Indians with wispy mustaches and chin hair down at the prison. Some were downright hairy but they didn't look as "Indian" as the others.

My God. She had gone from hating Indians—as an act of loyalty to her husband—to sleeping with one. She remembered thinking, before they made love, if it was going to be different. And she remembered wondering, years ago, how it would be to sleep with a Negro. She and several of her girlfriends had discussed it one night—white girls from northern Minnesota—and concluded that it would be different. One of the girls said if you slept with a black man, it would be all over for white men. She had heard that from a cousin from Illinois. They all squealed and wondered. Sleeping with Indians was out of the question because they were nearby and only sluts from poor families did it.

Was it different? In the dark she only remembered how fragile she had felt beneath him, but his weight was as light as a blanket over her. Her nipples hardened as she thought of his smooth chest brushing against them.

She slid her hand from his flat belly down to the beginning of his pubic hair. She lifted her hand and pressed down on it. Plenty of hair down there. Her fingers brushed his cock and she was surprised to find it erect so soon. she caressed the bottom side of it and it grew harder. For a moment she thought she was being too bold—she had forgotten what it was like to be with a man, she only been with two others, but he turned on his side toward her and ran his fingertips over her hip. She began to roll onto her back, but he moved his hand from beneath her shoulder to her other hip and lifted and pulled her on top of him. She guided him into her and she saw his large brown hands kneading her white breasts. She saw them in her mind for just a second and she felt a rush spread outward from her center and she thought, It's been so long, so long, so long, and she crushed herself down on him and threw her head back.

She slept and then she awoke and saw dawn through the thin white blinds beside the bed. She hadn't closed them last night. She pulled herself up on one elbow and looked around. The covers on the bed had been straightened and the other pillow fluffed. She traced a piece of stitching on the bright comforter with her finger, then glanced at the clock. 6:38. She had plenty of time to shower, put her makeup on, dress, and get to work.

She got out of bed and walked to the bathroom. She stopped before the full-length mirror on the door. She hadn't changed—her breasts were still there, the hair between her thighs hadn't changed color. But the hair on her head was a total mess. She put on her kimono and slippers and padded out to the living room. There wasn't a cushion out of place. She had led him through the dark into the bedroom and into her bed. She walked over to the picture window and looked out. A lone dog, as gray as the morning light, was trotting down the middle of the street. It had something furry in its mouth.

Patti Ann closed the drapes and wandered into the kitchen. She was floating this morning and had difficulty focusing on ordinary things. They hadn't really drunk much the night before, but she felt distant from her familiar life. She switched on the light over the stove. The handwriting on the grocery list did not look like her own; the toaster, the teakettle—she hadn't really noticed the curves of the oriental design. She filled the tea kettle and turned a burner on beneath it. She got down the tea bags and a cup, then some milk from the refrigerator. When she turned back to the teakettle, she saw the element behind it turning orange. She slid the teakettle back and she hugged herself against the chill and she felt intensely alone.

The whistling of the kettle startled her and she turned off the burner. But she did not pour her tea. She walked back into the living room and sat down at the small dining table. She still hadn't finished Myrna's suit and the fabric and patterns were scattered around. She picked up a piece of paper that had been torn from a small loose-leaf book. "We have to talk. I'll call you. Sly." And she remembered she had called him Sly. She had repeated it over and over. Now she said, "Sly." She said it softly, for it was dawn and the only sound was the extinguished burner clicking in the kitchen.

She put the note down. There was something about this day that disturbed her. She sat for a moment. Then she stood and walked back into the kitchen. She looked at the calendar beside the refrigerator. She had outlined in red marker the square that held the 7. October 7. Friday. It was the afternoon of this day that she would take off from work and drive down to the prison. She would see Jack. She should have felt guilty, dirty, fallen, but she didn't. She realized that she still held the note Sylvester had written. She pressed it to her breasts and closed her eyes and he hovered over her, in the dark, descending, and she accepted him.

CHAPTER EIGHT

Sylvester drove straight north from Helena through the Prickly Pear Valley on I-15, past housing developments and industrial parks, past the airport, past institutions and ranches and farms, until he was in a wide basin of rangeland populated only by herds of sheep. Then he climbed a steep hill and he was in the mountains. Off to his right lay the Gates of the Mountains Wilderness, an area bordered by the limestone escarpments of the Missouri River. He drove down the narrow canyon of the Prickly Pear and he knew it was not far from here where a small group of Blackfeet killed Malcolm Clark, which led to the eventual Massacre on the Marias and the subjugation of his people. He had never been to Malcolm Clark's ranch. He had only recently begun to show an interest in the history of the Blackfeet and he approached it almost clinically, reading books, studying maps, the way a hobbyist or academic would. He tried to remember the stories his grandmother and other old people had told, stories that had been handed down through the generations, stories told in the Blackfeet tongue, but he could only remember snatches of them and he felt ashamed of himself for not listening better when he was a kid.

But he had been more interested in basketball and cross-country and girls. Traditions, to him and many of the boys he grew up with, seemed foreign, old-fashioned, worthless. When he did accompany his grandparents to tribal occasions, he could not see what they had to do with his immediate life. He knew his lack of interest was a disappointment to his grandmother, but Sylvester's grandfather used to tell him stories of the days when his grandmother was a flapper, dancing her nights away in the numerous roadhouses of the period. Like many of her contemporaries, she had spent her youth trying to emulate the white people who lived all around, and sometimes on, the reservation, trying to forget that she was an Indian woman. It was not until her mid-forties that she sobered up and took a good look at herself and the others. Since then, she had been instrumental in restoring traditions and values to the Blackfeet. It was hard on her when Sylvester told her one night, during one of their many discussions, that he wanted to try the "outside world, the real world." From then on, she always felt shamed among her friends and she often blamed her daughter, Sylvester's mother, for laying this burden on her. It didn't matter that Sylvester didn't know his mother and that the other old ones told similar stories about their offspring. Little Bird Walking Woman loved her grandson as only a mother could (for she had raised him) and she boasted about his accomplishments, but the nagging shame would not go away.

Sylvester gunned the dark green Saab through the mountains until the country opened up and he was out on the rolling yellow plains. He breathed his customary sigh of relief to be out of the mountains, but this time the sigh was more exaggerated than usual. He was also driving faster than usual. He had almost called Shelley that morning, but then he didn't know what to say; instead, he called his office and told Doris that he wouldn't be in. He had planned to spend most of the day in the library anyway, so he was only missing two appointments. He also asked her to tell Ed Vance that he would have to miss their handball game. He knew Ed would think he had made it with that beautiful woman. Ed often kidded him about good-looking women with money whom Sylvester represented. It didn't bother Sylvester because he knew this was how Ed got his jollies—like a lot of his married colleagues, Ed fantasized out loud (and envied) Sylvester's love life. ("Hey, Sly, how was Chico Hot Springs? You know that hot water keeps sperm alive for days? Gonna be a whole lot of little Indians running around down there.")

This time Ed was right on target. Sylvester had made it with that beautiful woman and now he was running away to the only home he had ever known. Home is where they have to take you in. He had heard that somewhere, but he had never felt the truth of it until now. Until that moment he entered her bedroom, he had been in control, sometimes shakily, of his life. He had managed to keep all the balls in the air, but in the darkness of that bedroom the balls all came tumbling down, bouncing wildly away from him.

He put the speedometer at eighty, clicked on the cruise

control, and sat back. The air was warmer here, the sun brighter. He cracked his window and felt the wind rush through his hair. He had always loved the quiet fastness of the plains. To him, the country was not empty, but remote and secluded, even intimate if you were alone. Much of the time, if you were off the roads and highways, you could not see any sign of man's making and you were alone or with friends. Even with friends, if no one spoke, you were alone with your thoughts and your eyes. And you saw plenty, in spite of what newcomers and tourists said. They didn't see the colors, the shades and shapes, of the prairies, the various grasses and brushes, the occasional animal that made it all worth it. A place where you saw a badger or a golden eagle would be there always in your mind, even if you were a thousand miles away, preparing for your law exams or putting together a workman's comp case. Many times when he was far away, Sylvester had envisioned these plains, the rolling hills, the ravines, the cutbanks and alkali lakes, the reservoirs and scrublands, and he always saw life. He saw a hawk circling over a prairie dog town. He saw antelope gliding through, over and under fences at a dead run. He saw a rattlesnake sleeping on a warm rock, or coiled, tongue flicking, tail rattling, as it slowly undulated back away. He saw beauty in these creatures and he had quit trying to explain why. It was enough to hold these plains in his memory and it was enough to come back to them.

He stopped for gas at a convenience store in Great Falls and ate a soggy microwave sandwich. It was just after noon and he hadn't really slept in thirty-six hours but he was not sleepy. He had dozed for a time last night, because he remembered waking up and she was still draped over his body. But it was still very early in the morning when he gently eased from beneath her and covered her. He'd had to walk back to the parking lot behind the Power Block to get his car. Fortunately the gate was up and he drove home and watched sports on an all-night sports station. He hadn't tried to think then because he wasn't ready to. In the morning, he showered, put on faded jeans, a western shirt and boots. He packed an overnighter, then ate some toast. It was then that he decided to call Shelley. He didn't know what he would say to her but he wanted to hear her voice. She had been distant since their trip to Chico Hot Springs. In fact, they had seen each other only three times in the past two weeks. She said she was busy working the bugs out of the new fiscal program, but Sylvester knew she was working out their relationship in her own mind. Relationships. That was the other thing they talked about in Palo Alto—besides politics, law, and sports. It had become the buzzword for impending trouble, a rationalizing word to palliate a drifting away, usually by one spouse or lover. Sylvester had never heard the word used that way before. But then he'd had a relationship with Anita Talcott, or Sandoval, and it had turned bad or at least had evaporated away. And now, Shelley seemed to be in the process of distancing herself from him.

Sylvester couldn't believe what had happened last night, but he knew that he had wanted it. Why else would he have met with her in a bar? He had slept with a client. He had heard so many stories and he had always been disgusted by them. His colleagues laughed and told the stories with great enthusiasm. Now, Sylvester had joined the ranks of those they laughed at.

The worst part was that he hadn't really believed her tale about the contested will. She couldn't even remember the amount of money they had talked about. He had never had a client who didn't know the amount right down to the last penny. And calling him after two weeks—she worked in a government office, she knew about bureaucracy, knew things didn't move that fast. When she suggested meeting in a bar after work, he should have known something was fishy. She had offered to buy him a drink as compensation for inconveniencing him. They had both laughed at the idea, but she insisted.

At first, he thought it would be a good idea to invite Ed Vance a little early, ostensibly to talk about his run for Congress, but now he realized what a mistake he'd made. Ed had left them together and he would surely mention it around the office today.

Sylvester should have gone in today and acted as if nothing had happened. That would have taken care of it—there would have been the usual jokes but then it would have been forgotten. Now it was too late. He was a hundred miles from Helena.

Why would she make up a story just to see him—not just to see him, but to sleep with him? With an alarming clarity, he realized that she had seduced him. She had extended the evening to include dinner, then more drinks, and finally her bedroom. Why? Because she knew, from the day she walked into his office, he was ready for adventure? No, it had begun before that. It had begun before they met each other. The lie was just an entrée into his life. Who was she? And what had she to do with him?

Sylvester threw the sandwich wrapper into a waste can by the pumps, got into the Saab, and drove off, heading west, then north. Patricia Lowry. Patti Ann. Where had he seen that name before? He saw the sunlight striking her auburn hair and he felt her fragile weight on his arm just before he pulled her on top of him. He was not innocent in this affair, just stupid. And in love.

~~~~~~~~~

Mary Bird sat on her front step and watched the children walking home from school. A few of them lived nearby but most of them lived in the government housing west of Moccasin Flat. Virtually every day for twenty-nine years she had watched them, ever since Sylvester had entered the first grade. For the first month she had taken him back and forth to school; after that he had walked home with the other grade-schoolers. Most of the time she would hear the laughter and yells, the loud boisterous talk, before she saw them. Later, when Sylvester entered the seventh grade, she and Earl had given him a basketball for his birthday; after that, she heard the thump, thump, thump of the basketball punctuating the loud talk.

Then came the girls. Before, the girls and boys had pretty much walked in separate groups. By the ninth grade, they were walking together in one large group.

That was the way it should be, all of the kids together. But after the ninth grade, Sylvester stayed after school to practice basketball and run track and he came home alone, most of the time after dark. He would trot then. She knew that because the basketball would bounce faster and she could hear his sneakers on the frozen ground of the yard. It was just about that time that Earl Yellow Calf bought his first TV set. He would sit in the living room watching his TV, eating supper on a TV tray, while Mary and Sylvester ate and talked at the kitchen table. Sylvester would report on the day's activities and Mary would listen. She could tell a lot about families by Sylvester's report, the way the kids acted in school, what someone said about his father or grandparents, if a girl had been missing from school for several days. Later, she would clean up and wash dishes and interpret those reports. Sylvester would talk awhile with his grandfather, usually about basketball, then go to his room to study.

Things were different now. Mary Bird still got her gossip when she went shopping or visiting or to a ceremonial, but she missed those daily reports and her imagining at the kitchen sink. And, of course, she missed Sylvester. He had been gone for seventeen years and she missed him every day, even now, as though he had just walked out the door to the coach's car that took him off to college. She had packed a bag of sandwiches and some pemmican to eat along the way. And two apples. She could still see those two apples sitting on the counter before she put them in the bag. They were perfectly red and firm, like the ones you could get down in Great Falls if you paid a little extra. She couldn't remember where she got those apples. That was the trouble with old age. But she did remember the small medicine pouch that she had given him the night before. It had belonged to her grandfather and had protected him back in the days when a warrior needed protection when he went off to battle. A week later, she was cleaning Sylvester's room for something to do and she found the medicine pouch tucked behind some books in his bookcase. She never mentioned her discovery to him, but she put the pouch back in the trunk with her other old things.

The last of the children, in their bright jackets and basketball shoes, had walked by, but still Mary sat, feeling the sun in her bones. Although she was eighty-seven years old and a little heavy, she felt she was in pretty good shape. She got around still, her mind (except for her memory) was sharp. She didn't leave burners on or forget where she was or what she was going to do. A good thing too. Earl had had three small strokes in the past five years, the last one leaving him partially paralyzed on the left side. He spoke with great difficulty, but he could speak, and the older he got the more he wanted to talk. Quite often, he would speak right through a TV program, even though he had it on full-blast because he was hard of hearing. He spoke of many and various things. It was as though his mind was racing over old familiar courses and every now and then an obstacle would stop him and he would have to talk his way around it. Mary didn't mind. It beat paying attention to the TV.

Except for one time when he'd asked her, right out of the blue, if she loved Sylvester more than him. She had been stitching a star quilt for a friend's daughter's marriage. The question stopped her. She had lived continuously for sixty-five years with Earl and they hadn't talked about love for the past forty. Earl had been treasurer of the tribe for twenty-five years; after that, he had worked in the accounting department for the BIA at the agency for another fifteen. He was an educated man. He had gone to Carlisle Indian School just after Jim Thorpe and gotten better grades than he had. It was such a childish question that it made Mary sad to think that somewhere, a long time back, they had quit telling each other about love and each other.

"Of course I love you," she had said, hoping that would end it, and it did. Earl went back to his TV and Mary smiled to herself. To think that he still *thought* about love made her happy. She hoped she didn't die first. She couldn't stand the thought of him being put in an old folks' home.

She watched a dark green car pull up on the edge of the yard right in front of her. The driver sat there for a moment, then opened the door and got out. She couldn't see very well anymore, and she only saw the upper half of the man, but she knew it was Sylvester. She laughed and clapped her hands. It was always so good to see him.

〰〰〰

"I w a n t y o u to sleep with him."

Patti Ann sat motionless for a good ten seconds, staring at her husband, putting the words into a context that had nothing to do with what had already happened.

"I know. I'm asking you to do something that goes against everything you believe, everything you stand for. Believe me, it isn't easy for me. I've lain awake nights, thinking about this moment, wondering if I'd have the guts to ask you." Jack hung his head. "It's not easy asking your wife if she'll sleep with another man."

So this was it. This was what it was all leading up to.

"I'd never ask this in a million years—you know that—"

"I don't want to hear any more, Jack." Her voice sounded weak as she looked off to the edges of the visiting room. A child in a striped T-shirt was watching them. His small corduroys were in danger of falling down. Patti Ann thought she might have had a child that age.

"If there were only another way, Patti. But this is it. This is my only chance, our only chance to be together."

"Jack, I can't do it—even for that reason. It's wrong." The child waved at her.

"What other reason could there be? We're talking about a chance to be together. Isn't that reason enough?"

"But you want to do something bad to him. You want me to do something bad."

Jack leaned forward and shook a cigarette out of Patti Ann's pack. He tamped the filter end on the smooth plastic table. "You do love me," he said. It was halfway between a question and a statement.

"Of course I do. You know that." She looked at him. He looked smaller than he had a couple of years ago. Back then, he held himself erect and talked and laughed and held her hand. Ever since he had gotten stabbed, he seemed to hold himself within himself and grow smaller. And grayer. He was not the same man she had fallen in love with.

She was different too. Right now she was totally different and she could end all of this by telling him why. The funny thing was, she wasn't really ready for this complication, although she had been stupid not to see it coming. Now she was faced with the dilemma of sleeping with a man she had already slept with, and maybe loved, in order to help her husband, who maybe she didn't love anymore, get out. It was almost funny when she thought of it like that. But when she thought of Sylvester and last night, her mouth got dry and she had to look away.

The clock over the guard station said 5:40. Another twenty minutes.

Jack lit the cigarette and sat back. "I shouldn't have asked you," he said, exhaling smoke. "It was a crazy idea." He laughed. "I guess I'll just sit it out and hope nothing happens. You'll still be there, won't you, babe? Even if I'm not?"

Patti Ann's hand was trembling but she reached for his, twining her fingers between his. She remembered these strong hands. She used to dream about them. She lowered her head and kissed his hand. She was his wife. She was still his wife.

〰〰〰

Sylvester slept until 10:30. When he awoke, he sat up and looked out the small window. It was a habit from his childhood. It seemed like half the year the window would be frosted over and he would have to scratch a peephole in the frost to look at the world. Today, he saw a few wispy clouds high overhead, and the yellowing leaves of a cottonwood that had always been there were dancing in the wind. The one thing Sylvester hadn't missed when he moved away was the wind. It came from all directions, depending on the season, but the wind he remembered most often was the one that came down from the north pole. That was the wind of winter. That was the wind people dreaded, but after so many generations they had learned to live with it. They lived with snow that blew horizontally over the plains and through the town, snow so thick and violent that people died walking home from bars and cows were not discovered until spring. People dreaded but accepted such weather. Traditionalists said prayers to Cold Maker and asked his blessing, but they knew some among them had lived badly over the year and now he was punishing the whole tribe. Others were more fatalistic. Bliz-

zards were part of life and it didn't do any good to piss and
moan.

Sylvester rolled out of bed and sat and yawned. He had
slept a good ten hours but he still felt heavy and bone-weary.
He was only thirty-five and the handball kept him fit, but just
now he felt old and tired. He had stayed up until just after
midnight with his grandmother. She had told him all the
gossip about his old friends. To her, time was a continuum
and so people did not get older, did not drift apart, did not live
away. When they came home, the continuum went on. This
was home.

As Sylvester listened to her, he realized that was the way
with old Indian people. She had hugged him mightily, but
then she sent him to the store to get a chuck roast and some
potatoes, just as he had done many times while growing up.

Sylvester pulled on his Levi's and shirt. He heard the faint
buzz of voices and laughter on the TV in the living room.
Sounded like some kind of game show. He looked at himself
in the mirror above the child's dresser. His black hair looked
dull and his close-set dark eyes were foggy with fatigue. He
knocked on the scratched, sorrel-colored dresser top and noticed the pouch. He picked it up and felt it. The covering was
soft-tanned hide made hard by the years. The top was tied
shut by thin yellowing sinew. He held it before his eyes by the
two rawhide strings. It was completely unadorned and heavier
than Sylvester remembered. It was his great-great-grandfather's war medicine, the medicine his grandmother had
tried to give to him when he went away to college. He held it
to his neck and looked at himself in the mirror again. He tried
to see in the mirror a Blackfeet warrior, getting ready to raid

the Crow horses, but all he saw was a man with circles under his eyes, a faint stubble of beard on his chin, a man whose only war, skirmish, actually, was with himself. The new warriors. He remembered Lena Old Horn's brochures and articles about Indian lawyers. He wasn't even a new warrior. He was a fat cat lawyer, helping only himself, and some fatter cats, get richer. He put the pouch carefully on the dresser.

He had thought about calling Lena, but now he decided he would just drop in, Indian-style ("I was just thinking about you—"). His grandmother had mentioned Lena last night— she was still here, men came and went, she almost got married once but then the man beat her up, and she was still at the high school but she was looking old and tired. What was she, six years older than he was? Forty-one. He would eat something, then go over. It was Saturday and he knew she would be there.

〰〰〰

Lena Old Horn lived in a 1940s-style stucco house one block off the main street of Browning. She could walk out her back gate, cross a vacant field where a building had been demolished, and be downtown. It was a convenience she would rather not have had, for men, and some women, often drank in the alley off the field. She could look out her kitchen window and see men at all hours of the day passing a bottle around. They were relatively quiet at night, but she had kept the doors and windows locked since a couple of them came into her yard and serenaded her four or five years ago.

The backyard was a mess of weeds, paper bags, bottles, and beer cans. When she first moved in, twelve years ago, she had tried to keep the small patch of grass mowed and picked up, but the men in the alley had called to her and made obscene gestures with their fingers. She didn't go out back anymore, not since she had seen a woman, practically passed out, being raped by two men. Lena had called the police, then gone back to the window. The men were gone, and the woman lay against a building across the alley, with no shoes, pants, or panties, reaching for an empty bottle lying on its side.

Lena went out and helped the policeman pull the woman's jeans and sneakers on. Then she helped put the woman in the backseat of the patrol car. It stank of liquor and vomit. She recognized the woman. She was the mother of one of the boys she had counseled a few years back. One of the teachers had caught him sniffing paint from a paper bag in the locker room. It was common enough. Lena had learned to recognize the smell and the telltale misty sheen around the nose and mouth. Silver was the paint of choice because it had some intoxicating chemical property that she had forgotten.

Lena had watched the patrol car turn the corner at the end of the alley, and then she noticed the panties. They were black nylon with fringes of lace around the openings. She picked them up by the lace with two fingers and carried them to her garbage can. She wondered what the woman had expected that morning, or the morning before, when she put them on. That night Lena threw away two pairs of her own that she had bought because they were sexy. She also threw away a black lace bra that one of her boyfriends liked her to wear when they made love.

Lena put away the last of the groceries that she had bought down at the IGA. She had planned to drive to Cut Bank that morning because she was out of fresh vegetables and fruit, but the thought of the eighty-mile round trip enervated her completely. It was tough enough to shop at the IGA on a Saturday with all the families coming in from Heart Butte, Babb, and East Glacier. She knew virtually everybody after nearly twenty years. She was still an outsider, still a Crow in Blackfeet country, but the people now accepted her in her role. She had counseled them and their children and she would probably counsel their grandchildren. That was the part of her life she still liked. Many of the students had gone on to college, to professional schools, to military programs. Many more had dropped out of high school—but she could live with her failures because she was good and she cared for all her students equally. Early in her career—and now she saw the mistake of it—she had cared only for the bright ones, the sure things. She had spent too much time with them; sometimes she became too intimate with them. Now she found the right college or program for the bright ones, and she found the right help for the pregnant girl or the abused boy. It took her a while to realize that being a counselor on the reservation sometimes meant being a confidante, sometimes a conspirator.

The rest of her life had pretty much evolved into a disaster area. She had long ago given up the notion of going to law school, or later, graduate school in administration. She had had several bad love affairs—one with a married grade school teacher whose wife found out about and tried to have her fired; another with a man she almost married until he put her in the hospital one night with broken ribs and a broken cheekbone. The cheekbone hadn't mended right and her left eye was slightly lower than her right. Nobody noticed, or if they did they didn't think it so remarkable, but she noticed every morning. She had learned to mix the shadowing with makeup so it looked like one eye was a little brighter than the other.

She had been celibate for two years and, at first, she had felt like an alcoholic taking it one day at a time, waiting to fall off the wagon, wanting to fall off the wagon, but she hadn't. She had met some men that she was interested in, but they were either too young or not interested in her.

Now, a big night for her was to go with some of the other single teachers to the Palomino up in East Glacier to eat and get a little silly. She always went home alone, ignoring the advances of some of the studs in their tight jeans and cowboy hats, to her house and cat, Fraidy.

Fraidy threw himself against Lena's leg and she almost jumped. It wasn't the cat but the doorbell that startled her. She had been leaning on the sink, looking out the window at the alley, not really seeing anything but the images in her mind. Now she saw three young men, two of them squatting on their heels, the other standing, head thrown back, a bottle to his mouth. She closed the mini-blinds and hurried through the living room to the front door. "I'll feed you later, Fraidy," she called.

~~~~~

Sylvester rang the doorbell again. Third time's a charm. Sure enough, the door opened and there stood Lena. "Hi," he said.

She looked at him for a second or two. Then she said, "Come in, Sylvester," and stood back, away from the door.

"I got into town last night and I thought how nice it would

be to see you. It's been quite some time." Sylvester looked around the room. It was a long room, divided by an archway and two built-in cabinets that separated the dining room from the living room. Both rooms were dark, the windows covered with heavy drapes, but he could see light from the kitchen. He heard the slide of metal behind him and turned and saw that she had opened the drapes on the window overlooking the street. Two girls rode by on mountain bikes.

"Sit down," she said. "It has been a long time—I think you were in college the last time I saw you. You came home for your grandmother's honoring."

"I came home a few other times, but it's always been hard to get away. There's always been something."

"Would you like some tea? A drink? I'm afraid I only have decaf—"

"Tea would be great. How are you?" Sylvester followed her into the kitchen.

Lena shooed a big calico cat off a counter. "That's Fraidy, my constant companion. I said I'd feed you later, Fraidycat." Lena opened a cupboard. "Would you like Constant Comment or regular? I have some Red Rose—that's Canadian, I think. I just picked it up."

"Sounds great." Hadn't he just said that?

Lena filled a teakettle at the sink and put it on the stove. "Oh, I'm getting along. Life isn't too exciting around here. I spent a mad passionate weekend a couple of weeks ago judging a spelling bee. Good thing we had dictionaries. Some of those little cusses could spell the words before I could look them up. It was fun, though." She kept her back to Sylvester, rounding up cups and saucers, a teapot, sugar. She emptied a box of Chips Ahoy into a dish. "I seem to remember you liked your cookies."

Sylvester laughed. He couldn't remember an inordinate taste for cookies.

"I used to make cookies back in those days. Chocolate-chips were your favorite. Now I just buy them." She paused but still did not look around. "Isn't it funny? I just threw these things in my cart at the IGA this morning. And now here you are."

"I used to love your cookies." Now he remembered. She had always made him cookies and he had loved them. She had brought them along when they went fishing, the three of them, Lena, Stan, and Sylvester. Stan got Lena, Sylvester got the cookies. "I used to love those cookies," he said. He could almost taste them now. He did not think about the rest of it.

Lena turned and faced him. She had washed the teaball and was wiping her hands on a dishtowel. "What brings you around?"

"I just came up to visit my grandparents. They're getting pretty old. My grandfather's had three strokes. Grandma thinks he's just about done for—one more will probably kill him. I should come up more often."

"I see your grandmother every now and then. She came to a powwow up at the community college last month. Indian Awareness Week. She looked very good. She even danced a couple."

"She's got a lot of spunk, but she's afraid she won't outlive Grandpa. She's afraid of what will happen to him."

"It's tough to grow old," said Lena. "My grandmother outlived my grandfather by thirty years. She missed him all that time." Lena turned and poured the hot water into the teapot. "Of course, he was a fairly young man when he died. She didn't have to watch him grow old."

Sylvester glanced around the kitchen. It looked as if it had been freshly painted white. There were no pictures or calendars, no hooks to hang things from. "You've made this house nice. It's a lot nicer than the one you used to live in." The light from the mini-blinds gave the room a cheerful dimness.

"Oh, I'm an old maid now, Sylvester." Lena carried the tea set over to the breakfast nook on a silver tray. "All I've got is this house and old Fraidy. Sit down."

"What do you mean, old maid? You haven't changed a bit—you're still lovely."

"The man with the golden tongue. Eat your cookies and shut up." But she smiled for the first time.

Sylvester laughed. She hadn't changed. From his grandmother's description, he had expected to see a tired old woman, bent at the waist, hard wrinkles around the mouth. He almost hadn't come because he didn't want to see her like that. But she was just as lovely as he remembered, as lovely as the faded, grainy picture of her he had seen in the *Glacier Reporter*. Her cheeks were just as smooth as ever. The tiny wrinkles at the corners of her eyes gave her face a softness that he found appealing. Maybe he had been a little afraid of her when they were younger. He had never really thought of that but it was true.

"You've cut your hair," he said.

"Oh, I did that a long time ago."

"Not too long ago. I saw a picture of you with some kids in the paper. You had long hair then. You wore it exactly the way you used to."

"What's with this hair fetish? I just decided to have it cut one day. I got tired of sleeping on curlers." She touched her hair. "Don't you like it?"

Sylvester was pleased that she asked him. He had noticed her slender neck when she had her back to him. Now he noticed the tips of her ears, brownish-pink, through the black hair. He hadn't seen her ears before; nor her neck from the back. He suddenly felt more intimate with her than ever. Perhaps because he was grown-up and the years between them not so great. In high school he had been painfully aware that she was a woman and he a boy.

"It's fine. It suits you."

"Thanks for the overwhelming endorsement." She smiled at him in a teasing way. She stirred her tea. "Now, what brings you to see me?"

Sylvester pursed his lips as though he did not want to speak. There was a peacefulness in that Saturday Browning kitchen that he did not want to alter. He could hear the occasional car go by on the main street beyond the alley. He even heard children yelling in the vacant field. But there was an illusion of peace here—and he knew it was an illusion, behind which were men drinking in alleys, fistfights, knife fights, domestic fights, suicide, rape, murder, a whole panoply of violence that lay on the outer edges of that illusion. Nevertheless, the illusion was strong in that breakfast nook with its closed mini-blinds and fresh white paint.

Sylvester wanted to reach across the table and touch Lena, squeeze her small hand with the silver ring and clear strong nails. He wanted to stroke her hair, feel his fingertips on her delicate ear. He wanted to make up for all those times he hadn't touched her, for all that time he had never had. He wanted to lay his head against her breast and confess.

But he said instead, "Some people down in Helena want me to run for Congress." He said it softly, but the words broke the illusion and he was back on planet Earth. A car suddenly accelerated on the main street, roaring, squealing rubber. "They seem to think I could do a pretty good job representing Montanans and especially Indians. I've thought about it the past few weeks and I'm beginning to believe they're right. I think I could do a good job if I commit myself to it. And that's the problem. I know the commitment will have to be strong and unswerving. Once you throw your hat in the ring, to use an old cliché, you have to be prepared to run without slowing down or stopping. I don't know if I'm prepared to do that." He looked into her eyes. "That's why I came to you, Lena."

"Me?" She said it in a surprised but almost cynical tone. "I don't know anything about that kind of stuff. My God!"

Sylvester didn't know what he had expected, but he was taken aback by the disdain of her response.

"You *know* me, Lena. I guess—I thought you could tell me if I could do it."

"Sylvester, I don't know you—that way. We've only seen each other once since you graduated college. I think we talked for ten minutes with people milling all around." Lena looked off into the kitchen. She seemed to be assessing her own small world. "I've heard about you from time to time—law school at Stanford, you're in some big law office down in Helena, you're not married but you've got a girlfriend—your grandmother keeps me minimally informed. But, gee whiz—" She stopped and looked at him. She studied him as though she just now remembered that he had been her first bright light, the first one she had cared too much about. She dropped her eyes and ran her finger around the rim of her teacup.

"Of course you could do it, Sylvester. They're right, you should run for Congress." She looked up and smiled at him. "I'd be so proud of you, so damned pleased—"

"Would you be pleased, Lena? This is so important to me—I can't tell you—you've always been the one I thought of when I needed help with something or other. You don't know how many times I've almost called you. But I didn't want to burden you. I know how much others need you—"

"Don't get carried away, Sylvester. Life is too damned short to be killed by flattery. Let's just say that I'm glad you asked my advice, and yes, I know you will do a good job of it, and leave it at that. How about some more tea? And eat up those cookies. I bought them just for you, as it turns out."

"Don't you want to hear my platform?" Although the plaintive tone made him feel foolish, Sylvester didn't want to be dismissed just yet. He wanted her to hear about his ideas on treaty rights, water, mineral, fishing, hunting rights, education, industry on reservations. Suddenly he knew that he had been formulating ideas and plans in his head all along, as though he had already made up his mind to run even before he came to see Lena. He wanted her to listen to these ideas, to be impressed, to be excited and encouraging.

And down deep and far back in his mind there was a gnawing hope that she could help him with the problem that he would have to resolve before he did anything as high-powered as running for national office. He felt his enthusiasm ebbing, being replaced by a heaviness that seemed to settle on his shoulders and press him down onto the bench in the clean white breakfast nook.

"Lena—"

"I know you'll do the right thing, Sylvester."

"—could I talk to you again—sometime?"

"If you'd like. I'm always here when I'm not at school." She stood and carried the teacups to the sink.

"I've been so wrapped up with myself I haven't asked you how you are doing, really. Are you in touch with Stan at all?"

"I have some things to do, Sylvester. No. Not at all." She put the sugar away and laid the plate of cookies on the counter. They hadn't eaten any.

"I wonder what happened to him." But Sylvester didn't wonder that at all. He wondered what had happened to him and Lena. He knew that Stan had quit Browning almost fifteen years ago. His grandmother had told him. But could he have been afraid to see Lena, afraid that they would consummate something neither would really want? He had never allowed himself to even think this question. Now he saw the truth of the question but he couldn't answer it. He couldn't allow himself the possibility.

He slid out of the breakfast nook and stood awkwardly, watching her run water into the sink. He watched her back, her narrow shoulders, as she washed the two cups. "Goodbye, Lena," he said softly. Then he turned and left before she finished because he didn't want to face her. He didn't feel bad for what might have been but for what was. He let himself out quietly.

〰〰〰

Lena Old Horn pulled the living-room drapes shut, then sat down in a big old chair. It was her reading chair, but she didn't turn on the lamp. She closed her eyes and tried to think of her schedule for Monday. She had a girl coming in who was a marginal college candidate. Lena suspected that she just wanted to get off the reservation, to get away. Was that a good enough reason to go down to Missoula and fail? To come back after six weeks, three months, six months? Then what? What could Lena say on Monday that would make a difference in the girl's life? What about all the other lives that she would touch in the coming years?

Sylvester Yellow Calf. Young, squatting on his heels on the bank of Four Horns Reservoir, the wind lifting and blowing his thick black hair. He had been her friend in a way no one else had. He would never know it but he had made her feel confident, bright, a young woman of sex and substance. When he went away to college, she read about his basketball career in the *Great Falls Tribune* and she knew she had lost the little piece of his life that she had occupied. And she was hurt. He never contacted her when he came to Browning. She knew when he was in town. She had seen him a couple of times on the street but she never acknowledged him. Once she had come out of the drugstore and he was standing there, his back to her, signing autographs for some grade-schoolers. It would have been so easy to go to him and say hello. But she walked to her car and sat there, watching him banter with the children. When he turned her way, she leaned over, pretending she was looking for something in the glove compartment. At that moment, it became too late. They became strangers, and had remained so until today.

Why had she acted that way, then and today? Could she

have been that hurt that she couldn't give him her enthusiasm, her encouragement? And why had he come? Was it
really for her advice?

Lena rubbed her eyes with her palms and she could feel the
difference between them, the slightly depressed socket lower
than the other. She hadn't had much luck with men. Even
Stan. But she had dumped him, not long after Sylvester left
for college. For some reason, Stan was no longer interesting to
her. Surprisingly, when they did meet on the the street or in
some establishment, they talked about Sylvester, as though
he had left some gap between them that neither could cross
over. He had hurt them both. The broken nose became a
symbol of betrayal to Stan. He left town after the next school
year and she had not seen nor heard from him since.

Fraidy jumped up on her lap and she hugged him to her.
"Fraidy, Fraidy," she crooned. "Are you hungry, dear?"

~~~~~~~

Mary Bird watched the green car back out into the street,
then shoot away beyond the corner of the house. She listened
hard and she heard the gears shift once, then twice, the pitch
of the motor changing each time until she heard it no more.
She stood in the quiet yard until she got cold. Although the
morning sun was bright in the blue sky, there was snow in the
wind coming down from Cold Maker's house in the north. She
felt it in her bones, just as she had for eighty-seven winters,
but it didn't come any easier, nor was it any more welcome.
Mary pulled her shawl tighter around her shoulders. She
wished she could see the mountains. She could always tell the
weather by the way the mountains looked. When Earl first got

his TV set, he would watch the weather report, then come into the kitchen to tell her the forecast. But she always knew. And she knew when they were wrong too. She used to drive Earl crazy when she contradicted the forecast and turned out to be right. He expected a lot from his TV set, including the right to a wrong forecast.

Now Mary was sure he wouldn't last out the winter. She had told Sylvester last night that his grandfather, although he appeared stronger than he had in some time, was eating less and talking more about old times. For the most part, she enjoyed these talks—his ramblings—but she knew the signs, just as she knew the coming weather. Sylvester wanted them to come live in Helena where he could care for them, but she told him that old people needed to die where they had lived. Besides, she had been to Helena once when Sylvester first moved there to become a lawyer. There were too many people and the mountains were all around. The Blackfeet were not mountain people. They needed to watch Sun Chief rise a long way off.

Mary Bird walked back to her house and she felt stiff and tired. But she was determined to give her husband a proper burial among his people at Heart Butte. And she was determined to see her grandson become a big politician. She smiled to herself. A big chief in Washington. Now that was something to live for. Many of her old friends had felt sorry for her when she had taken Sylvester in as a baby. Some who were not traditionalists even thought the baby would be better off if it were put up for adoption. They felt Sylvester might have inherited his parents' ways and would end up breaking Mary's heart. But she knew different. She knew he would be her boy and he would make up for her daughter's wildness.

Now she could point to her Sylvester's picture in the newspaper again and tell them what it was like to be a big chief's grandmother.

Then she remembered something. Her step lightened and she padded quickly up the step in her soft-tanned moccasins. Once in the house, she went straight to Sylvester's room, past Earl and the blaring TV set, and her hand was trembling as she pushed open the door. The bed was made even though she had told him not to bother. She walked to the dresser and bent over so she could see clearly, her shaking hands sweeping the surface. Then she stood straight and saw an old wrinkled face, almost toothless, almost blind, an old Blackfeet face, laughing at the mirror. The war medicine was gone. Sylvester had taken it.

C H A P T E R N I N E

Buster Harrington heard the chiming of the bells atop St. Helena's Cathedral and he closed up the paper and looked at the clock over the fireplace mantle. 11:45 A.M. He stood and stretched, then bent at the waist to touch his toes. He bobbed up and down, each time trying to get lower, but he always came down three inches short. Fuck it, he thought, leave it to the younger men. He tucked his shirt tail back into his expansive cords and walked to the window on the other side of his desk. He had already worked for three hours that morning before taking a break to read the Sunday paper. A man of habit, he always worked for three hours on Sunday morning so he would have the rest of the day for other things. Trouble was, there were fewer other things as the years slipped past. He liked it when the legislature was in session. He and Maggie were famous for their Sunday brunches. They invited Republicans as well as Democrats, sometimes even members of the administration. It was good to work both sides of the street, especially on Sunday late mornings, which was a neutral time of the day and week.

But this was an off year for the legislature and the Republicans were in control of the administration for the first time in twenty years. Everything was going to hell up at the capitol, and he did not feel like inviting any of that gang into his home.

Buster pulled the lace curtain aside and looked out over the broad valley north of Helena. A snow had fallen during the night and had stuck. It was the first snow of the year, and although it was only mid-November, it was a sign of a long hard winter coming in. The steel-gray clouds hung low over the valley, obscuring the surrounding mountains. I should retire, thought Buster, move to Phoenix permanently. He and Maggie had bought a house in Phoenix nearly ten years ago when she first started whining about the winters. It was a small house in an expensive suburb. They had paid more for it than they had for their Helena mansion twenty-five years ago. Now Maggie spent January and February and part of March down there. Buster endured two weeks in February before he flew back north to disrupt the smooth flow of his law firm. Goddamnit, thought Buster as he looked out over the snowy valley, this time I'm going to do it. I'll join one of those health clubs down there, get all tan and healthy, show these bastards around here there's a little smoke in the old volcano.

The clock over the fireplace chimed twelve times, the final strike echoing throughout the large library. Then it was quiet again. Normally, Maggie would be home from church about now, but she had to attend a luncheon for a member of her Bible group who was moving away. South. To Phoenix. No flies on that old mare, he thought. Her husband had died only a couple of months ago and she was heading for Sun City or one of those other dens of iniquity. Buster had read stories about the fun and games in those places and the idea kind of intrigued him. He was only sixty-two and while he was a little portly, there was a pretty stout body in there. He bounced his fist off his stomach. Still pretty hard. He might suggest to Maggie that they get rid of that expensive house and move into a nice double-wide. Be with people who shared their interests. Instant community. Maggie liked people a hell of a lot better than he did. Wild sex. Where had he read that? Maybe he had heard it from one of his friends at the Montana Club. They were all getting old and talked of such things during pinochle games. But they all showed up every Friday afternoon. No one quit to take advantage of the randy widows of Sun City.

Buster sighed and dropped the curtain. He sat down at his desk and looked over some briefs. He was still the managing partner at the firm; in fact he was the only partner who took a hand in the business nowadays. Malcolm Lohn had retired last year, although he still kept an office and attended the Monday-morning briefings. Pinky Price was another matter. It had been a major mistake to take him on as a partner. He was fifty-seven and incompetent. He had taken a leave of absence to run in the Democratic primaries for governor and had gotten his ass soundly whipped. He hadn't been worth a damn since, if he ever was. Still, it wasn't such a bad move to run him. He had been a front-runner until one of his opponents discovered that Price had spent the Korean War shelling peas in the Matanuska Valley in Alaska. Pinky had emphasized his army record to veterans' groups around the state. To hear him tell it, he had captured Porkchop Hill all by himself. Buster laughed out loud. Goddam that Pinky. Buster had been seriously damaged himself, but the party needed him more than he needed the party. But he was stuck with Pinky Price and his whole goddam family of would-be politicians. Sun City. It was sounding better all the time.

Buster flipped through his Rolodex, found the card he wanted, and dialed the phone. He sat with his ear to the receiver and stared at his prize art on either side of the fireplace. He never had been too fond of the Charley Russell. It was an early watercolor of a cowboy on a horse in a snowstorm. The cowboy had his hat brim tied down with a scarf and the horse only had three legs as far as Buster could tell. But the Sharpe was something else. It was a painting of an abandoned cabin surrounded by trees of fall colors. It was one of those kinds of paintings where if you looked close, all you saw was smudges of pigment. If you looked at a distance, you saw the brownish-gray cabin and the yellow and red leaves and they looked real in a strange way. On his only trip to Europe, he had seen a lot of those kinds of pictures, especially in the galleries of France. It was a movement of some kind, but Buster couldn't figure out how Sharpe knew about it.

"Hello?"

"Mr. Yellow Calf—I was just thinking about you and wondering why you haven't invited me for a drink at the Montana Club later this afternoon. Winter is upon us and we need to speak of the future."

"What time?"

"Four."

"See you then."

"That's the boy. I know you've got things to tell me."
Buster hung up the phone and glanced down the room at the
Russell. It looked like a cartoon. Maybe it was art. It wasn't
very uplifting to look at with the first snow on the ground.

〰〰〰

Sylvester arrived at the Montana Club a few minutes
early. He climbed the stairs, touching the wood paneling as he
made the circle to the second floor. The dining room was
closed, but one had to go through the entrance to reach the
bar. All the tables were set with white linen and silver. The
sky had cleared off and the sun angled into the dining room
from the southwest, sparkling off a hundred water goblets
with their fanned napkins inside. Sylvester never ate there
unless he was with clients or other lawyers—or a date. He had
taken Shelley there the first time. He had been mildly surprised by how deferentially the hostess and waiters and some
of the other diners treated her. Even if she was the daughter
of Mel Hatton, she received more than enough attention. It
worked out all right, but after that they went to other restaurants.

But Sylvester had not been out to dinner with Shelley anywhere for over three weeks—not since their dinner together
at Chico Hot Springs. He hadn't called her for a week, but he
had been busy with other things. He had seen Patti Ann
Lowry three times that week and they always ended up in her
bed. Unlike the first time, there were no dinners, no drinks,
no excuses.

He found a table in a corner, away from the bar. He settled into a low black leather chair and ordered a beer. It felt a little strange to be drinking on a Sunday afternoon and the beer was bitter and he wished he'd ordered a tonic water. There were only seven other people in the bar—two middle-aged couples (Sylvester recognized one of the men, a criminal lawyer who practically lived in the courthouse), two men playing the electronic poker machines, and a woman, elegantly dressed in a white sweater and skirt, sitting at the bar. She had stared at Sylvester coming in and he saw a bored, reckless look in her eyes and kept his own straight ahead.

Buster arrived at ten after four. He was wearing a pink button-down shirt, a lavender sweater, and tan cords. He had hung his coat up outside, another of his ancient habits. The sweater was stretched to the limits, but there was a surprising lightness in his step. No one would have guessed that he was a high-powered lawyer and a maker of politicians. If it weren't for his slicked-back steel-gray hair and once-broken nose, he might have been mistaken for a rich old barfly.

He moved among the tables and few patrons with ease, just as he had done for thirty-five years. He might have been the off-duty owner, coming in to check the receipts. He waved to one of the men playing the poker machines and greeted the two couples as though they were longtime friends. Usually, he would have gone to their table and shaken hands all around and exchanged nonsense, but today a wave and a loud "Howdedoo there, folks" was all they received. The criminal lawyer had smiled expectantly, but Buster didn't have anything to do with criminal lawyers. Unless they were among the big boys, they were on their way to nowheresville.

"Sylvester!" Buster clapped him on the shoulder. "How

long has it been since we saw each other last?"

"Friday afternoon, Buster. Howya doing?" Sylvester stood and signaled to the barmaid, but she was already coming with Buster's Early Times ditch.

"Oh God, I just got bored sitting around that old house. Maggie had all kinds of stuff to do today and none of them included me. I figured it might be a good time for us to get together and get reacquainted——"

"Here you are, Mr. Harrington." The barmaid set his drink on a paper napkin.

"Hey, how's it going, Whitey? What are you doing working on a Sunday? You've got kids to look after."

"Swapping shifts with Joany. She's getting married today." The barmaid beamed.

"No kidding! Good for her. Are you still going with that deputy?"

"Nooo, we broke up a long time ago." Her voice trailed off wistfully. "He went down to Bozeman to the police academy. He wants to be a highway patrolman."

"Christ. Well, you just hang in there, kid. You can do better than that. Tell Joany I've got a big fat hug for her." Buster watched the pretty brunette walk over to the couples. "These poor girls. 'Life shore is tough.' I had a ranch hand years ago who used to say that. 'Life shore is tough.' Man of few but well-chosen words."

Sylvester smiled and nodded. He was used to Buster's busywork and most of the time he enjoyed it. It relaxed everybody, got them in the mood for a few hours of camaraderie—until Buster dropped the bomb.

"How's that gal of yours—Shelley?" Buster leaned forward and took a sip of his brimful drink.

"Shelley? She's fine, I think." Sylvester added quickly, "She's been involved in setting up a new fiscal system—"

"Still? You told me that a month ago. How long does it take to figure out a new way to bleed the poor taxpayer?" Buster leaned back in the black leather chair and glared at Sylvester.

Sylvester tried to read his boss's expression. There was very little difference in Buster's face between repose and anger—just another furrow in the brow, a slight opaqueness in the blue eyes. Had he heard something about Sylvester and Shelley? Sylvester ran his fingers across his forehead, expecting to find a small dampness. Ed Vance must have told him about Patti Ann. He would disapprove mightily—for any number of reasons. He would think that Sylvester was getting into something dangerous. Especially now. Any change in situation, in behavior, would be dangerous now. Sylvester almost surprised himself thinking in terms of danger, but almost from the beginning, he'd known there were too many things he did not know—about Patti Ann, about himself, about their physical attraction to each other.

He and Shelley had—or had had—a good love life. He enjoyed making love with her, being as close as he could to her when they were alone, and sometimes in public. She was the only woman he had ever really touched in public. It made him feel good—and possessive—to put his arm around her waist or on her shoulder at parties or in grocery stores. She always snuggled into his arm, tight against his side, and smiled at their public privacy. She liked their secrets, the lovely things they did to each other when they were truly alone.

Sylvester looked at Buster and decided that his expression

was one of thoughtfulness, a benign patron feigning interest in his underling's affairs. He couldn't be thinking of the new woman in Sylvester's life.

"I've decided to run, Buster. I've thought it over from all the angles I could think of and I see no reason not to take a shot at it."

If Sylvester thought that Buster was going to jump up and down, he now saw that he was mistaken. Buster took another sip from his drink. He did smile, but it was one of his patented noncommittal smiles.

"What do you think?" said Sylvester.

Buster chuckled. "You know how many times people have asked me that, Sylvester? Must be a hundred by now, maybe five hundred. I've backed some winners and some losers. Frankly, I've had my ass handed to me too many times to get too excited. If my candidate wins, he's a hero and I've strengthened my hand; if he loses, they say Buster backed a loser. It takes a long time to recover from a defeat, no matter how minor the office."

"If I run, and I will, I won't be looking to be defeated." Sylvester felt a tightness in his throat, an anger welling up, and he couldn't quite believe that he would feel this way toward his patron. He had never felt anger toward Buster.

"Have you called Fabares?"

"Not yet. I just made the decision this week."

"Have you told anybody? Shelley?"

Sylvester remembered that he had promised Shelley she would be the first one he told. He thought for an instant that he should call from the pay phone by the cloakroom. He should have told her, but there was no real opportunity. Dammit, he could have saved it, their relationship. But the distancing was too real. He could do it now. He could go to her, make her see him. He could tell her right now. Tell her what?

"You're the first, Buster."

Buster leaned forward on his elbows. His large, round face seemed to grow even larger. He smiled again, but this one was real. "Atta boy, Sly, atta boy. Now we're cooking. Now, what's next? Let's see, we gotta get ahold of Fabares. First thing in the morning—before the meeting. I want to announce something at the meeting." Buster picked up his drink and drained it in two swallows. He waved to the barmaid and pointed to their glasses. "Hot shit! Listen to me, son. Not a word to anybody. Mum's the word till we get this thing figured out." Buster looked around. The criminal lawyer was looking at him. Buster smiled. "See that prick over there? He'd love to know, wouldn't he?"

"Probably wouldn't make much difference to him, would it?"

"Ho, ho. He'd be trying to get his hand in your pants before you hit the door." Buster waved, almost knocking the drinks out of the barmaid's hands. "Sorry about that, Whitey. Listen, tell Scott to scare us up some potato chips or something, will you?"

When the barmaid had gone, Buster leaned back and grew thoughtful.

"I know it's taken me a long time to decide. Do you think Fabares, the national committee, will still be interested? They must be involved in a thousand projects more important than this one."

"Sylvester, there is no project more important than this

one. That's the second thing you're going to tell Fabares tomorrow. You're going to make him believe that you are the reincarnation of Abraham Lincoln. Hell, Mahatma Gandhi. Let's get all our cards on the table."

Sylvester laughed and he felt good, almost optimistic.

Buster leaned forward again, heaving his chair forward on its casters. "Let me tell you something, Sly. Throughout the years, I've picked up a little experience in the political arena, developed an instinct, you might say. I've had a few defeats, I'll be the first to admit a few failures, but, goddam, we've won most of them! We've kept Democrats in the governor's mansion and in Congress for twenty years or more. We've had mixed success over in the eastern district, but they're a bunch of scissorbills anyway. But we won't quit trying over there, goddammit. If I had half a notion that Jesus Fucking Christ could win that district, we'd take a run at it. But we'd lose. Your skin color would take care of that, sure as hell.

"What I meant to tell you, before I rudely interrupted myself, is that you have a chance to make a difference—not only in the state but on the national level. Think of it. How many Indians are there in Congress? One, two? You come from a state with a hell of a big Indian population. You know what that suggests to me? You run for the western district seat, but you conduct a statewide campaign. You'll visit reservations in the eastern district, you'll give speeches to sympathetic parties, you might even shoot a few baskets for the local photographers. Someday all that activity will pay off. When you get to Congress and you hammer together your first piece of legislation, you'll see. You'll make a difference, Sylvester. Your people will reap the benefits."

"What about the rest of it? Who else am I going to appeal to? Fabares didn't think much of my potential constituents. I think he thought I was a bit naive."

"You are! That's your strength, buddy, you said it. Jesus Christ, now I am getting excited. Well, we won't get into it just now. We have to put together a whole strategy and we don't want to get hasty. I've been doing a little work, finances, stuff like that. We haven't exactly been asleep at the switch, my boy. There's a storefront on the Gulch with a big back room, used to be a picture-framing place. The realtor who handles it owes me a big one. We'll move in a few desks, some phones, a couple of computers. We'll be in business before you can find a place to hang your hat. Where the hell are those potato chips?"

"What's the first thing I'm going to tell Fabares?"

"Huh?"

"You know, you said something about the second thing—"

"Oh! Hah!" Buster's round face beamed. "You're going to tell him that you really are Mahatma Gandhi and he'd better get his ass in gear." Then Buster surprisingly, almost theatrically, turned grim. His lips thinned over his teeth and the words came out flat. "You've got a lot to think about, Sylvester, and the first thing is, how badly do you want your life to change forever? You'd better come up with a good answer, because it's going to be one hell of a ride. For the next year, others are going to own you. People like Fabares are going to shake your dick every time you get done pissing. Then they're going to point you to the next stall. Your private life will be the five or six hours of sleep you'll get before somebody comes knocking on your door. They'll order your breakfast, write your speeches, and transport you to some of the godawfulest places you've ever been in. They'll tell you how to dress and how to act around the biggest assholes in the state and back in Washington.

"But, if you do everything they tell you to do, if you give yourself over to them, I think you'll be a shoo-in. Then you can start regaining a little control over your life."

"What about you?"

"You won't need me once you get started. These boys and girls are professionals—a slick bunch of bastards. I'll help get you off the ground, son; after that, I fade away, and the sooner the better. They'll tell you that."

"I thought you and I were going to talk about strategy, plan positions on some issues."

"Oh, we will! I figure we have about a month to do our own thing. I'll help you any way I can. I know you, Sylvester—they don't. Not yet. Maybe not ever. That's why I want you to think this thing through before you get caught up in the machinery. Once this machine gets wound up, there's no stepping off at the next corner." Buster shook his head and sat back, his pink scalp shiny beneath the slicked-back hair.

Sylvester looked off toward the windows beyond the table where the two couples had sat. They were gone and he couldn't remember what the criminal lawyer looked like. As he looked into the blackness beyond the shine of the beveled-glass windows, he felt confused and apprehensive about such an enormous undertaking. But he also felt a tingle of excitement at the prospect of changing his life. He had never liked fairy tales, but if what Buster had said was true, he was about to enter another world.

He leaned forward and clinked Buster's glass with his own. "Here's to it," he said.

The wind had kicked up but the snow was frozen and the yellow light from the streetlamp was as clear as a January moon over the plains. But Sylvester was in Helena, in the mountains, walking to his car, slightly drunk, wishing he'd worn a heavier coat. The relief and elation of telling Buster his plans, the panicky excitement and the four or five toasts thereafter, were beginning to wear off. Sylvester crossed the street, surprised at how icy it had become in the four hours he had been in the Montana Club. Downtown Helena was always depressing on a Sunday night, and tonight it was completely deserted, no humans, no dogs, no cars. He was hungry and thought briefly of stopping at the Overland Express for a steak. He hadn't been in since he'd met Patti Ann there that fateful night. His stomach growled and he almost changed directions, but he wasn't up to the Overland this night. In fact, he was trying to put all the things that reminded him of Patti Ann out of his mind. He had a new purpose now, a goal that required him to behave. In a week or so, his life would be on public display. He had wanted to tell Buster that he and Shelley were having a little difficulty, but on second thought he wanted to clear up that difficulty. That way there would be no need to tell Buster anything about his personal life that might haunt him in the coming months. If things worked out, he would be right back where he was a month and a half ago. He wanted desperately to be there.

He unlocked the Saab and slid onto the velour seat. Although it was only a year old, he had put a lot of miles on it, driving around the state, taking depositions and looking up records in the various county courthouses. He enjoyed that part of his job and always did it himself, although it was time-consuming and often a waste of time. But it got him out of Helena a few days a month and he got to see parts of the state, especially the far eastern and northwestern parts, that he had previously only seen on local TV news. But such segments were rare. It seemed as though nothing much ever happened in those areas.

A streetlamp cast a yellow glow through the back window. Sylvester turned and looked at the back seat. It was littered with old documents, Xeroxes of Xeroses, manila envelopes and folders. The floor was a mess of pop cans and candy wrappers and three yellow tennis balls. They belonged to Shelley's daughters. He had meant to return them all summer, but now it was winter and they were as motionless as yellow stones.

Sylvester started the car and pulled out onto the street. He touched his brakes slightly and the car slid down the incline toward the bottom of Last Chance Gulch. He managed to get the car stopped at the stoplight, but the incline before him glistened in the streetlamps. The street coming up the gulch was a one-way toward him. The other side was the beginning of the pedestrian mall. He sat through a change of lights before he decided to turn right and go down the one-way street the wrong way. There was no traffic and he drove two long blocks, then turned left and drove out past the Civic Center with its landmark minaret, the strangest building he had ever seen. He always half expected to see a dark man in a burnoose up in the minaret, calling the citizens of Helena to prayer. But not tonight. Tonight he didn't notice the illuminated minaret as he drove west through residential streets until he came to Shelley's old-brick ranch home. He eased the car to a stop on the opposite side of the street. The porch light was on and there was a dim glow from behind the living-room drapes. The rest of the house was dark. Shelley's bedroom was in the near corner of the house. Sometimes, when the girls were at a movie or a birthday party, she invited Sylvester into her room and they made quick, almost frantic love in the afternoon stillness of the stodgy neighborhood. She admitted once that she liked to sleep with his smell still in her bed. It was her naughtiest secret from her little girls, she said.

Sylvester almost groaned as he put the car in gear and pulled away from the curb. His stomach was now growling continuously, but he drove back toward downtown, taking a route that would lead him to the area of mansions just west of Last Chance Gulch. Again he pulled the car to the curb opposite a large sandstone mansion with arches and turrets and balconies, and a simple wooden carriage house. It was a fairly grotesque structure but historic, built by the madam of the biggest saloon-whorehouse in Last Chance Gulch just before the gold played out. She had lived in it for only a year before she followed the boom to the the next gold town. It had gone through a series of owners and deterioration before the Hattons bought it and restored it.

Sylvester could see the dining room, brightly lit by a crystal chandelier, from where he sat. Mrs. Hatton had signed the papers selling off the ranches beneath the chandelier. She and Sylvester and Shelley, whom he had just met, lifted a glass or sherry in honor of the sad occasion. Now he saw two small heads bent over something at the table. Probably homework. Amy and Marty. He had remembered earlier that Shelley and the girls always had Sunday dinner with Mrs. Hatton. The other rooms on Sylvester's side of the house were dimly lit. The drapes were all open.

Sylvester never quite knew where he stood with the girls. Amy, the older of the two, had once done a class project on the Blackfeet in particular, and the northern plains Indians in general. One of the segments in her workbook included a matching up of buffalo parts and their uses. Sylvester had failed miserably in his attempt to help her match them up. But together they did a good job in the history segment. After that, Amy looked at Sylvester with a wary awe. He had convinced her he was a real Indian and knew something about Indians if not buffalo.

Marty was another story. She was slight and a shade blonder than either Shelley or Amy. And she was pretty. At nearly ten, she had more boyfriends at school than she could handle, and people on the street stared at her and remarked after her. She was blasé about the whole business, noncommittal in the extreme, and this worried Shelley. She never talked with Shelley's friends and she barely answered their polite questions. For his part, Sylvester attempted a heartiness around her, joking about boyfriends and school and swimming, but she didn't respond. She just barely expressed appreciation when Sylvester brought the girls gifts. For a while, he tried more gifts, until Shelley made him stop. Then he gave up. He really didn't know anything about children, he said one night after the girls had gone to bed. You're doing fine, Shelley said, just be yourself, she'll grow out of it. But Sylvester knew Shelley was worried about their future together. And he thought it might have something to do with his being an Indian in such a white, white world.

Sylvester almost ducked down in his seat when he saw a

figure come from the kitchen and lean over the girls. It was a man in a dark crewneck sweater. He looked to be in his thirties or forties, tall, almost gaunt. He had dark hair, but Sylvester couldn't quite make out his features. The man stood over the girls for a couple of minutes, once leaning closer and moving his arm slowly from one side to the other, as though he were pointing to something on the unseen tabletop. Amy turned her face up to him and Sylvester knew exactly what her expression would be. Marty did not move and he knew that gesture, or lack of one, too.

Then he saw Shelley come in from the kitchen and stand beside the man. She put her hand on Marty's head and laughed at something the man said. Then they walked off together, toward the living room.

Sylvester sat in the car, listening to the heater's low hum, and he felt numb. He had forgotten his hunger and now it was just a dull throb in his stomach. He was running on empty and even the alcohol had worn off, leaving him with the beginning of a headache and a dry, sour mouth.

The sight of the man had depressed him more than he would have imagined. It seemed clear, from the man's easy manner with the girls, that he was not a stranger. With seeming ease, he had taken Sylvester's place at the side of the girls' mother and they didn't seem to find it as remarkable as Sylvester did.

He glanced toward the window as he put the car in gear and the two blond heads were gone. Just like that, he thought. He gunned the car into the street and nearly hit a police cruiser. He jerked the steering wheel to the right and waited for the rear end to slide out and clip the cruiser. But it held firm and the near-accident looked like nothing more than the nose-thumbing gesture of an overly aggressive punk. Sylvester drove slowly, looking into his rearview mirror. The cruiser kept on going, then turned right at the end of the block. He almost laughed but he wanted to cry. Then he did laugh when the thought struck him that he had just decided to run for Congress, that he was a member of the parole board, an upstanding member of the community, and a credit to his race. How far from being a punk could you get? But he knew that if the cop had stopped him and he had long hair and wore Levi's and a dirty shirt and drove a jalopy, he would be on his way to the police station right now. He could see himself, dropping the dime and calling Buster to bail him out. "We've got an Indian here who says he knows you . . . ."

Sylvester made one more stop that night. It was in a run-down neighborhood a few blocks behind St. Helena's Cathedral. The houses were uniformly built at one time, in the 1930s—all were tall, narrow, two-story houses with steeply pitched roofs, three cement steps up off the sidewalk, three more to the front door. Most of families were either young or old. Some of the men worked at the smelter in East Helena; others drove delivery vans or hung drywall in the new developments. The women stayed home and watched the kids or smoked behind closed drapes. None of the yards were fenced.

One structure stood out among these homes. It was a two-story brick apartment building with the first story dug partially into the ground. There were eight apartments in the flat-roofed building, which took up most of two lots. Patti Ann lived in the upper-left front apartment. Her lights were on.

Sylvester turned off the motor and sat for a moment. The last time, after making love in the small bedroom, they had actually had a glass of wine in the living room and talked.

They had both seemingly given up the pretense of the contested will, so they discussed autumn, her trusty old Honda, the suit she was making for a friend. Sylvester, at her urging, volunteered a little information about his work as a lawyer and a parole board member. Patti Ann seemed to find the latter exciting and questioned him about procedures, cases ("What was your hardest case?" "Have you ever had anyone who was, well, different, who didn't seem to belong with those other men?"), and whether someone who had been denied parole could request another hearing soon or "do you just throw away the key and forget about him?" Sylvester usually didn't like to talk about his work on the board or what it was like down at the prison, but her questions were intelligent, even knowledgeable in a not quite vague way. She was sympathetic but clear-headed, and, in spite of himself, he was pleased that she was interested in such a thankless task. Nevertheless, he changed the subject when the opportunity came about, and they drank another glass of wine, then he went home.

Sylvester realized that he had taken the keys from the ignition and his other hand was on the door latch. How many times had he done this without thinking? But now he thought about it and he knew if he opened the door he would be obliged, willing, eager to go to her. He almost checked his watch, but he knew that too would open up possibilities that had better remain closed. He placed his arms on top of the steering wheel and rested his forehead against them. He closed his eyes and he saw her naked body standing in the bathroom light, touching up her makeup as he toweled himself dry. He opened his eyes and the image dissolved into a snow-packed street and the whine of a gusting wind. He started the car and glanced at the warm glow of her window before leaving. He had been window-peeking for an hour, half intoxicated, he'd almost hit a police car, he had driven two blocks the wrong way on a one-way street. He had committed enough crimes in his mind, if not in actuality, to cause him to question his sanity. So many things were going right for him. There were a lot of inmates down at MSP who had fucked up in situations similar to Sylvester's. He and the other board members and staff always shook their heads in feigned disbelief at such self-destructiveness. Now he wondered if he had been on the board too long, had absorbed too much foolishness. Sylvester drove home very cautiously.

〰〰〰

The sun came up the next morning, a late-morning early-winter sun rising over the southeastern end of the Big Belt Mountains. Most of the leaves were off the trees, but the ones that hung on were a golden beige under a blue sky. The snow on the streets had turned to slush and patches of still-green lawns showed through the melting snow.

Sylvester Yellow Calf had gotten up before dawn, feeling good in spite of his strange night. He had drunk three cups of coffee, walking around his large apartment, thinking of the day ahead and the night before. He felt apprehensive about the day and relieved that he had not actually talked with either Shelley or Patti Ann last night. Especially Patti Ann. He probably would have stayed until dawn. He showered and dressed and ate a couple of hard-boiled eggs and an English muffin while he made a few notes to himself on a legal pad. One of the notes he made was to call Shelley that afternoon.

Sylvester called Fabares from Buster's office at eight sharp.
He sat on the edge of the bare desk, glancing around the
room, while the call was being put through. The office could
have been in a museum as an example of a turn-of-the-century
magnate's drawing room. The furniture was hard wood with
leather seats, except for the two overstuffed couches that
flanked a mock fireplace at the other end of the room. Maggie
had selected the furniture and pictures, had replaced the old
water-damaged wainscoting with new blond oak, and had re-
finished the fireplace herself. Three Persian rugs lay in per-
fect symmetry across the width of the oak floor.

Fabares's voice was cheeful, full of forced vigor and heartiness. His accent was more clipped than Sylvester remembered, but the image of Fabares in Buster's home study was as
clear as a bell, especially his face when Sylvester caught him
off-guard.

The phone call lasted less than five minutes. Fabares would
fly out the middle of next week and he hoped the party chairman would accompany him. A couple of days' planning session and Sylvester would be off to the races. Tell Buster to
round up a solid crew. We're going to fly with this one. Don't
say anything to anybody, don't announce anything. Congratulations, Sylvester, welcome to the wonderful world of Democratic politics.

The Monday-morning briefing session began at nine, as
usual, in the law library. Doris had made a pot of coffee and
laid out a cardboard box full of breakfast rolls from the bakery down the street. Sylvester was already seated and he
watched the group milling around the table, pouring milk,
selecting just the right roll. Most of the eleven members of the
firm were younger than he was, a couple of them a year or two

out of law school. He glanced at the back of Sally Ellmann.
She was the youngest, and the only woman, in the group. She
handled simple divorces and wills and domestic matters. She
was the one Sylvester normally would have given Patti Ann's
case to. She turned and caught Sylvester's eye and came
around the table. She sat down next to him.

"I hear there's big news afoot," she said.

Sylvester sat up with a start. "What?" he said. "What
news?" Only he and Buster and Fabares knew about his decision.

"Search me," she said, laughing. "Just a rumor. Don't be
so jumpy."

Buster Harrington strode into the room and closed the
door. "Okay, c'mon, let's go to work. Vance, if you eat any
more of those rolls they're coming out of your pay."

The group laughed and Ed Vance put down the roll, smiling sheepishly at Buster.

Sally Ellmann squeezed Sylvester's hand, then moved
down to her accustomed place.

"Okay, Rizzo, you're up; Vance, you're on deck; Yellow
Calf, you're in the hole. Let's get this game started." Buster
heaved himself into the leather chair at the head of the table,
splashing his coffee on a stack of folders before him. "Goddammit."

Sylvester hardly heard Lou Rizzo's report on a comp case
he was working on in Anaconda. It was big case and it had
been offered to Sylvester but he had been stuck on an appeal
of one of his own cases. He heard some familiar words and
phrases, but he was trying to figure out how Sally Ellmann
and the others had learned about his campaign. There was no
way. Buster loved a mystery and he would wait for a more

opportune time to spring it. Then he closed his eyes and felt a tingling in his scalp. Patti Ann. Ed Vance must have told them about Patti Ann. Big news, rumors. He opened his eyes and looked across the table at Ed. Vance was looking down at his own notes. Sylvester scanned the other faces but they were listening intently to Rizzo.

Sylvester sat silently through the rest of the meeting. He had nothing beyond a court date to report on his appeal. He tried to read the expressions on the faces as they listened to him. He tried to find a flicker of a smile, an exchange of glances, but nobody betrayed any emotion. He sat back, and for the rest of the meeting, stared at a large photograph of a pair of fighting buffalo bulls above Ed Vance's head.

Finally, Buster stood. "And to wind up, a little in-house business." He raised his empty Styrofoam cup. "I would like to propose a modest toast—I say modest because I am, normally—but I'm proud as punch to present this one, to our new partner here at Harrington, Lohn and Associates—Sylvester Yellow Calf."

Sylvester stood and looked blankly at Buster as the others toasted him, then leaned across the table to shake his hand and congratulate him. Then he grinned and he felt helpless and foolish—and so relieved he feared that he would collapse into a puddle on the floor. Malcolm Lohn had eased behind him and patted him lightly on the shoulder.

"You earned it, my boy," he said. "You bloody well earned it."

"Thank you, Mr. Lohn. Thanks a lot." But the frail old man was already excusing himself from the gathering.

Sylvester looked down the table to Sally Ellmann and shook his head. "How did you know," he said, but the words were too weak for her to hear. Then he looked across at Ed Vance, who was gathering up his papers. For an instant Sylvester thought of apologizing to him, but Ed would not know what for, and furthermore, he glanced up at Sylvester with a tight blank look of nonrecognition as he placed the papers in a leather portfolio.

C H A P T E R   T E N

Shelley Hatton Bowers sat with her legs up on the sofa looking out the picture window at the street, the houses, the fireplug on the corner. She lived on the edge of an upper-middle-class neighborhood of ranch homes, dandelion-free lawns, and middling-tall maple trees along the boulevards. "Comfortable" was the word she used to describe her life away from the job. She liked to sit with her arm over the back of the couch and look at the small park kitty-corner from her house. She and some neighbors had formed a committee and bought several lots there, then raised the money to create the park, the playground, the one-goal basketball court. Her girls had grown up playing there, until they decided it was too close to be any fun. But other, smaller children who didn't know any better played

there while their mothers sat on benches and talked of ecolog-
ical matters and the problems with the Helena school system.
It was that kind of neighborhood, young to middle-aged professional people who drove foreign cars and were up on everything. Shelley always felt a little guilty when she backed her
old Ford Fairlane that her father had given her before he died
out of the garage. It had started to burn a lot of oil in the past
year. The girls wanted her to get a new one. They tore out ads
from magazines for Cadillacs, Buicks, and once for a British
Sterling, and placed them on her bedroom dresser.

Shelley sighed and felt her forehead again. She had called
in sick because she thought she was coming down with something, and she was. The flu had been going around, the first
wave of the season, and four people from her department
were out with it. Now her. Shit, she thought. Her life had gone
downhill ever since her trip to Chico Hot Springs with Sylvester over a month ago. She still couldn't believe that she had
allowed this awful business to happen. One minute they were
as happy as clams, swimming, eating, making love; the next,
they were distant, polite, practically saying "Excuse me"
when they brushed each other as they packed up to return to
Helena. They had slept together that night after dinner. They
had even made love in the saggy old bed, but she felt a rigidity
come over her and she tightened up and waited for him to
finish. The next day he dropped her off and she was glad to
see her girls playing on the lawn in front of the house.

She had analyzed that weekend many times in the ensuing
month. She had analyzed herself, and Sylvester. She came up
with all kinds of explanations—her first husband had never
communicated anything to her about his background, his job,
the things he thought about when they rode around the coun-

try or lay together after making love. She had thought she was getting Sylvester to open up to her more and more, and she was shocked and hurt to learn that he shared her former husband's unwillingness to let her into his life. Then she thought she was just being too sensitive, that she was rushing things, that she wanted too much. After all, he was trying to be forthcoming. He had tried hard, but he couldn't tell her what he didn't know.

Shelley pulled her housecoat tighter and retied the sash as she felt another chill come over her. It was such a silly thing. She should have given him more room to make such an important decision—but she thought the reason for the trip to Chico was for him to announce his decision to her. Maybe more. After all, her dad always said a good politician had one good woman behind him and a bad one had several. It was the corny type of thing that politicians and public men say, but she had wanted to be that one. In spite of the fact that her daughters hadn't really warmed up to Sylvester in a necessary way, she had wanted to live with him, to marry him. And so she was bitterly disappointed when nothing more came of the weekend.

That was her best analysis of the situation, but she had another, darker explanation, and it had to do with her actions after the weekend. It came to her a couple of weeks later when she found herself at a party for a retiring coworker. She had been uncomfortable by herself but she had gone to parties alone when Sylvester had other plans or she thought he would be bored with company talk. This time she was uncomfortable because there was not a possibility that he would come with her. She had seen to that herself by being aloof on the telephone and making up excuses why she couldn't see him. But this particular evening, as she looked around the rooms at all the people, drinking, laughing, talking lightly or with great intensity, she was aware that there was not an Indian in the group. And she was further aware that she was the only one she knew who even went out with an Indian. Her mother had often pointed that fact out to her, even though Mrs. Hatton was fond of Sylvester and took some pride in his accomplishments. She didn't want her daughter to be hurt, that was all.

But as Shelley scanned all the faces at the party, she was struck by the thought that maybe she, deep down, had been uncomfortable by his Indianness and had found a way, or a time, to get him out of her life.

A flock of cedar waxwings swooped across the window, flew across the street, and lit in a mountain ash. They busied themselves eating the clusters of red berries, some hanging upside down on the delicate branches, others treading the air as they picked at the berries. Their antics, as they got drunk on the berries, always delighted the girls—until they started flying into windows, killing themselves instantly. The girls had already buried two waxwings this fall, their graves marked by popsicle-stick crosses. Part of growing up, thought Shelley, but she stood and walked into the kitchen, partly because she didn't want to see one of the birds flying right at her and then hear the loud pop against the window, and partly because she had to eat something.

She put on some water to make herself a hot Tang, then she looked into the refrigerator. Kentucky-fried chicken and a biscuit left over from last night. Two cold weenies from the night before. The sight of them depressed her. She couldn't even make the girls a decent meal—or rather, they didn't want a decent meal, and she allowed it. Thank God they ate at their grandmother's once or twice a week. She still fixed big ranch meals—meat and potatoes, vegetables and salad. She was always worried that the girls were not getting properly fed, especially Marty, who was so slight and pale. Shelley closed the refrigerator and picked up the wall phone. She dialed the number she knew so well.

"Harrington, Lohn and Associates."

"Doris? This is Shelley. Is Sylvester in?"

"Shelley!" Doris was always surprised to hear a familiar voice. She had been there for twenty-five years and she had seemed never to get over hearing a familiar voice. "Yes, so good to hear from you, I'll put him right on."

Shelley walked over to the stove, the long cord uncoiling behind her. She turned off the burner and looked out the window at the feeding waxwings. More had joined them. There were well over a hundred now, flashing, hanging, flying, landing. They were the only activity on the street.

"Shelley! Hi, how are you?"

"Not so good, Sylvester. I've got a touch of the flu. I'm calling from home. I called in sick today."

"I'm sorry. I know it's been going around. Are you sick to your stomach?"

"Everywhere. Wherever it's possible to be sick, that's where I'm sick. God, I feel weak."

"Do you have someone there? Your mother?" There was a pause. Shelley sat down on a stool by the breakfast bar. "I could come over. I could reschedule a couple of appointments."

"No, that's all right." If Shelley hadn't been so sick, she might have considered it. Now she felt downright ill. "I'm sorry. I didn't call to complain. I called to apologize—with my dying breath, I apologize for being such a pill the past few weeks."

"You're not a pill. I just assumed that you had other things—"

"No, you didn't. You assumed, rightly, that I was a pill. There's just no other way to describe my behavior, Sylvester. You can't treat people the way I've treated you. Can you accept my apology?"

"If that will get us over the hump, yes, I do—but only if you'll accept my apology for being so, so self-absorbed at Chico. I really let you down—I know I did. It won't happen again."

Shelley laughed. "Sylvester, you're so lovely. You just won't let me wallow in humiliation and degradation, will you?"

"Not if I can help it. You're too good for that, sweetheart."

"Thank you, Mr. Sly."

"Does this mean we're still—friends?"

"I hope more than that. I did some thinking the other day—I gave myself every reason for ending it, for just staying apart. I had a good start on being apart. I could grow lonely very gracefully, I decided, if it weren't for you. You were always there in the back of my mind to foul things up. I even saw a man—"

"Oh?"

Shelley was surprised at the control in his voice. It wasn't a startled "Oh," not even an apprehensive one; it was more a considered "Oh," as though he might have expected it.

"He was a minister, of all things. He just came to Helena from Portland. He's an assistant pastor at Mother's church."

"Sounds like a decent man."

"Oh, he was. Is. Mother invited him to dinner last Sunday night." A wave of nausea swept over Shelley and she felt her stomach tighten in response. She decided she'd better speed things up. "Sylvester, I had absolutely no interest in him. He could have been a potted plant. He just made me realize how much I missed you. I do. I miss you terribly."

"I've missed you too, sweetheart."

But Shelley heard something else in his voice—this time a definite apprehensiveness. Her face grew hot and she couldn't tell if it was from fever or something else. She could feel the strength going out of her body and she knew it had been the wrong thing to call him when she felt this way.

"So many things have happened in the past couple of weeks. We've got to talk. I have so many—"

"Not now, Sylvester. I don't feel well. I shouldn't have called you like this. I'm sorry."

"Will you call me when you feel better? It's important that we talk."

Talk. We have to talk. Not we have to hug, to kiss, to hold each other. She felt her spirits fall and this time she knew it was not the fever.

"I'll call you, Sylvester."

"Promise?"

Shelley stood and hung up the receiver. She walked around the breakfast bar and looked out the window. The waxwings were gone and she felt rotten.

Rotten to the core, she thought, as she padded back to her bedroom. She kicked off her slippers and climbed in under the comforter. Then she slept a long, hard, sweaty sleep alone in the quiet of the comfortable ranch home.

~~~~~~

PattiAnnHarwood hung up the phone and tried to make sense out of the brief conversation. The man said his name was Woody Peters and he was a friend of Jack's. Although it was early afternoon, the man seemed to be drunk or on drugs, and his sentences were almost incoherent and senseless. As much as she could understand, she thought he said he and another man, also a friend of Jack's, were going to get him out of the joint. Then he seemed to be blaming her for Jack's troubles, but she couldn't tell if he meant all his troubles in his life or just those in the prison. Two or three times she almost hung up the phone, but he seemed to anticipate this and become less aggressive if not more sensible. The last thing he said before hanging up on her was "We're going to get your husband out of there and you're going to help, whether you like it or not."

Patti Ann had been so shaken she didn't know if she had talked loudly or whispered her responses. What she did know was that he had done virtually all the talking. But how had he gotten her work number? She couldn't remember giving it to Jack. They had an understanding that she was not to divulge the fact that her husband was in prison. In any case, Jack had never called her at work and wouldn't. They probably had it in Records at the prison, for emergency purposes. But how could this Woody Peters, who said he'd met Jack in max, get it?

She glanced around her cubicle. The rust-colored fabric walls were bare. Unlike her coworkers, Patti Ann had no photographs, no pictures, no mementos on her walls or desk. She folded her hands on her desk like a schoolgirl to stop the trembling. What was happening? A month and a half ago, she was leading the quiet life of a prison widow, almost content in her emotional isolation, sewing dresses for Myrna, shopping at Buttrey's, sleeping alone in her small bed. Now she was sexually involved with one of the men who had denied Jack's parole and loving and hating it at the same time. Hating herself for all the duplicity—on both sides—that she was engaging in. She had never imagined that she could be so—what?—criminal? immoral? dirty? And now a strange, drunken man, a thug, had just threatened to pull her in deeper.

Patti Ann suddenly shuddered as she realized he must know about her and Sylvester. Jack had told him. But had she ever told Jack she would do it? She hadn't, she wouldn't have. But was there a moment of acquiescence, a nod, an affirming touch, a look that made him think so? Patti Ann recalled her last visit and she tried to remember it all, but all she could really remember was Jack's resigned voice when she told him she couldn't sleep with Sylvester, not for any reason—"It was a crazy idea. . . . I'll just sit it out and hope nothing happens."

But she had already slept with Sylvester, even then, even the night before she was to visit her husband in prison. And she had slept with him several times since, and Jack knew about it. And now this Woody Peters and his friend knew about it. Who else?

Patti Ann almost picked up the phone—there was a general clatter and murmur in the office, so it would be safe—but she couldn't take even the slightest chance. She couldn't use the pay phone in the hall because there would be clients hanging around, in groups or singly, waiting to see one of the counselors. She would have to call him after work when she got home.

You poor man, she thought, what have I gotten us into? Then she shivered violently as she recalled the man's ugly, drunken voice. ". . . whether you like it or not."

~~~~~~

Sylvester entered the apartment through the back door. He was always pleased when he put the heavy brass key into the keyhole of the bolt lock. The heavy thud of the sliding bolt, the opening of the solid oak door, and the closing of it behind him gave him a feeling of sanctuary, of a kind of permanence in his life. He had lived in the apartment since his arrival in Helena ten years ago. One of his new colleagues knew a woman who was moving out of an apartment and Sylvester moved in three days later. Because he was a lawyer with a prestigious firm, the landlord, who had followed Sylvester's career in the newspapers, didn't even ask for a deposit. He laid out the rules, handed Sylvester the keys, and shook his hand.

The building wasn't in one of the best neighborhoods, but it was a graceful old wood-frame house that had been divided up and added on to over the years. Each addition had been built to blend in with the lines of the original house; even at that, the house looked massive, full of angles and pitches that didn't quite add up to the landlord's vision of gracious living. But it was comfortable and light.

Sylvester set his briefcase on a chair, walked into his bedroom, just off the kitchen, and changed into Levi's and denim shirt. In ten years he had gotten used to wearing suits and ties and shiny shoes, but the first thing he did when he got home was to change into the kind of clothes he had grown up in. He left his office clothes lying on the bed and padded in his stocking feet into the kitchen. He got a can of beer from the refrigerator, then walked through the dining area into the living room, where he snapped on the TV to the local news. He sat back on the couch and put his feet up on the coffee table and took a long swallow of beer. It had been a long day. He had gone in at seven that morning to catch up on his work, just as he had for the past week and a half.

But it would soon be over. Thanksgiving had come and gone and Sylvester had missed it. At least, he hadn't celebrated it—he hadn't gone home to Browning or eaten with Shelley and her mother and daughters or gone to Buster's for the giant feast that Maggie always prepared for the "lonely guys," as Buster called them, regardless of sex. Sylvester had attended the dinner his first three years in Helena. In fact, the second year Maggie had found a single woman who was part Northern Cheyenne for Sylvester. She worked as a teller where Maggie did her banking. Sylvester went out with her two or three times before she tried to convert him to her Seventh-Day Adventist beliefs. He had been a little uncomfortable about celebrating Thanksgiving anyway—it wasn't really a festive occasion for Indians—but when she asked him to pray with her a couple of weeks later, he hit the ground running. After the third "lonely guys" dinner, he told Maggie he wasn't that lonely. It took her several weeks to forgive him and she never invited him again. He didn't do anything for Thanksgiving for several years after that, but he had spent last Thanksgiving with Shelley and her family at her mother's house. He met an aunt and uncle and several cousins who still farmed in Musselshell County, just out of Roundup. He was a great curiosity to them. Although Shelley insisted they were good people. Sylvester recognized the danger signals. Even such a simple question as "How did you figure you wanted to be a lawyer?" was filled with skepticism. They had had an Indian boy who worked for them for a year and a half until he just ran away. A white boy, or man, would have walked off or walked away. Sylvester knew all the signs.

A weatherman was standing in front of a map of the United States. There were snowflakes over Minnesota and northern Michigan. And one snowflake over southwestern Montana. The rest of Montana had puffy clouds with the top half of the sun peeking over them. Sun Chief. In Florida he had a happy face.

Sylvester had forgotten to turn up the sound, and as he sat trying to decide if it was worth the effort, the phone rang. He slid across the couch to an end table and picked up the receiver. In spite of a vague hope, he knew it wouldn't be Shelley.

"Hello?"

"Sylvester, it's me. We have to talk."

Hadn't he just heard that? Or was it last week he had told that to Shelley on the phone? But this wasn't Shelley.

〰〰〰〰

"Come in," she said. All the lights were on in the small apartment, and even that seemed wrong. He took off his light parka and Patti Ann took it from him and hung it in the foyer closet. "Come sit down. Would you like a drink?"

"I'd better not. I have some work to finish tonight." He sat down on the couch and looked up at her. She was wearing blue jeans, gray sweatshirt, and light-blue running shoes. Even in this informal dress, she was beautiful, her long auburn hair haloed by a floor lamp behind her. But there was a stark, almost plain look to her set mouth.

"What's up?" said Sylvester.

"It's a long story—I don't know where to start—and I'm not even sure now how much I'm going to tell you." She sat two feet away, facing him, one leg tucked under the other. She looked at him as though she were assessing his need to know; then she leaned toward the coffee table, picked a cigarette from a pack, and lit it with a plastic lighter. All the gestures were automatic, without thought, but her dark eyes, as she blew the smoke quickly into the air above them, were bright with concern.

"Oh God, Sylvester, I honestly don't know how to do this. I know you'll hate me."

"Is it about the will?"

"That and much more. I think you've guessed the will was a fake, a lie to get to know you, to figure you out. I had to do it."

"Why?"

"Somebody made me. Somebody wanted to know all about you—"

"Who?" Sylvester leaned toward her and put his hand on her knee. "Who, Patti Ann?"

She turned her head and tears glistened in the glow of lamplight. She sat like that, almost in profile, for a few seconds, the cigarette smoke curling into the light behind her.

Then she swallowed and turned toward him and the tears were lost in the shadows of her long hair. "My husband," she said.

Sylvester let his hand drop from her knee to the couch and he sat back and looked at it. He shouldn't have been surprised by the fact that she had a husband, and he wasn't. But he knew that was the simple part.

"Who is your husband?" he said.

She looked as though she were about to cry as she put the still-burning cigarette into the ashtray on the coffee table. But she didn't, and her voice didn't crack as she told him. There were long pauses, and she lit another cigarette that she left burning in the ashtray. Once she put her hands to her cheeks, and once she said "Oh God" when she told him how long her husband had been in, as though time, the length of it, had dawned on her in the telling.

Sylvester knew, early on in her story, what the point of it was. He had thought of it often—one night he had even dreamed about it, but he'd had lots of strange dreams in his first year or two on the parole board. Somehow it never seemed possible in real life. The distance created by the table between the board members and the inmates made the hearings, for the most part, polite, formal, almost impersonal. Once in a while the members joked with an inmate or made a special effort to help him get treatment or arranged contacts for him. Once in a while the hearing deteriorated into a yelling match, ending with an inmate stalking out of the room, telling the board where they could stick their parole. But it all ended there in the hearings room. There was no contact on the outside. When Sylvester drove home after the two days at

Deer Lodge, he was able to put MSP and its inmates out of his mind.

Blackmail. The real thing.

He realized she had told him all about her husband except for his name. "What's his name—what's your name?" he said.

She hesitated.

"What's his name?" he said.

She looked away and said, "Harwood—Jack Harwood. That's my last name too. The Patti Ann is real."

Sylvester rested his head against the back of the couch and closed his eyes. Will the real Patti Ann stand up? he thought. That was a game show he used to watch with his grandfather. One contestant was real, the other two were fakes. When the announcer would say, "Will the real so-and-so stand up," they would all shuffle their feet and place their hands on the edge of the table, but only one would rise. The real Patti Ann Harwood. He remembered the name now, from Harwood's file.

And of course Sylvester remembered Jack Harwood. He very seldom forgot an inmate of Harwood's caliber. It was the punks, the wimps, the seemingly endless parade of inter-changeable losers that Sylvester forgot. He forgot them the way one doesn't see grocery items that aren't on the list. But Jack Harwood was on the list. Bright, educated, clean-cut, good-looking, a mystery, maybe even a flake. He committed crimes because he was fascinated by crime. Sylvester almost smiled when he thought of Pete Higgins's reaction to this. Then he thought of something else. He opened his eyes and leaned forward, toward Patti Ann.

"He was stabbed by an Indian," he said. "In the library. A little over a year ago."

"And he hasn't been the same since. He's frightened, Sylvester. He wanted so badly to make his parole. He has to get out—I'm afraid, by hook or by crook. Don't you see?" Now her dark eyes were bottomless as she looked into Sylvester's. This time she touched him, on the thigh. "He has to get out or something bad will happen!"

Sylvester looked at the hand on his thigh, the rose-colored nails, the soft knuckles, one blue vein that ran back to the wrist. Another time, it would have been provocative, just there.

"And your role?"

"It's pretty obvious, isn't it? At least, it is now. In the beginning I didn't know what my role was. I was supposed to meet you, get some information, where you worked, are you married, stuff like that." Her voice was no longer beseeching. Instead, a bitterness had tightened her face and the voice was flat. "I honestly didn't know what the information was for. Maybe I thought he was going to write you a letter, or even hire you, I don't know. I don't know how things work in prison.

"Oh, God, if he had made his parole none of this would have happened. Jack and I would be sitting here right now. I never would have met you and gotten you involved." Again, her eyes became dark and deep. "Isn't there some way, Sylvester? Please, couldn't you do something, something to get us out of this mess? I know I'm to blame and I have no right—"

"There's nothing I can do, Patti Ann. God, I wish now there was something, but it would look suspect if I suddenly decided Jack Harwood deserved another look." Sylvester put his hand on hers. "I don't know, maybe I could get him an appearance at his annual review. That's less than a year away—"

"He'll be dead by then—don't you understand? He's afraid the Indians will get him—" Patti Ann stopped, her mouth still open, frozen by some kind of recognition that was only half formed.

"And he chose me to blackmail." Sylvester smiled and shook his head. "The only Indian on the board. Not only is he trying to blackmail me, he's getting his revenge too. Pretty neat."

"Jack wouldn't think of a thing like that. He's too—"

"Yes he would. He would think of exactly a thing like that." Sylvester was remembering the holdup money, the unaccounted nine thousand. He was clever, the way he attempted to shift the direction away from himself without being too obvious. "Just for information's sake, what became of the nine thousand? You needn't worry, it won't go beyond this room."

Patti Ann looked off. "It went for my operation. I had a hysterectomy. Jack didn't want me to be burdened with such a large debt."

"Did you know it was against the law to take it?"

"Yes. I didn't want it, but he was insistent. He was different then. I know you won't believe me, but he was a sweet man, in spite of his mistakes. He wanted to take care of me— even in prison."

"He escaped to be with you—when you had your operation."

She looked at him, then withdrew her hand. "I suppose you have lots of information about us in your files."

"Apparently not enough." Sylvester paused, not wanting to ask the next question but needing to. "When did you two decide to escalate this blackmail—to fuck me?"

Patti Ann looked as if she had just been slapped. Her eyes grew round and her cheeks reddened. "I never decided to—not that way! I didn't even know what he wanted! Not then! It was only later, but by then"—she folded her arms and hung her head—"we—we already had—made love."

"Do you expect me to believe that?"

"I don't know what I expect anymore," she murmured. "It's true, he wanted me to see you that first time. After that, I wanted to see you again, then again and again. I suppose I was lonely. I've lived alone, faithfully, for seven years. I don't even get out of this apartment much anymore. If I didn't have my job, I don't know what I'd do." She looked up and smiled wearily. "Maybe become a prostitute. They make good money. Would you pay for me, Sylvester? No, probably not. But I'd get better with experience—" And she broke down and cried. She buried her face and cried, not noisily, no great racking sobs, but quietly and steadily in her hands.

Sylvester wanted to reach for her, to cradle her in his arms and let her cry, but he was confused. He did not know if he was her lover or her enemy or a fellow victim. So he let her cry until she was through and then he handed her his handkerchief, but she stood and hurried into the bathroom off her bedroom without taking it.

He looked around the living room and he saw how simple and cheap her furniture was: a couple of ancient wicker chairs against the far wall, too-shiny veneer coffee and end tables, a dining set that looked secondhand, an old green sewing machine on the table. He looked at these things and he understood. A wave of sadness came over him and he was surprised to feel tears welling in his own eyes. He knew about the sadness of poverty, of hopelessness, of loneliness. He knew how exciting a bright, shiny thing could be—a watch, a toaster, a penknife, an unexpected love from another, for another. He had grown up that way. Even when he was in high school, the coach had to find him basketball shoes when his old ones either wore out or he outgrew them. When he got his letterman's jacket, red and black with BROWNING written in big letters across the back, he wore it for several winters, not because he was so proud, but because it was the only nice jacket he had. Now he wore suits and socialized with others who wore suits and fashionable dresses. He had become a heavy hitter in the legal world almost without realizing it. The partnership in the law firm was not unjustified. He had taken on large cases for Harrington and had won virtually all of them. But what did this mean right now, sitting in this poor woman's apartment, involved in something that had suddenly turned so shabby, so dangerous?

He believed Patti Ann. He believed that she had been a victim too in her husband's scheme of blackmail. He believed that she was a simple, lonely woman who had remained faithful to her husband—until Sylvester came along, until her husband decided to use her to get at him. He had been stupid to get involved with another woman. He could have patched things up with Shelley. He felt that would still happen. When she got better, he would go to her, he would make real friends with her daughters, her mother. He would try to become a part of their world. He would try hard.

Sylvester stood and walked to the hall closet to get his coat. He should stay until Patti Ann came back into the room, but he didn't want to see her again. He didn't want to see this apartment again. He didn't want to be reminded of the sadness of her loneliness, of his vulnerability. He had used her too. He had fucked her for his own selfish reasons. He remembered how he and his buddies in high school described the act—getting their horns trimmed. He had gotten his horns trimmed at her expense. And it had almost cost her—and him—dearly. Especially him, the big-time lawyer, the congressional candidate. But he couldn't see how the blackmail attempt could go anywhere. There were only three people involved, and he was confident that Patti Ann could not be manipulated by her husband anymore. She had been hurt too. Her sense of decency would not allow her to continue. So that left Jack Harwood, and what could he do now? He was smart enough to see that his attempt had failed and would probably pursue some other means—perhaps legal—of gaining his release.

Sylvester wanted to run for Congress now. He wanted to put all this foolishness, the sadness of her bedroom, behind him. His announcement was set for the week between Christmas and New Year's. He had less than a month to prepare himself for the event. He knew he would have to put this incident behind him—and forget about Shelley too. At least until after the election. If Shelley decided to come along for the ride, fine, but he couldn't take the time or the energy to devote himself to winning her. The campaign was the thing. As both Fabares and Harrington told him, he could make a difference. He could do something beyond himself. He now felt this in his heart—and he was anxious to get on with it.

He was just slipping into his coat when he heard the voice: "You can't leave just yet." He turned and saw Patti Ann standing in the bedroom doorway. She looked pale and thin against the darkness behind her. For an instant Sylvester thought she wanted to take him into the bedroom with her, and he smiled slightly at the absurdity of it. But she wasn't smiling. Her face was a pale emotionless mask. She had washed off her makeup, but that wasn't it, he thought. The halfhearted smile left his face and a quiet dread began building in his chest.

"We have one other thing to talk about," she said, and she came toward him.

CHAPTER ELEVEN

Sylvester Yellow Calf parked the Saab in the firm's private parking lot behind the Power Block. He turned off the headlights, locked up, and entered the building through the back door. He had become used to opening it with his private key lately and he was surprised that it was unlocked until he looked at his watch. 8:02. This was the latest he had arrived at work in three weeks, but he was still an hour early.

He walked the six floors up, taking the stairs two at a time, part of his conditioning program. The only time he rode the elevator was when he was with someone. By the fourth floor he was breathing hard; by the fifth, he was sweating; and by the sixth, his legs had just about used up all the oxygen in his blood. He climbed the stairs faster than he ever had, but he had a reason. At the top, he stopped to catch his breath and collect himself. Doris and the stenographers would be just starting work and he didn't want to appear hurried—or desperate. He sighed a deep, abrupt sigh, the way he had before a free throw back in his playing days. He tried to concentrate on what he must do and block out the emotions that had contributed to a sleepless night. At last, he pushed himself away from the balustrade and walked down the hallway to the Harrington, Lohn suite of offices. He paused, then opened the door.

Doris wasn't at her desk but her machines were uncovered. The two stenographers were already at work. They glanced up and smiled at him, and he waved, then walked down the hall toward his office. He stopped at the door to the library and peeked in. Doris was setting up the coffeepot.

"Good morning, Doris."

She jumped and turned in the same motion, her hand over her heart. "My goodness, you gave me a scare, Sylvester. I was tiptoeing around because I thought you'd be in your office. My goodness."

"I'm sorry I scared you. I should have knocked or something."

"Oh, I'm just getting jumpy in my old age. It comes with time, Sylvester. You'll see. One of these days, even you will get old." She laughed and turned back to the coffee urn. "I'll bring you a cup when this is done."

"Don't bother, Doris. I just wanted to tell you I'll be making a couple of phone calls and don't want to be disturbed until nine. I can get my own coffee."

"Until nine. You got it."

Sylvester unlocked his office and turned on the overhead

light. Three weeks from now would be the shortest day of the year. He couldn't remember if it was the equinox or the solstice. But the days had become shorter and colder and the whole Prickly Pear Valley had taken on that squeaky blue-gray light that people drove in to and from work, their exhausts cloudy over their taillights. It was the time of year for memories of childhood, walking home from school, sliding down hills until all the blue-gray light was used up, then home to supper. Even this morning, Sylvester remembered a girl from his junior high days, the evening they talked outside her house until long past the coming of night and the cold white streetlights. He had run all the way home with joy in his heart. Dolores Bullshoe. His first real girlfriend.

He hung his topcoat on a halltree in the corner, then took off his charcoal suitcoat and hung it on a hanger. He had to go to court today and the judge was an eccentric old man who insisted that the lawyers look like lawyers. He snapped on the desk lamp and removed files and folders and a small dictaphone from his briefcase. Then he sat back and decided how he would do this thing. Thank God, Patti Ann had had the presence of mind to write the man's name down. Sylvester folded his hands in a steeple before him and he almost said a prayer. Where was that Seventh-Day Adventist when he really needed her?

He leaned forward suddenly, picked up the receiver, and dialed the Board of Pardons office in Deer Lodge. He didn't use his parole board calling card because he didn't want that kind of record of his call.

On the second ring, a familiar voice said, "Board of Pardons, may I help you?"

"Hello, Sandy. This is Sylvester. Is Walt in?"

"Hello, Sylvester. He's out at the prison right now, returning some files to Records. You can probably reach him there. Do you have the number?"

Sylvester got hold of one of the clerks, and after a short wait, Walt Flaherty, the executive secretary of the parole board, came on and said, "How you doing, old man?"

"Can't complain. You?"

"Ugh. Busy, busy. We've got a big board this month. Plus we're being audited today. Can you believe that? The little guys always get it in the neck."

"I thought we were audited last year."

"We were! I don't know, these guys over in Helena don't have enough to do so they pick on the little guys. But you didn't call to listen to my woes."

"I'm afraid you're right. I've got a pretty big day myself." Sylvester paused, looking up at the ornate tin ceiling. "Listen, do you have anything on a Woody Peters? I don't know his real first name, but he apparently discharged his sentence, maybe out of max. I figured it would be in the prison files if not ours."

"Woody Peters, Woody Peters . . ." Walt made a practice of studying the movement sheets, as well as parole hearings dates. He talked to virtually everybody in the yard, inmate and officer alike, and he prided himself on knowing what was happening, who was doing well, who was trouble, what problems the officers were having with inmates and administration. There were always around a thousand inmates, and like a small-town politician, Walt knew them all. Even Woody Peters. "Yeah, a bank robber—I think three counts. He became eligible for parole three or four years ago, but he waived

his hearing. He wouldn't have made it because he had a rap
sheet and a string of write-ups as long as your arm—most of
them Class Twos for disobeying a direct order, being in someone else's house—but the biggie was a drug possession. They
found a ton of cocaine on him. He was working in the fields
and he had a girlfriend drop it for him when she came to visit.
Next day he picked it up. He'd have gotten away with it, but
there was some trouble in his unit. I don't remember what it
was, a fight or a weapon. Anyway they strip-searched the field
crew when they came in and they found the shit on Woody.
He had it in his shorts."

"So they sent him to max."

"And he discharged from there—I don't know, about four
or five months ago. I'll bet you dollars to doughnuts he has
some suspended to finish up. Or maybe a detainer. You want
me to look?"

Sylvester looked down to the end of the room with the large
lithograph of the Paradise Valley. A streak of light from the
window illuminated the strip of Yellowstone River. He and
Shelley had driven by that strip of river on their way to Chico
Hot Springs. That was a simpler time and they were happy.

"Actually, I was wondering if anybody is coming up today
or tomorrow. I'd like to look at his jacket myself." He paused
briefly. "I have a thing where I think he might help out."
Sylvester stared at the golden light off the river. Don't ask,
Walt.

"You're in luck, Sly. Kelly is transferring an inmate to the
county jail up there—Fritz Hennig. He's going to testify tomorrow in a series of burglaries."

"Could you have Kelly drop it off here?" Kelly, Kelly. The

name rang a bell, but Sylvester couldn't put a body to it. Then he remembered an incident. "He's not the one who got drunk with the inmate—"

"In the airport bar?" Walt laughed. "That was Olson. He went to pick up Carlucci on extradition and got drunk with him in the Minneapolis airport. No, Olson is long gone. Kelly's a good head. He's from Anaconda."

"How's Jack Harwood doing?" The words were out before Sylvester could think. The question had been burning ever since last night, but he had decided against asking it.

"He's doing fine. He took it real well when you guys denied him. He seems content to do his time, but I think you guys should give him an appearance at his annual. God, talk about a waste. He doesn't belong in here."

"No trouble with him?"

"Not a bit. He got his old library job back. He's a model inmate."

"Okay, Walt. Listen, I owe you."

"That's right. Maybe you could bump off one of these auditors. They're all a bunch of tight-ass crooks anyway."

"See you at the end of the month."

"You'll be getting your board book next week. Meanwhile, I'll send that file up with Kelly. He should get there around noon."

Sylvester hung up and breathed a great sigh of relief. Containment was the word here, just as in wildfire situations. Plot your strategy, then work decisively. He pulled a piece of paper from his shirt pocket, unfolded it, and looked at it for a moment. Then he picked up the phone and called the number on it.

"Parole and Probation. This is Molly."

"Hello, Molly, this is Sylvester Yellow Calf. Is Bill Leffler there?"

"Yes. Just a minute, Sylvester."

Sylvester could hear some sort of distant noise as he waited. Then he recognized it. Muzak. When did this happen?

"Sylvester. What can I do for you?"

"Hello, Bill. I'm calling for a little information. Do you have a client named Woody Peters?"

"Sure do. Not one of our bright lights, I can tell you. Fact he's playing around the edges a little too much. I was thinking of sending him down to you guys for a revocation hearing."

"We didn't parole him. He discharged."

"That's right. Sonofabitch has got me all discombobulated. He's doing his ten years suspended. I'm about ready to throw him in jail."

"What's he doing?"

"Lost his job, for starters. His own brother-in-law had to fire him. And he's drinking. Might be selling a little dope. He's just fucking around."

"Who's he hanging out with?"

"That crowd at the Shanty. Every known criminal in the fucking state drinks out there."

"Are you going to pick him up?"

"I kinda think we need something more solid on him. It's not a crime to get fired. But if we could catch him selling dope—even public drunkenness would do it. But he's a tricky bastard. He can hear cop feet coming a mile away. You know, I think he's dangerous, Sly. I want to get him off the street before the shit hits the fan. Speaking of shit, he's buddies with another sack of shit named Robert Fitzgerald. They discharged together and came to Helena together. Fitzgerald is supposed to be in a chemical dependency program, but he quit after the first or second session."

"What was he in for?"

"Knifed some guy over in Missoula. I think the guy was a bouncer in a club over there. Judge buried Fitzgerald. He had a mess of priors, virtually all violent. He and Peters are the Bad News Bears and they're going to make me step in deep spoor before this is done. I know it."

"I don't envy you, Bill."

"Part of the job, Sylvester. Long hours, low pay, and all the shit you can eat. But who's complaining? Listen, I've got a pre-sentence investigation. I've got to get over to the courthouse. Randy Edwards. You ever hear of him?"

"I don't think so."

"You will. Young guy. I'm recommending five with three suspended. Just give him a little taste of that prison chow. See you, Sylvester."

Sylvester hung up the phone and leaned back in his swivel chair. Nothing to do now but wait for the jacket on Peters. Jesus, what a mess. Sylvester thought of the night before, how after Patti Ann told him about Woody Peters and the escalation of the trap, he had held her—not as a lover or a fellow victim, but as a man who felt a kind of strength and cunning of his own. He had felt an anger and he recognized it from his basketball days, when he had gotten beaten badly by his man, a controlled anger and a resolve to make his man pay next time. Sometimes he did it legally, sometimes illegally, sometimes brutally. He felt that kind of resolve when he held Patti Ann and stroked her auburn hair and assured her that it would work out all right. It felt good holding her and he felt righteous, defender of a damsel in distress, but all the while he knew it was he whose ass was on the line. Patti Ann was just the means to the end.

No matter. Plan A. Get this Peters off the street and back in the joint. Fitzgerald. Sylvester looked down at the piece of scratch paper. Robert Fitzgerald. He had to be the friend of Peters that Patti Ann had mentioned. It would have been a lot easier to deal with one man. Two was a complication, but Fitzgerald seemed as shaky in his freedom as Peters. Sylvester was sure he could handle both of them legally with a little manipulation. He could get them sent them back to MSP, maybe with new sentences, surely with violations of their suspended sentences. Fitzgerald. If he had gone into a chemical dependency program, he must have had a suspended portion to do. No other reason a guy like that would do it. And if he quit the program, that was a violation. Dammit, I should have asked Leffler about him, thought Sylvester. Now it would be hard to call Leffler without raising some suspicion. Sylvester had used up his luck. It was up to him now.

He leaned forward and looked at the stack of files. He had witnesses to depose in court today. He was still a lawyer. He still had to win one last case before he took a leave of absence. He had to win it for luck's sake, for his own sake. He just wished it wasn't an appeal of a case he'd already won. But he would take it. He needed a running jump into the big race. He did not need any more complications.

Sylvester was back in his office by 4:30 that afternoon. Things had gone better than he had expected. The attorneys for the other side were making noises about a settlement. They hadn't come up with a figure, but Sylvester knew it would be a good one. He would probably encourage his clients to take it but he was tempted go for the win. He hoped his clients would see it that way but they were poor and had gone into heavy debt just to get this far. He couldn't put them through the wringer anymore.

He walked down to the library to get a cup of coffee. Ed Vance was sitting at the long table, looking through a volume of the Montana Code. He had a legal pad full of notes. He prepared his cases as well as anyone in the firm and he presented them in court with great care and thoroughness; yet he never won the big settlements. He just didn't have the killer instincts, and the other attorneys around town knew this. When push came to shove, if they had to lose, they would rather settle with an Ed Vance than lose in court, say, to a Sylvester Yellow Calf. That's why Buster Harrington kept him off the big cases.

"Ed—when are we going to get together for a game of handball? I'm so rusty I squeak when I stand up. I'll bet you could kick my rear end right now."

"Oh, hi, Sylvester. Yeah, we gotta do it one of these days. We really should." Ed went back to his notes.

"You working on that Howser thing?"

"Yeah. Not making much headway, I'm afraid. He worked for Treasure State Power for twenty-nine years, seven months, and two days when they turned him loose. But he doesn't want to push them. Can you believe that? He still thinks it was a mistake, that they'll give him the comp time to make his thirty."

"Assholes. What about his wife?"

"She has no compunctions. She's a feisty lady. She wants to hang 'em by the balls. Trouble is, we can't do anything without his cooperation. I have to be in court day after tomorrow, and so far I've got nothing."

"Well, hang in there. You'll come up with something. Nothing old Ed Vance can't do when he puts his talents to it."

"Yeah."

Sylvester took his coffee down to his office. There was something dispirited about Ed and it had nothing to do with the case. Ever since the surprise announcement that Sylvester had been made a partner, Ed had avoided him. And he had become cool toward the others in the firm. Sylvester had heard a couple of the younger associates talking about it. Usually Ed was very helpful to them, making suggestions, acting as a sounding board to their youthful problems. Sylvester couldn't imagine that he was the cause of Ed's coolness. Ed had always supported him and vice versa. They were buddies.

Must be the famous midlife crisis, thought Sylvester. Ed was probably ripe for it—married since college, three kids, no real advancement in the outfit. He always joked about Sylvester's and some of the others' love life, but maybe he was more than casually envious. He *was* in a rut, and Sylvester had to smile at the unintended pun but he found himself almost pitying Ed Vance, a man who had a nice family and made good money. Sylvester shrugged, as though there were someone else in the room, then sat down and opened the jacket on Woody Peters.

He studied the face sheet carefully. Alvin Woodger Peters. MSP Number: A107-967. Date of Birth: 8/11/52. Height: 6'1". Weight: 195 lbs. Eyes: Blue. Hair: Light brown. Identifying Characteristics: Two-inch scar on left cheek. Four-inch scar on right forearm. Tattoos: Eagle head on left forearm. Swastika on flap of skin between left thumb and forefinger Chain around right wrist. Crime: Armed Robbery. Current Sentence: 30 years (10 SS). Designation: Dangerous. Prior Felony Convictions: (8) 1971, Aggravated Assault; 1978, Criminal Mischief, two counts; 1979, Escape; 1981, Armed Robbery, three counts; 1983, Escape. Parole Eligibility: Anytime. Approximate Discharge Date: 8/12/88 at 0 good time.

Sylvester was puzzled. With the sentence Peters got, he should still be in prison. He should have had to serve at least nine or ten years with no good time starting in '83 or '84. Yet he was on the street, right here in Helena. He looked at the sheet again, and this time he noticed a small asterisk at the bottom of the page: "Sentence Review flattened sentence to twenty years (10SS) and designated subject nondangerous."

Sylvester rubbed his eyes and sat hunched over the file. Aggravated assault, a string of armed robberies. Nondangerous. He was used to the funny ways the criminal justice system worked. He and the other board members laughed and shook their heads at some of the sentences that were meted out in the name of justice. But the nondangerous one took the cake. There were murderers in MSP who had been declared nondangerous as a result of some fancy plea bargaining. It was all part of the game. But now Sylvester was directly involved in the game and it wasn't funny anymore.

He had only glanced at the mug shots prior to reading the

face sheet. Now he studied the face. The first thing he noticed was the long hair pulled back into a ponytail. Many of the inmates let their hair grow long in the joint, but Peters seemed to have had long hair on the outside. The face was expressionless and unremarkable, except in profile. Peters had a long, thin, slightly hooked nose and a long upper lip which made his jaw look weak. If Sylvester had to make a snap judgment on the man's character from his face, it would have been one of a perpetual whiner—a loser who always blamed others for his failures and had the lack of insight to believe that was the case. Sylvester had been wrong before, but in dealing with hundreds, even thousands, of inmates during his tenure, he had become a pretty good judge of the criminal character. Even the fact that Peters chose to discharge his sentence rather than take a chance with the parole board lent support to Sylvester's judgment. As he looked into the deep-set eyes of the impassive face, he saw a dangerous, cruel outcast, more at home in prison society than on the street. And he would return to prison. The only question that interested Sylvester was when.

He read the prison reports, the rap sheet, the various psychs prepared over the years of Peters's previous incarcerations, the trial transcript of the instant offense, and he put together a portrait that could have fit half the population at MSP. Abusive father, alcoholic mother, two brothers who had also done time. He had two children who had been taken away from their mother because of abuse and neglect while he was doing a shift in the Nevada State Prison. His most current psych stated that "Peters has a tendency to blame his former live-in girlfriend, the mother of his children, for pushing him over the edge . . . a passive-aggressive personality . . . keeps it bottled up until the pressure builds . . . acts out in a sometimes violent manner . . ."

Sylvester stood and stretched, then walked to the window. It was dark and it had begun to snow lightly, the flakes falling through the streetlights below. He looked at his watch and was surprised. 6:30. He thought he had spent about fifteen minutes reading the file. He had been looking for something and had not found it. He had had a gut feeling that Peters might have been involved in crime with Jack Harwood. They were both from Helena, about the same age, and both were bank robbers. But if there was a connection, the file failed to indicate it, or he failed to see it. He couldn't remember precisely, but there had seemed to be an accomplice that was never picked up or charged in Harwood's robbery of the savings and loan. The trial transcript seemed to suggest an accomplice that Harwood would not name. Peters got picked up for another bank robbery a year or two later. In Montana, even in a larger community it was fairly unusual for two bank robbers to be working the same territory. But Sylvester had been wrong about this kind of thing too. He had a tendency to make connections, to try to tie the knot a little too neatly. Probably Harwood and Peters met in the joint when they did time together in max. It wasn't unusual for a released inmate to do favors for a friend inside. Especially if the friend inside promised him something.

〰〰〰〰

Sylvester changed into Levi's, plaid flannel shirt, and worn rough-out boots. Then he stood at the kitchen sink and ate a peanut butter sandwich and drank a large glass of milk. He rinsed the glass and put it in the drainer. If he had a plan at all, it was so sketchy that it might as well have been an opportunity for a random encounter, just as one goes after a deer he had seen a couple of days before in a particular bend of the river. If he was in luck, one encounter might do, but that was wishful thinking. What he did know was that he couldn't afford too many. The chance that he would be identified would increase with each visit.

He called Patti Ann, then drove over to her apartment. He parked the dark green Saab behind her car, locked up, and looked into the driver's window. The keys were hanging in the ignition, just as she had said. He opened the door and slid behind the wheel. It took him a moment to find the lever that moved the seat; then he slid it all the way back. Her car had a little road grime and snow was beginning to stick to it. That was good. The inside was clean and neat and smelled of cigarette smoke. The smell reminded him of his grandfather's car before he had to give up smoking. He turned the key and the little Honda started right up.

He drove north out Montana Avenue, past car repair shops, fast-food joints, small shopping centers, bars, until he reached an area where the streetlights were farther apart and the pavement narrowed. Another mile and he saw what he was looking for. On the left stood a squat sprawling log building that had been painted a light green. The word "Shanty," flanked by a pair of shamrocks, was illuminated over the front door. Neon beer signs, some partially out, twinkled in the darkened windows.

He waited for a car, then turned into the parking lot. There were nine vehicles, most of them beat-up pickups and faded vans. He looked at his watch. 8:15. Early yet. He parked at the edge of the lot, just off the street, and waited. The snow was coming faster now, big flakes that wafted straight down, and soon his windshield was covered in a thin blanket of white. He could see the glow of the bar lights and he heard the coming and going of cars on the street, but none of them pulled into the lot.

Sylvester was just about to go into the bar when he heard a vehicle slow down, then turn into the lot. The engine noise was loud and throaty. He rolled down the window just as the engine died, and he saw two men getting out of a pickup. They stopped at the entrance and looked up at the sky. One wore a stocking cap and the other a baseball cap. Both were shorter than Peters's description on the face sheet. They turned and went into the bar.

Sylvester sighed and rolled the window back up. It's now or never, he thought. He had to go into the Shanty. Maybe Peters was there, maybe he'd show up later. Either way, Sylvester had to go into the bar. He wished more people had shown up before he had to put in an appearance. He wanted to see if any Indians, or Mexicans, or any dark people went in there. What if it was a complete redneck bar? What if it was the hangout of the local Aryan Brotherhood? A biker bar? A gay biker bar? Slow down. It's probably just a bar. He had handled situations where he was the only Indian among hostile whites. He had even gotten into a few fights when he was younger and had handled himself okay. The idea was to walk to the bar, preferably an uninhabited stretch of bar, and order a beer, a schooner, anything on tap, and not look around for a minute or two.

He put on a tired old boss cap with the word CENEX across

the front. He decided not to lock the car in case he had to beat a hasty retreat. He was glad he hadn't brought his Saab. The little Honda was conspicuous enough among the pickups and vans.

He pushed open the heavy wood door and walked in, prepared to walk slowly but determinedly to the bar, but the room was too dark to focus on anything like the bar. Only the lights from three poker machines and a jukebox against a far wall cast any illumination. He hesitated inside the door for just a moment until he could make out the recessed lights over the bar reflected in a long mirror. Then he saw a narrow aisle between two groups of tables and he moved forward. A man sat on a barstool in front of one of the poker machines, and another leaned over the jukebox. The others, ten or twelve of them, were seated at the bar. A few looked around at him with mild curiosity. There was no uninhabited stretch of bar, so Sylvester took the first stool he came upon, squeezing in between the two men who had just walked in and another, larger man in a sheepherder's coat. He had his back to Sylvester, watching the man at the poker machine.

The bartender had watched Sylvester come in and now wiped the bar with a bar rag. "What'll it be?" He was a short, well-built man with a shiny head, thick glasses, and pressed white shirt rolled up two rolls at the sleeves.

"Schooner. Whatever you've got on tap."

The bartender gave the bar one last wipe as he studied Sylvester. Then he moved a couple of feet over and began to draw a beer. "Still snowing?" he said.

"Coming down pretty good. Wouldn't be surprised if we had six, eight inches by morning."

Suddenly the bartender said "Shit!" and hit the side of the

tap with an open palm. He hit it again. "Goddam thing, nothing but foam. Shit!" He dumped the foam from the glass and moved down to the next spigot. "Hope you like Lite."

By now all the men in the bar were looking at the bartender. Sylvester leaned back and glanced down the bar past the big man. Three young men, obviously together, were laughing at the bartender. Another man farther down had his head cocked in the direction of the excitement. A cigarette dangled from within a heavy black beard.

The bartender set the schooner of beer on the bar and took the ten-dollar bill that Sylvester had laid out. "Sorry about that," he said as he rang up the till. "Fucking thing's been acting up all night. Worse than my old lady." He turned and laid the change on the counter.

"No problem," said Sylvester. He leaned forward and took a swallow of beer.

The bartender walked down to the end of the bar, picked up a bottle, and poured some whiskey into a shot glass in front of the man with the black beard. Sylvester looked toward the other end of the bar and saw two men talking and two others silently looking beyond their drinks into some middle space that only they saw. Sylvester had never been a bar drinker, other than going out with his colleagues once in a while after work. After two drinks most of them, including Sylvester, left for their own worlds of wives, kids, girlfriends, food, more work. It had never occurred to him that he could stay and drink until the bars closed, that he could go out night after night, that he could end up like the silent drinkers at the end of the bar. There was always too much going on, too much to do. He had heard stories about his father, before he was born, when his father was still around, stories that made him

sick to his stomach. The stories did not come from his grandmother; they came from acquaintances, old drinking partners,
old drunks around Browning who bummed Sylvester for a
dollar or two. They always began with "I remember the time
me and your old man . . ." and Sylvester remembered the sick
feeling and the burning shame, even as a young man, as he
listened to stories of binges that took his old man to Great
Falls or Spokane, car wrecks, hopping freights, fighting, waking up in strange places with his boots or watch gone, lying in
puke and shit—

Sylvester shuddered and closed his eyes and took a long
drink of his beer. He had learned to hate his father more and
more the older he got; each story filled him with hatred and
fear—fear not only of and for his father, but fear for himself,
what he might become if he slipped. He had nightmares of
waking up in the street, stark naked, alone in a crowd of
strangers, not knowing where he was or what had happened,
alone and naked and full of loathing of himself, his father, the
strangers—and his mother.

He had tried many times to understand why she had run off
and left him with his grandparents. She hadn't even nursed
him she was in such a hurry. By then, she and Sylvester's
father were not living together. She could have taken him
with her, or come for him later if she had to leave in a hurry.
He was twelve when his grandmother told him she was remar-
ried and living in New Mexico. That was practically the first
and only real information his grandmother had given him
about his mother. But when he wanted to write her a letter,
his grandmother said she didn't know her address. What if
she wanted him then? He would have gone to her and been
her son. He would never have been his father's son, but he

would have been hers if she had only asked. But she never did, and gradually he came to hate her too and imagined that she was dead, wished that she was dead.

Now, as he looked around the Shanty, he tried to imagine their lives in places like this. Perhaps they had even stopped here once on their way to wherever. Perhaps they were decent people once, the kind of couple other people like to be around, full of fun, good-looking, in love with the world and each other. He had seen other couples like that and he had enjoyed being around them. And he had seen their marriages break up; in his younger days he had represented one or the other partner whose marriage seemed made in heaven until it hit the skids. Usually it was the result of infidelity or abuse, but what made it happen? What made it happen between his parents? Why did his father become a bum and his mother go off without her son?

Sylvester caught himself looking at himself in the mirror. Perhaps that was the middle distance old barflies found—the mirror image of themselves somewhere in no-man's-land with no escape, no farther to go. He had learned to live with the fact that his parents had abandoned him. He had had a good life with his grandparents and he was proud of them for having raised him up to be a decent human being. He could not be a barfly and he could not hate his parents for whatever weaknesses led them into their lives.

Sylvester watched the heavy wooden door open in the mirror and he saw, beyond the two figures that entered, light and snow, clean and dry, and he wanted to be out in it. As he watched the door close, the figures became shadowy. They stamped the snow from their shoes, and the taller one took off his stocking cap and slapped it against his thigh, and although Sylvester couldn't see his face, he knew that it was Woody Peters. He felt his heart beat faster as they passed behind him, so close Sylvester could smell the wet wool cap, but they kept on until they found a couple of stools between the three young men and the man with the black beard.

The bartender waited for them, idly wiping the bar with his rag, as Peters slipped out of his faded army-green parka, which could have been prison issue, and hung it on a hook on a wall behind him. The other man, probably Robert Fitzgerald, sat down and blew into his cupped hands.

Sylvester was surprised to see that Fitzgerald was an Indian, or at least part Indian. He was shorter than Peters, about five-ten, and thin. His dark hair was long and wavy and his face was youthful, unmarked, and cheerful. He could have been the class cutup—Sylvester remembered such a kid from his own high school days—but Fitzgerald had stuck a bouncer in a nightclub over in Missoula.

Peters pulled himself onto a stool and ran his fingers through his receding hair. It was not as long as it was in the mug shot and it was not in a ponytail. But the hawklike nose and long upper lip were there. So was the whitish scar on his left cheek. There were too many people between them for Sylvester to look for the tattoos, but they would also be there.

"Double shot of Early Times, beer back," he said in a loud, deep voice.

"Double Cuervo," said Fitzgerald. "Gimme a beer too."

"How about Lite? The Rainier's fucking up. Worse than my old lady."

"Where have we heard that one?" said one of the young men.

"Yeah, anything. Jesus Christ, it's getting cold out there," said Peters, still running his hands through his hair. He turned and smiled at Fitzgerald. "How about you—you still cold, Bobby?"

"Nah, not me, man. I found me a nice, warm home." He looked around the bar, and Sylvester pulled himself down over his beer.

He wondered about Peters and Fitzgerald's relationship. Neither Walt Flaherty nor Leffler had said anything about Peters's sexual preference. A lot of guys fucked each other in prison but returned to the straight life when they got out. It was a little harder to get together in max, but a little money or a favor—a hop in the sack with a wife or girlfriend, or a bag of dope—could get you anything, even open doors at night.

Okay, big shot, now that you've got them exactly where you want them, what are you going to do with two hardened criminals who could eat you for breakfast? Pick a fight? Good. They're probably both packing knives. And it would look real good if the Indian lawyer was arrested for starting a fight with two innocent cons. An anonymous call to Leffler? In spite of his threat to pick them up for drinking, Sylvester knew he wouldn't. The prison was overcrowded now. Even if he did, the chances of their getting thrown in prison for the next ten years were pretty slim. They'd be back on the street in the morning. So, what? Sit here until they made a drug sale or mugged one of the middle-distance drinkers at the other end of the bar? Chances of either of these crimes were remote. They looked as if they were just in the Shanty for a good time.

Sylvester realized that he didn't know the first thing about the front end of the criminal justice system. He didn't know how criminals were caught. He knew about charges, trial procedure, prison, and parole—but he didn't know a thing about investigation and apprehension. He knew from the newspapers that undercover agents were often used in situations like this, but he couldn't picture himself going down the bar and asking them if they had any drugs for sale. They'd laugh at him—or worse. Drugs were very serious business.

He could confront them with the truth, tell them he was Sylvester Yellow Calf and he knew about the blackmail plot they were involved in and they'd better stop harassing Patti Ann. He could threaten them with immediate arrest. Maybe they would think a parole board member had the same arresting authority as a parole officer did. Maybe they also believed in little green men from Mars.

That left one alternative. He could follow them when they left, find out where they lived. That would be something. He had used up his dime with Leffler—no more information there without complications.

In fact, Sylvester was starting to feel uncomfortable in the Shanty. He was still nursing his beer. The bartender had come by a couple of times and wiped imaginary puddles off the bar in front of him, looking all the while at the half-full schooner. Sylvester glanced at his watch and realized that he had been sitting there for an hour and a half. Several times he had tried to pick up the voices of Peters and Fitzgerald, but there was too much conversation and the music was too loud. He drained his beer in two swallows and caught the bartender's eye.

"How about a shot too."

"Whiskey? Tequila? Schnapps?"

"Whiskey will be fine. And a beer back."

The big man next to him turned away from the blinking poker machines and looked at Sylvester. He looked him up and down, then said, "Whiskey will be fine."

Sylvester looked at him. "You want one too?"

The big man laughed. "Whiskey will be fine," he said. Then he said, "Where you from, chief?"

"Great Falls." That, at least, was part of the plan.

"Great Falls is a real shithole. What's your name?"

"Bill."

"Abner. Put 'er there, Bill." The hand was large and spongy and strong. "Pleased to meet you, Bill."

The bartender brought Sylvester's drinks. "I see you've met Abner. Abner's a wrestler, aren't you, Abner?"

"Fuckin' A."

"Bring Abner a whiskey," said Sylvester. "You want a beer back?"

The bartender laughed for the first time that night. The laugh was harsh and rapid, a long ha-ha-ha-ha-ha-ha-ha, as though he'd been given laughing lessons to practice. Then he stopped. "How about it, Abner, you want a beer to go along with that whiskey?"

"Ah, fuck you, Karl—a-a-and the h-h-horse you rode in on. Just b-b-bring me another Coke."

Sylvester watched Abner's mouth with his own mouth wide open. The man had just started stuttering for no reason.

The bartender walked away, laughing, and Abner looked down at Sylvester's drinks. "H-h-he knows I can't drink."

Suddenly Sylvester remembered Abner. He'd been paroled a couple of years ago. He was from back east, Connecticut, Massachusetts. He *was* a wrestler—he had wrestled all over the country until he got into a car wreck or something. Sylvester remembered because the board members couldn't believe that the big, pudgy, brain-damaged man had once been the Masked Marvel or somesuch. After the wreck, he had continued to travel the country, but this time on the bum. He had a rap sheet filled with misdemeanors—bad checks, several counts of defrauding an innkeeper, vagrancy, public drunkenness, indecent exposure—and one negligent homicide. Sylvester couldn't remember what the particulars were, but it had something to do with Abner's strength and lack of mental capacity.

Abner was looking at Sylvester again, but it was with an animal curiosity, not recognition. It had been clear during the hearing that Abner would probably not recognize his own mother. He had belonged in the state hospital, not prison, but Warm Springs did not take people from the prison. So Abner had been warehoused until his parole date. The board sent him to a pre-release center in Great Falls and paroled him out of there. He must not have liked Great Falls.

Sylvester looked at Abner and Abner smiled. "Whatcha thinking, Bill?"

Sylvester felt like saying that you're doing all right out here, Abner—you know the bartender's name, you know you're not supposed to drink, you can talk without stuttering all the time like you did in prison. Lil Abner. That was his name, his wrestling name.

"Oh, I was just wondering . . ." Now was the time. Abner didn't recognize him. He could do it. "I was wondering if you knew those two men down there, those two buddies, three or four stools down?"

Abner leaned forward and craned his neck.

"I just thought I recognized them," said Sylvester. Abner's

short-term memory seemed pretty good, but he'd been out for a couple of years. Maybe a few brain cells were starting to regenerate. Sylvester started to get nervous as Abner continued to look down the bar. "Forget it, Abner, probably no one."

"Yeah," said Abner. He sat back on the stool. "Yeah, those guys. They come in every night almost. I seen them before, before here." He rubbed his bushy head, trying to think.

Sylvester leaned forward. Peters was talking to the man with the black beard, who was nodding. He had a serious frown. Sylvester got up and walked down the bar. He walked slowly and when he got behind Peters and Fitzgerald, he stopped and looked at a painting of the Shanty. He had seen some bad prison art, as well as good, and this rivaled the worst. But he wasn't there to criticize art.

"He's a shit. He ain't got nothin' you want. Man, all his stuff is sad shit. Now me, I can get you a reconditioned four-barrel dirt cheap. . . ."

Sylvester moved on toward the men's room. His legs were weak from the tension of standing there, not more than two feet away from Woody Peters, the man who was out to get him. He closed the door behind him and leaned against it. Leffler was right. The place was a den of thieves. How many others out there had been in prison? How many had come up for a parole hearing? Sylvester breathed deeply, then let the air out in a slow hiss. It was just a matter of time before somebody recognized him, if not tonight, then another. He had seen parolees on the street downtown, but there was an unspoken rule that you did not acknowledge them and they didn't acknowledge you. You both passed along with the smallest flicker of recognition. But this was dangerous. He was on their turf and he was stupid and fair game. This was definitely not the way to deal with Woody Peters and Robert Fitzgerald.

He opened the door and walked out into the dark room. He kept his head down but as he passed behind Peters, he looked up slightly and he saw Peters's blue eyes looking directly into his. There was a grin on Peters's face. "Howdy, pard," he said, and the grin broadened.

Sylvester kept walking, his heart pounding in his chest, until he reached his stool. He reached in for his shot, but the glass was empty and nearer Abner than it had been. The several dollars he had left on the bar were gone too. Abner had his back to him, again watching a couple of men playing the poker machines. Sylvester hesitated for a moment, then turned and walked deliberately toward the door. He wanted to, but didn't dare, look back toward Peters and Fitzgerald. He pushed open the door and walked out, letting it close silently behind him. The snow was coming down harder and there were a good five or six inches of light powder on the ground. He kicked his way through it and thought of the tracks he was leaving, from the door to the Honda, which was parked on the edge of the parking lot. Sylvester did not turn around until he reached the car and opened the door. He glanced back but they had not followed him. He leaned over and wiped off the windshield with his bare hand, then got in and fumbled with the keys. There were seven keys on the chain and he tried three before the fourth went into the ignition. He turned it and the car started right up and Sylvester almost crumpled into the seat in gratitude, but he put it in gear and let out the clutch. Once on the street, he drove slowly back toward town and he began to relax. He couldn't quite believe he had done this thing, had actually gone to a bar he knew would be dangerous, not only to an ordinary citizen, but especially to a parole board member who had turned down and revoked many paroles. Inmates had a lot of time to think in the joint and quite often they thought of revenge. He was absolutely sure that Peters knew who he was. The question was how he knew. He hadn't come up for parole. There had been no official contact between them. The only other possibility was that Peters had been told who he was by Harwood and had made a point of finding out what Sylvester looked like. He had stalked him and had been much better at it than Sylvester had been at stalking him. Woody Peters had been invisible.

Sylvester stopped for a traffic light on Custer Avenue. The street widened here and was lit by strip business signs. Most of the businesses were closed but there was enough light from the red, yellow, green, blue signs to comfort Sylvester. The snow even seemed lighter here. He drummed his fingers on the steering wheel and looked to his left and right, but there was no traffic. Two cars waited across the intersection. He glanced in the rearview mirror. Nothing. He saw, out of the corner of his eye, something glint in the overhead arc light on the passenger seat. He looked down and saw an empty pint bottle. He picked it up and turned it over: Early Times. He hadn't noticed it when he drove out to the Shanty and it dawned on him that it hadn't been there. He was sure of that. As he felt the cold glass, something else dawned on him. "Double shot of Early Times, beer back."

The light had changed, but Sylvester sat still, hearing the strong, deep voice, and he saw Peters running his fingers,

over and over, through his longish, thinning hair. "Howdy,
pard." The broadening grin. Then Sylvester noticed the green
light and he let the clutch out and the tires spun, then caught,
and the Honda crept forward. He leaned over and rolled down
the passenger window and threw the bottle out and away with
a backhand flip. There was no sound of breaking glass as
Woody Peters's calling card lit in the soft snow and disappeared.

CHAPTER TWELVE

Harwood got the call from Nine LeDeau just as he returned to his unit from the chow hall at 6:15 P.M. Nina was on his cleared list of callers. He had just walked by the glassed-in duty station when he heard the phone ring and one of the officers call his name.

He thought it might be Patti Ann. He hadn't called her since her last visit a few weeks before. He wanted to put some pressure on her, but he was a little pissed when she didn't call him in that time. He was also a little worried because he knew what was going on with Yellow Calf and he didn't like it. She seemed to have entered into the conspiracy with a great deal of enthusiasm—after all that high-and-mighty crap.

The officer handed Jack the phone. "Not too long, okay?"

"Yeah. Thanks." Jack waited until the officer had returned to the cubicle and settled down with a paperback. "Yeah, this is Harwood."

"Jack—it's me, Nina."

"Oh, hi, Nina."

"You sound kind of surly there."

"I'm sorry. I thought it might be someone else." Jack glanced out a mesh window. From here he could see the lights of Deer Lodge, four or five miles away. "Things have been a little touchy in here lately."

"I can imagine. Jack, I'm going to put you-know-who on. Just a minute."

The lights were clear but not very bright because of the moonlight reflecting off the snow. Another winter, he thought, going into my eighth winter in this godforsaken shithole.

"Jack—how's it going, man?"

The deepness of the voice always startled him.

"Like shit. How do you think it's going?"

The voice laughed, low, throaty chuckles. "C'mon, don't be like that, man. We're going to get you out of there. Just exercise a little patience, my man."

"What's up?" Jack turned and looked at the officer in the cubicle. He had his feet up on the desk and was turning a page in the paperback. Jack figured he had about five minutes.

"Hold on. Nina, could you get me another Coors?" Jack knew that was for his benefit. A couple of seconds later, the voice said, "Your wife is fucking the big Indian, just like clockwork. Yeah, we got the skinny, man. Bobby watched him go into her apartment the other night, came out two hours later, looking rather rumpled and a bit sneaky. This was after

I called her at work. I think we shook 'em up, man. They're running scared."

Jack closed his eyes and leaned his shoulder against the wall.

"But get this, you better sit down, man, 'cuz this'll fucking floor you—the big Indian comes into the Shanty last night, bigger'n shit—actually, he was already there when me and Bobby got there. He's sitting there, drinking a beer, being cool, but I spotted him right away. I knew he was in there, see. Bobby recognized your wife's car from the couple of times he staked out her house. I couldn't believe it, man. He took your wife's car—I don't know, maybe he thought it would be less noticeable than that expensive piece of shit he drives.

"Anyway, there he is. He made us, man, he's a sharp dude. Your wife must have given him my name, and he must have called Leffler or one of those other dudes at Probation and got the skinny on me. Leffler knows about the Shanty from way back. The cops busted Garner there six months ago for dope, but it's cool there—except for the Indian. Okay, so here's the situation. We know about him and your wife, he knows about Bobby and me and he knows about you and you know about him. It's all on the table, man. Everybody knows about everybody."

"You're absolutely certain about him and my wife?"

"I haven't actually been in bed with 'em, but, yeah, certain as shit. He doesn't go over there as often lately—Christ, first couple of weeks he was over there practically every night. That old lady of yours must be something, Harwood. She's got this goddam Indian slobbering like a running dog." The voice laughed that deep chuckle. "She's in heat, man. We got to get you out of there before all the other dogs come sniffing around."

Jack's jaw tightened and he had to calm himself down. He was used to this shit but he didn't like it. Back in the old days when she came to visit him, he'd had to listen to all the raunchy stuff about what a good fuck she must be and somebody was getting it on the outside. It used to make him think, drive him crazy, but he knew she was faithful—until now. And it hurt worse now. He was an Indian, big-shit lawyer or not. I'm in here getting harassed, practically killed by Indians, and she's out there fucking one, he thought. He turned and looked out the window and he heard the voice say, "Thanks for the Coors, Nina." The lights of Deer Lodge were far away.

"Okay. I want you to turn the heat on now. Get face to face with the Indian, tell him you know about him and—my wife. Make fucking sure he understands you but don't mess with him. Not for now. We don't want to scare him into something irrational." Jack turned back and he saw the officer look up from his paperback. The officer pointed to his watch. "You know the rest, just like we talked about. I want to be out of here in the next couple of months."

"Yeah, I want you out too, man. Me and Bobby are just about broke. We need the big one like yesterday."

"Be patient. I promised and I'll deliver." Jack watched the officer stand up. "I gotta go. Let me know as soon as the shit goes down. I'll be here."

"Yeah, I'll bet you will, Jack. Here's Nina."

"Jack?"

"Yeah, it's been good talking to you, Nina. Thanks for

calling, and you take care." Jack hung up and the officer sat down.

As he walked down to his house, he thought of the day he had arrived to paint Patti Ann's house nine, ten years ago. He was on parole then, but it didn't matter. He had done his crime, he had done the time, and now he was going straight. He would paint houses that summer, then think about going back to school. He figured he could get accepted into the engineering program down in Bozeman winter quarter. He was eligible for a Pell Grant and he could live on that and his savings. He had enough credits that would transfer so he could probably finish up in a couple of years. He had felt good about himself then and he was anxious to get on with his life, maybe in Alaska. He'd heard a guy with a degree in engineering could go just about anywhere he wanted. He'd be off parole status then too.

The crew had scraped her house for two days before he caught a glimpse of Patti Ann. He was working near the kitchen window when he saw her mixing something in a big bowl. He'd heard about her from the foreman but he wasn't prepared for what he saw. She was wearing white shorts and sneakers and a striped tube top. It wasn't so much that she was sexy or built like a brick shithouse, but she had a litheness, a slender grace, that set her apart from other women in his life. Her auburn hair was long then, parted in the middle and combed straight down with a trace of curl at the ends. She had a frown on her face and her tongue stuck out as she labored with a wooden spoon, but she was beautiful, and Jack felt guilty for staring at her but he didn't want to stop. Finally she stopped and wiped her forehead with the back of a slender hand. He ducked away from the window and continued to scrape away the blistering paint, but he knew he had to talk to her, to see if she sounded as pretty as she looked. Jack had never been much of a ladies' man, although he never had any trouble finding a woman for the short term; he just had never been interested enough to look for a woman he might like to live with for the rest of his life. Later, in his one-on-ones with Larson, the prison psychologist, he had learned that might have been his problem. He was cold, manipulative, he used people and avoided long-term relationships. But Larson couldn't figure out why. And if it was true, neither could Jack. Larson even suggested that Jack had robbed the savings and loan in order to get arrested, so he wouldn't have to develop his new relationship with Patti Ann. Jack had laughed and shrugged in mock innocence then, but now he wasn't so sure. Larson had been on the money all the way around. Jack wasn't with Patti Ann; instead he was manipulating her and, in turn, Yellow Calf. He even had Peters and Fitzgerald working for him on the promise of a big stickup when he got out.

But he didn't feel cold toward Patti Ann, not then, not now. When he did find an excuse to talk to her, the next day, he fell in love and she seemed to feel something toward him. He found excuses to talk with her several times over the next few days, asking her if she wanted the storm windows fixed up, if she wanted him to rake under the front porch and paint that too—the other three guys on the crew laughed at his eagerness and the foreman got pissed at the extra work he was doing. But he didn't care. One day he asked her if she wanted him to come back that evening, after she told him she was fixing the place up to sell, and help her plan her packing. He was taking a chance and he was ready for rejection, but she surprised him by saying yes. He didn't know then that she was desperate for money, and the real estate agent had a buyer almost locked up.

So he came back that evening, and the next evening, and after the job was done and the house sold, he helped her move into a small apartment out on the flats and store the rest of her furniture in a mini-warehouse. After they got all the furniture moved in and the bed set up, they lifted the box springs and mattress in place. She smiled and said something, blew a strand of hair from her face, and he kissed her. She put her arms around him, and they kissed for a long time. Again, he was surprised by her acquiescence, by the way she leaned into him, until he gently pushed her back onto the mattress. She was wearing the same tube top as she had when he first saw her and he didn't know whether to push it up or pull it down. She noticed his hesitation and pulled it up and off over her head. He had no trouble with her faded blue-jean cutoffs. But he hesitated again, this time to look down at her white cotton panties, the tan thighs and stomach, and he knew he had never seen anything so lovely in his life. A tiny part of him would have been content to stop there, perhaps to run his fingers over the panties, to feel the soft firmness of her thighs and stomach, but he was soon beyond aesthetics and they made love and it was over almost before he knew it. He started to apologize but she stopped him with a finger on his lips and they lay and rested on the mattress in the hot afternoon.

Jack left the next day to paint a country schoolhouse out of Great Falls. He was gone all week and when he came back Friday evening he went to her apartment but she wasn't there. He was crushed, because he had thought this might be the real thing, the start of something beautiful that could go on for a long time. He waited in his car until a little after nine and when she still hadn't returned, he went to a bowling alley and bowled a few lines and drank Coke. He had nothing more in his life, no real home, no friends. He would have gotten drunk but his parole officer liked to give random urine tests and he would have been sent back to the joint if he turned up dirty. He wasn't ready for that so he bowled and drank Coke for a couple of hours and then he swung by her apartment again but there were no lights. He went back to his basement apartment and read a couple of magazines until he fell asleep.

The next morning he went back to Patti Ann's apartment and banged on the door. When she opened it, he almost pushed her aside but she stepped back and he walked in, looking into the bedroom and bathroom as he did. Then he turned to her and she asked him what was wrong. Although her eyes were puffy from sleep and her long hair mussed, there was an edge of alarm in her voice. She was wearing a short white terry-cloth bathrobe and nothing else. Jack looked down at her long brown legs, her delicate feet, and he became almost sick with desire. But he sat her down on the arm of the sofa and walked a couple of steps away and told her everything that might drive her away—that he had been in prison, was now on parole, and was mindlessly in love with her. He expected her to tell him to get out of her apartment, out of her life, and he would have. He was taking a chance but he had to do it before anything further developed.

She sat silent for a moment, knees together, twisting a small gold band on the little finger of her right hand. Jack tried to will her to look up at him, he wanted more than anything for her to look at him, he was tired of being a number, a name, another inmate, another parolee—but she didn't look at him and he left, closing the door quietly behind him. He felt empty and strung-out as he walked down the sidewalk toward his car. No more, he thought, no more. He kept repeating the phrase to himself, but just as he stepped onto the boulevard grass, he heard her voice. He turned and saw her standing in her door, her fingers touching the jamb on either side.

"Will you come back tomorrow?" she called.

Jack smiled to himself as he entered his house. He had gone back the next day and four months later they were married. He leaned over and looked at her picture taped above the small built-in desk. It was taken the day after their wedding day at Canyon Ferry Reservoir. Patti Ann was sitting in the bow of a skiff they had rented, the Gates of the Mountains Wilderness as a backdrop. She had gone to a hairdresser the day before the wedding and her hair was long and wavy and wild-looking. He liked it and she had worn it that way ever since. Jack sat on the edge of his bed and rubbed his eyes with his fists. They'd spent less than two years together before he got busted on the savings and loan job. Why'd he do it? They were happy together, they loved each other and couldn't get enough touching, holding, sex. Patti Ann once joked that she didn't know marriage was a contact sport. She said this after he had wrestled her into the bedroom, giggling and screaming, fumbling with buttons and zippers, until by the time they collapsed on the bed, there were no clothes in vital areas.

But they were poor. Patti Ann had an entry-level job at Human Resources and he worked sporadically, seasonally as a painter. Each of the two winters they had spent together they lived off her salary and his unemployment until it ran out. Finally he'd had enough of their hand-to-mouth existence and he convinced himself he had to do something—for her.

Jack stretched out on his bed and stared at the ceiling light. He was about used up. If this blackmail thing didn't work, he'd just serve out his shift and hope to hell Patti Ann would wait for him. He smiled ruefully. He was the one who had involved her, and as a consequence, might lose her to the very man he wanted to hurt. What a fucking joke.

"Hey, man."

Jack looked over and Peter Quinn was standing in the doorway.

"What's going on, man? I haven't seen much of you lately."

Quinn was wearing his medium-security khakis and a T-shirt. He had a blue bandanna around his head and a new tattoo on the underside of his right forearm. It was crude and Jack couldn't make it out, but it was clear enough that Quinn had joined the club. He looked like an inmate.

"What do you say, Quinn?"

"Not much. I just dropped in to say goodbye. I got a custody reduction. I'm going to A Unit tomorrow."

"Congratulations."

But Quinn did not look happy and Jack knew why. He knew that Quinn was fucking his housemate. It was around the yard. Guys would whistle and hoot and make suggestive comments to them. But Quinn didn't seem to care. He gave as good as he got and even managed to protect his friend from the bulldoggers.

"Jack, could I ask you—"

"Get the fuck out of here."

Quinn had entered his room. He jumped back quickly. "I'm sorry. I forgot." It was a Class Two to enter somebody else's house.

"What do you want?"

"I'm worried about Freddie, what'll happen to him when I'm gone. I was wondering—"

"He'll get along. In a week he won't even remember your name. There's a lot of action in this unit."

Quinn looked down at his foot as though he had caught it trying to sneak back into Jack's house. "I don't suppose you'd look out for him?"

"Quinn, it's hard enough doing my own time. Contrary to popular belief it doesn't get any easier with time. I've got an old lady waiting for me out there and I don't need any more grief. So look out for your own ass, get out of here, and don't come back. Leave Freddie to fend for himself. He'll make it, he's got something to offer, guys like him always do."

"Yeah, you're right, you're right. I don't know, I just thought—forget it." Quinn turned and looked down the hall. "Well, goodbye, and good luck. And thanks for helping me out there in the beginning. It helped." He started to step away, then he turned back. "Isn't it strange what happens to you in here?"

Jack listened to Quinn's steps echo down the hall, then he closed his eyes against the glare of the light and he saw the lights of Deer Lodge twinkling against his eyelids. What did you expect, he thought, in a shithole like this? Strange is normal, and normal is someplace way out there, beyond even the lights of Deer Lodge. Then the lights faded and he dozed off with his arm over his eyes. It was cold and white and dark and quiet in the Deer Lodge Valley and Jack didn't think or dream. He became the night and it was the best part of doing time.

~~~~~~

Woody Petrs watched his sister Nina work on her needlepoint. It seemed to be a flag blowing in the wind, and he remembered drawing a flag when he was a kid and it looked just like the one Nina was working on. He was a pretty fair artist back then. He could draw horses and airplanes that actually looked like horses and airplanes. The knees were the hardest on horses, while getting the wings just right was the toughest part in drawing a plane. He had spent night after night, after coming home from school and eating, drawing things on the backs of old mimeographed papers the teacher had given him. Then one night, he went out and stole his first car and that was the end of his art career.

He looked up at the high cathedral ceiling, at the two fans slowly turning, the three lights suspended from the beam, and he shook his head in disbelief. He had learned to live in an eight-by-ten cell in the new max. Before that, his cell had been even smaller in the old one. But he had gotten used to it and had been uneasy when he got out and came to live with Nina and her husband. All the furniture was in the middle of the cavernous room and he felt naked, exposed—especially with the front of the house being all glass. Now he was used to this, and as he looked out the front to the lights of the Prickly Pear Valley, he kind of liked it this way. It would be hard to go back. But he did easy time in the joint, he was used to it. The only thing he missed was the freedom to be with Bobby anytime he wanted. They had a little run-down house out on York Road, half a mile away from the nearest neighbor, and they often walked around in their shorts, nothing else. He liked to turn Bobby on. He turned himself on sometimes, just thinking about how he must look to Bobby, especially when he thought about it and made himself hard. It had taken a long time for him to admit he enjoyed being with men more than women. The fact that he was with men most of the time made his denial even stronger. He couldn't stand queers on the outside and he beat the shit out of the few who approached him. But it was a part of life on the inside, something men do when there are no women around, but he had abstained from that kind of stuff. Then Bobby moved into the cell next to his and they hit it off right away. Bobby was young and good-looking, but he'd been around the block a few times. Somehow, this made him attractive to Woody. He wasn't your basic fruit, weak and soft, trying to catch your eye, looking to get into your pants. The first time they did it, it was easy and natural, although Woody didn't quite understand the mechanics of the ritual. He let Bobby initiate the action, and then they were doing it right on his bunk in max, nothing really heavy—that came later—but good and more satisfying than anything he could remember. About once a week Bobby managed a visit. Woody didn't know exactly when Bobby would come, but he knew it would happen when a particular officer was on duty. He learned to look for that guard with great eagerness.

"What are you thinking about, Woody?" Nina had glanced up and seen him looking out the glass at the valley.

"Oh, nothing, just—nothing."

Nina put her needlepoint on the sofa beside her. "What are

you and Jack planning? I get the distinct feeling that you two are up to something and I don't like it. What is this 'big one' you need?"

Dammit. He shouldn't have been so careless, so reckless. That's what always got him in trouble. But Nina was all right, they had few secrets from each other. She was two years older than he was, and they really had only each other most of the time while growing up. They tried to protect each other from beatings, mostly by their father but sometimes their mother, and usually ended up getting beaten themselves. Their mother got beaten worse than either of them and she was still with their father. They had a starvation ranch over by White Sulphur Springs, but neither Nina nor Woody ever went back after leaving, a couple of years apart but both while in their teens. Their mother visited Nina and her husband once or twice a year, but she never asked about Woody. She had written him off years ago. The old man wouldn't allow his name to be spoken in his house.

Sometimes Woody thought about killing them. Over the years, sitting in one cell or another, he thought he would like to get out, steal a car, drive to White Sulphur Springs, and kill them. Do the world a favor, especially Nina. She still thought that down deep they loved her and Woody. Woody was amazed several times over that Nina was so naive and sweet. He wondered how she could have turned out so good and him so bad. Sometimes, just for an instant, he would become angry at the injustice of it, but the feeling would pass and he would be happy for her. Except for that prick she'd married. He had never liked Woody, never, but after much wrangling with Nina, he had agreed to hire Woody on as a roofer. He had even agreed to let Woody stay with them while he looked for a place to live. He'd advanced Woody the money for a couple of months' rent. Anything to get his worthless brother-in-law out of his house. Woody smiled. He had thought about killing him too. Especially after he fired Woody after only two weeks on the job for a couple of things that weren't even his fault—running out of gas and not making it to work that morning, for Christ's sake—leaving his tools on the job site one afternoon, forgetting them, only to have them stolen. A few things like that and the guy blows up and thumbs him down the road. His own brother-in-law.

Woody had been thinking of killing him, along with Woody's parents. That way there would only be Nina and him—and Bobby. They could all live together in this big wooden boat. The guy probably had insurance up the ass, not to mention a fat bank account.

"Well?"

"We're not up to anything, Nina. Jesus, we're just trying to help Jack out. He's at the end of his rope and Bobby and me are trying to help him get out of the joint. No big deal."

"What's this 'big one' you were talking about?"

"Just a job. Jack has a job waiting for him when he gets out and he thinks he can put me and Bobby on too." Woody smiled. "Hey, I told you I'm through with that other crap."

"I wish I could believe that, Woody, I really do." Nina leaned forward and touched his knee. "Vernon thinks you're riding for another fall. He doesn't like your friend."

"Fuck Vernon. What does he know? He just hopes I'm going to fall. He fired me just so I would fuck up. He'd love that."

"Well, he's going to be home tomorrow. He's finishing up that job in Columbia Falls, so I guess you won't be able to come around for a while. He's got a big job over in Missoula, a gymnasium, but that won't start for a couple of weeks."

"No big deal." Woody stood. "I gotta go. What time is it?"

Nina looked at her watch. "Seven-fifteen. You just got here." She started to rise. She was a little on the heavy side and it took some effort. "Let me fix you something to eat, at least."

Woody put his hand on her shoulder and prevented her from getting up. She struggled slightly, then sat back. Woody leaned down and kissed her on the cheek. "I'll call you," he said.

"Do you need some money? I've got some." Again she tried to rise and again Woody held her down.

"I'm okay for now. I might call you on it sometime, though." He looked down at Nina's pretty, pudgy face. She hardly ever left the house, but she always made up her face and combed her hair nice. In her bright orange muumuu and silver slippers, she looked like a Hollywood movie queen gone to fat. She was a far cry from the skinny girl Jack had experimented with when they were kids on the ranch. He couldn't smell hay and manure without thinking about how she had given him his first orgasm in the horse shed, the tight sweet warmth of her hand between them. "I gotta go," he said.

He let himself out the kitchen door and backed the van down the driveway out onto Le Grande Cannon Boulevard. The full moon was bright off the snow and the air was crisp and still. His tires spun slightly, then caught, and he drove down off the side of Mount Helena, down toward the valley and Patti Ann Harwood's apartment. He'd promised to meet Bobby there. Poor little fucker's probably froze stiff, he thought. It did seem a bit pointless to keep spying on Harwood's old lady, but what if something happened? What if she put it all together, panicked, and decided to run? What if she and the Indian decided to run off together? Besides, it kept Bobby occupied, and that was the main point. He got restless real easy.

As he drove across town, he began to think about Jack Harwood and how down he had seemed on the phone. He was the most intelligent guy Peters had ever met, and when they began comparing notes on their various stickups, Peters realized that Harwood was too smart for his own good. It was a game to him, or a challenge, or something. And when it was all done, he let them catch him. Like that was part of the game too. But Christ, why? Taking a thirty-year fall was no joke, especially when you had a sweet piece like his wife on the outside. Besides, he could have made it in the straight world, no question. He had a brain that wouldn't quit and he talked so reasonably, so sensibly, about education and jobs. And why the strong-arm stuff? He was an accountant, he could have cooked the books and made himself probably a lot more than he got from his stickups. White-collar crime was where it was, man. Those guys made a lot of money and a lot of them never got caught. Or if they got caught, they did short time in the letter units because they were part of the bullshit system. No, Harwood was a mystery, a self-made loser.

And now he was down, broken way down. Peters could hear it in his voice. He knew when a guy was broken, he'd seen it a lot in the joint. One minute a guy'd be joking around in the shower or chow hall, then he'd get a write-up or some bad news from home, his old lady'd been fucking around or his dad died, and the next minute all the air went out and he'd be bitter and broken. But there was usually no way out. Even if he wanted to quit the life of crime, he couldn't because he had no social or work skills, no connections, usually no family, and no idea how to function in the straight world.

But Harwood had all these skills and the knowledge and he blew it. He carried the game too far. It caught up with you sooner or later. Peters was still full of piss and vinegar but he knew it could happen to him too. One more bust, one more stretch, and suddenly, poof! The air goes out. And you sit there and you know you've lost the game and you're a loser.

Peters was uncomfortable with the current situation. Even if this half-baked idea worked, even if Harwood got sprung, who's to say he had it in him to plan and pull off a job and get away with it? Peters got the impression from the phone call that it was touch and go with Harwood. Maybe—and his eyes narrowed as he thought this—maybe Harwood was just using him and Bobby to get himself back on the street. It was bad form, against the con code, and dangerous. He would have to know that Woody and Bobby would have to do something about that. It was a matter of honor.

No, Harwood was too smart to back out on a deal with them. He might be down but he wouldn't want to die. What's the point of getting out if you had to die?

Peters almost didn't recognize the next thought that flashed through his brain. He was waiting for a light to change on Last Chance Gulch and looking in a display window of a western store. It was only after he started up the incline on the other side of the gulch that the idea came around again, as though it were riding a merry-go-round in his brain. This time he saw it, the brass ring, and his breath caught in his chest.

Shit oh dear, he thought, could it happen? Could me and Bobby pull it off?

The big score of the century. The idea almost scared him it was so fresh and clear in his mind. Who needed Harwood? Harwood was a loser—and besides, his way could take months to get all their shit together, and the way Harwood seemed to operate, they'd probably all get caught anyway. Peters was thinking so hard he didn't even notice that he had to bear left or right to go around the cathedral at the top of the gulch. He just did it, to the right, and he found himself driving past the county lockup, the dim lights in the high windows of the cellblock. Peters had been in there two or three times waiting trial or sentencing. The building looked cold and ominous to him, and another idea crossed his mind—he and Bobby could make the big score and be in Mexico thirty-six hours later if they drove straight through. The idea appealed to him just then. The farthest south he'd ever been was Colorado and he had spent most of that time in prison. Mexico. Fuckin' A. Señoritas, man. He and Bobby weren't above making it with the ladies. Peters drove past the lockup and laughed and pounded the steering wheel with his fist. Then he grew sober. He had to figure this thing out. One thing was sure—the Indian had to have a lot of money. He drove a fancy car, he was a lawyer with a fancy-ass outfit, he was single and lived in an apartment, not too ritzy. He and Bobby had scoped it out, even thought of crawling the place as a kind of joke. Jesus, good thing they hadn't. They didn't need him getting paranoid, not just yet. Patience. Just like he told Harwood—only now Harwood was out and he was the brains and he began to feel uneasy. He had never been the brains of any outfit; in fact, there had been no brains in any outfit he was involved with. They just went and did it when they needed money, and sooner or later somebody got caught and rolled over on the other guys. The only thing that separated Peters from the other punks down in the joint was that he robbed banks while they held up convenience stores and motels. He went for the big stuff. That gave him status down there. He didn't run with the heavies, didn't play games, but they knew better than to fuck with him. Even the bulldoggers looked up to him. Maybe that was why he didn't mind too much being sent down. But he was getting too old for that shit. He wanted status on the outside, and what better way than to make a big score and show up places with a roll of bills?

Blackmail. That wasn't a status crime in the joint, but who gave a shit? If he and Bobby could pull this off right, they'd be long gone before anybody ever caught wind of it—if anybody ever did. Who's going to tell about it? The Indian? He more than anyone else would want to keep it quiet. Harwood's wife? She'd probably just want it to be over with. He'd scared her something bad that time on the phone. Harwood? Who'd believe him? Besides, he'd implicate himself if he went to the cops in the joint. Maybe. Maybe it wasn't a crime to plan a blackmail. Harwood. He could be a problem—he'd be more than pissed. In his frame of mind, he could go off the deep end. What would he have to lose? His chance of getting out would be gone, and he'd sounded a little freaky on the phone.

Peters saw the blue Pinto beside the curb and he couldn't remember having turned onto the dark residential street. He pulled the van in close behind the Pinto and cut his lights. He left the motor running and reached into the jockeybox for his pint of Early Times. He unscrewed the cap and took a long pull, his eyes closed, feeling the warmth all the way down to the pit of his stomach. When he opened his eyes, he saw Bobby standing in front of the windshield, making a face at him. He laughed and took another shot.

Bobby opened the door and slid up onto the plastic seat, pounding his gloved hands together. "Man, where ya been? It's fucking cold sitting in a car with no heater. I smoked my last joint two hours ago. We gotta score a cap tonight or I'm through with this shit."

Peters laughed again and reached over to tousle Bobby's hair, but Bobby pulled away from him. Peters handed him the pint. "Try this, you little shit." Then Peters looked toward the apartment window. "Any action?"

"Naw. She came home around five-thirty. Yellow Calf hasn't showed. Let's get the fuck out of here, go out to the Shanty. I need a cap of weed."

Peters wanted to tell Fitzgerald than he'd buy him a whole bale of weed soon, but he needed to think things out a little more. He knew Bobby would want to call the Indian tonight and demand dinero. That was the way Bobby was, and Peters loved him for it. But he had learned to be cautious in what he told Bobby.

"What time is it?" Bobby was trying to see his watch in the dim glow of a streetlight behind them.

"Relax. Seven-thirty, eight. You say nobody else has come around?"

"Yeah, a few people went into the apartment building, but they seemed to live there. They were carrying sacks of shit. One lady had a little dog about the size of a rat—one of those fucking wiener dogs, only real little, littlest one I ever saw. Man, can you imagine the personality on them? Little fucker had a little suit on too."

"Christ, I send you over here to spy on Harwood's old lady and you give me a rundown on a wiener dog." Peters smiled in the dark and he felt Bobby's hand squeeze his thigh. And the image of that first night flashed in his brain. Sitting side by side on Woody's bunk, talking in whispers and grunts, and suddenly Bobby's forearm was resting on top of his thigh and the fingers were brushing lightly along his inner thigh. Woody had looked down at the fingers and he could have sworn he saw trails of blue electricity in the dark where the fingers stroked. Wow, he thought. He still couldn't believe it had happened so naturally and it was happening even now. He felt the familiar stirring in his groin and he slapped the hand away. "Later," he said. "I'm going to look around a little, then we'll go to the Shanty and get you a cap."

Peters got out of the van, smiling to himself. He liked to make Bobby wait. Bobby was the one who usually got things going, but he knew who was really the man. "Later for you," he said, laughing, and he heard the harsh whisper, "You fucker," as he eased the door closed.

A small wind had kicked up and Peters buttoned his parka up to his neck. The snow squeaked underfoot as he climbed the concrete steps up from the sidewalk. He walked quickly and assuredly until he reached the apartment steps. He thought about turning and waving to Bobby, maybe flip him off, but that was pretty amateurish. That's something Bobby would do—but Peters found himself tempted to do stupid things lately, and sometimes he gave in to those impulses, like when he'd said "Howdy, pard" to the big Indian the other night in the Shanty. He had thought about that acknowledgment often and he couldn't decide if it had been the right thing. He was sure Yellow Calf had walked by because he knew who Woody was and wanted to get a good look. It seemed only right that he and Yellow Calf should know who each other was. Woody almost spooked himself thinking this through. He had to be smart, he had just become the brains behind this thing and he had to be cautious. But how cautious do you have to be? Could he have already blown it with that stupid greeting? Goddammit, Harwood, what now? Then it dawned on him that he was casing Harwood's wife's apartment, but she was no longer Harwood's old lady, she was just a woman now to be used—and abused. Where did that thought come from? Then the memory came to him of the old con he'd done time with in Colorado. He'd said that—that's what women were for, to be used and abused. He was a scary old fucker. He'd cut up two women, a lifer with no parole and nothing to lose. He liked to describe how he'd cut pieces off the women while they were kicking and screaming—he'd recount every detail while they were eating in the chow hall, and Peters had seen more than one hardass have to get up and leave the table. One evil old dude.

But what if he nailed Harwood's wife, maybe abused her a little in the process? That would send a message to Harwood to keep his fucking mouth shut or she'd get more of the same, maybe a little worse. It would also scare the shit out of the lawyer, knowing they were that close and capable of something violent. Peters was used to lawyers, especially the ones who dealt with criminals. He knew they liked to act breezy, speak the lingo, pretend that you're their friend, but underneath they were always a little scared of you because you pointed guns at people and maybe beat the shit out of people who crossed you. The Indian lawyer might be on the parole board, might have seen a lot of criminals sit in the hot seat, but probably none had actually made a run at him. It was one thing sitting across the table from a criminal, but it was another when one of those criminals came after you on the street.

Peters liked what was going through his mind. The plan was a little risky—what if he really hurt the woman, or what if she crossed him up and went to the cops, or what if the Indian or Harwood went to the cops? Yeah, there were risks, but everything he had ever done had had risks. Besides, there was a lot of money involved in this thing. If he and Bobby made it to Mexico, it'd all be over, they'd have it made in the shade for a good long time.

A gust of wind blew a sheet of snow across the streetlight above the van. Peters looked upward but all he saw was light reflected off the low ceiling of clouds. He glanced behind him and saw the light in Patti Ann Harwood's living room. It was less than eight feet from him. He turned and opened the apartment door and took the four steps up quickly and quietly. There was a small piece of heavy paper taped over the door buzzer to his left. It said P. Harwood. It was yellowed and warped but the name was distinct, typewritten. Neat. Peters thought of taking it as a souvenir, maybe swinging by the Indian's place and taping it to his door. Pretty fucking slick. That would turn up the juice a little.

But Peters turned and left as quickly and quietly as he had come. Once outside, he turned up his collar and hurried down the walkway toward the street. He could feel the snow lighting on his bare head. Got to be cautious. Got to be patient.

Sounded like a song. Better not cry, Santa Claus is coming to town. Yeah, Christmas, about a week away. Unbelievable how it slips up on you, first in the joint, or joints, then out on the street. He thought about his kids and wondered if they were doing okay. Ned would be, what, fourteen, fifteen? Faith would be a year and a half younger. Were they together, maybe in a foster home together, maybe adopted by some good people? Naw, they wouldn't be together, it didn't work that way—kids were like puppies, nobody wants two from the same litter, especially with the kind of parents they had. Bad bloodlines. A criminal and a drunk. Here's to you, Edna. I hope your fucking bones are rotting under some barstool in Winnemucca or Elko. Poor goddam kids.

Peters crossed the boulevard in front of the van. He had to make himself be calm. That fucking Edna was still driving him up the wall fifteen years later. Christmas presents. It was too late for the kids, it always had been, but he could give Bobby one, shit, two. The big score—and Patti Ann Harwood. She'd make one hell of a present, kind of a combination Christmas and going-away present. Bobby would love that. Then it's off to Mexico, bye-bye, you cold sonofabitch, hello señoritas. Yeah.

CHAPTER THIRTEEN

Sylvester Yellow Calf made his announcement two days before Christmas on the steps of the administration building of the Pinehurst School for Children. It was a surprisingly warm day, the temperature around fifty degrees, the result of a chinook that had blown through the valley the night before. The snow had melted on the smooth tan surfaces of the hills and bottoms and lay only in the gray crevices of the limestone cliffs of Mount Helena and on the peaks of the Elkhorns to the south. Sylvester faced into the wind and took one last look at these mountains before he began his speech. It was 10:30 A.M.

He wore his best gray suit, a plain white shirt, and a maroon tie. His thick black hair rippled in the warm wind as he spoke slowly, unsmilingly, of his goals and desires, of the needs and rights of Montana and its citizens, its special-interest groups (indicating with his arm the Indian delegation behind him to his right, then the parentless children behind to his left) as well as the individual, of the need to preserve the land, to protect the rights not only of the conservationist but of the responsible developer as well. He spoke of the right of women to control their own bodies so that unwanted children are not left to face the darkness alone (he hastened to praise the efforts of such institutions as the Pinehurst School for Children). As he spoke, a somber silence fell over the audience, punctuated only by scattered polite applause. Behind him, Senator Will Beecham, a man not much older than Sylvester but in his third term, nodded wisely at the supporters and reporters and TV cameras. Next to him, Congressman Tillman Oakes smiled wanly. He had been in poor health for nearly two years, had been ineffectual for twelve years, and had announced his retirement a year ago. He had agreed to appear at the last minute, having been talked into offering at least token support of Sylvester by Buster Harrington and Fabares. In exchange, Oakes would be seriously considered as a consultant or liaison to a couple of Pacific Rim countries who were interested in the timber industry in Montana. He had only met Sylvester twice and didn't think he had the right stuff. He couldn't say why, but the man didn't have it. Now he gulped against the pain of the hiatus hernia, which, accompanied by severe angina, kept him in a state of perpetual anxiety. He felt put upon, impotent, and manipulated, and he sure as hell didn't like standing out on the steps of an orphanage, listening to the man who was taking his thunder away from him. But he smiled and nodded to a young female TV reporter he'd been flirting with, in his old man's way, for a couple of years. She didn't notice him.

Behind the congressman and senator and a little to the side, on a higher step, stood a small group of children, residents of the home. A nun in civvies stood behind them, somehow on the same step, beaming at the audience. One of the children, an Indian boy, seven or eight years old, in clean, pressed turtleneck sweater and plaid slacks, held a large wooden cutout of a peace pipe that he was to present to Sylvester after the speech. The novelty of his role had worn off even before it began and now he looked both frightened and bored.

On the other side of the congressman and senator, several members from the various tribes of Montana, including the Blackfeet tribal chairman and the cultural historian, looked dispassionately at the activity below them. They were dressed in suits or western clothes. Only the cultural historian wore anything resembling Indian paraphernalia: Pendleton capote, leather gloves with beaded gauntlets, braids, and dark glasses.

Sylvester read his speech from three sheets of paper which kept blowing back over themselves. The podium was too short and he had a hard time both reading and remembering to look out at the audience. He felt as if he were in high school speech class again and he didn't like it. In fact, he didn't like the whole spectacle, the way he was using the children's home for his own gain. He had been instrumental in raising funds for the home for several years and had been playing Santa Claus for the past three, but he now felt bad that he had let Buster and the others talk him into announcing his candidacy here.

The only thing he could be grateful for was that he didn't have to wear his Santa Claus outfit. Somebody had suggested it, for Sylvester would be passing out Christmas presents in the dining room afterward. The photographers and TV people would be there and it would be a great opportunity. Even Buster had blanched at that one.

What Sylvester disliked the most was the timing of the announcement, three days before Christmas. The announcement was supposed to come during the week between Christmas and New Year's Day. He felt that would be the time when the people of Montana would be interested in and receptive to such an announcement. But Buster had had a brainstorm, a mega-brainstorm. ("What's the name of that kids' home you been playing Santa Claus in, aren't there some Indian kids there? Hell, you were an orphan yourself—almost.") And so the idea was to appeal to the Christmas spirit, to strike while the families were feeling warm and good. ("Before good old Uncle Harry goes out and splatters his brains along the roadside with the other New Year's drunks.")

Sylvester had lost that one, mainly because he believed in Fabares, and Fabares had gone along with Buster. Now, as he remembered to look out at the small crowd, he saw the posters bobbing over the faces, red and blue with white lettering, YELLOW CALF FOR CONGRESS, and the large buttons on topcoats and wool jackets, and he became excited by what he was actually doing. All the planning, the strategy, the issues, which had seemed so academic to him, gave away to the reality that he was actually running for office, that he was qualified, not in the politician's way but in his own beliefs and values. He felt a great wave of anticipation sweep through his body and he thought, I am on my way, I will make a difference because I am Sylvester Yellow Calf and I do count. He suddenly felt as though his life had inexorably led him to this moment and he wanted it to be momentous.

He was on the last page and he heard his voice rise and he smiled as he accepted the call to duty with great pride and humility. "I am a candidate for the congressional seat of the western district of the great state of Montana!" Then he was waving and smiling at the bobbing posters and the applause and hoots and the clicking cameras and a hundred faces, most of them familiar, all of them seemingly happy. Shelley was standing near the front and off to the side. He waved at her and she held her hand up, as though she were waiting to be called upon. She smiled at him and it was a warm, subdued smile, and Sylvester wondered for an instant if she would be with him during the next year.

Then he was caught up in a swirl of activity. Will Beecham grasped his hand, then put his arm around his shoulder and turned and waved at the photographers. Oakes stepped down and stood on the other side of Sylvester. He was nearly as tall as Sylvester, but thin and pale. He raised both arms and made the victory sign with his fingers. He was suddenly, hugely relieved that he would not have to face too many more gatherings like this one. He turned and slapped Sylvester on the back, then hugged his shoulders. Tillman Oakes was thinking about China, Taiwan, Japan, Korea. Hell, they all needed timber. He remembered reading that log cabins were a big item in Japan. He grinned and shouted, "Good luck and God bless!" to the small assembly.

Sylvester didn't even feel the tug at his pantleg at first. It was only after the second, third tug that he tore his eyes away from the crowd to look down at the small boy in the turtleneck

and plaid pants. It took him a moment to realize what the boy
was there for. The boy had the plywood peace pipe under his
arm like a crutch. The nun behind him poked him in the back
and the boy handed the peace pipe up to Sylvester. Sylvester
laughed and picked up the boy. He held the boy in one arm
and the peace pipe in the other hand and displayed them.

"What's your name?" he said to the boy.

"John."

"See those cameras, John? They're taking your picture.
Give them a wave."

But John was too shy to wave. He wiped his nose with the
sleeve of his sweater and stared at the cameras. "Will it
snow?" he said.

"Do you want it to?"

"Yes."

"How come?"

"For Christmas."

Then the nun lifted the boy from Sylvester's arm.

"Thank you, Sister."

"It's a happy day for the children, Mr. Yellow Calf." And
she led John by the hand to the other children.

After that, Sylvester posed with the Indian leaders, Beecham and Oakes again, some of the children and staff of the
children's home. Somewhere along the way, he realized that
the peace pipe was gone and he hoped a campaign staffer had
taken it. Then he saw the cultural historian walking down the
steps with some of the other leaders. He had the peace pipe
under his arm. Sylvester tried to figure out what that meant,
but the leaders had seemed genuinely pleased to have an
Indian run for Congress and pledged their support. A holy
man had burned a braid of sweet grass and blessed Sylvester

with its smoke. Caught up in the moment, Sylvester wished he had worn his greatgrandfather's war medicine. Then he thought that would be condescending, but he was now glad to have it in his possession. Just knowing that it was there made him feel aggressive and confident. Maybe the cultural historian had taken the peace pipe to put into some sort of archive.

Later, in the cafeteria, Sylvester passed out presents and circulated among the children as they ate their cake and drank orange drink. He was a little surprised at how subdued, how shy they were. Especially the older children. He wondered if they were thinking about their lives, their futures, and he remembered, when he was their age, wondering if he would have real parents like the other kids and wishing, hoping that someday . . .

By now all the politicians, the Indian leaders, the administrators of the home, and most of the staff had gone. A small clutch of adults stood at the far end of the cafeteria, paper cups in hand, talking among themselves. Sylvester glanced at them and he stopped in his tracks. Shelley was standing with the group, watching him.

"It's about time, Sylvester."

He turned and recognized the young woman. "Oh, Debbie."

"We have to be downtown in fifteen minutes for a brown-bagger. Then it's off to Missoula by two o'clock, then on to Kalispell for the Knights of Columbus Christmas party. Five-thirty."

Sylvester looked at Debbie. She was an older student at Carroll College, probably twenty-four or -five, majoring in political science. She'd been in the Peace Corps in Zaire for three years. Maybe that's where she developed that serious cheerfulness, he thought, suddenly on, suddenly off, whatever the occasion demanded.

She tapped her watch and went from cheerful to serious.

"Be with you in a minute, Debbie." He picked his way through the tables, his eyes straight ahead. Shelley saw him and walked away from the group to a corner lit by a high basement window. Sylvester veered in her direction.

"Well," she said, "this is a fine showing. A captive audience. The other thing outside was nice too."

"Do you think it went okay? I felt a bit foolish."

"You'll get used to it. First few times are the hardest. Pretty soon, your people will have to tell you where you are and who you're talking to. That's when it gets easy. You just shift gears and tell them what they want to hear."

"You learned a lot from your father."

"He was a real politician."

"Shelley, I have to spend the night in Kalispell—I have to speak at a dinner—but do you think we could have dinner together tomorrow evening?"

"You'll be in Billings tomorrow night—"

Sylvester whirled around and flashed a look of irritation at the hand on his sleeve. It had become this way in the past three weeks, as more and more staffers came aboard. He wasn't used to being pushed and pulled, guided and being spoken to in level, condescending tones. Buster had warned him, but he hadn't mentioned that they would all be young and bright, almost like religious groupies.

"—speaking to the Indian Alliance there." Debbie had a small notebook in her hand and a smile on her face.

"Oh—Debbie, this is Shelley Bowers, a friend of mine."

"Daughter of Senator Hatton. I saw you at political rallies. I was a Young Democrat."

Shelley laughed. "Pleased to meet you, Debbie." She turned and extended her hand to Sylvester. "Well, Mr. Yellow Calf, I'll be honored to have dinner with you, whenever you find the time. I'm in the phonebook. Maybe after Christmas."

Sylvester took her hand and smiled helplessly. Christmas seemed a long way off.

"We have ten minutes, Sylvester." Debbie took his elbow and steered him past Shelley and up the concrete steps leading outside. "She's nice," she said.

〰〰〰

Sylvester returned to Helena the following night after his speech to the Indian Alliance. It had gone well. In spite of his fear that many Indians would feel that he was an opportunist, suddenly embracing the Indian way of life after years of living out of it, the people at the dinner seemed quite pleased to have him talk to them, talk with them. They had presented him with a star quilt and a certificate of appreciation. He in turn presented certificates of achievement on behalf of the Indian Alliance to several young people who had gone a whole year of alcohol and drug abstinence. He had promised in his speech to mount an all-out war on all intoxicants on all reservations and Indian communities.

His small chartered Cessna got in a little before midnight and Sylvester walked in the back door of his apartment a little after. He was pleasantly exhausted, still slightly high from the success of the evening. He threw his topcoat, coat, and tie on a chair in his bedroom and walked into the kitchen. He opened a beer and drank half of it in four swallows. He felt mildly guilty but he was parched from the airplane trip. He took the can of beer into the living room and almost turned on the television, but it was too late for a local news report. He hadn't seen a TV set in two days, so he didn't know how extensive the television coverage was of his campaign. He had made the front page of the Helena and Billings newspapers, the two he had seen. The other state papers would be down at his campaign office. He could look at them tomorrow. Tomorrow—he looked at his watch, check that, today—was the day before Christmas. He hadn't thought of presents; in fact, he didn't know who he would give presents to. Shelley? The Harringtons? His grandparents? Maybe he could give the star quilt to Shelley. It occurred to him that he didn't have the star quilt. Another disappearance.

He put the beer on the coffee table and opened the door into the front hall. The wood floor was cold under his stockinged feet. He opened his mailbox and took out a sheaf of envelopes and flyers. There were no catalogues for a change.

He shut the door behind him, sank down on the couch, and began to leaf through the mail. Christmas cards, bills, a letter from the Standing Rock Reservation in North Dakota, two-for-one pizza special from Domino's, Yellowstone Boys' Ranch, an envelope with just "Yellowcalf" typed across the front—no stamp, no address, no return address. Sylvester swallowed hard. He stared at the envelope for a moment, then laid it carefully on the couch next to him. He glanced at the rest of the mail, shuffling the envelopes faster. He didn't even see the writing on them.

He picked up the envelope carefully by the edges and slit it open with his small Swiss army knife. He fished out a piece of plain white paper and unfolded it. The words were typed in caps: SAW YOU ON TV. YOU LOOKED GOOD. WILL CALL SOON. Sylvester looked into the envelope but there was nothing else.

Sylvester stood, holding the note, and walked through his apartment. He went to every room and studied every detail, even looking in the shower and oven, the refrigerator, the laundry hamper in his bedroom. He put the note on top of the antique dresser and went through all the drawers, feeling under and behind the clothing. The sock drawer was a mess but it had always been a mess. The others were more orderly. He looked in the closet and slid the suits and coats from side to side. His shoes were lined up neatly on the floor of the closet. Nothing out of place.

He walked over to the dresser and picked up the note. The letters were all quite clean and sharp. He snorted, almost a laugh. If this was TV, one of the letters, maybe the O, would have a distinct smudge or flaw. But this wasn't TV. This was Sylvester's real, suddenly fucked-up life. A quick thought came to him—maybe the note was from a friend, an acquaintance who didn't know how else to get hold of him, maybe someone from Browning down for the holidays. Lena? His heart quickened with hope, then just as quickly sank. Yellowcalf. Everybody he could think of knew it was two words. He glanced at himself in the mirror. Still the same face, still Yellow Calf. Blackmail. Maybe it hadn't sunk in yet. He didn't look like a cornered rat—maybe a tired rat but definitely not cornered. He glanced at the medicine pouch hanging from a mirror support. He touched it and he wondered what was in it to make it so hard, almost like a leather-covered stone. Certainly something as simple as a stone couldn't be the war medicine. It occurred to him that he would never know what was in the pouch. War medicine was a very private matter. Why hadn't it been buried with his great-great-grandfather? He hadn't asked and his grandmother hadn't volunteered that information. What had happened to the old Blackfeet warrior? Maybe he had been killed in a battle and his fellows just had time to snatch away his medicine before it got into enemy hands. "There are enemies all around." Wasn't that part of the scalp dance song?

The telephone rang and Sylvester quickly pulled back his hand. He dropped the note and ran into the kitchen to the wall-hung phone by the breakfast bar.

"Hello!"

"Sylvester?"

It took a moment to recognize the voice. He sighed and sat down heavily on a stool.

"Are you all right?"

"I'm fine, Debbie. What is it?" He placed the phone in the crook of his neck and shoulder and rubbed his eyes.

"I'm sorry to call you at this hour but I wanted to catch you before you went to bed." The voice went from concerned to no-nonsense. "One of the workers down at headquarters, Margie, got a very strange phone call this afternoon. I though you'd like to know."

"Yes?"

"You know Margie—the little Indian girl from Poplar. A man called, drunk or on drugs or something, very slurred voice—anyway, he said, 'Tell the Indian we need fifty big ones.' I assume 'the Indian' is you. He made Margie write it down."

Sylvester rubbed the heel of his hand against his forehead. It felt greasy. "Did he say anything else?"

"He was quite abusive, especially when Margie asked him who he was. She thinks he was just some drunk—but he made sure she got it right. He was quite insistent. That's why she called me."

"Does anyone else know about this?" Wrong thing to ask. Sylvester could almost feel Debbie tighten up. "I mean, I'm sure it was someone in his cups, playing a little joke. No need to get anyone else stirred up over a prank. Right?" He forced a laugh. "I think we're probably going to get a few of these cranks, a few racial slurs. Goes with the territory, Debbie."

There was a pause on the other end. Finally, "I wish it didn't have to be like this, Sylvester. When I came back from Zaire, I thought, at least America is civilized. The political situation there was awful. Here, the social situation is awful. Which is better? Will either get better?"

"You sound tired, Debbie. Go to bed and we'll just forget this ever happened. Good night, Debbie."

"Oh, one other thing." The practical Debbie. "Don't forget we have a strategy session tomorrow morning. Ten sharp. Shall I pick you up?"

"I can make it downtown all by myself, Debbie."

"I didn't mean that!"

Sylvester laughed. "Good night, Debbie. Sweet dreams."

Sweet Jesus. Things were completely out of hand.

He released the hook and listened to the dial tone. Then he dialed a number he didn't know he knew by heart. He leaned back and glanced down the hall. All the lights in the apartment were burning. He couldn't remember having turned them on. By the fourth ring, he decided he didn't know the number by heart. He reached up for the hook just as a voice said, "Hello?" It was tentative and small, a little girl's voice.

But he said, "Patti Ann?" His own voice sounded husky.

"Yes?"

"I'm sorry to disturb you. I know you were asleep. This is Sylvester."

"Hi."

"Were you asleep?"

"Yes."

"I'm sorry." He decided to plunge right in. "I heard from our friends. I got a note saying they'd be in touch. I'm afraid it's Peters and Fitzgerald—that's the name of Peter's friend—and I'm afraid it gets worse. Peters called my headquarters today and told a staffer he wanted fifty thousand dollars. The staffer doesn't know any more, nobody does, but he's getting dangerously reckless. If I don't stop him somehow, it's only a matter of time before it's all out in the open."

He heard Patti Ann clear her throat, then there was a silence.

"Are you okay?"

"Yes, yes, Sylvester. I'm just stunned. I don't know what to say." Then she said, "I saw you on TV yesterday." She paused. "Sylvester, I didn't know, I had no idea, you never told me—"

"Yeah, the stakes are a little higher now." He felt an anger rising within him, a steady rising that made his voice tight. "These friends of your husband's could shoot me out of the water in a big-time way. I'm not just talking about my political ambitions, I'm talking about my career, my livelihood, something I've worked hard for."

"I know, I'm so sorry, Sylvester."

"Patti Ann—" He wanted to say, You're the one who got us into this mess, but he held himself back. Instead—"I want you to do something. It might work and it might not, I don't know much about your husband, you do—or at least did. I want you to call him tomorrow. I want you to tell him to call off the dogs. Don't editorialize—I'm not threatening him and I'm not promising him anything. See what his reaction is. For now, that's all I want. If he agrees, we might have a chance. If not, I'll deal with that."

"He'll agree! I'll make him. I'll leave him!" Her voice rose with passion, half anger, half wishful delusion.

Sylvester smiled at the pale cupboards. His own anger had passed and he felt a sudden warmth again for this woman. Even under these circumstances, he recognized the frail courage that had drawn him to her in the first place and he wished he could be with her right now. But he couldn't allow himself to feel this way.

"Patti Ann, that's the last thing I want you to do. Do not threaten to leave him. His hope is our only chance to come out of this thing unscathed. You have to make him believe that you will remain his wife, that things will return to normal if he gives up this nonsense." Sylvester glanced at the window over the sink. There was nothing but blackness beyond. "Whether it's true or not," he said softly.

"I don't know what's true anymore. God, at one time I was a small-town girl from Minnesota. It wasn't a particularly good life, but now it seems like heaven on earth." She laughed. "I could be married to the local plumber, have a bunch of kids—oh, Sylvester, where did I go wrong? Why did I have to meet you? I could handle the rest of it, but I can't stand the thought of hurting you, of wrecking your life, and not even for love. I know you don't love me, how could you, and somehow that makes it worse—"

"Don't do this, Patti Ann. I feel more for you than you think. Another time we could have been a hot number, kid."

She laughed ruefully. "Thank you, pal. If we come out all right, could we be pals, even if you're way up there and I'm still—still here? I would like to think that much before tomorrow."

"Yes, of course, a man needs pals through thick and thin."

"So does a woman." But she sounded wistful, as though she were thinking beyond tomorrow.

"Are you still sewing that dress for—what's-her-name?"

"Myrna? No, I finished that last week. She loved it."

"Well, I guess we'd better say good night. Good, I'm glad." Sylvester was too tired now to think clearly.

"I'll do fine tomorrow. I promise."

"I know you will."

"I'll call you, probably late afternoon."

"Good night, Patti Ann. I do love you, you know."

"Yes."

Sylvester hung up the phone, turned off the kitchen lights, and walked slowly toward the living room, reaching into each room he passed and flicking off the overhead lights.

He picked up the can of beer from the coffee table and put it down again. He turned on the television set to the all-night sports channel, then flopped on the couch. Fifty big ones. He probably had that much in savings and stocks and bonds, maybe more. If it was a one-time shot, he could do it—but who knew? They could come back again. Or if they got caught, they would probably spill the beans, use it as a bargaining chip.

He had meant to tell Patti Ann what was really in his mind, perhaps out of spite, but when he heard her voice and thought of her sad life and the increasing sadness he had brought her, he couldn't do it. He had no spite for her in him, only a kind of tenderness that bordered on pity. That's probably why he couldn't really love her. He would always see her somewhere between courageous and pitiful.

He was quite sure that Jack Harwood was out of it, whether he knew it or not. He had put the forces in motion, he was the wellspring, the trickle of clear water, but now those waters were roily, high and muddy, a torrent out of control. Woody Peters and Robert Fitzgerald were in it for themselves, and they were stupid and vicious. It went beyond money now, and certainly beyond the notion of springing Harwood. It had to do with hatred and perversity and a desire to hurt somebody. Sylvester had seen this kind of criminal before, they had sat across the hearings table from him, polite, repentant, earnest—and wicked with hate. They didn't know that you could see through their eyes to the blackness of their insides and you shuddered to think that such evil exists. They were the ones who cut the throats of families or hitchhikers because they just wanted to do it, to see how it felt drawing the blade of a knife across the windpipe, the jugular, the soft flesh below the ears. They wanted to know how it felt to smash a skull into pulp, to blow a hole through a face, to degrade and destroy a human body. He had seen them and he had shuddered.

And now he sat alone in his apartment, listening to the roar of race cars on television, thinking of Patti Ann's vulnerability, his own, his sudden fall from grace. It had seemed so simple in the beginning when all he had to worry about was

Harwood's half-baked plan. He could have stopped it then, gone to the police and reported it. It would have been embarrassing then, he might have had to take a leave of absence from the law firm, there might have been a hearing before the ethics board for sleeping with a client whose husband was a convicted felon, but he would have come out safe on the other side. Lawyers made stupid, even if unwitting, mistakes. But he was now an announced candidate for Congress, in the public eye, seeking the public trust, and he was being blackmailed by thugs. He was playing in their world, and that was unforgivable.

My God, he thought, it was just yesterday morning that I announced my candidacy, pure as the driven snow on the steps of the children's home. Ironically, Sylvester's only real opposition in the primaries, a high school teacher from Butte, had agreed to give up his run in exchange for promises that were part of Sylvester's platform anyway. And Buster and the others had no doubt he could beat any candidate the Republicans threw at him. He wasn't quite a lock, but if he campaigned correctly, maybe slipping over the line once in a while, giving the timber, mining, and ranching interests enough attention, he would win. The western district, in spite of the Reagan/Bush years, was still largely Democratic.

Sylvester idly opened the Christmas cards—most from colleagues and clients, one from Lena Old Horn (without a note)—and the letter from Standing Rock. It was from the tribal attorney, on behalf of the tribal council. It noted that Sylvester had done some pro bono water rights work for the Blackfeet and Fort Belknap reservations—would he consider doing the same for the Standing Rock Sioux. It had to do with the flooding of tribal lands, sports fishery, and the periodic drawdown of the Oahe Reservoir on the Missouri River. The letter assured Sylvester that the work would be interesting and innovative and a landmark case in Indian Country. Of course, the tribe would pay his expenses, supply an "enthusiastic" staff of two law students from the university, and provide him with a "pitifully small" stipend.

Sylvester laid the unfolded letter on the couch on top of the Christmas cards. He stood and walked to the bay window that looked out over the street. He opened the mini-blinds and stared at a small tree in the yard across the way. Colored lights blinked on and off in the glow of the streetlamp on the corner. The rest of the neighborhood was dark. There were three cars on the street and Sylvester studied each one.

CHAPTER FOURTEEN

On Wednesday, three days after Christmas, Patti
Ann had Myrna over for dinner. It was a celebration because Myrna had just learned that her husband had an
early parole date in January. He had been a model inmate
for three years and would make it on his first try. He already had a parole plan to go to Billings to work for a
sheet-metal outfit. He had a substance abuse counselor all
lined up for his booze problem. The only hitch was he
might have to live in a pre-release center for five or six
months, but he could eventually gain passes, eventually
overnight passes, and he wanted Myrna there.

"God, it's been so long. First thing I'm going to do is buy
him a whole new wardrobe, colorful shirts, Hawaiian
shirts! I haven't seen him out of prison khakis and blues

for over three years. Oh, God!" Myrna spread her arms before her and looked up at the ceiling. "My God, I can't believe it!" she shouted.

Patti Ann laughed. "Maybe we should get drunk or something," she said. She handed a glass of champagne to Myrna.

"Just this once I want to get drunker'n shit. Because after this, no more. Kaput. No booze, no pills, nothing." Myrna looked at the bubbles in her glass, then she looked up, and Patti Ann thought she saw doubt, maybe even fear in her eyes. "Do you realize I haven't missed church once since Phil got sent down? I don't know why but there you have it. And I haven't played around, except twice with that guy from Institutions, Marty what's-his-name, and you know why?"

"You don't have to tell me, Myrna."

"Drunk. I was drunker'n a skunk and he took advantage of me."

"Myrna, I didn't mean literally we had to—"

"I know, baby. I just wanted you to know the only times I cheated on Phil I was drunker'n a skunk both times. Oh well—" She clinked Patti Ann's glass with hers and took a healthy swallow. "Oh, that's good. You won't take advantage of me, will you, honey?"

Patti Ann laughed again. She had truly grown fond of Myrna in the two years they had been working together. Big and blond with too much makeup and cheap jewelry, Myrna kept the whole office staff entertained with her snide remarks and colorful language. The only time Patti Ann had felt uncomfortable around Myrna was the night Myrna mentioned that she had tried to take some Polaroid shots of herself for Phil. Myrna had been over for a fitting of the first dress Patti Ann had sewn for her and was standing beside the dining-room table in her bra and panties and purple high heels, watching Patti Ann tack the hem.

"You ever try to press that little red button with your toe?" she had said. "Phil said my thighs looked like two whales that had been out in the sun too long, and my boobs—he said they looked like two faces on Mount Rushmore, my nipples looked like noses."

Patti Ann had laughed, but she was astonished—not by what Myrna had said, but what Jack had said a few months before. He told her that some of the guys on his unit had their girls and wives taking Polaroids of each other. A couple of them were showing them around the unit for three cigarettes a customer. They had gotten a lot of customers.

Patti Ann had only known Myrna a couple of months back then and she had a hard time with the pins because her hands were shaking. She was afraid Myrna would ask her for a favor, perhaps to take some Polaroids of her, perhaps something more. Myrna had only laughed. But that night Patti Ann had had dreams about her and Myrna and she was afraid of how she felt the next day at work.

"Six seventy-five an hour. You can't even keep a cat on those wages. That's the trouble with these big shots, they think a guy coming out of the slammer is going to jump for joy at their pissy offer."

Patti Ann, for the hundredth time, wondered how Myrna could go to church every Sunday and still talk the way she did.

"But we'll manage. I'm hell on wheels with a word processor. If I can't find a decent job right away, I'll work down at the Dairy Queen. I've done it before, honey."

"Have you given Mr. Webster your notice?"

"Tomorrow. Why spoil the Christmas afterglow, right? We'll have a good time tonight. I'll deal with Webster in the morning, maybe I'll give him the old moon shot, he'll like that, won't he?"

Patti Ann opened an expensive bottle of Beaujolais to go with their dinner. It was real French wine and had cost her two hours' pay, but when she hesitated in the grocery store, she thought of how she would have felt four months ago if Jack had made his parole, and she put the bottle in her cart. She wanted Myrna to feel that way tonight.

As she poured the wine into two fresh glasses, she thought again of her phone call to Jack and she felt herself come down all over again. She had told him about the blackmail business and when she was finished, he didn't say anything for a long time. She said, "Jack?"

And he said, "Shit." Then he said, "It's all over for me, Patti, I'm out."

"Isn't there something you can do? Can't you get hold of this Peters and make them stop? I'm frightened, Jack."

"I'm sorry, Patti. I should have known better than to get mixed up with those two. They're totally out of control. It wouldn't matter what I said or did."

"But aren't they breaking the law? Isn't blackmail illegal?"

"Illegal as hell if you get caught. Remember, you and I are a part of it, or were, at least part of the first plan." He let that sink in. "Does Yellow Calf have that kind of money?"

Patti Ann had heard the amount from Sylvester and had told Jack the amount, but she hadn't really thought of the money. It was a lot. "He didn't seem too concerned with how much it was. He was more concerned with his career and his political campaign."

"Yeah, I can imagine."

"Jack, listen to me. Would you at least try to talk them out of it? You could get all of us out of this mess." Then Patti Ann had gotten an idea, a good idea. She stared at the phone for a second. "You could tell them that Sylvester had agreed to parole you—soon—in exchange for their backing off. Peters said on the phone that you were his friend."

"That was before they thought of blackmail money. I'd have to give them something." There was another silence. "Maybe if Yellow Calf really agreed to get me out of here."

"I'm sure he would. Talk to them, Jack. I'll talk to Sylvester. I'll make him see it's the only way."

"Patti—you and Yellow Calf—are you seeing him?"

Patti Ann suddenly realized what *she* would have to give in this arrangement. She was standing in the kitchen looking out through the living-room window at the street. In her excitement she had almost forgotten she was his wife. Now she saw a large black van move slowly down the street, its exhaust blowing up and across the taillights.

"No, Jack," she said softly. "I slept with him, as you guessed, as you wanted. It didn't mean anything, at least not to him."

"And you—you sound like it meant something to you."

"I don't know, maybe it did, but right now it just seems like a long time ago. The only thing I really know is he's a good man and he doesn't deserve what you—and I—and they have done to him. We're in the process of ruining a decent man's life."

"What about us, Patti—our lives? You and me?" His voice had had an edge of real concern. She barely remembered that part of him. Then he said, "I got a message the other day—from the Indians. Walker and that bunch I was telling you about. They haven't forgotten the money. Patti, they still think I have it and I don't think they're going to let up until I come up with something. I'm going to have to pay them something. Will you tell Yellow Calf that much? It's getting real serious in here, Patti. I need you to help me."

Patti Ann filled the glasses half full and set the bottle of Beaujolais in the middle of the table. She had lit two candles. She sat down, looking at the red wine in the candlelight, and waited for Myrna to come back from the bathroom. She had said, yes, she would try anything to help him, and yes, if he wanted her, she would wait for him, no matter how long it took. He said he wanted that, it was the only thing that kept him going, and he sounded genuinely grateful. So there it was, right back to where it started.

Now Patti Ann couldn't believe that she had entertained a notion of freedom these past two months. Even more, she couldn't believe that she had thought for a brief week or two that she was in love with and loved by Sylvester Yellow Calf. Putting the two together, she had actually thought of spending a long lovely life with him, but even as she thought that, she knew it would never happen. She would always be on the outside. Later, when she saw him on TV, announcing his candidacy, she almost wept with embarrassment at her foolishness.

"Hey, why the long face, kiddo?" Myrna was standing in the shadows of the living room.

"Oh—come sit, Myrna. It's nothing."

"Well, God, I hope not. This is a celebration."

Patti Ann lifted her glass. "Here's to the happy occasion, to you and Phil and a new life together."

"And to you and Jack—someday."

Patti Ann smiled and sipped her wine.

Myrna swept her napkin off the table, popped it open with a flourish, and laid it on her lap. "What's in the pot, sweetheart? It smells heavenly."

Patti Ann removed the cast-iron lid with a hot pad and set it on the kitchen counter behind her. Steam rolled in waves away from the kettle.

"Stew! Oh God, I love stew!"

"Beef Bourguignon," said Patti Ann. "I hope it's good. I've never tried it before." She felt a sudden emptiness inside at the futility of her small lie. She had made it before. She had made it for Sylvester when she thought they were happy. But they hadn't eaten it. Was that the night after the first phone call from Peters? No, it had to have been before. Sylvester just hadn't shown up. No, the Peters thing hadn't broken them up, it was something else, it could have been anything else, but she knew now what it was. There was nothing to break up. She had tossed the whole stew in the garbage the next morning, disconsolate and sorry for herself, as if anyone cared.

"Hand me your plate, Myrna. We have to eat this whole pot tonight."

"I'm up to it," said Myrna. "I have to build up my strength. That man is going to be an animal when he gets out. He says he thinks continually and obsessively of making love with me—only he doesn't call it making love. I think you get my drift. Thanks, honey. Ummm, smells yummy. Oh, look at the little carrots. I might have to wear some chain-link undies after that first night, just like in days of yore."

"I don't think he'll be that brutal." Patti Ann had met Phil in the visiting room a couple of times, and he seemed a little shy, even timid. "If anything, Phil should worry about you."

Myrna tried to laugh around a mouthful of hot stew and ended up swallowing it. She picked up her glass and drank half the wine. "Oh, God, that's hot. I'm burning up inside." But she laughed and Patti Ann laughed and they ended up having a good time, in spite of everything.

~~~~~~

Late the next afternoon Patti Ann returned from work and the store with a small sack of groceries. She set them on the counter and shrugged out of her wool coat and tossed it over the back of an easy chair in the living room. She snapped on a floor lamp beside the easy chair, then walked over to the picture window to close the drapes. As she reached for the cord, she saw, in the fading light of dusk, a van pull over to the curb a little short of the steps leading up to the apartment building. It was a dark color, either black or dark blue, and beat-up. She pulled the cord slowly and the drapes drew slowly across the window until they were open about an inch. Patti Ann hurried back and switched off the floor lamp. Then she looked out the crack between the drapes. The light had faded completely, but a streetlight twenty feet behind the van came on suddenly, its white light shiny on the top of the van. The windows were dark and nobody got out. There was no exhaust rising in the streetlight. The street was quiet, no traffic, no kids or dogs. Patti Ann's own car was parked under the carport in back.

She watched the van for several minutes and once she thought she saw a small orange light, as though somebody had lit a cigarette. But the light was too small to reveal anything.

She closed the drapes all the way and turned on the floor lamp. She turned on all the lights she could, except for the bedroom lights. Then she put the groceries away. She put on the teakettle and leaned back against the counter and watched it. When it started to boil, she poured the water over a tea bag in the teapot.

Then she walked back to the window and lifted an edge of the drape. The van was still there. For the first time since the whole blackmail business started she got scared, really scared. She had talked to Jack two days before and he said he couldn't reach Peters. He had called Peters's sister—their line of communication—but her husband was home and she was brusque on the line. She hadn't seen him in several days, didn't know where he was, didn't care. She told Jack he couldn't call there anymore and hung up. Jack was convinced that Woody Peters was on the verge of acting out something that could end badly. For the first time in a long time, he seemed more concerned about Patti Ann than himself. "I'd feel a lot better if you stayed with Myrna for the next few days, maybe the next couple of weeks. I don't want you alone in that apartment."

But Patti Ann had downplayed the danger. She hadn't even seen Peters and his friend, her number was unlisted, and she always locked the doors and windows out of habit. Jack insisted that they would know where she lived—and locks didn't mean a whole hell of a lot to them. Finally she agreed to talk to Myrna, and she had meant to last night, but the right time never came, and Myrna had been so happy. Patti Ann had been happy too and she didn't want to spoil the mood. It had been a long time.

Now she was afraid. She was sure that Peters and his friend were in the dark van, waiting, watching, and she suddenly felt exposed. How long had they been watching her? Had they followed her from work, stalked her in the grocery store, followed her home? How many nights had they sat out there? They had only called her at work once, never at home. Probably they didn't have her home number. But they had been watching her. They could have gotten to her anytime. Jack was right, they did know where she lived, but what did they want from her? She wasn't the target, she didn't have any money. Then the thought came to her, the word right along with it, and she said it aloud: "Kidnapping." Such a funny word, not at all like the act. But the act, and the motive, came to her as clear as a bell. Peters had been escalating the pressure on Sylvester, very subtly, dropping the right clues at the right times. They were working their way up to something, and Patti Ann knew that she would be involved in that something. She had nothing to offer them but herself. Blackmail payoff and ransom, one and the same to them, but the pressure on Sylvester would shoot off the scale.

Patti Ann let the drape fall shut and walked into the kitchen. She poured a cup of tea and tried to think of all the reasons she could be wrong. For one thing, she didn't know that they were in that van. Maybe there were teenage lovers or beer drinkers or pot smokers in the van. Even if it was them, were they smart enough to think of the kidnapping angle? Jack had said they were stupid and vicious, Peters too dumb to do a job right and the other fellow, Fitzgerald, a thrill-seeker. But they really didn't have to be too smart to think of getting to Sylvester through her. She shook her head. If she could only tell them that she and Sylvester were not close anymore, that they were in contact only because of them—

She had talked with Sylvester two days ago, just after Jack had called. After she told him what Jack had told her, he too wanted her to get out of her apartment. Surprisingly, he too had mentioned moving in with Myrna for a little while, until this was all over.

She picked up the wall phone and started to dial Myrna's number. Then she hung up. Not Myrna, not yet. Instead, she dialed a number she had known by heart since the first time she called it.

"Sylvester, this is Patti Ann. They're outside my apartment right now, in a dark van. I know it's them. It just pulled over to the curb twenty minutes ago and nobody has gotten out. It's got to be them."

"Stay where you are, Patti Ann. Lock the doors and don't let anybody in until I get there. I've got to make a phone call, but I'll be there in fifteen minutes."

Patti Ann hung up and walked through the apartment turning off lights, except for the light over the kitchen sink. Then she lifted the edge of the drape with her finger. The dark van was still there, like an enormous shiny beetle. A light snow had begun to fall.

Sylvester pulled over in front of the van, walked back to the driver's side, and flung open the door. The front fender behind the wheel well had been creased and the door caught halfway open with a screech, then sprang wide. Sylvester braced himself on the balls of his feet, prepared to jerk Peters or Fitzgerald out before they had a chance to react. But there was no one there. He leaned in and looked in the back. The streetlight shone through the back windows, illuminating a mechanic's toolbox, several long-handled implements, and a blanket spread over a long object. Sylvester swallowed hard and climbed between the front seats. He pulled back an edge of the blanket, expecting the long auburn hair, the flawless white skin that he had run his fingers over those nights in her bed, but the object turned out to be several pieces of scrap insulation. The insulation was compressed in several places, as though somebody had used it for a bed.

Sylvester sighed, almost moaned with relief. He climbed out of the van, sliding across the cold plastic driver's seat. He forced the door shut with a loud pop, looked up and down the street, then walked up the steps to the front door of the apartment. There were at least three sets of footprints in the dry snow cover. Sylvester backtracked down the steps to the sidewalk, then the boulevard beside the van. The footprints started from there.

This time he took the steps in two leaps, but then made himself slow down. He had lost the element of surprise. He walked to the front door, opened it, and walked up the three steps. He hesitated outside Patti Ann's door, put his ear to it. Nothing. He knocked.

Patti Ann opened the door as though she had been waiting

with her hand on the knob. She was wearing a blue sweater dress with matching blue high heels. She hadn't changed into her sweatshirt and jeans. He tried to read her face, but there was little expression on it.

"Come in," she said, and there was little expression in her voice.

Peters and Fitzgerald were sitting on the couch a couple of feet apart. They both looked a little uncomfortable, in spite of their smiles, as though they weren't used to dealing with victims up close.

"I think you know these two," said Patti Ann.

"Evening, Senator," said Fitzgerald.

"Congressman," corrected Peters. "This man is going to be our new congressman, Bobby."

Sylvester glanced back at Patti Ann.

"I invited them in," she said, closing the door. "I wanted both of us to hear what they had to say."

"That's right. All very civilized. We're not trying to horn in on your action, Mr. Congressman. We're businessmen, not lovers." Peters actually had a tie and sport coat on under the green parka. "Sit down. Perhaps we could prevail on our hostess to bring some refreshments."

Sylvester turned a dining-room chair around and sat with his arms over its back. He was wearing a Pendleton shirt underneath an anorak, Levi's, and rough-out boots. "What do you want?" he said.

"How about a beer?" said Fitzgerald.

"No," Peters laughed. "I think he means, what do we want on a grander scale, don't you, Mr. Yellow Calf?"

Sylvester decided to take a chance. "Bill Leffler knows

about you two. He's been waiting for you to fuck up so he can take you down. He knows you're mixed up in drugs down at the Shanty."

"Well, then, it's up to you to protect us, brother."

"He and I had a long talk the other day. I didn't mention any names, but I left him with the impression you two are trying to blackmail somebody prominent. I told him you found out something in the joint that could be damaging to that person. He didn't like that. He doesn't like trouble but he said it was up to him and the police to protect citizens from people like you and he didn't care how they did it." Sylvester decided to let it all hang out. He had made up his mind coming over that he would try to bluff them. He had actually tried to call Leffler, but the probation officer had left the office and wasn't home yet.

Peters sat forward, patting his parka away from his sides, like a gunslinger getting ready for some action. "You know what I think, Mr. fucking Indian lawyer? I think you're full of shit and you're wasting our time."

Fitzgerald laughed. "Listen to the man. You trying to pull our chain, man?"

"I'm not done yet," said Sylvester, ignoring Fitzgerald. He was in too deep to back away now. "I can get you out of this. You said it, I'm a lawyer. I'm pretty sure I can persuade Leffler to let it go. He's probably down at the police station right now. You know a probation officer doesn't need any paper to take you guys off the street anytime he wants. He says you violated probation, you're on your way back to Deer Lodge, no more shots of Early Times, no more fucking around with your buddy there."

This time Fitzgerald shifted forward. He looked at Sylvester with his mouth open, his dark almost-pretty face suddenly flushed. "Hey, man . . ."

"Shut up, Bobby. Just sit there." Peters smiled. "Okay, pal, if you're finished with this bullshit, let's talk business. Fifty grand and we're on our way to Mexico, out of your life for good, adios. You have my word on it, as a businessman and a gentleman."

"You don't seem to understand, Peters. I'm giving you a chance to fold this thing up quietly. You can disappear right now, tonight——I can get Leffler to issue you a transfer to another district, maybe out of state later. All legal and no questions."

"Cut the shit, man. We got you over a barrel and your pants are down around your ankles. Check it out, Bobby. This dude is in serious trouble and he doesn't even know it."

"Maybe we ought to show him what kind of business we're in." Fitzgerald looked at Patti Ann and grinned. "You'd like to see my business, wouldn't you, Mrs. Harwood?"

"Cool it, Bobby." Peters laughed. "Bobby has a serious personality disorder. He's highly impulsive, that's what they told him in the joint, highly impulsive and prone to acting out. One dangerous motherfucker."

"The alternative is another shift at MSP. You've got ten years to do on your probation. Your friend there has a pretty good stretch too." Sylvester glanced at Patti Ann, who was standing tensely behind the easy chair. The light from the kitchen haloed her auburn hair. He really wished she wasn't there, but it was too late. He had to go on. "You see, I figured it out the other day. I'm not so committed to running for office that I have to take shit from guys like you. In fact, I've decided to drop out, right now, this very moment. I'm no longer in the running. I have nothing to lose. My law career might suffer a bit, I might even have to move to another town to practice, but that's all right too. The change will do me good."

Peters sat back and stared at Sylvester. He ran his fingers through his long, thin hair, and Sylvester saw the swastika on the flap of skin between his thumb and forefinger. He remembered it from Peter's jacket. That was another thing. Sylvester would have to resign from the parole board. He could definitely live with that.

"Five thou," said Peters. "Enough to get us on the road. You don't have to drop out of your fucking race, you don't have to leave town, you can shack up with Harwood's woman here—"

Sylvester didn't say anything for a moment. He looked from Peters to Fitzgerald, then back at Peters. Peters was smiling. Sylvester heard the refrigerator kick on, and it was the only sound in the apartment.

Finally Fitzgerald said, "Better take it, man. I can guarantee you I'm gone. This is the last this state's going to see of me, you better believe it. I'm gone." Fitzgerald was talking fast. "You and Harwood's squeeze can fuck your brains out for all I care. Knock yourselves out."

Sylvester remained silent. He knew he was taking a chance, but this was the crucial moment. He watched Peters's smile freeze on his face, no longer easy, no longer menacing.

"You'd better just leave." It was the first time Patti Ann had spoken since letting Sylvester in. She spoke softly, almost inaudibly against the noise of the refrigerator behind her. "It's over."

And just like that, it *was* over. Bobby, who was perched on the edge of the couch, looked up at Patti Ann. He seemed confused, as though her tone of voice belonged in another conversation. He frowned, then stood quickly. "C'mon, man, they're wacko. I'm not ready to go back to the fucking joint, not for something like this. I mean it, Woody."

Sylvester stood too and walked over to Patti Ann. He put his arm around her, and they both looked at Peters, who was still slouched on the couch. He watched his fingers drum a deliberate beat on a doily. Then he heaved himself up, smoothed his tie, and walked to the door. He had to pass in front of Sylvester, and he stopped less than three feet away. He was a couple of inches shorter than Sylvester, but his gaze was firm. "You're fucking lucky, you know that? I've thought of killing people for less than this, just for being assholes." Then he turned and opened the door and walked out, Fitzgerald warily dogging his footsteps.

Patti Ann started to say something, but Sylvester put his finger to her lips. He locked the door, then walked over to the picture window. He stood looking out at the snowy street. He watched Fitzgerald sweep the snow off the windshield with his gloved hand. Peters was already inside and the motor was running. Finally Fitzgerald jumped in and slammed the door against the cold wind that had begun to move the snow horizontally. The black van crept off and Sylvester watched it until he couldn't see the taillights anymore.

He dropped the drape and turned. Patti Ann was holding a bottle of Canadian Club by the neck. "Please," he said, and watched her pour a half inch into two water glasses.

She crossed the room and Sylvester studied the blue dress, the slim legs, the bright blue high heels, and he wondered what his life would be like from that moment on. She handed him his drink and they clinked glasses, each looking into the other's eyes as they drank.

Patti Ann lowered her glass and tilted her head back, her eyes closed. "We did it," she said. "You bluffed them," and Sylvester wanted to reach out, to stroke the lovely white neck, to take the empty glass with the faint lipstick mark on its rim from her hand, to fold her in his arms, but he suddenly felt weak and chilled, as though a great wind had rushed through his life and he hadn't yet assessed the damage.

He did reach out and take her hand and it was warm. He was grateful, and relieved that he hadn't taken more.

CHAPTER FIFTEEN

Sylvester called Buster Harrington the next morning at seven-thirty. The snow and wind had quit sometime during the night. The day had not lightened enough for Sylvester to tell whether it was clear or not, but a thin drift of fog moved through the streetlights' glow, a sign that the sun would be out by late morning. The street beside his house had become an arterial in the past half-year for a large housing development to the north. He watched the early-morning headlights begin and for once he didn't mind.

"Buster, this is Sylvester. Hope I didn't wake you. I know you don't generally go in on Fridays."

"Sly. Oh, yeah. No, I'm awake. What's up?"

"I have to see you today."

"What about?"

"Everything."

"Ten o'clock. My office."

"Great."

"This is bad, isn't it?"

"Not good."

Sylvester took a long hot shower and he caught himself whistling a tune that he had learned in grade school, way back in grade school, first or second grade. He sang. "Did you wash your neck and ears, Billy boy, Billy boy, did you wash your face and hands, charming Billy . . ." He stopped and tried to remember the rest of the words, but the only phrase he could come with was "I am wise for I do know my health habits." Not a great song, but instructional, part of the reservation health plan.

Sylvester dressed and fried a couple of eggs and made toast. He couldn't remember when he had gotten the eggs, but the bread was a gift from one of the women at his campaign headquarters. It was only slightly stale. He carried his breakfast into the living room and sat on the couch and ate off the coffee table. He listened to Morning Edition on public radio. One of the features concerned a drought in Navajo country. The sheep were starving and the crops had dried up. As always, there were a lot of sound effects, rustling stalks, footsteps over what seemed to be gravel, wind soughing through the brush. The voice was dramatic and impersonal at the same time, a style that often irritated Sylvester. But this time he listened carefully. He pushed his plate away and he felt a heaviness in his chest. As he listened to a Navajo official emphasize the severity of the drought, he leaned back on the couch and thought, I have failed. After all these years of taking, I had a chance to give and now it won't happen. I have failed these Navajos who won't even know I was almost in a position to help. But the Indian people in Montana will know. They'll read it in the newspapers, hear it on radio, see it on television. They'll say, he was a basketball player, now he's a big-time lawyer making all kinds of money. He doesn't want to quit that gravy train to help out his people. He was just looking for an excuse to quit the race, to quit us.

In the few days of his campaign, Sylvester had visited four different groups of Indians and they had all looked up to him. They had looked upon him as a possible answer to their various problems, their lack of communication with the outside world. They had made him feel good about the things he could accomplish, for them, for others. Now he was quitting.

Sylvester glanced out the bay window. It was light enough to tell that the day would be clear, cold, and still. He stood and carried his dishes back into the kitchen. Earlier that morning, he had wallowed in his aloneness, his timeless privacy, but now he felt truly alone, as only a man who has fallen from grace can.

He put the dishes in the sink and ran water over them. The clock on the stove said 8:50. He decided to go down to the office to clean up a few details. It felt strange to have nothing to do, no case to take his attention from the extraordinary events of the recent past—and the ordinary sameness of his days at home.

The phone rang.

"Good morning, Sylvester, this is Debbie. I just wanted to go over next week's schedule with you."

"It'll have to wait, Debbie. I have an appointment right now."

"It won't take a minute. Some friends are picking me up in half an hour to go cross-country skiing. I'd like to get this done."

"Can't do it, Debbie. Call me when you get back. Burn up those trails, Debbie, that's the only way to do it."

Debbie hesitated, then laughed uncertainly, as though she had just gotten the joke if there was one. "I'm going to my parents' ranch for New Year's, but I'll call you from there."

"Happy New Year, Debbie." He hung up.

The phone rang again.

"Hello?"

"I've got your puppy," sang a cheerful voice.

"Puppy?"

"The little golden. She just had her shots and you can pick her up anytime."

"I'd like to, but I'm afraid she doesn't belong to me. You've got the wrong party."

"Two four six, three eight three two?"

"Nope."

"I'm sorry."

"Happy New Year."

〰〰〰

Sylvester sat in his office until ten. The suite of offices was practically deserted. The only people he had seen were Doris, who brought him a cup of coffee, and Sally Ellmann, who was doing research in the library. He tried to sneak past the library door, but Sally was alert.

"The old campaigner. How's it going?"

"No complaints. You?"

She frowned at the legal pad before her. "Depressing. How did you maintain your sanity when you were doing divorces?"

Sylvester laughed. "Look on the bright side. Those people are going to be a lot happier without each other. Take the long view, Sally."

"I don't know. I think some of these people are going to miss all the bullshit they put each other through. Trouble is, I'm the one who gets all the scratches and bruises."

"Poor Sally."

"I read in the paper where you're going to address the cosmetology convention in Billings next week. That should be fun." She smiled sweetly.

"They vote too. Besides, I might get you a free perm if you treat me right."

"Yeah, right." She stroked her short straight brown hair.

"Happy New Year."

"You going to Harrington's bash?"

"I don't know yet."

At ten sharp, Sylvester walked down to Harrington's office. He was not at all nervous or filled with dread. The half hour alone in his office had restored the feeling he had had when he awoke that morning, a feeling somewhere between apprehension and hope. He did not feel like a man going to his own funeral; rather, he felt like a man whistling past the graveyard and having just about made it.

All that changed when he entered Buster's office and saw Shelley standing beside the fireplace, looking down at a brass fan in the opening. Sylvester's footstep on the bare wood between the hallway carpeting and the Persian rug echoed in the cavernous office. She looked up, alert but composed, as though he had merely interrupted an interesting thought.

"What are you doing here?"

"Hello. I might ask you the same thing, but I imagine we'll get to that. Buster asked me to come over."

She was facing him now, her hands in her pockets holding the black wool coat together. Beneath the light makeup, her cheeks were red, emphasized by the fuzzy white turtleneck and her soft blond hair.

"You look cold," said Sylvester. "Can I get you a cup of coffee?"

"No thanks." She turned back to the fireplace. "I wish this thing worked, though."

Sylvester crossed the room, glancing down at her high-heeled brown boots. Like most of her clothes, they were simple and expensive. On their second date, he had told her how lovely she looked, and she whirled around, her pleated skirt flaring, and said, "Not bad for a kid from Roundup, huh?" It was a moment of unabashed immodesty, her slender thighs shiny in tan pantyhose, and she'd been that way until the trip to Chico. Now she held the dark coat closed and looked down at the brass fan.

Sylvester stopped five feet away. He tried to think of something to say.

"Ah, there you are! I was just down to the can. This one in here—" Buster walked across the room and threw an arm in a disgusted gesture toward a doorway beside the high windows. "It's on the fritz again. I told Maggie I didn't need a can in here in the first place. Hello, darling." He wrapped Shelley up in a bearhug, then just as quickly turned to Sylvester, slapping him on the arm.

"How about a drink?" He veered off toward a sideboard

that Maggie had converted into a liquor cabinet and wet bar. "Shelley?"

"No thanks, Buster."

"Sit down. Sly?"

"You got a Coke in that thing?" His throat was dry. He knew Buster's breezy manner was very close to aggression. He often thought about how much he had learned about behavior since sitting on the parole board, how "normal" the inmates could make themselves seem, shy, chatty, confidential, earnest, friendly, but how often those manners disappeared when they didn't get what they wanted; on the other hand, he had seen how people on the outside, social beings, could use these very same attributes to disguise aggression, even hostility. The difference was that those on the outside acted out in acceptable ways, at least in ways within the law. At the moment, Sylvester couldn't tell which was better. He seldom admitted to himself his grudging admiration for the honesty of some of those outlaws in Deer Lodge.

Buster handed Sylvester a Coke from a small refrigerator in one of the lower cabinets, then poured himself half a tumbler of Jim Beam.

"Hair of the dog that bit me. I played cards with some of the boys last night. A couple of them are taking off for Arizona next week. You remember Willie Steingass—used to be on Metcalf's staff back in Washington—I'll bet you didn't know he and I used to drive ambulances during the war. France, Germany." Buster heaved himself down on the couch next to Shelley and patted her on the leg. "How's your mother doing?"

"Just fine. She's fine."

Sylvester had seen her flinch away from Buster's hand and he almost remembered a story, a party, a conference, something. He wanted to get Shelley out of there.

"So, Sylvester. You wanted to tell us something." Buster sat back, resting the tumbler of bourbon on his belly.

Sylvester noticed that the door was closed but he didn't recall Buster closing it. Doris must have done it discreetly, as though she sensed something unusual was going on. He sat down in a wing-back chair.

"I really think Shelley should not hear this," he said.

"Nonsense. I asked her to come. I figured between the two of us, we could talk you out of whatever it is that's bothering you." Buster patted Shelley's hand without looking at her.

Shelley was looking straight at Sylvester, her eyes devoid of any emotion. She did not flinch this time at Buster's touch.

My God, she knows something, thought Sylvester. Just as quickly he realized that she couldn't, but her look sent a chill through him. She senses something, he thought, she senses what has happened to me these past months.

"Shelley, are you sure you want to stay? This isn't good, what I am about to tell you."

She stood and Sylvester thought she was going to leave. He almost tried to will her to walk to the door. But she walked instead to the bank of windows and stood with her back to the men. "Go ahead, Sylvester," she said.

Buster fidgeted on the couch, sliding forward to put his drink on the coffee table. For the first time, his pudgy body stiffened with concern.

Sylvester told them everything, starting with the day Patti Ann had first come to his office with the story of the will. He left out very few details of the escalating events, with the exception of their times in bed together. He called it "going to bed together" but the image that came to his mind was of her standing naked, water beads on her shoulders, combing her hair in front of the bathroom mirror, while he toweled himself dry behind her. He told them about her husband, Jack Harwood, whom the board had turned down for parole, his desperate blackmail attempt, and finally the involvement of Peters and Fitzgerald, the scene in Patti Ann's apartment yesterday. He made it clear that Patti Ann had been a pawn, and in fact, had acted with courage and good faith through the whole thing.

Shelley had continued to look out the window, motionless, her hands in her pockets, while Sylvester told his story. He had watched her back when he said that he and Patti Ann had gone to bed together a few times, but nothing had betrayed any emotion. He wanted to see her face, but he needed to tell this story completely, without interruption, even without emotion. And he did, and when he was finished, Buster stood and walked to the bar behind him. Sylvester heard the splash of bourbon in the glass, then the clink of the bottle on the glass top of the sideboard. Beyond Shelley's head, he saw the sunlit top windows of the Montana Club, less than half a block away. The day had turned out to be nice.

"Who else knows about this?" said Buster, as he passed Sylvester's chair. He had unbuttoned his vest, and his white shirt, paisley tie, and belly moved before Sylvester's eyes in slow motion.

"The participants—Patti Ann, her husband, Peters and Fitzgerald. I got some information about Peters from a probation officer I know in town, some more information from the executive secretary of the parole board, but they don't know anything. I suppose they could put something together if this story came out."

"How long did this business last?"

"Patti Ann came to see me the first time on September fifteenth. I have it on my calendar. So, three and a half months altogether."

"Jesus, I wish—no, I won't say it. But dammit, we could have nipped it in the bud, or somewhere along the line—"

"It's too late, Buster. I wish I could say it was a seedy little affair, over and done with, but it'll surface. I know Patti Ann and her husband won't talk, maybe Fitzgerald won't, but Peters—I'm afraid he'll use it to cut a deal next time he gets picked up. I don't think anybody would make a deal on such soft information, but he'll try."

"What if we sent somebody to talk to him, see where he's at? Sounds to me like you scared him pretty good, threatening to send him back to prison."

"Guys like Peters have a pretty short memory. Prison won't seem so bad to him after a while. Guys like that don't get straight until they've truly had enough of wasting their lives in prison. Peters has a way to go."

"So you think it's inevitable that he'll drop the bomb one of these days?"

"Yes." Sylvester glanced at Shelley. She was facing him now, leaning against the window ledge. Because of the brightness of the sun outside, he couldn't see her eyes clearly.

"Damn, damn, damn." Buster slumped back and closed his eyes. "You've got yourself in a hell of a pickle, son."

"I know. I'm sorry. I've gotten everybody—you, Shelley, everybody—who trusted me in a hell of a pickle." Sylvester looked down at the Coke can. He was almost surprised to see it in his hand. "If I had only turned her case over to Sally or one of the others. It was a simple contested will—or it purported to be—"

"Does this mean you're going to quit?" Shelley pushed away from the window ledge and walked slowly to the couch where Buster sat. She stood behind it. Her face had lost the color it had had when Sylvester first walked into the room. Somehow her features had grown softer too, almost blurred. Her eyes seemed less flat.

"What choice does he have?" said Buster without looking around. "The press and the GOP would turn him inside out if they got ahold of this thing. Didn't your daddy teach you anything, honey?"

"And what do you say?" She looked at Sylvester with such simple directness that he looked down at the white sweater.

He shook his head. "I suppose there is always the possibility that Peters will get run over by a car or killed in a shootout. That would be nice, I guess, but not very realistic. I'm sorry, I didn't mean that." He looked into Shelley's eyes. "I'm just terribly sorry that I blew an opportunity to do something good for people who need something good in their lives. There are people in this state, this country, who could use a man like me. It sounds arrogant, but I feel that way. You know, when we went to Chico and I couldn't talk to you, couldn't let you in on what I was feeling, it was because I was ashamed of myself. I didn't want you to know that. I felt like an impostor, a poseur, an opportunist who would pay lip service to the issues involved in order to get himself something he hadn't earned. I guess, in some dark but surprisingly decent corner of my mind, I didn't want you involved with that man.

"It wasn't really until I was standing on the steps of that children's home, speaking, feeling the presence of the children, the Indian leaders behind me, that I felt I did have something to offer, that the job didn't require a saint, just a person committed to making some lives a little better, a little easier. I wasn't an opportunist. My past successes only gave me an opportunity." He shook his head again and sighed bitterly. "And that's the shame of it. I had my chance and I messed it up."

"There will be other chances, Sylvester, believe me." Shelley was smiling and her eyes were deep. "You'll see."

"Your damn right!" Buster slapped the tops of his thighs with his thick hands. He looked up at Shelley. "See, this is the fellow who came to work for me those many years ago. I saw something then that made me think he was going places and I don't see anything different now." He looked at Sylvester and his eyes were bright. "We'll unwind this thing—it'll be delicate, make no mistake about that, but you'll get through it—then we'll see where we're at. My suggestion would be that you continue your sabbatical, at least until June. By then the legislative session will be over and this town will be somewhere near normal. Why don't you take a trip, go to Europe, Hawaii, just have some fun for a change. Wouldn't that do him some good, Shelley?"

"I'm sure it would." She wasn't smiling now. She buttoned her coat as she walked to the door. Both men rose.

"Shelley—"

"Not now, Sylvester, not right now." She opened the heavy oak door and turned. There were tears in her eyes. "Call me—in a week—okay?" Then she walked out.

Buster put his arm around Sylvester's shoulder. "Women. You gotta love 'em," he said sweetly.

〰〰〰〰

Thenextmorning, Saturday, at 7:30 the calls began and Sylvester had to switch his answering machine from four rings to one ring. Then he had to listen to his recorded voice over and over again. "This is Sylvester Yellow Calf. Please leave your name, number, and message. Thank you." All of the major and some minor (the *Glacier Reporter* in Browning among others) newspapers and the radio and television stations asked for confirmation of the AP story that had appeared in the morning papers.

Sylvester was still stunned at how fast Buster had acted. He looked at the article again: "Helena attorney Sylvester Yellow Calf has canceled his run for the U.S. House of Representatives, The Associated Press learned Friday night. The Democrat is scheduled to explain his decision at a news conference here Monday morning. A source told the AP that Yellow Calf is 'in the process of defining his other priorities, which include working with reservations and the so-called landless Indians. The timing is right for Montana's Indians to present a strong united front in Washington.' Yellow Calf could not be reached for comment."

Sylvester had to smile. He had told Buster that the Indian people he spoke to had talked of uniting behind him. The story went on to list Sylvester's accomplishments, including his basketball career, the other possible Democratic candidates, the two Republicans in the race. Farther down, the source was quoted as saying that "Sylvester has decidedly not ruled out another run for Congress in the future."

He could handle the news conference Monday morning. He wasn't sure how he would handle the weekend. Tonight was New Year's Eve. Tonight was Buster and Maggie's bash and Buster had reinvited him that morning of the meeting. Something perverse inside him told him to go, to mingle with all the politicians, the movers and shakers, to make them deal with him. He wanted to make them uncomfortable. But he knew that Buster had only reinvited him out of courtesy. Buster did say that Sylvester was still a vice-president of the firm and, as such, he should be there. But Sylvester had an image of a dark bird, ever present, circling slowly over the festivities. He had a hunch Buster saw that vision too. Maybe that's why he had called the AP reporter last night, to get it out in the open, to remove Sylvester's presence from the Democratic scene as early and cleanly as possible. Just in case the shit really did hit the fan. That's politics, son. You don't drag other people and especially the party down with you.

Shelley would probably be there. So would her mother. The problem was, Sylvester didn't know if he could handle the evening alone. He'd be okay on New Year's Day—he could draft his statement and watch football games. He could drive out of town and hike. He could go out to the Shanty and drink beer with the other outlaws, with Lil Abner. Maybe Peters and Fitzgerald would be there. He would tell them it had all been a joke, that they were buddies after all.

Patti Ann. It was a crazy idea and it was the best idea he'd had in days. He glanced at the answering machine as he dialed her number. He'd already gotten eleven calls that morning. Entirely too many for a sunny Saturday morning.

"Patti Ann. This is Sylvester Yellow Calf. What are you doing tonight?"

"Tonight?"

"New Year's Eve. Do you have plans?"

"No. Nothing."

"Would you like to celebrate together?" Sylvester had his elbow on the counter, his arm raised, his fingers crossed.

"Do you really want to?" Her voice rose in wonder. "I read the paper this morning—"

"There's no one I'd rather celebrate with."

"But what would we celebrate?"

"Endings and beginnings of one thing and another. It's New Year's Eve. Please say yes."

"Oh, Sylvester, you're a sucker for punishment." She laughed. "Of course I will."

"Thank you, thank you, Patti Ann." Sylvester looked up at the ceiling, as though he could see blue skies and beyond. "We'll do it here. I'll get champagne, party hats, the works. Wear your best dress."

"Really?"

"Something colorful and gay. I'll pick you up at eight."

"I'll be ready, Mr. Yellow Calf. I'm going to go look through my extensive wardrobe right now."

"Patti Ann?" Sylvester wanted to say something, something both exhilarating and sobering, something about what had happened to them, who they were now. Endings and beginnings for both of them.

"Yes?"

"You make me awfully happy. Isn't that the strangest thing?"

CHAPTER SIXTEEN

Earl Yellow Calf suffered his final stroke in April of the following year. Sylvester had been living in a kitchenette unit in Bismarck and commuting down to the Standing Rock Reservation. The two law students from the University of North Dakota lived in a more modest motel on the western edge of town. He would pick them up every morning at eight and they would drive down the Missouri River through a game preserve, and he always felt the same sense of peace, no matter what the weather. And there were always waterfowl, ducks and geese, sometimes swans and pelicans, cranes and osprey. Deer and antelope watched their car pass with only mild interest. He was always surprised that an area of North Dakota could be so beautiful, so lush and abundant, even in winter. He had driven across the state, east and west, and had thought of it as nothing but wheat fields and prairies. He loved that kind of country and became very attentive in it, as though a discovery would be made over the next hill, down in the next swale or wash. But this country, the slow wide river, the bare trees and brush, the battered reeds and cattails, the bright bunches of willows, held every color, every texture, under the sun or in the snow or rain. Sylvester began to think of the hour-and-a-half drive as his dreaming time. He drove down every morning, and even in the two or three blizzards, as he crept along at thirty, his mind was concentrated on both driving and dreaming, and the things he dreamed were minute and ordinary—times when he was growing up, fishing or shooting baskets, listening to the radiators clank in the old grade school, watching a muskrat preening in the reeds of one of the potholes around Browning. Other times he thought of college in Missoula, the evening walk with the sorority girl, the runs up Mount Sentinel in the fall to get himself in shape for basketball, the smell of pizza in the dorm. He dreamed of Palo Alto and Stanford, the dry hills, the long nights in the law library, the warm early-spring evenings he pedaled home on his bicycle. Even Helena was becoming a dream to him but the dreams did not come as easily. When he dreamed the small bakery that served good bread and soup, he saw faces and he did not want to see faces, so he stopped the dreams and concentrated on the small slick blacktop road or the sudden flight of geese lifting from the wetlands.

In the three months he had been there, he had thrown himself into the case and had gotten a circuit court date for a hearing on the issues, a small triumph in itself. He and the tribal attorney and the two law students spent most of their time researching prior decisions, taking depositions, filing informations, rounding up expert witnesses. Indian irrigators and tribal recreation people were protesting the periodic drawdowns of the immense reservoir, the diversion of water to downstream farmers and ranchers and hydropower concerns. The state maintained that the modification of the prior appropriation law did not apply to this particular case because most of the reservation water was unused. As far as Sylvester could see there were no new wrinkles in either side's arguments; it was simply a matter of convincing the circuit court that the Winters doctrine and later court cases had established that the Indians could protect the amount of water necessary for future as well as current use. But he read all the pertinent water rights cases affecting Indian property. He knew that each case had to be argued on its own particular merits, that it would have to be argued again and again all the way to the Supreme Court if necessary.

At first he didn't know if he wanted to become so deeply involved. It could conceivably take years to settle the case, but the more comfortable he became with the reservation people, the more he got to know the individuals involved, the more he realized he would see it through to wherever it ended—even if it meant giving up his new partnership in Harrington, Lohn and Associates. Lately, it had begun to seem like a small sacrifice.

The telephone call from the priest reached him at the tribal offices in Fort Yates. He and the two student lawyers were eating lunch in the lounge with the recreation specialist. He took the call in the receptionist's area, then called a travel agency in Bismarck.

The next morning he boarded a small commuter plane to

Billings, then a Northwest flight to Great Falls. By one o'clock he had rented a car and driven through Great Falls on I-15 on his way to U.S. 89 and Browning. It was April 16th, one day after the tax deadline. His grandfather had died on the 15th. Sylvester smiled as he thought of the irony of the tax deadline and the fact that his grandfather had been an accountant all his working life.

As he approached the Rocky Mountain Front, he noticed that the country was greening up, even the foothills as they rolled toward the mountains. The fires of last summer had burned through the Scapegoat and Bob Marshall Wilderness Areas but there were no visible scars along the Front. He could barely see the lower slopes of the mountains below the dark clouds. He headed north and west on 89, passing through squall after squall of rain, sleet, and pebbly snow. The area along the Front was the last in Montana to give up winter, forming a natural corridor for the weather that began in northern Canada and swept south in massive violent storms. But today the weather consisted of spring squalls, and Sylvester was grateful to be going home in such beauty.

〰〰〰

The funeral was in the Little Flower Catholic Church in Browning. Although Earl Yellow Calf had not been a church-going man, Mary Bird wanted a church service for him. She had rejected a traditional service because Earl had long ago rejected the traditional way of life. He was a rational man and did not believe in that hocus-pocus, he had once told her.

Sylvester sat in the front row with his grandmother and

several of the elders, listening to the organ music, smelling the smoky incense, and staring at the closed casket. Finally, all the shuffling behind him ceased and he glanced back and saw that the church was full. People were standing along the back and side walls. He was both shocked and pleased that his grandfather, his grandparents, had been important in the community they had never left. North Dakota, Bismarck, Standing Rock seemed a long way away, Helena even farther. He had come a long way home to the simplicity and peace of his birthplace.

He wondered if the priest had called his mother in New Mexico. Neither Sylvester nor his grandmother had mentioned her last night, and that seemed to be that. But it was his mother's father lying up there in the casket and she surely would have come if she had known about it. But there had been no late arrival of a strange woman, a woman who might have looked like Sylvester, a woman who might have touched him like a son. He tried to imagine what she would be doing this spring day in New Mexico, but he couldn't, and he realized that he did not want to see her ever because she might want something from him and he had nothing to give her.

The incense lulled him pleasantly and he thought of Patti Ann Harwood and he realized that in his subconscious he had connected her with the fires of the summer and fall before. Even now he smelled the smoke and saw the orange glow against the night sky. There had been smoke in the air that first morning she came to see him, and all that early fall he smelled it when he stepped from his car in front of her apartment.

He had gotten a letter from her in the middle of February.

She thanked him for all he had done for her and her husband.
He was now in the Maximum Security Unit, having decided
he could live there until his discharge or parole if she would
stick by him, be there when he got out. And it wasn't so bad,
at least he had peace of mind knowing he would be safe until
then. Myrna and Phil were together in Billings at long last,
and she, Patti Ann, was plugging away at her job, neither
happily or unhappily. She thanked him for their chaste New
Year's eve, which meant more to her than he would ever
know, and she wished him, belatedly, great success in the new
year. She closed with "your loving pal."

The priest gave a short talk, mentioning Carlisle School for
Indians, the years put in as tribal treasurer, then as accountant for the BIA, the fact that Earl loved to fish, the many
loved ones he left, the respect and esteem of the community
toward him. Finally he commended Earl Yellow Calf's soul to
heaven and led the throng in a final prayer.

Sylvester sneaked a look at his grandmother. She was smiling.

~~~~~~

Lena Old Horn had just finished Sunday dinner with a
family, the Fine Shields, who lived in Chinatown, so named
because of the curious roof design of the government housing.
As she started her car and pulled away from the yard, one of
the children yelled after her, "You're draggin' a dog!" She
laughed but looked in the rearview mirror, just in case. It was
an old Browning joke, based on the fact there were so many
loose mongrels around town. It hadn't taken her long to get
used to the sometimes crude humor of the Blackfeet; her own

Crow people were nearly as bad. She looked back and waved and the family, standing on their spotty brown lawn, waved and laughed.

She passed two teenage girls riding double on a big liver-colored mare, and ducking low so they could see her, waved up at them. For an instant they looked surprised, then they covered their mouths and giggled. They were the Aims Back twins, as silly as girls get at that age, but they were good students and already planning to take nursing down at the college in Bozeman. Lena had helped them pick out the program, just as she had helped their mother select a secretarial course twenty years before.

Lena felt good about herself today. She had come to a big decision two nights ago and it still felt right. The incredible thing was she had only thought about it that night. There was no agonizing, no hemming and hawing, no big guilt trip. She came home from school late Friday afternoon, changed into her sweats and sneakers, took her customary walk out the Starr School road, came back, went to the grocery store, fed Fraidy, cooked some frozen cod and canned new potatoes, then sat down in her reading chair with a glass of wine and watched the children across the street play in the deepening dusk until it was time to go in. She continued to watch the street until all she could see was the reflection of the table lamp beside her chair.

It was probably the coming on of spring—it always made her restless and excited and vaguely happy, as though the nearing of the end of another school year would finally reveal a great adventure. And it did once, the time she took a group of juniors to Russia, but usually summer meant a month at home with her mother on the Crow Reservation, sometimes college classes at Eastern, maybe a trip out to Seattle or Portland if there was enough time before classes resumed in the fall.

Or it could have been the funeral earlier in the week. Something about how life is short and how quickly the end comes, although for Earl Yellow Calf the end had been a long-drawn-out affair. Mary Bird had told her how happy she was that Earl had finally passed on. Seeing Sylvester sitting beside his small indestructible grandmother in the front pew had made her tremble and she couldn't explain why.

But last Friday night, as she stared at her reflection in the picture window, she made the decision to leave Browning for good. She felt like the alcoholic who has hit rock bottom and the only way to go is up—or in her case, out—out of this school, this town, this country. She liked her decision because she felt good about all three. Browning had become her home, the country her inspiration, the children her life.

She had called Harley Matt, the principal, that night, and in spite of his entreaties, had stuck to her guns. Finally, he backed off and said he would personally miss her and the school would not be the same without her. When she hung up, she cried with joy and sadness. But she meant it and she would endure, even enjoy, whatever happened these final two months.

She geared down to second for the incline up past the old grade school. Although it was past the middle of April, a driving sleet had fallen while she was eating dinner with the Fine Shields. It had now turned into slush and had even disappeared on the bare ground and grassy patches of the yards. She was a nervous and careful driver and the slush made a hissing sound beneath her tires as she crept up the incline.

Lena was less than half a block from the playground of the grade school when she noticed a tall rangy man shooting baskets. Impulsively, she pulled over to the side of the road and stopped. She watched the man dribble to the front of the basket near where the free-throw line would be, pull up, and shoot a jump shot. It swished through the chain net. She turned off the key and set the emergency brake. She leaned back against the headrest. The basketball court was at the top of the hill, nearly in front of her, so she had a clear view of the basket, the man, and the cloudy mountains far behind him. She watched the man dribble farther out, slowly, almost thoughtfully, and suddenly turn and hit another jumper from the top of the key. He raced in, picked up the ball off the bounce, and made a reverse lay-up with his left hand. She watched the beauty and grace of the man on the court for the first time since high school. She held her breath as she watched the moves that she still recognized—the left-handed jump hook, the delicate finger roll, and of course the raining jump shots from the top of the key, the corner, the flank. She thought of all the basketball games she had seen in Browning, all the kids who played with grace and intensity, but there had never been another Sylvester Yellow Calf.

As Lena watched, the clouds grew lower and thicker and the first splotches of sleet hit her windshield and she could not see the mountains anymore. She started her car and crept up and over the hill. She glanced over at the basketball court, but Sylvester didn't notice the car. Nor did he notice the sleet, the freshening of the wind from the north. He was going one on one against the only man who ever beat him.